To hate Adam Connor

Ella Maise

Editor: Editing by C. Marie
Cover Designer: Sarah Horgan
Proofreader: Lawrence Editing
(www.lawrenceediting.com)

This book is for everyone who had—at some point in their life—trouble believing they were worth the trouble.

CHAPTER ONE

LUCY

I believe in love. Wholeheartedly.

Seriously, don't shake your head like that. I do.

I can picture those of you who already know me snickering. Well, don't.

There is no need for that, and frankly, it's kinda rude, don't you think?

Here, I'll say it again: I genuinely believe in love. I know all about its magic. Good and bad. I know the world seems bigger when you're drunk on love. I know it mends broken hearts, makes you deliriously happy, excited, hopeful...terrified, sick...a whole list of things that make this complicated world we are living in a better place.

For example, my best friend Olive. She has loved her husband ever since she was a wee bitty kid. She even asked Jason to marry her when she was six years old. She was six, people—six! Isn't that just the cutest thing you've ever heard? Then when they found each other years later, his movie star self swept her off her feet. Love works for her, big time, and it looks good on her too. She deserves all the love in the world.

Me? Love hangs a bit loose on me. Essentially, it's not quite the best fit.

So...what I'm saying is, love can do anything and everything...as long as you don't have a curse hanging over your head like I do. Oh, and you have to be willing to let love into your life, open that heavy door that leads the poor guy into the maze that is your heart, so to speak.

That's the tricky part, isn't it? You have to let love in. You have to open yourself up, share your least lovable parts, the deepest, darkest corners of your soul. That's the only way to experience real love. They feed us that shit as early as possible, or so I've heard. Our surroundings are an ongoing commercial for love. Share yourself with someone, be true, be honest, and if they love you for who you are then you are golden.

Enjoy the confetti shower that just blasted in your face.

You found real love. Good for you.

Sucks for the rest of us.

Now...do *I* let love in? Nope. I try my hardest not to, thank you very much. Been there, done that. If you are asking me what my problem is if I do indeed believe in love...well, if you are so curious about it, my problem is that my dear old friend '*love*' doesn't love me back. Never did. Probably never will.

I'd say it's quite rude of her, but...I've made my peace with it —at least I thought I had until I went and fell for Jameson.

Enter the hot bad boy covered in ink. College love.

If you haven't guessed it yet, I have all kinds of daddy and mommy issues. As if all of those weren't enough to fuck up my life, I have grandma issues to top it all off.

Blah blah blah...

Now you're starting to think I'm boring, and we can't have that.

Let's talk about one-night stands instead. Those are fun, right? You're skirting around love, smiling at each other, feeling all dizzy and ditzy with the excitement that you might score a good one, enjoy the feeling of having someone else's skin on yours, his hot breath, the heat, that blasted bliss you get to experience for a few seconds when he manages to hit that sweet spot—*if* he hits that sweet spot. Those are all awesome things, I agree. Hell, I encourage you to experience all those feelings, especially if he has some good inches on him.

Don't be a bitch; be a calm, happy waterfall.

Roar at life. In life.

Don't be closed off; be as free as a raindrop.

Most important of all: *live*.

My greatest advice to you all is, whatever you do, don't go back to the spectacular one-night stand you had just to satisfy your traitorous body's needs if you're trying to stay away from love, have your fun, live a little, love someone for a single night and then move on. Because if you keep going back to the same guy, oh, I don't know…about a hundred times…eventually what *will* happen is that you'll start to have feelings for said guy.

Look at that—I have a heart after all. Didn't expect that, did you? So you start to fall in love just like I did. Slowly. At first, you might feel a trickle of something you can't name because of how well he wields that huge cock of his (by the way, that's called an orgasm, not love). He'll zap you with all kinds of feelings when he is using it on you. And yes, he'll be that good; heart-breakers tend to be good in the sack.

More for you to cry over when they're done with you. Goody, right?

But then you'll foolishly start to put more meaning behind the Big O you experience every time he is near you with that monster cock. And then his smile will start muddling the waters, or the way he touches your face, or the way he looks at you when you take off your shirt in front of him—all smoldering and shit. Then those wicked words of his will make their way into your heart *and* brain. And maybe, just *maybe,* you'll start to feel safe because he seems to genuinely care for you. Then somehow, before you have the chance to back up…before you even realize what your heart is doing behind your back…

Boom!

You're in love.

Congrats. And, well, fuck you, dear heart!

Now you can thoroughly enjoy the misery that will surely follow suit.

Of course, I can't speak for everyone, but at least that's what happened between me and Jameson, my one and only college love, so go and blame him for the love vomit.

It had been exactly six days and twenty-one hours since he'd left Los Angeles and moved to Pittsburgh to start his stupid new job at his stupid new firm, leaving me behind, a little heartbroken, and essentially homeless.

If you're wondering how I managed to fall in love with this Jameson who broke my heart…let me rewind a bit. I met Jameson in a study group for our economics class. Contrary to popular belief, I wouldn't jump into bed with someone I'd just met—and I didn't. At first, I just enjoyed the view and chose to somewhat salivate over him…because that's always fun, isn't it? Oh, the anticipation, the coy looks, all those knowing smirks. Then a few weeks later we just tumbled into a bed that was nearby. Just like that, I swear.

Completely accidental, I tell you.

I recall seeing some ink on his chest and forearms, and then he turned around and I saw those tight buns. Suddenly we were in a bed and he was giving me and my lovely vagina the time of our life. I've already mentioned how good those monster cocks feel, haven't I? I wouldn't have minded if he were a tad bit thicker, but, oh well…I guess you can't have it all in life.

So, I went back for more. I remember telling myself, *Just one more time, Lucy, and that's it*. I sincerely thought it would be a crime not to experience that level of hotness again, and I'm no criminal. What could *possibly* go wrong, y'know…

Then somehow we ended up having those one-night stands a few times a week. So, technically he wasn't a one-night stand, but I'd still like to call him just that. He also proved to be a tough cookie when he started to fall asleep in my bed before my brain would start working enough to remember why I needed to kick him out of it.

Funnily enough, that's how I used to end up going for sleepy time on my best friend Olive's boobies. Sleeping and cuddling with your one-night stand is a big no no. The best part; Olive's boobs were The.Best.Freaking.Pillows.In.The.World! Trust me on that. So soft, yet so firm. It was basically magic, but that's a story for another time.

Long story short, I'd started to fall for Jameson. I thought maybe it was time for me to give good ol' love a spin and see if I was still cursed or not. True, I wasn't necessarily expecting a happily ever after at my first try because real life is rarely all unicorns flying around and farting rainbows in the clouds, but hell, I hadn't been expecting a sudden cut and run either. I was just dipping my toes into the water, not trying to electrocute myself.

So, yup, still cursed.

No love for this gal. Hurray…I guess.

"Hello? Lucy? Ah, there you are. Is there a reason you're talking to yourself?" Olive asked as she appeared at the end of the hall where I was dumping a trash bag filled with Jameson's clothes. I straightened up and let out a deep breath as I took in her appearance. The yoga pants and baggy white shirt she was wearing were practically her uniform when she didn't want to think about what to wear. And baggy or not her boobs still managed to look good. Her strawberry blonde hair was in a messy bun on top of her head and looked like it had seen much cleaner days. My guess was she had come straight from her writing cave.

"No reason at all. Just entertaining myself," I answered, clearing the invisible sweat off my forehead with the back of my hand. "What are you doing here this early? I thought you were coming around later. And is there a reason why you look like you haven't showered in a week?"

She was in the process of looking through the trash bags I had lined up against the wall that contained the clothes Jameson had chosen to leave behind. At my question, Olive's head snapped up and her lips spread into a wide grin.

"Not a week, but maybe two days? I only have a few chapters to write then it's officially The End for the story." She shrugged and went back to her rummaging, looking for God knew what. "Who has time to shower anyway?"

It wasn't a question, but I answered her anyway—under my breath of course. "People who like to be clean instead of smelly like you maybe?"

"And to answer your ungrateful question," she continued. "I came early because I'm *the* best friend anyone could have. Why do we have to go through his clothes? Why didn't the bastard take them with him?"

"*We* aren't going through his clothes, *you* are. I've already gone through them. I'm just gonna leave them outside. Jameson texted to say his friend was coming over to take care of them. I don't care either way."

"Or we could burn them to make a statement." She kicked one of the bags toward the door and reached out to lift up my small, bright yellow weekend bag.

"And what statement would that be exactly?"

"I don't know…to show him that we are a united front against him? And it would be therapeutic for you, too."

"Right. How about we stick to moving me out of here as quickly as possible instead."

She shrugged and grabbed the bag I was holding out to her. "By the way, I'm pretty sure Jason would've said something if I smelled. And look who's talking—you look like death warmed up. Your beautiful blue eyes are practically dead. Even your dark hair somehow looks…darker."

I clasped my hands over my heart and batted my lashes. "Aww, thanks, my little green Olive. You look lovely too, with your greasy hair and sleepy eyes. Combined, it all does wonders for your complexion."

A small smile playing on her lips, she shook her head and carried the bags downstairs to her car. I opened the bathroom door and checked the medicine cabinet to make sure I hadn't left anything behind. Then just to be safe, I checked the bedroom again. When I was sure everything was packed and ready to go, I carried my last suitcase into the living room where Olive was waiting for me with a full bottle of tequila.

"I brought this," she said, using her hands to present the bottle to me, as if that baby needed any extra presenting.

Taking a few steps to make it to her side, I snatched the bottle from her hands, ignored her gasp, and plopped my ass down on the shit-colored sofa, as I liked to describe it.

While I was busy trying to screw the top off, Olive sighed and dropped down next to me. I took a quick gulp and screwed up my face when the precious liquid burned my throat then handed the bottle back to her waiting hands.

She'd been my friend for three and a half years, and I doubted anyone else knew me better than her. She was a writer—a crazy successful author who'd made the bestseller lists with her very first novel. My favorite part was that she was the lucky, lucky wife of the hottest actor in Hollywood, who had also been her childhood crush. You'd think that shit would only happen in books, but nope, she did it. She scored the hottest guy. I liked to think I'd given her a small nudge in the right direction, encouraging her to go after what she wanted, but her chemistry with the guy was off the charts, so I knew with or without me, they still would've ended up together. And, well, despite being a hotshot celebrity, Jason Thorn was one of the good ones. He was completely in love with Olive—otherwise I would have totally organized a sneak attack on him to get his paws off my best friend.

"So…" Olive started after she took her own gulp of tequila and coughed a few times. "What was the subject of the conversation you were having with yourself when I walked in?"

I took another sip, a big one. That one definitely went down easier. "Actually, I was reminiscing about your pretty boobs and thinking how come you're so selfish about sharing those puppies."

She quirked her eyebrow at me and pulled her legs up to get comfortable. "Who said I'm selfish? I share very nicely with my husband."

I gave her a genuine smile. "Are you ready to share exactly *how*? As in with details? Like what's his favorite position? Doggie? Does he take care of your boobs? Is he nice to them?" I knew she wouldn't share—I had tried before; I didn't understand why, and it never stopped me from trying to get answers. Plus, it was fun watching her squirm. That's what friends got for hoarding important details like that.

"Sorry, no bueno."

Doing my best to give her my version of the evil eye, I offered her some alcohol. She passed, which was good for two reasons. One, more for me—yay—and two, well, she got out of hand when she got drunk.

"Not to sound like an ungrateful friend, but I thought you said you'd come around two PM, not ten AM. And you came bearing gifts too. Are you being nice to me 'cause I'm a victim?"

She looked clueless as she glanced at me. "A victim? A victim of what?"

"A victim of love, of course," I returned, acting outraged. "I got chewed up and spit out—and not in a sexy way."

She rolled her eyes and gave her attention to the phone buzzing in her handbag. After checking the screen, she sighed. "Sorry, my poor victim of love, I need to take this. I'm scheduling meetings with potential agents."

"You go ahead and do that, and I'll keep doing this tequila."

As soon as she left the room, I closed my eyes and let my head rest on the back of the sofa.

So Jameson was gone. So I wasn't in a relationship anymore. Whatever, right? I'd never planned to get into one in the first place. I should've been happy. I should've felt better knowing I'd been right about the existence of a curse on our family.

Did I feel anything like happiness at that moment?

Not even close. But I knew I would live, so there was no point in acting like my life was over. Thanks to my family, I'd seen worse. Jameson was a saint compared to them.

When Olive came back, I tried to avert my gaze so she wouldn't focus on my watering eyes.

Oh, shush! I hadn't been silently crying or anything, I was just allergic to the damn apartment.

"How about we get out of here?" Olive asked softly.

Apparently I hadn't been quick enough to look away. I wiped away a lone tear and took my last sip from the bottle. As much as I wanted to get sloppy drunk with my best friend and possibly start a big fire and make voodoo dolls with big junks, we couldn't. Adulting sucks big balls.

"Yeah. We should do that," I agreed.

Olive reached for the bottle in my hand, and I reluctantly gave it up, after a short struggle, of course.

"I'll hold onto this, and we'll continue later."

"Promise?"

"Promise." She narrowed her eyes on me. "Hell, you know what? I'll even let you cuddle me."

Perking up, I wiggled my brows at her. "And while I'm cuddling you, will you be cuddling your pretty husband?" I sat up straighter. "Olive Thorn, are you granting me a cuddling three-some because I'm a victim of love? If so, I'll totally take that."

"No, you little perv. Jason has a shoot tonight. I'll cuddle you until you go to sleep. Then I'm sneaking out of your room to sleep with my pretty husband."

"Ah, now you are just twisting the knife that's already been lodged into my heart."

"Good. I'm still angry at you, you know."

I made a miserable face. "Me? What did I do? I'm the victim here."

"And I'm your friend. You waited six days to tell me what that asshole did. You robbed me of my friendship rights."

"Oh, come on. You can't get angry at me for that. I just didn't want you to be miserable with me. I gave myself one week to cry my eyes and heart out, and I did just that. It didn't even take a week. Now it's done. Over. Tonight, we'll celebrate my singleness. I saved you the best part: the celebrations. We'll have a Tinder party and swipe right on every one. As far as I'm concerned, I'm a kickass friend."

She offered me her hand and pulled me up. "Nope. You robbed me. It's as simple as that. I didn't get to cry with you *or* curse at Jameson for leaving you. Now how am I gonna make the transition from sadness to anger and then straight to celebration? I'm still pissed. And I'm sad, too. Because my emotions are all over the place. I talked Jason's ear off the entire night after your phone call. He agrees with me completely. You definitely violated my rights."

I tilted my head and patted her arm. "Aww, you love me. I'd hug you, little Olive, but you smell even worse up close."

She gave me a hard push. Laughing, I fell back on the couch. "No need to be an angry waterfall, Olive. Be a lake. Like me. Look how calm I am. Fine," I added when she kept standing over me with a raised eyebrow. "If it'll make you feel any better, I'll probably cry some more tonight, so you'll still have your shot at being miserable with me."

"That's more like it. Thank you. Do try to cry at the beginning of the festivities, okay?"

Shaking my head, I got up on my own as we started a logical discussion of how long we should cry before starting the celebrations.

After Olive helped me carry the last suitcase to her car, I left her with the bags and went upstairs to do a last check, which was how I found myself alone in the living room, just gazing around. Remembering.

When Jameson had had his motorcycle accident a few months before, Olive and I had rushed to his side at the hospital. That had been the first time I'd accepted that I loved him.

When it became obvious that he was gonna have trouble looking after himself with all those stupid broken bones, I'd asked him if he wanted me to move in with him so I could help him out. When he smiled that sexy, confident smile—the one that encouraged your brain to do some stupid shit—and said he thought I'd never ask, I was relieved for two reasons.

One, I wouldn't have to beat him to a pulp until he realized he needed me while he was already in a hospital bed. Because, let's face it, that wouldn't look good for me, and, yeah, I liked his face a little too much to mess it up. Two, I'd get to move out of an apartment I was sharing with two very stupid people—stupid ex-friends to be exact, both to Olive and me.

Because of my quick move, I hadn't brought a ton of stuff with me. I didn't own many things anyway, and at the age of twenty-two bordering on twenty-three, being the owner of just a few suitcases worth of stuff was a bit depressing.

When I thought about it, I realized I was now the proud owner of new memories. Memories that wouldn't go away in a puff. Memories I wished weren't mine, because none of them, none of the I love yous I'd gotten out of Jameson would keep me warm at night.

No. These memories would play with my mind and remind me what I would never have in my life.

Because, yes, you guessed it...the freaking curse.

"Man, those stairs are kicking my butt. Are we done here?" Olive asked as she came in to stand next to me.

"Looks like it," I replied, wiping off my clammy hands on my leggings. "You ready to get out of here?"

"Shouldn't I be the one to ask you that?"

"I don't know. Should you?"

She eyed me for a few seconds, probably trying to figure out if I was messing with her.

"Nah," she said eventually, linking her arm through mine. "No need to ask; you are ready to close this door. This is already ancient history, right?"

I took a deep breath and laid my head on Olive's shoulder. "I wish I were as sure of that as you are, my little green Olive."

"You mean to tell me Jameson isn't ancient history?" Her voice softened. "It's okay if he isn't, Lucy. You know that, right?"

"Oh, the heartbreaking, panty-stealing bastard is most definitely ancient history, but I'm not sure our memories and all the I love yous he whispered to me within these walls are. And isn't that how it goes? You get over the guy way before you get over the memories."

She rested her head on top of mine and gently asked, "Are you sure you're okay, Lucy? I love that you're coming to live with us—"

"Temporarily," I spoke over her, but she pretty much ignored me.

"—because I'd hate it if you left the city, but why didn't you? I mean, Jameson was the first guy in four years who managed to put a dent in those walls you've built around your heart. I know you loved him. I saw it."

"I did love him," I agreed after a moment of silence. I had asked myself the same question multiple times after he'd left. "But I told you already, he never asked me to go with him, Olive. He never sat me down and explained his plans, or asked about mine for that matter. He just informed me that he had a job offer and that he had to leave. Oh, and he added that he would miss me like crazy. That's it. That's all he gave me. I'm not about to go after someone who doesn't want me with him."

"Would you have gone with him? If he had asked, I mean?"

"We'll never know that now, will we? Hell, it was all so civil. I didn't even get the chance to throw a vase at his head or anything. Never had the chance to have back-scratching breakup sex. I feel robbed by that. He just informed me of his plans and told me the lease for this place would expire at the end of this month. It was all so...I don't even know what it was. The only thing I do know is that he never asked me to go with him, or if I would consider going with him. I didn't factor into his plans, which is why I say fuck him. I wasn't about to beg the guy just because he gave good orgasms, that's for sure." I straightened from Olive's shoulder and turned my back to the living room. "Yeah, fuck him and the horse he rode in on. I'll stay with you guys until I find a job, then I'll be out of your hair."

"Are you going to call your grandma—"

"That is the *last* person I'm planning on calling. I broke up with a guy; it happens every day. I'd much rather call Jameson than call Catherine. I'm not suicidal."

After giving me a hard look, she opened her mouth to say something, but I grabbed her arm and ushered her to the door.

"It's over and done with, Olive. Obviously Jameson wasn't the right one for me. Not everyone gets their happily ever after, and that's totally okay. I'm totally okay with that fact. Now can we go and continue this unnecessary conversation at your place? Preferably when I have some more alcohol in my bloodstream?"

She huffed, but exited the apartment without me having to push her all the way to the car. I grabbed the key on my way out and gave the apartment a last look.

"Just so you know," I said to Olive, who was standing right behind me, probably so she could catch me if I decided to throw myself on the ground and bawl my eyes out. I guess she really was looking forward to being miserable with me. "I'm never saying I love you to any other guy again. Mark my words. The moment you spill the words, they screw you over. So I'm done with that. I don't even care if he is a God in bed, or if he has a foot-long in his pants. No more I love yous."

She made a strangled sound, so I looked over my shoulder. "A foot-long? Ouch, Lucy."

I gave her a devious smile. "Not ouch, that's actually a *come to mama* moment, but even the foot-long guy won't get an I love you from me. His penis might, but not him. If I ever make the mistake of doing that, give me a good pinch or dump a bucket of cold water over my head, anything to snap me out of it."

I locked the door, faced Olive, and waited for an answer from her.

"Fine." She sighed, pulling me away from the door. "I'll hurt you."

"Great. Now that that's out of the way, did you think about what I said way back?"

"What?"

"About you and your husband adopting me. Now…I've spent some serious time thinking it over, and I believe it can be beneficial for all parties involved."

"Oh? Please, do tell about these benefits."

"First benefit: so you know how much I drool when I see your husband shirtless on the big screen? I'll stop ogling your husband when he is shirtless on the big screen."

"That's a good start, I guess. Tell me more."

"Second benefit: you'll have to give me cuddle time more frequently, because, well, I'll be your daughter. You'll have to show me love with cuddles."

"Interesting. Does anyone else besides you benefit from this adoption? Because you just said—"

"Well, I haven't thought that far ahead yet. Geez, Olive. Victim of love here, remember?"

"Right…"

Another Hollywood Marriage Bites the Dust

Two months ago we brought you the sad news of Adam Connor (28) and Adeline Connor (26) calling it quits, and it was no surprise that it shocked everyone in the industry. To be honest, some of us were thinking it was a PR setup to promote Adeline's latest movie, but unfortunately, today we got news that the couple signed the final divorce papers that ended their love story, which started almost six years ago.

After all these weeks, we still have no idea what the breaking point was for the stars. Sources close to the couple have different views as to what went wrong in the marriage, but so far we can't confirm anything. There is only one thing everyone agrees on and that is that there was no cheating going on. To that end, through their short-lived marriage, neither Adeline nor Adam have been caught with another love interest by the herd of paparazzi that always follows them around.

To jog your memory, the love-struck couple got married after dating for over a year. Adeline Young was only twenty-one years old when she said yes and quietly got married to the attractive actor in Paris with only a few family members in attendance, and only seven months later she gave birth to their now five-year-old son, Aiden. As you all know, Adam Connor is the son of Helena

Connor and Nathan Connor, the legendary Hollywood couple. While their daughter, Victoria Connor, didn't follow in the footsteps of her parents by becoming an actress, Adam Connor has been in the acting world since he turned fourteen and his first movie The Poison of Family became a blockbuster.

Despite all the drama they must be dealing with, Adam prefers to stay quiet when presented with questions about his marriage. However, an insider told us, "After months of being heartbroken about the breakup, Adeline is finally ready to move on. To do so, she is getting ready to do a press conference and answer all the questions the media has about her marriage to Adam and why it had to end."

On the flipside, when we tried to reach Adam Connor's reps for a comment, we couldn't get an answer about anything related to his marriage to Adeline. All we could get out of the family's longtime friend and publicist was that Adam wanted to give all his focus and attention to their son, Aiden, during and after the divorce. The pair has joint custody of their son, but from the whispers we've been hearing, we're not so sure it will stay that way for long.

Who wants full custody and why? That seems to be the million-dollar question here. If the couple really were on good terms after their divorce, why would they prepare to fight for custody over their only son?

On a better note, we just confirmed that Adam Connor has purchased the estate next to our favorite newlywed couple, Jason and Olive Thorn. The hot, brooding star was photographed leaving the premises of his new house with his son, Aiden, just yesterday.

If you have good money tucked away, we would suggest you to look into buying a house, a shed, whatever you can get your hands on in Bel Air. Two of the sexiest movie stars in Hollywood *living side by side with only a stone wall separating them? Sure, okay, one of them might not be available anymore, but Adam Connor is free as a bird, ladies. Wouldn't you give all your life savings to be his neighbor? We certainly would!*

CHAPTER TWO

LUCY

"Shhh, be quiet," I whispered urgently.

"Shhh yourself! I didn't do anything."

"I didn't say you did something, I said be quiet. You're gonna ruin this before we even get the chance to see anything," I hissed at Olive. She huffed, probably annoyed with me, but stayed quiet as we carried the enormous ladder toward the stone wall of their property.

Hours had passed since we left Jameson's apartment, and I had officially moved into my friend's guest room. As promised, we'd already celebrated the move *and* the breakup with multiple shots of tequila and several margaritas each. We might have also used the screening room as our own karaoke bar and slaughtered a few songs along the way, but we chalked our bad performances up to bad weather because normally we slayed any and all songs.

While we were lying around and examining the ceilings, Olive got a text from Jason saying he would be late to our little pity party, which was exactly when I remembered it was a bad idea to let Olive drink more than four shots of tequila. After I consoled a crying Olive—she was crying because Jason was going to be late—she decided it was a brilliant idea to get the ladder we'd seen the gardeners use earlier and check out Adam Connor's side of the wall—the hottie movie star who had moved in a few months ago. Who was I to say no to such a good plan? Our plan didn't include spying on him or anything—I mean, obviously we weren't stalkers, we just wanted to see what his house looked like, you know, because houses are really important. It's always a mark in the winning column if you have a roof over your head.

And if by dumb luck we saw him walking around half-naked —or hopefully fully naked—well, it wouldn't be our fault we were looking then, would it? The blame would lie solely on his shoulders.

So that's how we ended up in Olive's backyard, carrying that damn ladder.

"What if he is naked, Lucy? What do we do?"

"Umm, make sure he is naked by his own will? It's practically indecent exposure, but we'll skip calling the cops, I think."

"Are you being serious?"

"Of course I'm not! Be careful, watch where you're going— there's a tree behind you."

After giving me the stink eye, she glanced over her shoulder and narrowly avoided the trunk of the tree. "Oh, thanks."

I smiled and shook my head. Jason was about to get one hell of a surprise when he found his wife drunk off her ass.

When we were close enough, I slowly lowered my end of the ladder. "Don't let go, okay? We need to lean it against the wall."

"I know what we need to do, stop bossing me around. And will you please stop hitting my bush!"

"Geez, Olive, I'm getting shredded by your stupid bush here, and you're not even worried that I might die from severe blood loss."

"Don't worry, you won't die from a few scratches. Plus, this whole thing was your idea, I'm gonna keep repeating that when

Jason comes home and busts us." She sing-songed her last sentence while I was trying my best to get away from the deadly bush.

"My idea?"

Groaning, I helped her prop the stupidly heavy thing against the wall. When it made a loud thudding sound, I winced and dropped my ass to the ground between the bush and the stone wall.

"Shit," Olive whispered and hugged the ladder. "Do you think he heard it?"

"Who?"

"Adam Connor."

"I think the whole neighborhood heard that, but let's hope Adam has hearing problems."

"Come on then, get up. I wanna have a look," she ordered as she jumped from one leg to the other and looked up at the wall. "We'll look just for a second, though, okay?"

"Yeah, yeah. You said that already. And it's not like we're gonna make this into a routine. We'll just look this one time and that's it."

"Yes. That's it, Lucy. I'm so relieved you said that."

As far as walls go, it wasn't exactly the highest wall out there, which was sad for the wall, but also weird considering how obsessed rich people are with security. Then again, I guess when two equally hot and successful movie stars became neighbors, they didn't have any reason to suspect each other of stalking.

I quickly tied my shoulder-length hair up in a ponytail. Holding on to the ladder, I lifted my butt off the soft soil.

"So, how do we do this?" I asked as I dusted off my jeans. The steps were actually wide enough to hold both of us, but climbing up them at the same time would be impossible—considering we were both intoxicated, quite possibly deadly too.

When I met Olive's sparkling green eyes, she shrugged and

motioned for me to go first, so I did. "When I'm at the top you can come up too. You're taller than me, so you stay on the lower step, okay?" When she didn't answer and just kept jumping around, I frowned and whispered, "What's wrong with you?"

"I need to pee, but I'm holding it. Come on, let's do this already."

"I'm going to remind you that you said that if it becomes necessary, and try not to pee on me while you're at it."

I grabbed the ladder on both sides and took my first step up as Olive placed her hands on my ass and started to push me up.

"I'm not a pussy."

"What are you even talking about, Olive?"

"Come on, go faster already!"

"Jesus, fine," I exclaimed, looking down at her. "Calm your tits, woman."

When my head reached the top of the wall, I stopped and looked down at Olive, who was already climbing up. "Move your ass to the left a little," she ordered in a huff before grabbing my ankle as leverage.

"Are you sure you're oka—"

"I'm sure. Go up one more step. I can't see a thing."

"Now who is the bossy one, I wonder," I murmured, climbing up one more step so I could peek over the wall. While the lights were on in the house, from what I could see, nobody was out in the backyard. Still, I wanted to play it safe and not look like a legit peeping Tom by actually hanging over the wall to try and see inside the house better.

"What are we looking at?" Olive asked when she finally made it up.

"*I'm* looking at an empty backyard and what looks to be an equally empty house. What are *you* looking at?"

"I think I'm looking at the same thing. Bummer, don't tell Jason, but I just wanted to see him once, you know. Of course we drool together every time we watch his movies." She shook her head and lifted it a bit higher while I tried to stay steady on my feet. "It's been months since he moved in, but we never run into each other. On top of everything else, Jason isn't exactly being cooperative about this. I already asked him to introduce me to—"

I gave her a sharp look. "You asked him to introduce *us*, right? Not just you."

"Us, right. Of course I said us. Sharing is caring. Oh! Lucy, look!"

She rested her chin on the wall so I did the same thing to get a look at what she was seeing. "What? Where is he? I don't see him."

"Not him," she whispered urgently.

"Who the hell did you see? Tell me!"

"I think...wait, there! Look at the window behind that big plant on the right."

I craned my neck higher, exposing my entire face. "Oh, is that his son?"

"Must be. Oh, he looks so cute, Lucy." She awwed next to me, her voice going all wonky.

"Oh God, please don't start crying again, not while we are teetering on the edge over here."

"I told you I'm not a pussy. I'm not gonna cry."

In the quiet of the night, we watched the little boy press his hands against the window and look outside with the saddest expression on his little face. After a few seconds passed, he abruptly turned around and looked up as if he was talking to someone. As much as we tried to, we couldn't see who was standing behind him.

"Don't lean on me too much," I said urgently as Olive's shoulder pressed against mine in an attempt to see who the kid was looking at.

"I think it's him," she squeaked, ignoring my warning.

While I was doing my best not to fall off the ladder, our mystery person stepped forward and lowered himself on one knee.

"It's him," I whispered to Olive.

We watched Adam Connor ruffle his kid's dark blond hair and nudge his chin up with his knuckles. If I said my heart wasn't doing all kinds of jumping and flip-flapping, I would be lying. After all, he was a handsome bastard, and it wasn't my fault my heart was weak. We couldn't see their expressions *that* clearly, but we saw Adam's lips start moving and then the kid throwing himself in his father's arms and hugging his neck.

"I feel like we're doing something bad," I said as the kid suddenly let go of his dad and ran away, out of our sight.

"We *are* doing something bad. That looked like a private moment, Lucy. We should get down."

"Yes, we should." Even though we agreed it wasn't cool of us to intrude, neither one of us moved. We couldn't.

Adam hung his head for a moment after the kid ran away, then he was up on his feet, walking closer to the glass windows.

Both Olive and I tensed, ready to disappear from sight if he decided to come out, but he simply stood there, his hands stuffed in his pockets, his gaze focused on the dim lights coming from his pool.

"Holy shit," Olive said quietly, and suddenly I remembered I wasn't alone.

I shivered and glanced at my friend. "What?"

She looked at me, then back to Adam Connor. "Nothing." She shook her head. "I mean, we can't really *see* him, see him, but he looks good from this close. And...and he looks sad too. The divorce must be tough on him and the kid."

"I read that they both wanted the divorce. You think he still loves her?"

"After everything they wrote about me and Jason, you should

know better than to believe what you read online. They have a kid together; it's never simple when there is a kid in the middle of everything. I'm pretty sure we know nothing about what's been going on in their lives."

"That's true. In that case, I could offer him my shoulder." I paused to think about that statement for a second. "Or better yet, my boobs." Olive's head turned to me in a sharp movement. "Don't look at me like that. It's just so he can, you know, cry. My lovely boobs aren't as comfy as yours, but I'm still rocking an almost C cup, and I'd be so gentle with him. Pat his head, put him to bed, maybe warm him up if he is cold from all the crying. Sharing body heat is a very important process. We could snuggle up under the covers…play hide the pickle to get his spirits up."

"I thought you said you were done with guys."

"I'm done *falling in love* with them, and even if I do, I sure as hell won't let them know that I've done so. I never said I'm done falling on top of certain body parts. They have many, many other uses that don't require me falling in love." Ignoring Olive's eyes on me, I shrugged and kept watching Adam. "You know what they say: to get over someone you should get under someone else. We can get over and under each other. I'm not picky at all."

"Okay, let's get down before you crawl over the wall to get to that poor guy. I don't like the look in your eyes."

"What look?" I asked, giving my best friend an innocent look, complete with a sweet smile. "I'm an angel."

She laughed and patted my head. "More like the devil."

"Hey! I take offense to that."

Just as we were bickering, Adam Connor suddenly reached up to loosen his tie, causing a softly uttered curse word to leave my lips.

"What?" Olive asked.

"I find it extremely hot when a guy takes off his clothes in slow motion."

We silently watched him take off his suit jacket and throw it on something we couldn't see clearly from our point of view.

"Is it getting a little hot?" Olive mumbled.

"Shhh," I whispered, completely focused on seeing what the six-foot-three hunk with the broad shoulders would do next.

When his fingers started unbuttoning his white shirt's left sleeve as he kept his eyes on the horizon with an unreadable expression, I had to swallow down the lump in my throat. Slowly but expertly, he started rolling it up, exposing his forearms—forearms I would've killed to see closer. Then he started on his right sleeve, repeating the same process while Olive and I watched the whole thing without a peep.

"Holy shit," Olive finally whispered when Adam was massaging his temples with his fingers, his head bent down, those thick arm muscles bulging even to our eyes.

"I think I've just creamed myself," I admitted.

"What do you mea—oh my God, Lucy!" she yelled loudly enough to wake up the whole neighborhood, then started laughing. Evidently, bursting my eardrums wasn't enough, so she hit my arm too—hard, almost causing me to lose my balance.

"Hey!" I shot back, laughing quietly. Before I could topple over, I grabbed on to the wall.

"Oh my God, I hate you!" she seethed when she had calmed down enough to speak. "Why would you even say that?"

Giving her a hurt look, I rubbed the spot she'd hit. "What? The guy almost took off his shirt, loosened his tie, and then rolled up his sleeves. I just think the whole thing was sexy. There is something called forearm porn. You know that, right? Besides, it's not my fault my body reacted to the guy."

"You're impossible."

"Thank you, I try to stand out. And relax, I was just messing with you. If I were closer to him, I might have creamed, but nope, the distance between us and the fact that I couldn't hear his breathing ruined it. I still wanna jump him, though."

"His breathing? You think you would learn—"

We heard a click and then a sliding sound. Olive stopped talking and grabbed my arm. Both of us had that 'oh shit' look on our faces, and if you were wondering, we wore it pretty damn well.

"Dan? Is that you out there?"

Olive squeaked and then slapped her own hand over her mouth to muffle the noise before we were completely screwed. Our only saving grace was that our side of the wall was pitch-dark and there was no way in hell Adam Connor could see us. I motioned for Olive to lower her head, and she obeyed without argument.

"You better be a goddamn raccoon because I'm not in the mood to invite the cops into my home," the voice said from the other side of the wall.

Olive looked at me in alarm, but I shook my head and pressed my index finger to my lips so she wouldn't speak. We knew there was no way Adam could know there were two girls hanging off a wall on the other side of his property, but the fact that we could hear his footsteps coming closer toward us didn't help me relax at all.

Silence fell again. Another few seconds ticked by, then the footsteps started retreating. After we heard the telltale sound of his sliding door, Olive released the breath she was holding.

"We are not doing this again," she whispered, taking a step down on the ladder.

When I didn't agree with her immediately, she tugged at my shirt to get my attention. "Did you hear what I just said?"

"Yes. Yes. We're not doing this again."

"I'm being serious, Lucy."

"Excuse me, Mrs. Thorn, but weren't you the one who first mentioned we could take a peek over the wall?"

"I didn't hear you say no—the opposite, actually. I remember you congratulating me on my great idea. Come on, get down."

I felt another tug on my ankle as she kept descending.

I slowly raised my head up to see if the fine specimen was gone, and to my dismay there was no sight of him. Lights were still on, but no eye candy. I looked down to see a frowning Olive looking up at me.

"What?"

"You remember the girl who hid in our hotel room in London, right?"

"Don't worry, my green Olive, I'm not planning on breaking into his house."

Not that it hadn't crossed my mind, but I drew the line at breaking and entering; I wasn't that crazy. I had thought about taking a peek through one of those gigantic windows, but like I said, the line had to be drawn somewhere, and looking over the wall was where I drew it.

Don't judge me. Tell me, what would you do if you ended up being the neighbor of one of your favorite actors? Of course you'd spy on the guy...or at least you'd attempt to. Don't even try to deny it.

Despite his legendary parents, Adam Connor was a closed book. Of course, everybody knew about him—even before he landed his first movie—but he was still somewhat of a mystery. Who doesn't love a mysterious guy? Certainly not me.

He was a quiet guy, one of those actors who smiles at the cameras when he doesn't want to answer a question, one of those hot guys who only talks when he has something good to say, wildly successful at his job, married at twenty-three, a seemingly good dad, possessor of an out-of-this world body...and those were just a few of Adam Connor's attributes. Of course, how much can you really know a public figure just from stalking them online every now and then…

"Lucy, you can't break into his house."

"Didn't I just say I had no plans to do such thing?" I asked Olive in a quiet voice as I took a step down.

"You even mentioning it scares me. It means it crossed your mind at some point."

When I was finally standing on solid ground, I gave all my attention to Olive. "I'm not stepping foot on the other side of this wall, cross my heart. Okay?"

She narrowed her eyes at me, and I gave her a reassuring smile with a thumbs-up. I really wasn't planning on jumping over the wall, so I wasn't actually lying to my friend. Now, if I ended up climbing the ladder again…well, I couldn't see any harm in that.

Done with the intense eye contact Olive was making, I reached out and forced the edges of her lips upward with my fingers. "Smile, Olive. Show me your teeth." Just to help her along, I gave her a big grin. "Come on, you can do this. I know you can. I've seen you do it before."

When she cracked and started smiling on her own, I took a step back and almost fell over another damn bush. "What was the point of surrounding the whole damn place with these things? To kill me?"

"You'll have to ask Jason about that," she said, pulling me away from the greenery. "I'm feeling a little dizzy, I think. Let's just sit down for a while."

Heading toward the pool, we plopped down on the grass when she found a spot she was happy with.

"Are you going to call Jameson?" Olive asked after we quietly watched the stars for a while.

"Why would I do that?"

"I don't know. It was a stupid question, forget about it."

I glanced at her from the corner of my eye and felt uneasy when I saw her expression.

"Olive, are you okay?"

"Nope. I'm still angry."

"Angry? At me?"

"No. At Jameson." She turned her head and frowned at me. "Why would I be angry at you? Anything else you're keeping from me?"

"Nope. No reason." I sighed and glanced back at the stars— the few we could see above the city lights. "I'm sorry for not telling you before. I didn't want to bother you since I knew you were getting close to your deadline. And maybe...maybe I didn't like the fact that I couldn't just shrug it off and move on like he didn't mean anything to me."

"I know what you mean, but you don't have to do everything on your own. And, Lucy?" She paused, so I looked at her again. "I'm your friend. Your sister from another mister. Nothing is more important than you. I don't care how deep I'm buried in words, you always come first. And now that you know it, you can never use that against me again." She turned her head back toward the sky and added, "Which means if you take away my friendship rights again, I'll have to kick your ass."

I let out a small laugh and looked away too. "Gee, Olive, I had no idea you were looking forward to being miserable. I promise, the next time someone breaks my heart—which is pretty unlikely since I'm never falling in love again—you'll be the first person to hear it."

"Good."

"You know you're my person, right?" she asked a minute later.

A small smile played on my lips. "Grey's Anatomy? Like Christina and Meredith?"

"Yes."

"Yeah, you're my person too, my green Olive."

And she always would be.

"Good. Lucy?"

I glanced at her again. "Olive?"

"Don't tell Jason I said this, but I think Adam is seriously hot."

"Is that so?" someone asked from right behind us; both Olive and I let out a shriek that echoed through the night. If the neighbors around the property hadn't heard Olive's first scream, they were sure to hear that one.

"Jason!" Olive yelled at him as she struggled to get up.

I pressed my hand to my chest. "Did you want to give me a heart attack just because I'm staying over for a few days?" I asked, helping Olive stand up. "Why would you sneak up on us like that?"

"I wasn't sneaking up on anyone. I simply walked into my house to hear my wife admit"—he paused to give Olive a look— "how 'hot' she finds this guy…this guy who is *not* her husband."

"Jason," Olive repeated in a completely different tone as she started walking toward him. She was drunk off her ass and had stars in her eyes, pretty, shiny little stars.

Jason took a few steps forward to catch his wife so she could fall into his arms instead of falling on her face. Glancing at me, he asked, "I take it the celebrations went well?"

"She is angry at me for not sending her an invite for my very own pity party, but she kinda got over it after the second shot of tequila."

He caught Olive in his arms and let her pull down his face to give him a long kiss. Looking at them, so beautifully in love, I caught myself smiling and realized once again that I loved very much how beautiful love looked on my friend. For me it had never been like that.

"I missed you," Olive whispered, or more likely thought she

whispered—she was still yelling. "And you missed our impromptu concert. We were so good, Jason."

Gently pushing the hair out of her face, he gave her a warm smile, one that clearly said, *I'm deeply in love with you*, and kissed her lips again. "I'm sorry, sweetheart, we had to stay late to wrap things up on set."

"I think it's sleep time for your wife, Jason," I said, interrupting their private little bubble, and they both turned to look at me. "I'm planning on waking her up pretty early, and I know for a fact that she's going to hate that, so…"

I wasn't trying to get rid of them, not necessarily, but I didn't want them to feel awkward around me, or feel the need to keep me company when I knew they had much better things to do—like get their freak on in their bedroom before I made it to my room that was right across from them. Not to mention, it wouldn't hurt to be alone for a short while.

Olive let go of Jason and walked back to my side to give me a hug. "I love you, Lucy Meyer," she said, still holding on to me. "And I promise you'll fall in love again." Taking a step back, she looked me in the eyes and added, "And you know what? When you do, it's going to be epic, and not just your plain old epic, it'll be out-of-this-world epic."

I grinned at her, and she nodded with a straight face.

"Now, don't go to bed too late, and we'll talk more about this in the morning."

"Okay, *Mom*," I yelled as I watched them walk back into the house, hand in hand. "By the way, thank you so much for adopting me, guys!"

"God, no," Jason said as he got ready to close the door. "We're not adopting you, Lucy."

"So, you're thinking about it? Great! I can't wait to call you *Daddy*, Jason!"

With a smile playing on his lips, he shook his head and slid the glass door closed.

Laughing to myself, I lay back down on the grass, closed my eyes, and took a deep breath. It was a beautiful night—not too hot, not too chilly, perfect temperature for September. I kept my eyes closed and imagined myself standing on the edge of a cliff, my arms wide open as the wind caressed my skin and played with my hair, a big smile spreading across my face.

CHAPTER THREE

LUCY

"I'm sorry, Lucy."

"Can you two please stop apologizing? I told you it's okay. Jesus, you're leaving me in a palace; I'm pretty sure I'll manage to survive without you two," I assured Olive for the tenth time as I sat cross-legged in the middle of their bed.

Olive gave me an apologizing look and glanced back at Jason while she continued to throw random clothes into a big suitcase. "Flying to London for the promotion stuff wasn't on the schedule for at least another week. Why did they switch the timeline at the last minute like this?"

So...remember how I mentioned my talented friend writing a book that made the bestseller lists in no time? Well, that book, *Soul Ache*, also got made into a movie. The leading actor? Jason Thorn, of course. How did you think they met again after so many years? She wrote a goddamned book inspired by him and voila! She got the dream guy with her dream job.

"You don't have to hurry, Olive," Jason said as he captured Olive's hand and dropped a kiss on her palm. "We still have two hours until they pick us up."

"You think two hours is enough time to decide what to take

with you for a weeklong trip? They'll follow us everywhere; I don't want them to write a whole damn article about how messy I look next to you and that maybe I should get my nose out of my books if I don't want to lose you."

"They already wrote that, Olive," I chimed in, just to be helpful.

"That's exactly my point!" she exclaimed as she started taking clothes back out of her suitcase. "I don't want to read that again."

Jason grabbed her attention as he zipped up his own small suitcase, which he'd packed in ten minutes. "I love it when you look messy. It reminds me of how good you look after I love you a little."

"Ah," I groaned, trying to hide my smile and doing a piss poor job of it. "Your kid is in the room. Gross."

He pressed his lips against Olive's hair, and I noticed how her body relaxed a little. "But," he continued, "I think I'm gonna wait for you in the living room. I need to call Tom anyway."

Tom was his agent, and even though he probably did need to call him, I would've bet a thousand dollars he was more interested in fleeing the scene than discussing his potential next project with his agent.

"Chicken shit," I murmured; he gave me a quick wink before exiting the room.

"Help?" Olive asked, looking at me hopefully.

"Oh, I guess I can help," I relented. "But you're not taking that black dress with you. You're not going to a funeral. This is your movie, more than it is his, actually. And this is not the premiere, right?" I crawled off the bed and headed toward her gigantic closet. Olive was right behind me.

"It is still happening, the premiere in London, I mean, but it is after the LA and New York premieres. This London trip is just interviews and a few talk shows."

"You're doing the shows too?"

She shook her head. "As much as Megan would've loved that, I said no to live shows. We'll do a few of the recorded interviews together, but that's it. I don't want to be seen that much. That's his job, and that's all the excitement I can handle anyway."

"Well, okay. Then you definitely don't need this floor-length dress," I said, fishing out another black dress she wouldn't need at all.

Half an hour later we emerged from her bedroom with enough clothes packed to hold her over for at least a month.

"The car is here," Jason said as soon he saw us wheeling two suitcases toward the front door.

"Already?" Olive and I asked at the same time.

"Yes," Jason said, reaching to take the suitcase out of Olive's hand. "There was a change in the schedule."

"Oh, I'm gonna miss you." She gave me a tight hug and followed Jason outside. "I'm really sorry for leaving you like this. I swear as soon as I'm back—"

"You'll make it up to me," I said, finishing her sentence before she could get into another long-winded apology. "It's only a week, Olive. Pray for me while you're over there so I can find a job by the time you guys come back."

"About that," she murmured as she sat down on the bench right outside their door to put on her shoes. "I sent you an email with a few contact numbers attached to it. While we are on our way to the airport I'll forward you some emails too."

"And what do you want me to do with those emails again?"

"Not much. I want you to play my agent."

Done with her shoes, she got up and stood in front of me.

"Play your agent?" I asked, confused.

"Look, you don't want to be an accountant. There. I said it. You might be good with numbers, but that's not your calling. And before you say no—"

"Olive?" Jason called out, holding the passenger door open

for his wife. Olive looked over her shoulder. "We have to leave. Can you call Lucy on the way to the airport?"

"I'm coming, just give me a second."

When she turned back to look at me, I had a frown on my face. "Olive—"

"I'm not doing it for you, Lucy. I'm asking for your help. You flaked on me when I needed to talk to the movie studio the first time, so you can't say no to this too. I talked to a good number of agents, and we don't see eye to eye. I doubt they even read my book. You inhaled every line of that book; if someone has to sell it, I want it to be you. And before you say it, if I start negotiating for future book and audiobook deals, I won't have a single minute to write. You'll help your friend out, right? 'Cause you're the bestest of the best friends, right?" She lifted her eyebrows, waiting on an answer from me.

"Olive, I have a business major. I know nothing about being a literary agent."

She started to back away from me and lifted her hands up. "Just add up some numbers then multiply them, do whatever the hell you do with numbers, and find out which deal is better for me. I have to make a decision before I'm done writing."

"I don't think the numbers should be your only worry, Olive," I yelled after her as she headed toward the black car. "What are they offering you in terms of marketing? Are they planning something you couldn't do yourself if you were to self-publish again?"

Reaching Jason's side, she yelled back, "See? You already know the right questions to ask. Just talk to them, okay? I'll call you when we land." With those last words, she hopped into the car.

"I don't like your wife very much right now," I grumbled loudly enough so Jason could hear. His eyes found mine, and he smiled.

He glanced into the car then looked back at me with a bigger smile on his lips. "She says she loves you, too."

I rolled my eyes and waved at Jason, ready to get back inside.

"Lucy?" Jason called out.

"Yes?" I answered, peeking behind the door.

"Take care of yourself, okay? Call Tom if you need anything at all."

"Aw, you love me too." I pressed my hands against my heart and sighed, dramatically. "I knew you secretly wanted to adopt me. I'm the daughter you never knew you wanted, aren't I?" I asked, batting my eyelashes.

Jason just shook his head before hopping in next to Olive.

———

THE DAYS FOLLOWING Olive's departure to London passed as you would expect them to: fairly uneventfully.

The number of job interviews I'd had: two.

The number of phone calls I'd gotten from Olive: countless.

The number of phone calls I'd gotten from my grandma, Catherine: three.

And let me tell you, that was three phone calls more than I wanted. As much as I wished I could, I couldn't avoid her for eternity, but I did put off talking to her as much as I could.

And, umm…the number of ladder climbs I'd done in the first few days after Olive left…well…that would be eight. By day three, I'd climbed that ladder a total of eight times. No eye rolling, please. What would you have done? Don't tell me you wouldn't be curious. There is no fucking way you'd shrug and say whatever, I'll just pretend he doesn't exist—not if the next-door neighbor was Adam Connor.

Anyway. I didn't see the guy until the fourth day anyway, so you can hold off on the judging.

I had just ventured outside, a pretty coffee mug in one hand

and a printed copy of one of the offers Olive had gotten from one of the big five publishers in the other when I heard the unmistakable sound of a child's giggle. Obviously, I had to drop everything and go investigate, because that's what good housesitters do. What if it wasn't a kid's giggle but thieves I'd heard? Things like that totally happen all the time, and since I'm a good friend, I looked into it. Obviously my only intention was to protect my best friend's house.

I tried to be as quiet as possible when I neared the wall and started climbing up. Raising my head just enough so I could see what was going on on the other side, I spotted my prey just stepping out into the backyard.

"Holy mother of…"

Trying not to lose my balance, I reached for my phone—which I had of course concealed in my bra—found Olive's name, and hit dial.

"Hello?"

"I'm in love," I admitted in a rush.

"That was quick. I thought you were never saying those words to another man again."

"This one can have anything and everything he wants from me."

"Who's the lucky guy? And did you have to find him when I wasn't there to approve?"

I ignored her question and instead said, "I have a question for Jason. Could you please be so kind as to relay it to him?"

In an amused tone, she said, "I'll try. Hit me."

"Where do they breed these Hollywood people? Like, is there a farm we can visit to pick out the ones we like best? I would just like to have a look-see. If there is a place like that and you've been keeping it from me…I'm not sure I can be your friend anymore."

Olive laughed. "I'm not aware of its existence, but I'll ask for you. Did you have someone in mind?"

"Yes, actually. How nice of you to ask, my beautiful and smart friend. And before you get mad at me, just look at this," I said before quickly taking a shot of what was happening in front of my eyes.

"What? What did you do, Lucy?"

"Nothing. Have a little faith in your friend. Just sent you a pic. Open it."

"Okay. Give me a sec."

I lowered the phone and kept my eyes on the duo in front of me. Oh, you wanna know what I was seeing, too?

I was looking at a half-naked Adam Connor. He had these loose shorts on that sat dangerously low, and he was showing me those impressive arm and shoulder muscles as he did pushups with a giggling kid sitting on his back. It was a private show just for me.

How considerate of him, I know.

"I might've just drooled a little bit. My God, those arms," I groaned.

"What are you even talking about?" Olive asked. "I'm trying to open the picture—shit."

"I zoomed in on those muscles. You can thank me later."

"Lucy…" She sighed.

"What?"

"You shouldn't be up there."

"Not without you, you mean."

There was a short silence, then she said, "Yes, and that is only because best friends don't let you do stupid things alone."

"Riiiight. I'll let you stick with that."

The kid hopped off his back and screamed, "You did it, Daddy!" He clapped his hands excitedly. His daddy had definitely done something to my panties, all right. Adam Connor, that mountain of a man, got up off the ground and smiled down at his kid, ruffling his hair. The kid jumped up and they high-fived, then he said something to his hot-as-fuck dad and ran inside. Leaning down, Adam grabbed a towel from one of the lounge chairs and started wiping off the sweat from his chest and abs.

"Dear Lord, I'm done for," I whispered into the phone.

"What's he doing? Tell me," Olive whispered back.

"I wanna lick him up, Olive. Like really bad. I wanna peel him like a banana and…"

"Tell me!"

"Jesus, don't yell," I said quietly before I started to describe what was going on just next to her backyard. "His son ran inside, but he is wiping off his abs with a towel right now. He's so sweaty. Olive…he has a V! He has a damn near perfect V."

"Is there a different kind?"

"Yes. Yes, definitely. Some just look wrong. But his…my green Olive, those shoulders…I think I've died and just stepped into heaven. Even his hair is fuckable. Does that even make sense? Not a huge fan of blonds, but his dark honey blond hair is doing it for me. It's almost brown anyway. Jesus, I wanna get under him and hold on to those shoulders and just let him pound—"

"Lucy, calm down and don't you dare finish that sentence," Olive warned, but it was too late.

"I have to," I said, whining a little. "I have to say it so it can come true. Pound me. I wanna hold on and just let him pound me."

"You're…I don't even know what you are," she said, laughing.

"And there is a bulge, Olive." I groaned quietly as Adam faced me and started stretching his arms with his eyes closed and his head thrown back. "*Sweet Jesus*, even his throat is sexy. And there is a big bulge, Olive."

"Is he *hard?*"

"No—hell, I don't know, but it couldn't possibly be that big when he is soft."

Oh, dear Lord, please don't let him have big balls and a small dick...

I wondered if I would get arrested if I just hopped over the wall, ran to his side while his eyes were closed, and pulled down his shorts. They wouldn't count a case of extreme curiosity as a crime, right? Hell, maybe what he was packing in there would be worth the time I'd spend behind bars, daydreaming about his cock.

His kid came running outside, and I shook my head to clear my mind. The kid was wearing the exact same shorts his dad was wearing. The only addition was a white shirt, probably to protect him from the unexpected chill. Never losing the big smile on his face, he handed his fuck-able daddy a water bottle, and I watched him gulp it down in one chug.

I could've used some cold water myself, but was anyone thinking about me? Nope.

Then I watched Adam slowly lower himself down again, this time on his perfectly bite-able ass.

"Lucy? You still there?"

"Yeah. Awww, look at that."

"What?"

"He is doing sit-ups now and the kid is hugging his knees with his little arms and counting."

"Awww. Picture. Picture."

"Okay, hold on."

I took another photo and sent it.

"There is definitely a bulge," I added as I tried to shift on my feet to get a better look. "He is definitely hung."

"His kid is there, Lucy."

"And? How do you think he created that kid? Do we have to talk about where babies come from again?"

Olive laughed in my ear, and I smiled, picturing her shaking her head at me.

"Oh, shoot. Jason is coming up; I have to go."

"Up? Where are you?"

"In bed. There were some fans camped out in front of the hotel when we came back from a late dinner, and he went down to sign a few things for them so they wouldn't spend the night out there."

"Got it. Well I'll let you go then, have fun with the crazy fans."

"You too. Oh, he is here. I'm hanging up now. Get down from there."

And the line went dead.

I spent a few more minutes watching the perfection that was a dad and his son spending time together, then reluctantly got down and went inside to work on those offers some more.

After that encounter, I spent most of my time up there, checking things out. Was I proud of myself? Eh, maybe not so much. But do you know what's hotter than watching Adam Connor work out in his backyard every day? Watching him spend time with his son. Instant reason to jump his bones. *Instant.* He was practically dangling himself in front of me, daring me.

Certainly it wasn't my fault that I was a weak human being, and as long as I didn't hurt anyone, it couldn't be that wrong, could it?

So it was my last day alone, and I was up on my perch again, watching my temporary neighbors as discreetly as I could as Adam jumped into the pool. The little version of him sat on one of the lounge chairs playing with his iPad, kicking his little legs every now and then. Holding on to the ladder, I rested my chin on the wall and stayed vigilant. Repeating the process every day for the rest of the week.

Because you never know, right?

CHAPTER FOUR

ADAM

I swam to the other end of the pool and came up for air. My arm muscles were burning, and the pounding in my head was getting worse as the hours slipped by. I wiped the water off my eyes and spotted Aiden sitting in the same exact spot he'd been occupying for the last thirty minutes, eyes focused on his iPad, face happy.

I looked over his head and my eyes caught sight of his nanny, Anne, standing just outside the door of the house. We had two nannies. The other one was Marta. She stayed with Adeline, half nanny, half assistant to Adeline, and Anne stayed with us when it was my week with Aiden. She gave me a shy smile, and I nodded at her. It was good that she was keeping an eye on Aiden.

Leisurely, I swam back to my son's side, making sure to splash some water close to his seat before I got out. He was looking over his shoulder and laughing at something. When he realized I was close, he took off his headphones and grinned at me.

Just looking at him constricted something in my chest.

"What's up, bud?" I asked, walking toward him.

"I'm bathing in the sun, just like Mommy."

I chuckled. "Good for you."

"Are you ready to do pushups now, Daddy?"

"Not today, buddy," I said as I reached his side and grabbed my towel.

He lost the big smile on his face and gently put his iPad down. "Am I not a good teacher?"

"Not teacher, trainer," I reminded him.

"Did you find a new trainer? I can do better. I really can, Daddy. I can work you harder."

I laughed quietly and sat next to him. "Why would I look for someone new when I have you? You're working me really hard, little man. I can barely keep up."

The worry in his eyes disappeared, and he patted my arm with his little hand. "Okay, you can rest today. Can we do pushups tomorrow if you rest today?"

"I have to take you back to your mom today, remember?"

Copying me, he sat up and rested his elbows on his knees. His feet didn't even reach the ground yet. After giving me a quick glance, he smacked his hand on his knee. "Oh, man. Tomorrow? Will you come and take me tomorrow so we can do pushups?"

"You have school tomorrow, Aiden."

"Oh," he whispered, and his eyes dropped to the ground. "You think Mom will let me come back here after school so I can help you do pushups?"

"How about we work out together when you come back next week?"

"Can I tell my friends I'm your teach—trainer?"

"Of course."

He jumped down and started bouncing on his feet, everything okay in his little world again. "They're gonna be so jealous when they see my muscles!" He lifted his arm up and flexed his impressive little muscles, pressing and prodding with his index finger.

The more I looked at him, the more persistent the ache in my chest got.

Christ!

Why would Adeline do this to me? Why would she hurt me by limiting my time with *my* son when she had no interest in spending time with him?

Almost six months before, she'd sat right across from me in a hotel room in Canada and told me she needed to get a divorce. It was completely unexpected; hell, I'd fucked her hard and fast only twenty minutes before that. Thinking she was messing with me, I was stupid enough to laugh, get up from my seat, and press a kiss on her forehead.

I remember jokingly saying, "You're breaking my heart, sweetheart," but when she rose up and faced me with that serious look on her face—that look where she stayed silent until you understood what she wanted, what she needed, and gave it to her —I knew she meant it.

We talked until the sun came up, and she told me becoming a mom so young had killed her creativity. She told me she wasn't as passionate about her career as she used to be, and that it was Aiden's fault, that he was taking over her life. She explained that she wanted to go back to the times where she didn't have to audition for the movie she wanted to be in; she wanted them to be handed to her. She explained in not so many words that she was starting to regret the decision she had made five years before, that she had made the wrong decision, that she couldn't bond with Aiden. And then she reminded me, again in not so many words, that while she was happy our marriage didn't seem to have a negative effect on my career, it was time for her to be the most sought-after actress in Hollywood again.

Aiden hadn't been in our plans, not when we were both at the peak of our careers. We were young, successful, and in love. The world was our playground, but then a pregnancy changed everything. Adeline herself made sure it changed everything. Before I could wrap my head around being a dad, I was married. Sure, I was in love with her. She was my world and all that crap you believe at the age of twenty-three, but when I watched her walk down that aisle toward me, it didn't feel as right as it should've felt.

It was early.

I felt trapped.

It was a setup, and it was necessary.

But I learned to ignore that gut feeling I'd had for that brief moment and told myself there was no reason for us to wait when we loved each other enough. A few years down the road I would've married her anyway, right?

So I married the girl I loved for an unborn little baby because we couldn't have a scandal as big as Aiden. That was what my own family had told me.

My face must've hardened, 'cause I felt tiny fingers pulling on my face and patting my cheeks. "Can we swim now, Daddy?" Aiden asked, looking into my eyes.

"I thought you didn't want to swim."

"I didn't, but now I do. SpongeBob is over, so we can swim now."

"We have three hours to get you back to your mom, Aiden. It's gonna have to be a quick swim, okay? Then you'll help Anne pack the toys you want to take with you."

He nodded eagerly and gave me a quick kiss that melted my heart.

"Go get your arm floats," I said in a gruff voice, and he ran off, squealing.

Aiden's version of swimming was sitting on the second highest step, splashing water, playing with his toys, and pretending to be swimming for a total of ten seconds as he kicked and punched the water. Our old house—the house that was now

Adeline's—didn't have a pool, so when he first came to stay with me and saw one, he was ecstatic. Learning how to swim, however…he didn't like that at all.

Five minutes into our pool time, Dan came out.

"Dan, look at me! Look!" Aiden yelled, pumping his arms furiously as he showed off his swimming skills to our longtime bodyguard and friend. At least I had gotten him out of the divorce.

"Look at you go, big man," Dan said as he came to stand next to us.

"Slow down, Aiden," I said, helping him sit down on the steps before he hit his chin. He glanced up at Dan and gave him a big grin.

"Did you see me? Did you see how good I was?"

"I did. Well done, big man."

"But did you see how fast I was?"

Dan nodded. "You're practically a fish now."

Aiden doubled over and laughed, his eyes big and happy. "I'm not a fish, Dan." He got up and lifted his arms. "I'm a boy, look!"

As his laughter died down, he focused on his toys and made all kinds of noises as he dipped his plane in and out of the water.

Leaving Aiden with his toys, I moved to Dan's side. "Something wrong?"

Frowning, he looked over his shoulder then turned back to me. "No. Michel has been lighting up your phone for the last hour. I thought you'd want to know."

"Fuck," I groaned. "I forgot about him."

"You want me to handle it?"

"No, it's okay. I need to ask him something first." Turning away from Dan, I dragged a complaining Aiden out of the pool and took off his arm floats. "Dry yourself off, then you're going in to help Anne."

"But I *just* got in, Daddy. Please! Five more minutes."

I crouched down in front of him and wrapped him in a big towel.

"You'll have more time next week, okay? I'll teach you how to swim without the arm floats."

The closer we got to the time I'd have to drop Aiden off at Adeline's, the moodier I got. I'd spent my entire morning closed up in a studio, going over some voiceovers the director wanted me to redo. The second Matthew had said he had what he needed from me, I'd raced back home so I could be with Aiden for the last few hours I had him. Since our divorce had been finalized, all I'd been doing was running around, trying to make enough time for Aiden while juggling all the shooting and promoting. Thankfully, we were getting closer to wrapping things up for *The Only Hour*, and I was looking forward to taking a breather and spending some time with Aiden. First I had to do something about the custody issue that was always in the back of my mind.

Aiden was a good kid. He'd always been that way, even before the divorce, but lately the mess we'd made was starting to get to him. He didn't act out, didn't throw crying fits like other kids would've done, but every time I dropped him off at Adeline's place, he'd get this scared look on his face, as if I was leaving him there for good and this would be the last time he'd ever see me. Every night I made sure to call him so he could hear my voice before he went to sleep, and every single time he broke something in me by asking if I would promise to come get him soon.

Especially hearing those unsure words, thinking about an entire week where I wouldn't have him with me…fuck, but it was starting to get to me.

Trusting Aiden would listen to me and follow us inside, I headed back in with Dan.

When I saw Anne in the kitchen with her phone in her hand, I reminded her that we would have to leave soon. She nodded and walked past me toward the backyard.

"Give me five. I'll check the front gate to see if there are any paparazzi hiding around—I flushed out three this morning. Then I'll get the car ready," Dan said and walked outside.

Nodding, I returned Michel's calls.

"Where have you been? I've been trying to reach you since this morning, Adam."

"What do you need, Michel?"

"I talked to your parents and they think it's a better idea to go ahead with the press release to cut off the rumors about the custody issue, Adam. We need to deny it, and we need to deny it today. You should consider doing this their way."

Michel was the head of the publicity team that had handled the Connor family business for the last ten years, but our time together had come to an end. It would've been better if I'd had the time to handle it face to face, but I didn't have time to go to his office and fire him there in person. I gritted my teeth and listened as he explained what they had come up with.

"Michel, I'm done doing things the way my parents want. I've told you that a thousand times. Look where they got me with their plans."

"I understand where you're coming from, Adam. Still, think about it and get back to me." Either he was ignoring my words or just dismissing them entirely. "If you think a press release won't be intimate enough, we'll secure you a few interviews on a few select shows. With the amount of requests we're getting, you can have your pick of them. Let me see who'd be the best choice in this situation."

"Michel—"

"Give me one second. How about James Holden? He just took over the late night show and his numbers are going strong. We'll provide him with the questions so things won't get out of hand."

"Michel," I started again as he fired more names at me. I opened the fridge and reached for a water bottle. Michel had been a family friend even before becoming the head of the PR team, which was why my parents were okay with him knowing almost every secret they were trying to hide from the media. It wasn't that the guy wasn't good at his job; actually, he was one of the best in the industry. He already had a long list of clients waiting for him to take them on, and I was about to make someone's day by opening up a spot for them. "With everything that's been going on, I forgot to ask—are you still representing Adeline?"

The line went quiet for a beat. "What do you mean am I still representing your wife?"

I ground my teeth. "Ex-wife."

"I'm sorry, Adam. It takes getting used to, you know. Well, of course we're still representing Adeline. Actually, I talked to Helena earlier today and she thinks it's smarter for you two to get in front of the cameras together and show the world that you're a united front, that you'll always do what's best for Aiden and stay friends, but I assumed you wouldn't go for that. Is that why you asked?"

"No." His use of the word 'world' raised my hackles again, as if I gave a shit what the world thought of my relationship with Adeline. I managed to keep my anger under control and continued. "There won't be any need for scheduling interviews, Michel." I tapped my knuckles on the counter after I put the water bottle down. "I know you're good at what you do, and I wish I had the time to do this face to face, but I've decided to get a different PR team."

"Give me a second, my office is too crowded right now." I heard a door click shut. "What do you mean? Is that why you asked about Adeline? I can put together another team to handle her PR if that's the problem."

"That's not necessary. You can keep her on. I just think it's time we went our separate ways. You do a great job for my parents, and from what I can see in the media, for Adeline too, but I don't think we're a good fit anymore."

"Adam, why don't you come down to my office so we can talk about what you want? This isn't the right time for you to make big changes like this or to be irresponsible in your life. You need to focus on your image and let your team handle the rest. I highly suggest we create an opportunity where they can snap some photos of you and Adeline with Aiden."

I let out a long, humorless laugh and shook my head. "You really have your priorities straight, don't you? Unfortunately, you're not that high on my list, Michel. Yes, I've had to make big changes lately, but this is definitely not one of them. I'll have my attorneys contact you about our contract, and we'll take it from there. You're a beast, Michel, you really are a PR guru, but it's just not working anymore."

Ignoring his words, I ended the call and felt like a huge weight had lifted off my shoulders. This was the easy step. Finding another PR firm was going to be a different nightmare altogether, one I didn't care for but knew was necessary.

Noticing Dan come back inside, I headed for my room to take a quick shower and change.

CHAPTER FIVE

Since my feet were starting to kill me from standing on the ladder for almost an hour, when I saw Adam heading inside, I was just about ready to get down and head inside myself so I could bake some chocolate chip cookies for Olive and Jason before they arrived—or at least give it my best try—as a thank you for letting me stay with them.

But instead of following his father, the kid stayed back, so I assumed Adam was coming back too. However, that didn't happen. Instead of Adam, the girl I'd seen around a few times—presumably the nanny—called out to the boy and then disappeared back inside.

Pretty sure the day's festivities were over, I took a step down. When my eye caught the kid glancing back at the house and then back at the pool, I hesitated. Why would they leave him out there alone? Thinking a few more minutes wouldn't hurt the cookie-making process, I decided to wait. Suddenly the boy smiled and reached for the arm floats Adam had taken off him.

Speaking of taking things off, I might have pictured him taking something—anything really—off me a few times here and there. I'm shameless, I know. Can't help it; the guy looked too lickable for his own good when he was half-naked.

After a few tries, the kid managed to pull one of them on, leaving it around his elbow. However, the second one…despite multiple attempts, he couldn't get that one on. So as any other kid his age would, he gave up and chucked it away. When he took his first step into the pool from the shallow end, I started to get nervous. *Surely he knows how to swim, right?* I mean, sure he had arm floats on whenever I saw him get in the water, but they would've taught him, right? They probably had an Olympic pool at their house—the one his wife was living in right now—not that I was keeping track or anything.

When the water reached almost to his chest, I started to panic earnestly. That float didn't look secure on his arm at all, and if he didn't know how to swim, would one arm float even keep him above the water? On top of all that, the kid didn't look too sure in the water.

Risking getting caught, I tried to get his attention.

"Pssssttt! Hey, kid! Hello?"

He finally heard me and looked straight at me.

Did he know I'd been staked out over the wall for days?

Grinning, he waved at me.

Shit!

Before I had enough time to panic and get down from the damn ladder, the kid just went for it and hopped in, face first, arms splashing and legs kicking. From what I'd seen the last few days, that was pretty much his style, but when the float slipped off his arm because of the way he moved…my heart just about stopped.

At first he seemed okay and I was able to breathe again; he knew how to swim after all…but then it all went to hell. He panicked, his head disappeared under the water, and it was quiet for a second…a stillness that was too much for me to take. Then he came up—or more like his head came up while his arms flailed, eyes big with fear.

"Shit." Cursing, I climbed the last two steps and looked around. Nope, no one was coming out. Hell, no one even knew anything was wrong.

"Shit! Fuck! Shit!" Making sure I was cursing repeatedly—because, trust me, the situation most definitely required that—I straddled the wall as fast as I could and basically tumbled down the rest of the way.

I landed on my hands and knees, my phone a few feet away, my face inches away from the ground, and before I could get up, the kid disappeared under the water again.

"Jesus," I moaned before getting up and blindly running to get to him. I yelled, "Where the hell are you, people?" but didn't see anyone coming out of the damn house. When I hit the water, his head came up again, his arms barely splashing water anymore as he gulped for air. If he had just stayed calm, he would've noticed that he was able to stay afloat, but how can you expect a five-year-old not to panic and get scared when he couldn't find his footing?

I jumped in and swam toward him. It had all happened in maybe fifteen seconds, twenty tops, and when I caught him under his arms and held his head above the water so he could breathe, my heart was just about ready to fly out of my chest.

Those few seconds had shaved off *at least* ten years of my life. Hell, my youth was practically gone. I was fully in the right to demand payment from the sexy-as-hell dad in the form of orgasms.

Finally I hit the steps and gathered him in my arms. The kid, probably scared out of his mind, threw his arms around my neck and held on for dear life as he coughed and took big breaths of air in between. Out of the pool, I dropped down to my knees so he could feel safer when his feet hit the ground, but even then he didn't let go of me.

"It's okay," I assured him. I had to untangle his arms from my neck so I could take a look at his face and make sure he was all right. "It's okay. You're good."

He took a step back, looked at me with those big green eyes, and then nodded as his lips started wobbling. I pressed a hand to my rapidly rising and falling chest and dropped on my ass. "You practically gave me a heart attack, kid."

His face crumpled and the tears started coming down. It sounded pretty bad too as he was still having a hard time catching his breath.

Not knowing what else to do, I hugged him, and he buried his face in my neck. "Ah, don't cry, kiddo. You're okay now."

Then there were shouts and Adam Connor was running toward us. Aiden heard his voice and let go of me, propelling himself into his father's arms as his sobs became louder. Then the bodyguard and the nanny came running just behind him. I got up and tried to force a smile on my face, but I was *not* feeling smiley at all.

I wasn't sure if I should start yelling at the idiot nanny or the DILF himself.

Adam crushed Aiden against his chest and wrapped his legs around his waist, all the while keeping his palm at the back of his head. The kid looked even smaller in his father's arms as his body rocked with barely held back sobs. Adam's eyes met mine, and the stupid me thought he was thankful, so I smiled a little bigger. And…well, don't shoot me, but the guy was seriously one of the finest guys I'd ever laid my damn eyes on, so there might've been some tingling going on in the lower regions of my body, too.

The smiling, though…wrong move.

"Dan." Adam gritted his teeth and the giant of a bodyguard

stepped in front of them like a big bear protecting his cubs. "How did she get in here?"

Ticked, hurt, *and* dripping wet, I said, "*She* is standing right here, and you're welcome."

His eyes threw daggers at me as if I were an unwelcome rat in his house—and, well, when you put it like that, maybe I was, but I hadn't tumbled into his backyard for shits and giggles; I had just saved his son's life.

Keeping Aiden in his arms, he turned to the ditzy nanny and ordered, "Call the cops, Anne. Tell them we have a situation with a stalker."

"A stalker?" I balked, coming out of my trance.

Adam sliced his eyes to me and then barked at Anne. "Do it!"

"O-kay. Okay. I'm so-rry, Mr. Connor."

"You should be sorry," I said, taking a step forward. Her eyes met mine, but then she quickly looked away and got on with calling the damn cops. Taking a step toward them was apparently the wrong move. I didn't even get to fully take my little step because the giant put his hand on my shoulder and pushed me back.

"Hey!" I screamed as I tumbled back, my hand rubbing the spot. "Are you crazy?"

"Step back."

While I was fighting for my life, Anne finally did something right and invited the cops to our little party. I wanted them to come and arrest someone. Adam turned and handed the crying boy over to her and told her—not so nicely—to get him inside. I'm telling you, the whole thing was playing out like a bad movie, and somehow I had ended up being the villain.

"I just saved your son, you idiot, and this is how you say thank you? By calling the cops?"

"Don't talk," the giant said, standing like a brick wall in front of me, his arms crossed over his chest, obscuring my view of Adam.

"What do you mean don't talk?" I asked, my voice getting higher. "All of you just left him here, and he was going to drown. Look at me!" I yelled, opening my arms wide and looking down at myself. "I didn't just decide to break in to take a dip in the pool. I was trying to save his son."

"So you admit to trespassing." The bodyguard shook his head while looking at me like I was the nastiest bug he'd ever seen.

Goddamn it!

"I've had it with you people," Adam said finally, coming to stand next to his bodyguard. He looked just as majestic next to the giant.

Imbecile hormones.

"Look," I started, trying to calm the situation down. "Why don't you go in and ask your son? I'm sure he'll tell you exactly what happened."

"The hell I will. Do you know how scared he gets when something like this happens? I tolerate this shit when it happens to me, but you went too far by getting close to him, touching him."

"Oh my God, touching him? You're making it sound like I was doing something to him! Are you all crazy? He was all wet too, didn't you see? He got in the pool after you left. I just scaled a damn wall to get to him because you idiots are the ones who left him here alone."

Adam shook his head and gave me a disgusted look. "Tell your story to your lawyer when he visits you at the station."

I groaned and ran my hands through my wet and tangled hair. "You're not hearing me," I said through my gritted teeth as anger pulsed through my body. "Your son was drowning. I saw him panic and disappear under the water."

"You saw him? So you were watching us. Great." He turned

his head and said, "Dan, find her camera. I don't want any shots of Aiden to leak."

The bodyguard left, and I stomped, actually stomped. The other option was to do something else, something that would cause bodily harm, and I assumed that wouldn't go over too well with the bastard and the giant.

"*That's* what you heard from what I just said? On top of everything else, are you deaf too?"

Something changed, sharpened in Adam's face, and I clamped my mouth shut.

"I found her phone, boss."

My hand flew to my chest, and I realized my phone wasn't nestled in there anymore.

Adam's eyes narrowed on me. "Check her photos."

I avoided his eyes and went for my phone. Adam's hand clamped on my wrist, and he stopped my forward movement by twisting my arm up and between our bodies. The second I tried to wrench it away, his fingers tightened, and he pulled me to his body, holding his face inches away.

"I wouldn't do that if I were you."

Take a deep breath, Lucy. Calm down.

Clenching my fist, I drew in a deep breath and released it before speaking. "You have no right."

He raised an eyebrow and looked deep into my eyes. *Shit!* He had no right to have such deep green eyes. What a freaking waste on this schmuck. Hottest celebrity my ass.

"Right? You're talking to me about what right I do or do not have?"

Okay, maybe that wasn't the best argument to make, but he still had no right to go through my phone. *Right?*

I gave him the dirtiest look I'd ever given any living or dead creature and quietly said, "Fuck. You."

A muscle ticked in his jaw. "That's why you're here, isn't it? You'd do anything to take your fucking."

My mouth dropped open. The audacity of the asshole! Before I could say anything, his bodyguard came to stand next to us.

"Looks like there are a few pictures of you with Aiden, Adam, and not all of them are from today."

Adam's hand tightened around my wrist, and he glared down at me.

I lifted my chin high up and didn't give any explanations.

"The cops are here." Anne's voice came from inside the house, interrupting our stare down. *Little bitch.* The asshole should've thrown her to the cops, not me.

"I don't want them to walk her through the house. Tell them to come back here through the side," Adam instructed, and Anne scurried away.

"You can let her go, Adam. Go and tell them what's going on. I'll make sure she stays put."

He met my eyes again, but spoke to his bodyguard. "No, I got her." I hated him for making me shiver. Thinking I was trying to shake him off, he pulled me flush to his chest. "You go."

Nipple alert!

I looked away from Adam's accusing eyes and watched the giant leave.

The whole thing was turning into a nightmare.

"Look." I sighed and looked up to meet his ridiculously green eyes. "I'm not your stalker." He opened his mouth, but I talked over him. "I know. I know what it looks like, but I'm telling you the truth. My name is Lucy. Lucy Meyer. I'm staying next door. Right there." I pointed toward Olive's house with my shaky index finger. His expression didn't change a bit, the handsome bastard, but at least he was listening, so I continued with my explanation. "Jason Thorn? Heard of him? He is an actor just like yourself, only he is a lot more good-looking than you are and actually has a kind heart, ring any bells?"

No answers, no acknowledgements. Apparently he had no humor.

"He got married this year. To Olive. She is my best friend. I'm their friend. I'm staying with them. You can ask them yourself."

"And where are these best friends, Lucy Meyer?"

"Jason had a promo thing, so they've been in London for the last couple of days."

"How convenient for you, isn't it?"

I tried to take my arm back, but it was still firmly in his hold. I gave him an annoyed look.

"Let me go."

"No."

"They're flying in today. You can ask them yourself."

"You're facing charges. You're not getting out of this that easily."

"For God's sake, are you even listening to me?"

"I already saw what I needed to see."

My breathing quickened, so I hung my head and tried to keep myself calm by closing my eyes and counting to ten.

His fingers around my wrists tightened to the point of causing pain, so I gasped and looked up sharply.

"Don't even think about crying. It won't work."

I wasn't about to cry; it hadn't even crossed my mind, but somehow when I saw the officers coming toward us, my eyes started to well up.

"Great timing," Adam murmured when he saw my blurry eyes, and something snapped in me.

"You jerk," I said quietly. "Go ahead, press charges. I'm pressing charges too. You shouldn't be a parent. If you didn't know, child endangerment is a felony. If I'm going down, I'm taking you with me! That kid deserves a better dad, a dad who cares about his safety, you...you smug son of a bitch!"

He almost crushed my wrist, but stopped and dropped my hand when I winced.

Maybe you're thinking I sounded a little dramatic, but I can assure you, I wasn't being a drama queen. He had practically left his kid to die out there. I should've been the one who called 911, not them.

"Mr. Connor," said one of the officers as they came to stand next to us. After Adam explained what was going on and that he was pressing charges, they didn't even listen to me as they cuffed me.

Cuffed me!

Five minutes later, I was sitting in the back of a police car, heading to their precinct. I was ready to kill the bastard. If I ever got out of the jail they were about to put me in, I was going to kill the guy for sure.

———

It was five hours later—five!—when Jason and Olive came to bail me out. It was all quiet in the car, and I was still seething.

"Lucy," Olive said as she twisted her body to look back and talk to me.

"I hate him," I repeated for the tenth time since I'd gotten into their car. "I want to kill him. I'm gonna press charges to save that kid from him and then kill him."

"Is this contagious, Olive? Should I be worried?" Jason said from the driver seat. Our eyes met in the rearview mirror, and I frowned at him. His lips twitched.

"What's he talking about?" When I glanced at Olive, she was trying to hide her own smile. "What are you two smiling about?"

I shouted. "Sure, maybe I was in jail for five freaking hours, but I seriously doubt I have an infectious disease."

Olive's smile widened. "Of course not. He is talking about something else. Don't mind him."

"What? Don't keep secrets from me, Olive. I'm very vulnerable right now."

"I'm not keeping anything from you, Lucy. I was promising to kill you when he was driving me back from the studio executives' office. You know, the day I had the meeting? The day you left me all alone? He thinks we enjoy going for killing sprees."

I glanced at Jason. "Don't do inside jokes right now. Be cute to your wife on your own time. She is all mine at the moment. I was in jail. I need my friend."

"I'm assuming we're gonna keep hearing about the fact that you were in a holding cell, alone, for a very long time."

"How about you keep your eyes on the road so we don't die before I can kill that smug son of a bitch?"

Placing his hand on Olive's leg, he said, "She is all yours, little one."

"Thank you," I said sarcastically and then repeated, again, "I hate him."

Olive put her own hand over Jason's and a loaded moment passed between them. They were cute, so I let that one slide. "I think we already got that," she said. "And don't chop my head off because I hate to say I told you so, but…"

"I'll give him that much," I admitted reluctantly. "It was wrong of me to spy on him. But I wasn't stalking. There is a distinct difference. I just climbed a freaking ladder, and if he happened to be out in his backyard I watched him for a few minutes. That's it."

"Privacy is really important to us, Lucy. You should know that by now," Jason joined in on the conversation.

"I'm not saying it wasn't wrong, but if I hadn't been watching, that kid would be dead right now. Doesn't that count for something?"

He remained silent.

Realizing something else, I slid forward on my seat. "You do believe me, right? Please tell me you believe me when I say the only reason I jumped over that wall was to save the kid from drowning."

"Of course we do," Olive promised.

"Jason? You do believe me, right?"

He met my eyes again and sighed. "I do, Lucy, but that's not important."

"How can it not be important! The douche should've dropped to his knees and kissed my feet for being there."

Kissing other parts would've been acceptable, too, but not anymore. I wouldn't let him come near any of my lady parts, let alone accept kisses.

"I meant, what I think doesn't matter. The fact is that Adam thinks you're a stalker."

I hate him. I really, really hate him. I slid back and crossed my arms against my chest.

"What will happen now?" I asked when the silence became too much.

"I'll talk to him and make him drop the charges," Olive replied.

"And how do you think you'll make that happen?" Jason piped up, giving Olive a sideways look.

"I'll explain that Lucy was just trying to help. I don't know, be her character witness in a way."

"No," he said, in a firmer tone this time.

"I'm not gonna offer myself to him so he will drop the charges against Lucy, Jason."

"Good to hear," Jason drawled.

Finally, we got home—well, their home—and drove through

the gates. It was pitch-dark, just like my hatred filled heart. Jason killed the engine, but none of us got out.

"I'll talk to him," he said a few beats later. "I'll handle it, Lucy, but you can't go up there to watch him again. Are we clear?"

"Are we clear?" I mimicked, a small smile forming on my lips. "We're very clear, my brand new daddy. I promise I won't spy on stupid boys anymore. Now, tell me, am I grounded or what?"

CHAPTER SIX

ADAM

It had been almost a week since what we'd begun to call *the incident*, and I was still pissed. Pissed at Aiden for not listening to me. Pissed at Dan for not being on top of our security. Hell, I'd fired Anne that evening after I was able to get the whole story out of Aiden, yet I was still pissed at her too.

But more than anyone, I was pissed at myself. How I'd been so careless as to take my eyes away from my son—it didn't even matter that he was a good kid, I was the one who was responsible for him. I should've been on top of things. I should've...I guess I should've done better.

The gates buzzed open, and I walked in hand in hand with my son. His little fingers squeezed my hand, so I looked down at him.

"Are you ready, Daddy?"

My lips twitched, and I nodded. "Are you?"

He nodded solemnly then looked up at me quickly. "Do you think she hates me?"

"Why would she hate you?" I asked distractedly as we neared the house.

"'Cause I caused big trouble. I think she hates me. I think she doesn't wanna see me again."

"I doubt it, buddy, but you'll ask her yourself so you can be sure, all right?"

"She was very pretty," he added quietly. "I hope she doesn't hate me."

I remained silent. I wanted to go and apologize to that infuriating woman like I wanted a bullet in my head, but from what I'd heard from Aiden and then later Jason Thorn, she had saved my son. Still, if Aiden hadn't insisted on seeing her again, I would've never stepped foot in the house where she was staying.

Dropping the charges should've been more than enough for the little stalker.

God, thinking about her was making me crazy. Every time someone mentioned her name—and Aiden mentioned her name a lot—I was back in our backyard, scared out of my mind that some crazy stalker or reporter was hurting Aiden. I could still picture her stormy gray eyes glaring up at me as if she had a leg to stand on when I had her delicate wrist in my grip. I remember wanting to squeeze her pretty little neck with my bare hands every time she opened her mouth to talk.

Yea, seeing that my pulse was starting to speed, seeing her again wasn't gonna be as easy as I'd thought it would be.

Before I could knock, Jason opened the door.

"Hello there. How can I help you two gentlemen?"

"Are you a movie star?" Aiden asked before I could explain what the hell we were doing at his doorstep.

Jason's face softened, and he kneeled down in front of Aiden. "I am an actor, just like your dad. And you must be Aiden."

Aiden's eyes widened, and he glanced up at me. "He knows who I am, Daddy," he whispered.

Jason chuckled and offered his hand. "I've heard a lot about you, Aiden. It's nice to finally meet you."

Aiden looked at his outstretched hand then up at me. "Can I, Daddy?"

"Go for it, buddy."

He gave me a big smile and shook hands with Jason. "It's nice to meet you too, mister. My daddy is a big movie star. He signs lots of things. Did you play in lots of movies too?"

"I did. And you can call me Jason."

"Are you my friend?"

"Would you like me to be?"

Another glance at me. "Can I be friends with Jason, Daddy? I like him, and he lives so close to us, so we could play games."

I gave him a short nod. "How about you tell your new friend why we are here before you make plans for a play date."

"Would you play with me, Jason? Sometimes Daddy can't."

Oh, Aiden…

"Aiden…"

Finally, looking down at his feet, he murmured, "We came to see Lucy because I don't want her to hate me."

Jason straightened up, opened the door wider, and invited us in.

As we walked through the narrow hallway, Aiden's eyes took in everything around us and I had to drag him with me.

"Lucy, you have visitors," Jason announced.

"What?"

"Who?"

Two distinct female voices responded back at the same time.

And then the stalker appeared with a wooden spoon in her hand. She spotted me and her face fell, a small crease appearing between her brows.

The other one, who I assumed was Jason's wife, appeared from behind her and smiled at me, covering her surprise very well.

"What are you doing here?" Lucy asked in a hostile voice. She was voicing my feelings exactly; the only difference was I couldn't act hostile toward her, not when I had Aiden with me.

Christl I still wanted to kill her, though. I ground my teeth to restrain myself.

"Trust me, I'm not all that fired up to see you either," I admitted.

That got me an eyebrow raise.

"Then by all means, please leave," she replied, gesturing at the door with a wave of her hand.

Both Jason and Olive were carefully following our conversation as they stayed silent and watched the interaction between us. I wished they'd interfere in some way; I would have much rather spoken with them instead of this madwoman who managed to spark something inside me. I narrowed my eyes at her and then felt someone pulling on the pockets of my jeans.

Aiden. Right.

"My son has something to say to you," I said pointedly so she'd get that seeing her wasn't my idea of fun. When Aiden decided to go all shy on me and hid behind my back, I was forced to take a step to the side so Miss Stalker could see the person responsible for our visit.

"Oh, hello. Hi there," Lucy said, her expression softening when she finally saw Aiden. This time, instead of hiding behind me, he was hugging my leg to ensure I wouldn't go too far away.

Aiden wasn't normally a shy kid, but being around strangers wasn't something he was used to. With all the media focus on us, we tried to keep our family life as private as possible, meaning Aiden wasn't used to meeting new adults—not when we were so particular about his security.

"Hello," he greeted in a small voice, giving her a small wave right before grabbing my leg and hiding his face.

Lucy took a small step forward, but when our eyes met, she stopped. I would've much rather taken my kid and gotten the hell away from her, but it was too late for that.

"Aiden," I prompted so we could get it over with and leave. "What did you want to say to Miss Lucy?"

He'd been talking my ear off about seeing Miss Stalker again ever since I'd picked him up from his mom the day before.

"I want to ask her something," he whispered.

"Go ahead then."

"Can you ask her for me?"

"I would, buddy, but I have no idea what you want to ask her."

"But I just told you, Daddy. On our way over here, remember?"

"Aiden, I told you—"

"Please, Daddy. Pleeeaaase."

My lips twitched as he repeatedly nodded and widened his bright green eyes.

Without meeting Lucy's eyes again, I said, "He was wondering if you hated him for getting you in trouble."

She looked at me with eyes full of hatred, which was admittedly a look I wasn't used to getting. It only accentuated those unique bluish-gray eyes of hers, eyes I had no place even noticing.

She shook her head as if she was disappointed in me. "Is that what you told him?"

Just as I was trying to figure out what the hell she meant, she handed the wooden spoon to her clearly amused friend and started sashaying toward us.

"Be nice, Lucy," Jason murmured as he casually leaned against the wall and watched us.

Instead of answering him, she gave me a pointed look that pretty much said, *Do you mind?* and without waiting for an answer, lowered herself to sit cross-legged in front of me.

"Hi," she said to Aiden again.

"So? Do you hate me?" he asked, his arm tightening around my leg as he waited for his answer.

"Nope."

"Not even a little?"

"Not even a little. In fact, I'm very happy to see you again."

Happy with the answers he was getting, Aiden let go of my leg and stood in front of Lucy. "You are?"

"Yes. I was worried about you after I left, so it's good to see you here, standing strong."

Charmed by her, Aiden threw his arms around her neck and awkwardly hugged her. "I don't hate you either. I promise. Not like my dad does."

That earned me another look.

Oh, the joys of having a very honest five-year-old.

"That's okay," she reassured him with a pat on his back. "I promise I don't hate you like I hate your dad either."

As if I cared. I rolled my neck to get rid of the sudden stiffness.

"Am I your friend now?" Aiden asked as he looked at her with a serious expression. "Jason just agreed to be my friend, so maybe if you are my friend too you can come and visit me with him?"

"Come on, Aiden. That's enough," I said, putting my hand on his shoulder.

Looking up at me, he asked, "Is it your turn now, Daddy?"

Goddamn it!

He was looking at me with such expectant eyes that I couldn't deny him anything, not even an apology to the person I had pretty much loathed since the first moment I'd laid eyes on her.

When Aiden looked up at me, Lucy's gaze flicked upward too. I met her eyes. I met her eyes and...couldn't think of anything to say.

"Daddy, you promised we would do this together."

I hadn't made any promises about anything, but since we were already knee-deep in this...I took a deep breath and exhaled as Lucy got up from the floor and took a few steps back.

"Aiden told me what he did and what happened after," I started in a rough voice. Hearing how scared he'd gotten when he'd lost his arm float and started swallowing water had been particularly difficult for me. "I don't like what you did. I don't like any of it." Narrowing her eyes at me, she lifted her chin ever so slightly and crossed her arms against her chest, pushing her boobs higher.

Look away, Adam.

"Other than the fact that what you did probably saved my son's life. For that and *only* that, I'm thankful."

Suddenly her eyes softened, and she dropped her arms. She looked over her shoulder and sighed. "You're right," she admitted. "Even though I didn't mean any harm, it was wrong of me to get up there and watch you. That being said, I'm glad I was there at the right time."

At least she was honest enough to accept the fact that what she had done was wrong. I relaxed a little and nodded. "Thank you." I looked down at Aiden's smiling face. "Are you ready to go?"

"One more minute? Please?"

Curious as to why he needed another minute, I said okay, and he ran toward Jason, stopping only inches away as he tilted his head back. He whispered something I couldn't make out, and Jason laughed.

"Yes, I know her. Would you like me to introduce you two?" Jason asked as he ruffled his hair.

Briefly glancing at Jason's wife, Aiden nodded. Jason chuckled, and they walked toward his smiling wife.

"Looks like you have a fan," he said to his wife.

"Hello, Aiden," she said and leaned down to Aiden's eye level. "I'm Olive."

Aiden's eyes widened and a surprised giggle escaped his lips.

"Olive? Like an olive?"

"Yup, just like an olive."

Another giggle and I relaxed further, exhaling a deep breath. I was happy to see him having fun, but we'd have to leave soon so I could make it to set early to go over some last minute changes in the script.

Lucy looked at me over her shoulder with a smile on her lips, but when our eyes met, her gaze turned into a cold stare. So much for our truce. Since I wasn't planning on seeing her again, I was completely fine with it.

"Would you like to have coffee?" she asked. "They have this complicated espresso machine; I'm sure you have something similar, so you'll enjoy that."

Now what the hell was that supposed to mean? I tilted my head to the side and studied her for a short beat. What exactly did she see when she was looking at me with those unwavering eyes? She didn't look like a star-struck woman, that was for sure. She didn't act like all the other women did when they had me this close. No, not this one. She met my gaze head-on, not even blinking under my hard stare. So then what the hell had she been doing watching me over the wall?

"No," I replied curtly and watched as Jason leaned down so Aiden could whisper in his ear this time.

"Ah, little man, are you trying to steal her from me?" he asked, acting all wounded when Aiden was done with whatever he was saying to him.

Aiden shook his head and gave Olive another coy look.

Fuck me, but he was crushing on the man's wife.

Jason lifted him up and sat him on the kitchen counter. "Tell her yourself. I'm sure she'll love hearing that."

"She will? You sure?" Aiden asked in a low whisper.

"Believe me, girls love hearing that."

Aiden nodded and made his deep thinking face, considering what he'd just learned. I couldn't help but smile as I watched him soak up all the attention he was getting.

"What? Tell me already," Olive said, getting closer to them with an unsure smile on her face.

"You're very pretty," Aiden said, and I groaned.

"Aiden…"

"Isn't she so pretty, Daddy?"

"Of course she is, buddy, but it's time for us to leave now. I'm sure your new friends are busy."

Ignoring me, he kept his eyes on Olive. "Would you like my daddy to sign a picture for you?" He glanced back at Jason. "Girls love that too."

Lucy burst out laughing with Olive. Thrilled, Aiden started giggling too. Jason's eyes were on his wife, and he was smiling at her.

I shook my head. Fool.

"Looks like you're raising quite the player," Lucy said when her laughter died down and the Thorns' were busy talking to Aiden.

Sliding my eyes to Lucy, I raised my brow.

She murmured something inaudible, and I could've sworn her pink lips mouthed *asshole*.

"Whatever happened to the attentive nanny?" she asked before I could figure out something to say in response to that uncalled for remark.

I looked away from her lips. "Got fired."

"At least you've done *something* right," she mumbled.

"She was supposed to be out there with him. Contrary to what you believe, I didn't leave him alone out there."

"Oh, right. The nanny. Does she wipe your precious ass too?"

"What is your problem with me?" I asked, taking a step toward her. She was a short thing compared to me, and I easily towered over her.

Did she back up like any other sane female would? Of course not. Not this one.

"I could ask you the same question! What the hell is your problem with *me*? I even offered you coffee after you had me thrown in jail! What more should I do?"

"That's called a holding cell. As much as I wish you would have, you didn't make it that far. You weren't even processed."

"And *I'm* sure you tried your best to make that happen. I spent five hours behind those bars, thanks to you. And that's what I got for saving your son's life!"

Grinding my teeth, I got closer to her. "I told you I didn't know Aiden was in trouble." I glared down at her, and she glared right back at me. Oh, if I could just grab hold of her and shake some sense into her. Maybe that way her presence wouldn't aggravate me anymore.

Her eyes dropped to my lips for a brief moment, and I realized how hard my breathing was.

Noticing the thick silence, I looked over her head and saw Aiden watching us with great attention.

"That escalated rather quickly," Olive said to no one in particular.

I shot a look at Lucy, frowning when I realized how close we were standing, then addressed Jason. "I'm sorry for interrupting your day, Jason, but I think it's time for us to leave."

Giving Lucy a wide berth, I helped Aiden down.

"Goodbye, Olive," he said shyly and waved at her. When Olive leaned down to give him a kiss on his cheek and invite him over again, he gave her a tight hug and thanked her.

"They want me to stay, Daddy. Can I stay?"

"They didn't say that, Aiden. They invited you over for another time. I have to go to work, so we need to leave."

"But you said Anne is gone, so who'll stay with me?"

"I have to drop you off at your mom's, Aiden. We already talked about it this morning, remember? She is meeting with her people at the house so she'll look after you today."

We'd almost made it to the door as Aiden chattered next to me, but when I mentioned his mom, he pulled me to a stop.

"Please, Daddy. Please."

I looked back at everyone behind us and then got on one knee in front of him. "What's happening here, Aiden?" While it was obvious he liked everyone in the room, the way he was acting wasn't his usual behavior. He wasn't a spoiled kid at all; something was wrong.

As soon as I was down on his level, he wrapped his arms around my neck and held on. "I don't wanna leave you. Please. Can't Dan stay with me?"

"Aiden, Dan has the day off." I unwrapped his arms from my neck and looked at his red eyes. *Shit.* "You can't do this to me, Aiden. I have no one to take care of you when I'm on set until I find someone new, little man."

He wiped at his dry eyes and nodded. "I'm gonna miss you again."

Lucy broke into our conversation by saying, "My heart is breaking."

Right, because her fucking heart was so high on my list of things about which I gave a fuck. My jaw ticked. "Can you give us a moment?"

She talked right over me. "Since your heart is probably carved from stone, you can't understand how that feels, but I just wanted to let you know that multiple hearts are breaking right now—not that it looks like you care about that."

"Lucy!" Olive whispered heatedly from behind her.

"What?" she asked her friend as if she were as innocent as an angel. In my eyes she was more like the devil reincarnated. "I'm just telling the truth. Look," she began, getting closer. "Olive and Jason have to leave for a meeting in an hour or so, but I don't have any job interviews today. Why don't you leave Aiden here with me? You'll pick him up as soon as you get back from wherever it is that you have to go, and since we established the fact that I mean no harm to your son, seeing as how I already saved his life once…"

No. That was my immediate answer, but before I could voice my opinion, Aiden ran to Lucy and gave her a hug—or more like gave her legs a hug. Her naked legs. Her smooth, toned legs. I looked up and met her eyes, already shaking my head.

"I wanna stay," Aiden repeated for the tenth time.

"She is right, Adam," Jason agreed. "Olive and I will be back here in two hours tops. It'll be fun. We'll take care of him until you come back, don't worry."

I sighed and rubbed my eyes. "I don't like this, Aiden. You can't get your way every time."

"But I like it here, Daddy, and if I stay here I can stay with you. You'll have to come back to pick me up."

"I always come back to pick you up, Aiden. And you've only been here for ten minutes."

Since his play wasn't working, he tried a different tactic. "I like Lucy."

"And Lucy likes you, little human," Lucy interjected into our back and forth and pointed at something I couldn't see on the other side of the kitchen as she whispered something in his ear. When Aiden went off to check it out, Lucy walked toward me.

"Clearly he doesn't want to go."

"Clearly."

Closing her eyes, she took a deep breath, and I watched her lips press into a straight line.

"I'm sorry for watching you, okay," she grumbled. "It was the biggest mistake of my life. You're not even that hot from this close. If I could take it back, *trust me*, I would. You are nothing like what I thought you'd be."

"Thanks," I drawled. "And here I was hoping you were in love with me."

Another fake smile. "I don't do love, and you're not my type anyway, sorry."

Like I'd believe that after I saw the pictures she'd taken of me half-naked. "My heart is fucking broken, sweetheart."

"As it should be, and don't call me sweetheart."

I chuckled and shook my head. The nerve.

"Anyway," she continued. "How long will you be gone?"

I ran a hand through my hair, thinking. "At least six hours."

"And you can't pick him up from his mother?"

"She is leaving the city tonight. We already talked; if I drop him off, she's not gonna wait around for me to pick him up again." And why was I so willingly giving her all this information again?

"There you go. He'll stay here until you come back."

My eyes found Aiden, and I caught him showing Jason his arm muscles. I smiled. I couldn't leave him there, could I? I knew Jason from the few times we had talked, and I definitely didn't know this mess of a woman who was standing in front of me with an impatient look. But, if I gave him back to Adeline, I wouldn't get to see him for another whole week. I was already missing him too much, and sending him away with Adeline so he could miss school and sleep in trailers…well, it didn't seem like the better choice at that moment.

"Aiden, come give me a hug," I said.

His head jerked to me and his face lit up. "I get to stay?"

"You get to stay. Just this time."

He came running. "Thank you. Thank you. Thank you."

"I love you, buddy. Be nice, okay?"

"I love you, Daddy. You can go."

With that he let go of me, turned his back, and grabbed Lucy's hand, pulling her away from me.

When she looked at me over her shoulder with a smile stretching on her lips...for a moment I thought she looked beautiful.

———

WHEN YOU HAVE A KID, everything changes. Your social life, work life, even the dynamics of your family shift. There was a time where I used to go without sleep for days on end to get in the shots we needed, but lately, especially after the divorce, I had to plan everything around Aiden. Make him my priority. Be a better dad. Be fucking everywhere. Be fucking everything.

It took me seven hours to wrap everything up at the studio. Our director, Matthew, wanted me to stay for another ten hours so we could shoot some of the night scenes I had left with Jamie Wilson, but because of Aiden's situation, I had them reschedule everything. The last thing I wanted was for him to spend the night in a strange home.

"I'm really sorry about this. I'm sure you guys had other plans today," I said as I walked through the door and into the hallway of Jason's home.

"It's okay, man. Olive and I just got in a few hours ago. Your little guy was already tuckered out."

"He fell asleep?"

"Woke up when he heard us come in—or more like when he heard Olive's voice—but he fell asleep again a little while ago."

We walked into the open living area and my eyes were searching for Aiden as I noticed Olive come in from the backyard. She hugged Jason's waist as she greeted me. "Hi, Adam."

"Hi. I hope Aiden didn't cause too much trouble."

"Oh, he didn't. We're practically in love with each other. I might even consider letting this one go if he doesn't up his game soon," she said with a genuine smile as she patted Jason's chest.

Jason put his arm around her shoulders and drew her closer. "I'm gonna have to keep my eyes on your son, Adam. With the way he is flirting with Olive, I don't think I have a fighting chance otherwise."

I laughed and winked at Olive. "It's good to know he has good taste in women."

She blushed a little and looked up at Jason with a big smile. Jason groaned and shook his head in return. "You can head out back; he is outside with Lucy. I think I'll keep my wife away from you Connors for today."

How long had it been since Adeline looked at me the way Olive was looking at Jason? Years? When had everything changed to the point where she was barely looking at me at all? With those unwelcome thoughts, I stepped outside to find my son sleeping on a chaise lounge, arms and legs wide open, peeking out from under a soft nude-colored blanket.

Frowning, I looked around. Hadn't Jason said Lucy was with him? I heard a faint voice coming from nearby, so I followed it to the side of the house.

"I told you I was staying with Olive, Catherine. No. Well, then I told your voice mail I was staying with Olive. No. How could I have known you wanted to do something for my graduation? You're right, I'm sorry."

The tone of her voice and the way her shoulders slumped forward were in such contrast to the woman I'd seen thus far that it made me stop in my tracks. Clearly it was a private phone call, and I wanted to give her privacy. I should've, but as far as I was concerned, turnabout was fair play. Instead of leaving, I leaned against the nearest tree and listened in on her side of the conversation.

"I'm actually helping Olive, Catherine. I didn't say that. I know. I know." She started pacing, and if she'd turned her head just a little she would've noticed me, but the night cloaked my presence. "That's the problem. I don't think I want to be an accountant. Yes, I'm aware of that, but the only reason I chose that major is because you wanted me to. I remember quite clearly the day you said you'd stop paying my tuition if I even thought about changing it. Yes, I know."

She stopped, and I held my breath.

"I'm sorry for all the trouble I caused you, Catherine, but I was just five years old when she left me with you. I had no say in the matter. I never did. I wish you could be proud of me." A long pause. "I understand."

She twisted her body and thanks to the moonlight, I was able to see her face more clearly. She was so fucking beautiful, even more so in the soft moonlight. Unfortunately, she was also a spirited lunatic—a beautiful one, sure, but still a lunatic. She tucked her short hair behind her ears and closed her eyes.

For a brief moment, I wondered how her skin would feel under my fingertips. Would her lips be soft? Would she smile at me like I'd seen her smile at my son? I remembered the day I found her in my backyard, dripping wet and fuming. If I was honest, I'd liked the feel of her body against mine, her breathing hard, eyes murderous. For a fraction of a second, I'd thought she was as hot as hell. If I'd met her on the street, in a coffee shop, or even on set, I wouldn't have minded fucking her brains out. Shaking my head, I got rid of those unwelcome thoughts. She was the last person I'd ever consider being with. I wasn't suicidal. There were millions of beautiful women out there.

"Sorry I turned out to be just like my mother, Catherine," she said after another long pause. "Olive wants me to be her agent, but I'm still going to look for a job. Okay. Okay maybe I'll go and talk to the firm you mentioned."

A few seconds later she ended the call and rested her forehead against the side of the house. While I was okay with intruding since she'd done the exact same to me, somehow this didn't feel right. Even so, I couldn't walk away. I crossed my arms and waited for her to notice me silently watching.

To my surprise, it didn't take her long to shake off the effects the phone call had had on her; as soon as she spotted me, her game face was on again—and by game face I mean the little dragon was ready to spit fire.

"What are you doing here?" she asked, coming toward me.

"Are you going to keep asking the same question every time you see me?"

"If you're somewhere you're not supposed to be, yes, I think I will."

"You actually enjoy this, don't you?"

"What?"

"Making people miserable," I explained. "Since you're so good at it, I'm assuming I'm not the only victim."

She kept her calculating eyes on me for a beat, then I watched her walk past me without a second look. "Everyone loves me, thank you very much."

I had to laugh at that. She turned her head to look at me and her frown deepened. "Instead of sneaking up on me, you should've stayed with your son."

"He is sleeping," I reminded her. "Not to mention, once he is out, nothing can wake him up until he is ready to wake up. Should I remind you that you're the one who left him alone?"

"I left him with Olive, and no matter what you say, he could wake up and walk right into the pool. You should take better care of him."

I moved from my spot and caught up with her before she

could make it to the opening where Aiden was sleeping. I grabbed her arm and spun her to face me.

"This is the second time you've insulted my parenting skills," I said through gritted teeth as I lowered my head to her. "You won't like what happens the third time." How was it even possible that she managed to push my buttons almost every single time she opened her mouth?

"I dare you to try." Her eyes narrowed on me, and she twisted her shoulder to shrug me off. "Take your hand off me."

I was ashamed to admit that I had to force myself to let her go. I took a step back. God, she made me so angry. So far, every attempt at a civil conversation had brought us right back to where we'd started. "And to think I was considering offering you a job."

Her forehead creased, and she tilted her head. "What job?"

"Who were you talking to?"

"What job?"

"Who were you talking to, Lucy?"

"What job, *Adam*?"

"Did anyone ever tell you how insufferable you are?"

"What can I say? You seem to bring out the worst in me."

Our eyes locked, and we stood perfectly still. I decided to ignore how her gaze flickered to my lips twice and took another step back. I had a feeling if we stood too close to one another for more than a few minutes, she'd burn me right up with her.

We glared at each other. It was inevitable when she was around.

Then, she huffed and rubbed at her eyes. "You really do bring out the worst in me. I just don't think I like you," she admitted.

Such honesty. "I don't think I like you that much either, so you don't have to feel bad about it."

"I wasn't feeling bad, but thanks."

Jesus, she was a handful.

She took a deep breath then visibly shook herself, presumably to relax her muscles. "I was talking to my grandma. We don't talk all that much, so I'm a little...tense, I guess."

"I gathered that. So you're looking for a job?"

"I think so."

"You don't know?"

"I'm looking. I've *been* looking. I'm also acting as Olive's temporary agent for the moment, trying to get a deal for her upcoming book or books, depending on the deal, of course. So far I'm not that impressed with what they're offering." She shrugged. "I'm not sure what I'm doing, but she seems to trust me, so I couldn't say no. I'm just trying to help, so I hope I'm not messing things for her."

Since she was behaving like a fairly normal person, I relaxed into the conversation. "Sounds like you're doing everything a good agent would do."

Another half-shrug. "Maybe. I majored in business, not sure how good I'd be as her agent. Anyway, I accept," she announced and waited expectantly.

"You accept what?" I asked, confused.

"I thought I'd save you the trouble."

"What in the world are you talking about now?"

"Aren't you gonna ask me to watch your son while you're away on set tomorrow, or whatever it is that you people do? Jason spends most of his time on set, so I assumed you were—"

I lifted my hand to stop her mid-sentence.

"How did you—you know what, never mind. Actually, I was planning on asking you if you could look after him for a few more days. For some unknown reason he seems to like you." I'd called twice to talk to Aiden during the day, and he couldn't stop talking about how cool Lucy was long enough to even listen to me. Standing in front of me, Lucy gave me an overly fake smile, and I would've bet millions that she was cursing at me like a sailor in her mind, or quite possibly plotting my untimely death. Either way, I was starting to enjoy goading her. "I'm only asking because I couldn't find anyone I want to keep long-term." After the divorce, Adeline had kept our assistant, and I still hadn't had the time to find one. "While I do see the irony of asking a stalker to look after my son, there is the fact that you already saved his life once, so I know you'll keep your eyes open. That's like stalker 101, isn't it? Plus, I don't have any other options right at this minute, not when his mother is out of town."

"First of all," she started, her eyes flaming. "Why do I feel like you're expecting a thank you from me? I already apologized for being curious."

"Oh, so that's what we're calling invading privacy these days, is that it?"

I doubted she even heard me as she kept talking. "I'm not gonna apologize over and over again, so stop calling me a stalker and I'll happily be the temporary babysitter for a week. That's all I'm being these days anyway. Temporary Lucy." She turned around and started walking in quick steps. "As long as you're not present, of course. I don't like you very much."

I followed her. "Have you ever had a boyfriend? Because I'm having a really hard time imagining anyone putting up with you." As I was insulting her yet again, my eyes took notice of the way her dark jeans hugged her full ass. Nothing flat about her at all— not her ass, and definitely not her personality either.

She stopped, and I nearly walked into her. I also almost grabbed her hips, but we can skip that part.

"And I can see exactly why your wife divorced you, Mr. Connor," she exclaimed, oblivious to what was going on in my mind. "I didn't have a hard time figuring that out at all. When you have the time, please give me her number so I can call and congratulate her on making such a wise decision."

Why did my dick jump when she called me Mr. Connor? Why did I even notice her ass in the first place? Regardless, we shared hostile glances and then kept walking as if we hadn't just insulted each other while I was checking out her ass.

"Of course, I'll be paying you for your time," I continued.

"A glorified babysitter. Awesome. How much will you pay me? I'd like to remind you that I was emotionally scarred by those five hours spent in prison."

I ignored the jab. "Dan, the head of my security—or body-guard, whatever you'd like to call him—he picks Aiden up from kindergarten then drops him off at home, so you won't be with him all day."

"I can pick him up too if you need your bodyguard to protect you from your excited fans. God forbid they lay their eyes on you or anything. What will you do without him?"

I spotted Aiden's sleeping form and, not too far away, Olive sitting on Jason's lap. Since they were keeping an eye on him, I reached out to grab Lucy's arm to stop her. I told myself it was only because I didn't want Aiden to hear my voice and wake up. It was mostly because of that.

When I touched her skin, it was cold. She was cold. I dropped it before she could shrug me off.

"You'll need to sign an NDA."

She opened her mouth to argue about it as I expected, but then closed it without saying anything. Studying me, she remained silent as she rubbed her hands up and down her arms. I could already see small goose bumps appearing on the length of her arms. "Let's go inside, you're cold."

Why would I even think she would listen to me? She stood her ground and sighed. "I'll sign it. I don't plan on talking to anyone about you."

"It's not just about me. You can't talk about anything you hear while you're with Aiden to anyone. Not even your friends."

She glanced toward her friends and something changed in her

expression. I didn't like it, especially those calculating eyes of hers. Nothing good would come of it.

"I'll look after Aiden, and I'll sign your stupid NDA, too, but I have a request of my own," she said finally, her eyes meeting mine.

"I'm not hiring you to be his full-time nanny. You don't get to have requests."

"I do. And I'm requesting to sleep over at your place for the week. I'll spend my time with Olive after you come home so you won't see me, but I'm coming back to sleep."

Genuinely confused, I frowned down at her and asked, "Why?" Didn't Jason want her in the house? I mean, I wouldn't blame him for it, but from all he'd said about her when he'd come to talk me out of pressing charges and getting a restraining order, I'd assumed she was somehow important to him.

"Look at them," she said, motioning toward Jason and Olive with her head.

I looked and saw what I'd already seen just a minute before: Olive sitting between Jason's legs as they smiled and whispered to each other. "And?"

She sighed and rolled her eyes. "They love each other."

As if that explained everything. "I wish I understood your language, 'cause I'm thinking a lot of things would make sense then, but I don't, so you'll have to spell it out. Why the hell would you sleep in my home because they love each other?"

Those goose bumps made an appearance again, and she forcefully stuffed her hands in her back pockets, unknowingly thrusting her breasts out.

I snapped my gaze up.

"I was dating this guy and we were living together, but after we graduated he left the city."

"He left you, you mean. Smart man."

Her eyes shot sparks, and she pressed her lips together.

I smiled. "I'm sorry, that was uncalled for. Go on."

"My name wasn't on the lease, so they wanted me out. Since you're *such* a smart guy, I'm sure you already know that I'm not close with my grandmother. If I'd gone to stay with her…I don't even want to think about that. Let's just say, she drains me, of life, positivity, everything. So, of course, Olive took me in, and I've been here for more than two weeks now."

"I still have no idea where you're going with this, sweetheart."

"Don't call me sweetheart. This is the second time I'm warning you. I hate it when people use that word with that tone."

Watching me intently, she shifted her weight from her left foot to her right, hands still secured in her back pockets, shoulders tensed and high up.

Before crossing my arms over my chest, I motioned for her to go on.

"Like I said, I've been here for more than two weeks now, and this is their home. Granted, they were in London that first week, but still, what if Jason wants to fuck her brains out in the kitchen?"

My arms dropped down.

"Well, he can't," she continued. "He can't because I'm in the house. Not that I'm trying to listen in on them or anything, but I don't even hear a moan at night and trust me, Olive is a moaner. Anyway, Olive waited a very long time for that guy, and she deserves to have loud, earth-shattering sex, so I'll be staying at your place. That'll give them a week to do whatever they want to do wherever they want to do it. I'm hoping to find an apartment as soon as I get a job anyway."

Frozen in place, all I could do was lift an eyebrow at her. Had I lost my mind, thinking Aiden would be fine to spend a few days with her? Clearly satisfied with the eyebrow lift, she nodded and turned around to join her friends—only she tripped on something and didn't have enough time to free her hands to balance herself. I caught her by her arm a second before she would have face-planted into an actual plant.

Did I get a thank you? That would be asking too much.

"Goddamn it, Olive," she yelled into the night. "I'm gonna cut down all your bushes with my own hands!" Then she turned to me and shrugged me off before I could take my hand away. "And what is it with you and my arm for God's sake? Every chance you get, you latch onto it. Do you have a fetish or something?"

I didn't remember saying yes to her request, but she'd somehow managed to invite herself to stay at my place.

CHAPTER SEVEN

LUCY

With every passing day, I hated Adam Connor even more; how that was even possible...don't ask me. It had somehow started to become a passion of mine. Why? Because he was...a sly bastard, because he worked out shirtless in his backyard, because he made his son laugh, because his arms were all masculine and sexy, because his arms were peppered with hair, because there was something called forearm porn, because his voice had the ability to give you tiny orgasms, *annoying* tiny orgasms that forced you to cross your legs or apply some kind of sneaky pressure. I hated those orgasms; they left me unsatisfied and only reminded me that I hadn't had sex in weeks. Weeks, I tell ya! Leave sex aside, I hadn't even had a kiss. A freaking innocent kiss. Can you even imagine what that does to a girl? Your body reacts differently to all kinds of things.

Adam Connor being one of them.

Tingles.

Everywhere.

Long.

Short.

Painful.

Pleasure-filled tingles.

You ever had a tiny orgasm just because a guy said—no, whispered, *I love you, little man,* to his son while he was tucking him into bed? No? That's just me? Well, excuse the hell out of me then. You should visit your doctor to make sure everything is all right if you don't get the tingles when you hear Adam Connor telling his son he loves him. So yeah, Adam Connor was an asshole for making me tingle—and that's me being frugal with my bad words.

Do you finally see where I'm coming from, or do you need me to go on with the list of why I hated Adam Connor so much?

All in all, his voice sucked. Whether he was professing his love to his little man or talking to his ex in hushed tones, his voice sucked just as much as he did.

The first day of my unexpected babysitter job didn't suck that much, though; I hadn't had the full effect of him at that point. I had spent most of my day glued to my phone talking to and emailing back and forth with publishing companies, trying to hammer out the best deal for Olive's books. And you know what, as much as I'd thought I wouldn't be any help to her, I was starting to realize that I wasn't half bad at it. So my little green Olive was right after all. The deals that were on the table—I had four so far—were already better than what the other agents had promised to get her. So I was doing a bangin' job at being the temporary agent.

Then around three o'clock, the big bad bodyguard dropped Aiden off and rudely told me to keep him safe and inside the perimeter of the house, as if he were trusting me to protect the president—not that I wouldn't protect him, but he was a five-year-old kid, for God's sake. Still, the rest of the day and the evening went smoothly. We had fun and talked about all kinds of things, from his friends at school to the girl he liked sitting with to why he didn't like sleeping in trailers. At some point, Olive came out of her writing cave, pushing pause on the edits she was working on for her latest book and joining us for ice cream.

I wish you could've seen the way Aiden got all shy around Olive, giving her all kinds of looks. He was going to be a heartbreaker, that was for sure. Just like his asshole father, except Aiden wouldn't be an asshole; he was too cute for that.

It was fun. The little human was fun, cute, and smart—everything his father wasn't, and I was maybe a tad bit in love with him. The son. Not the father.

Definitely not the father.

Because who'd want to fall in love with a bastard who had a voice that could give you orgasms, right?

Right.

Anyway, I'd given up on love completely, hadn't I? Better to stay away from the curse at all costs.

So, it was all great until *he* came to pick up a sleepy Aiden. We barely said two words to each other, but he made sure I signed his stupid NDA and told me he had a room ready for me to stay in. He said the next day I should spend my time with Aiden at their place instead of at Olive's. I just nodded and disappeared from sight as he chatted with Jason in hushed tones, and Aiden promptly fell asleep on his shoulder.

The second day, I got a call from an unknown number as I was emailing Tom, Jason's agent, to get his opinion on something. It was Dan the Man giving me a particularly sharp order to come next door. Ticked off because he had hung up on me before I could open my mouth, I marched over to their place, only to find he'd already left. I let it go. Barely.

Seeing Aiden's happy face helped too. It was going to be my first day spending the night at his place and when I told him about it, Aiden seemed to be the happiest person about my sleeping arrangements because according to him, I was going to be his first sleepover, and we were going to have loads of fun.

Again, everything was perfect until Adam showed up. As he listened to his son chatter about our day, he carried the little human to bed. Thinking he wouldn't be back any time soon, he found me just as I was climbing up the ladder I'd secured against his side of the wall earlier that day.

"What the hell are you doing?" he asked, almost startling me off the ladder.

"Singing 'Hakuna Matata'," I replied without looking down at him. You never look the devil in the eye. I could already feel him shaking his head in disapproval anyway. *Judgy bastard.* "You don't expect me to walk in and out of the gates every time I want to go next door, do you?"

"That would be what a normal person would do."

"Normal is boring. You're welcome to do so. This…" Reaching the top, I straddled the wall and finally looked down at him—not his eyes, though; that was too much. "…is much faster and easier."

"If you wanna break your neck, be my guest," he said, crossing his arms. He looked so majestic, the ugly douche.

I gave him a big, fake smile, showing all my teeth. "How thoughtful of you. I'm touched." As I was about to climb down, he called my name, so I looked back at him.

"At least be considerate enough to break your neck while you're on the other side of this wall."

I gave him the finger with a sweet smile and ignored the faint twitch of his mouth.

Just as my feet hit the ground on the other side of the wall and the stupid bush grazed my arm yet again, I heard his voice.

"If you want to sleep over here, be back in an hour or I'm activating the alarm."

"Give me the code," I said, raising my voice so he could hear me.

"No."

Then I heard his retreating footsteps on the stone pathway. By the time I had climbed up to say I don't even know what—maybe yell at him for a yet to be determined reason—he was already back in the house.

I trash-talked him to Olive the whole hour I had, had a late dinner with her and her cheeky husband, and went over the wall again.

When I knocked on the glass door, Dan let me in with a barely held back frown. I marched right into the room the last nanny had slept in and went to sleep grumbling to myself. To say that I wasn't welcome was an understatement. He wasn't welcome in my heart either...not that he was interested in my heart, but...

Let's just move on.

The third day was a Wednesday, and it was a happy day. Adam wasn't coming home from the set, and the bodyguard had actually talked to me in sentences. Exactly three sentences, but who was counting, right? I could've sworn I saw a smile, too, but then again maybe that was just wishful thinking. Around that time, Aiden learned that his father wasn't coming home, and he started crying. It must've been my off day or something because when I saw him crying so earnestly without even making a sound, my heart broke a little, and I shed some tears with him.

So, yeah, Adam Connor not coming home...didn't mean a happy day. It was a sad, sad day.

The fourth day was a mellow day. Olive joined us again, and I briefly mentioned the deals I'd rounded up, not going into the details. The rest of the day, I spent an awful lot of time watching SpongeBob SquarePants and making sure Aiden was smiling. Avoiding Catherine's calls was also one of my major achievements of the day.

I fell asleep while we were watching *The Lion King* in the living room. When I woke up, Aiden was no longer lounging on the carpet, kicking his feet up as he kept his focus on the humongous flat screen. I was snuggled comfortably under a thin blanket that hadn't been there when I'd first closed my eyes. Shrugging it off, I got up and went to bed. I told myself Adam Connor wasn't thoughtful enough *or* kind enough to cover me up.

I didn't see him at all that day.

It was kind of a sad day.

The jerk.

The fifth day…

The fifth day, Adeline Young, Adam's ex, Aiden's mom, took his son from school. Adam called me to let me know I wouldn't have to look after him that day. He sounded angry, so I didn't push for answers.

The sixth day, I didn't see any of the Connor boys. I was only supposed to look after Aiden for a week, so it was my last day with him. With them.

It was…it was a…normal day, I guess.

CHAPTER EIGHT

ADAM

Despite Dan's objections, I felt I'd made the right choice asking for Lucy's help. Yes, as far as we knew, she didn't have any kind of background with kids, but I'd watched her with Aiden, and I'd heard *plenty* about her from Aiden. He was happy around her, and I wanted him happy. All of that aside, I knew she would keep him safe. She'd already done that once. Besides, Dan had done a background check on her the minute she'd left the house with the cops that day.

She was clean as a whistle.

The first day she was supposed to look after Aiden, Dan had insisted we put a small listening device on one of Aiden's toys and make sure everything was okay throughout the day. I didn't object; it was the safety of my son. Overkill? Who cares; my mind was at ease.

When I was over at Jason's place to pick up Aiden, I was running on three hours of sleep. I had a grumbling Lucy sign the damn NDA then grumble some more, and I got out of there as soon as possible.

The second day, after I spent some time with Aiden, I found

Lucy's very firm ass climbing up the wall that separated Jason's property from mine.

Apart from being a pain in the ass, she was doing her best to stay out of my way, which was a surprise for me considering she'd watched me and my son without our knowledge for God knew how long.

It was going to be the first night she'd spend in my house, and I preferred her to keep her distance as much as possible. I'd accepted her request only because I was out of options. Aiden had a tendency to disappear into himself when he wasn't happy, and taking him to the set with me was out of the question. I would never forget how much I'd hated it when my parents took Vicky and me with them, only to forget about us for hours while they were lost in their own world. Sure, they had their assistants check up on us to make sure we were still breathing and behaving, but some days we barely even saw their faces. However, we made good props. Vicky, with her golden hair and big green eyes, was my mother's choice of accessory. She used to dress her up and make sure she was seen, just so the paparazzi would get shots of them and talk about their fashion choices.

It was a similar thing with me and my father. Sure, we didn't make the cover of tabloids with our fashion choices, but that wasn't the point, was it? The Connor family was a brand and that was it.

Our best memories were the ones where we wouldn't see our parents for months when they had location shoots. It wouldn't be the same for Aiden. That was the whole point.

The third day, it was a very long day. Between trying to find a new PR firm to shooting extra scenes for the movie, I was swamped. Add in an argument with Adeline about Aiden, and another argument with the studio about my contract…and my day was completely fucked.

It was early morning when I made it home. Despite having

been awake for more than thirty-six hours, I made sure to spend some time with Aiden before Dan drove him to his school.

The third day, I didn't see Lucy Meyer's smiling face.

The fourth day, when I came home, I found them sleeping on opposite sides of the same couch as Simba rolled around with Nala on the screen.

I stopped myself from going to their side and just watched them quietly.

Aiden was sleeping with his mouth wide open as always, his hands under his head. He murmured something and then softly kicked Lucy's legs as he struggled to turn to his other side. My gaze strayed, and I found myself watching Lucy's face. She was curled into herself, her knees tucked in. Her shoulder-length hair was tied up in a bun, giving me a clear view of her face. I could see a hint of her shoulder through the small opening of her T-shirt. She looked so innocent, the complete opposite of her usual loud self. If I hadn't been listening in on Aiden and her, I don't think I would've felt safe leaving him with her, but since I knew exactly how they spent their days through Dan, I was okay with my hasty decision.

The door behind me opened and closed, and Lucy stirred. I kept my eyes on her, waiting for her to wake up and accuse me of something, but other than the initial twitch of her shoulders, she stayed still.

"They're down already?" Dan asked, coming to stand next to me.

"Looks like it."

"She is good with him," he said in a soft tone as he kept his eyes on the duo. "She is teaching him how to sing with her friend, and he is teaching them how to act. He is quite demanding, too."

"Sounds like you had fun listening in on them."

"Right," he said shortly, and I smiled at his tone.

"She is a handful," I commented, having trouble keeping my eyes away from her.

Dan grunted, so I forced myself to glance at him. I noticed his eyes were on Lucy, too.

I cleared my throat and headed toward the kitchen. After a second of hesitation, Dan followed me.

I opened the fridge to get some water.

"Everything looks okay. No one was waiting around tonight."

"That's good. They are on Adeline more than me."

"How did your talk with her go? You think you'll be able to convince her without going to court?"

Sighing, I leaned into the fridge. "You want something to drink?" I asked, taking out a bottle of water.

"I'll skip."

"No, she isn't taking me seriously. I don't know what she's playing at, but it's not gonna be as easy as we thought. I'd thought she'd be all over it since he is the reason she asked for a divorce in the first place, but maybe that wasn't it at all. I have no idea what's going on in that mind of hers."

"Maybe she needs time. Maybe she is worried about what the public will think of her if she doesn't fight for the custody of her son," Dan suggested, casually leaning against the doorway.

"Maybe," I said. I took a few sips of water. "Maybe that's it. Maybe she'll come around."

God knew what the public thought of her, what her friends said behind her back mattered very much for Adeline. She wouldn't be able to explain Aiden's sudden absence from her life.

"Don't worry, she will. Besides, it would be hard on Aiden if he just saw her over the weekends."

"I want him with me, Dan," I said, meeting his eyes. Dan was one of the very few people who knew almost everything about the Connor family, all the good and the bad.

"I know you do, boss, but these things take time. Let her be for a while. Let's see what she'll do now that she is free from all that was holding her back."

Adeline's words, not his.

I nodded and stayed silent.

Dan straightened and looked over his shoulder into the living room. "If you have everything under control here, I'll leave."

"Sure. I'll call you later, but you don't have to pick up Aiden tomorrow morning. I promised him I'd drop him off at his school. Then I have the meeting with the new PR firm." I glanced at the clock on the wall: 11:00 PM. "Take the morning off if you want to. I'll be on set after my meeting anyway."

"I thought you were wrapping things up this week. Still shooting?"

"Yeah, Matthew—who was the director—wants to try a different ending and extend it with a few added scenes."

"Okay, we'll talk before I pick Aiden up," Dan said, then paused at the mouth of the living room. "Do you need help carrying one of them to bed?" He lifted an eyebrow and waited for an answer. I had a guess at which one he was referring to, and I didn't like it.

I threw the water bottle into the trashcan and walked to his side. They were still sound asleep.

"No. She'd probably make a scene and accuse us of assaulting her in her sleep."

Dan chuckled. "True. True." Turning his back to the view, he put his hand on my shoulder and gave me a serious look. "Be careful with her, Adam. She might be good with Aiden, but that doesn't mean she'd be good with you."

"What the hell is that supposed to mean?"

"Just warning you."

"About what?" I asked, my voice hardening.

He lifted his hands up, palms out, and headed out after saying,

"I see how you watch her. Just take it as advice from a friend, nothing more."

I couldn't be sure if he was warning me off because he was interested in the spitfire himself, or for a completely different reason. I shook it off and gathered Aiden in my arms as gently as possible.

His eyes fluttered open as I was tucking him into bed.

"Daddy?"

"Shhh," I murmured, combing his hair back with my fingers.

His eyes barely open, he asked, "You won't die yet, will you?"

The effects of *Lion King*…

"I won't, little man. It's time to go to sleep now."

"Kay." He nodded readily and pulled the covers up to his neck. "Lucy cried when Mufasa died, so I hugged her and told her it was all made up and she was being silly. I was right, wasn't I?"

"She cried?"

"Uh-huh. Like really cried with tears and all, not fake cry like Penny from my class does. I hugged her and patted her back and made her laugh."

"Good job, buddy," I said, smiling. "Now, go back to sleep."

"But I was right, wasn't I? I did good?"

"You did good, Aiden."

"Love you, Daddy."

I pressed a kiss to his forehead. "Love you, too, Aiden."

In seconds he was out.

As soon as I turned off the lights in Aiden's room, my feet took me back to Lucy's side.

So she cried for Mufasa…after all the times she told me how much she hated me, she had a heart after all.

I kneeled in front of her and waited for her to wake up and scream at me. When she didn't, I surprised myself by reaching up and gently touching her exposed wrist. Maybe I *did* want her to wake up and scream at me. Maybe I did enjoy seeing that heat in her eyes, that flash of *something* I couldn't exactly put a name on. My thoughts strayed to Adeline, how calm she was, how...soft, for lack of a better word. How much she had changed in just a few years...was I missing her? The old Adeline? Is that what this was?

Don't get me wrong, Lucy looked soft in all the right places, but there was something about her that was solid. Real. For all her crazy, she was also normal, and I envied her for that freedom.

She knew who she was, and she had no problem showing herself to the world.

When she made a soft noise in her sleep, I got up, threw a thin blanket over her, and left her alone.

As much as I seemed to enjoy going head to head with her, I had to stop myself from getting close. Short or long, meaningful or meaningless—any kind of relationship with a fan was a bad idea, and Lucy Meyer was the worst kind of fan, the kind that wasn't afraid to get in your face and force you to recognize her. My only focus was getting full custody of Aiden and giving him a new normal, and I had to remember that at all times. None of it mattered anyway; I'd find someone to look after Aiden while he spent his week with Adeline, and we wouldn't see Lucy again.

I wasn't looking for a quick lay—I'd had enough of those to last a lifetime—and I wasn't looking for a relationship either. What I was looking for was my bed. I was tired and sleep-deprived. I needed to get at least a few hours of sleep in before another day started and we did all the same things all over again.

CHAPTER NINE

LUCY

"Olive, are you one hundred percent sure about this?"

"Why? Come out so I can see."

"Are you sure you gave her my dress size and not some imaginary girl you cooked up in your mind?" I looked down at myself, yet again, and tried to make a decision. "Once you see this, it can never be unseen. Don't say I didn't warn you."

"Lucy, come on. Get out of there."

"As you wish, my green Olive." I shrugged, tried to take a deep breath, and stepped out of the bathroom.

It was around ten o'clock in the morning and we were in Olive's bedroom, where she did bad, bad things with her pretty husband that she didn't share with her friend—share as in *tell*—trying on dresses for the LA gala for *Soul Ache* we were supposed to attend that evening.

A short while before, Jason's stylist had dropped off ten different options for both Olive and me, and we were trying them on until we found the right ones.

"Oh my God." Olive breathed out when she lifted her head up from her phone, her eyes glued to my chest. "Oh my God. What's happening to your boobs?"

I frowned at her and put my hands under my boobs, glancing down for a short moment. "*This dress* is happening to my boobies. What does it look like from there?"

"Oh, it looks…it just *looks*, you know. Like a *lot*."

"Well, I warned you. Can't say I didn't." As I was walking to the full-length mirror, I pushed my thumbs between the thick fabric and my breasts and tried to pull it up higher. The only issue was that nothing was budging. I looked at myself in the mirror, and then glanced at Olive over my shoulder.

"You know, I think I can actually motorboat myself in this dress. How fun would that be?"

"Lucy." She groaned and sat up on her knees on the bed. "Come here. Let me see if I can pull it up."

"I already tried that," I said, but I still turned around to walk over to her. "I think this is as high as it can go. My poor boobs can't even breathe in this thing. How do you even manage to walk with your puppies? I mean, sure, they're good to sleep on, but this"—I lifted my boobs even higher with my hands—"this is just ridiculous. They're almost touching my chin, for God's sake! Help me get out of this before I explode."

"But the strapless looks so good with your short hair."

"Try, Olive," I said, giving up and letting go of my boobs as I stood in front of her. "Just try to make it work then."

She bit her bottom lip and just kept looking at my boobs.

I snapped my fingers in front of her face. "Excuse me! I'm not just some piece of meat."

"I'm sorry." She laughed. "I'm sorry, but I just can't look away." Eyes still on me, she started to yank up the fabric.

"Well, thanks," I drawled when she managed to make it even worse. "I always wanted to know how it would feel if my chin disappeared between my boobs."

She laughed and let go of the dress, watching my boobs

bounce in the aftermath. Then she reached out with her finger and pushed at the swell of my breast.

"It feels nice, right?" I asked, pressing with my own finger at my other breast. "Like a soft cloud. That's why I love sleeping on yours."

She nodded absently. "You definitely look like a D."

"I'm not a D. Barely a C."

"Well, the dress makes you look like a D." She pulled back her finger and looked up at my face, then back at my boobs. "Huh."

"Huh, what?"

"Actually your face looks smaller than your boobs. It's weird. I hope I don't look like that when I'm wearing a strapless dress. If I do and you never said anything…"

"I will definitely tell you if your face looks ten times smaller than your boobs." I walked back to the mirror just so I could see if there was even a small possibility of me wearing it that night. The dress was beautiful; the way it hugged my body actually did wonders for my waist and hips, but there was no way I could go out in public and quite possibly in front of cameras looking like I was about to eat my own bosom. "If I didn't have short hair, I might've actually considered wearing it, just to get people's attention—and when I say people, I mean hot men. No, not hot boys, hot men." I managed to let out a sigh. "Because hot boys suck. Jameson was a hot boy with a big dick and tattoos, but I want hot *men* and their—hopefully—big dicks." I thought about that for a moment, then looked at Olive. "Okay, that's not fair. I'll share with the rest of the women in the world. I'll settle with only one hot man. I won't love him, but I'll use him for sex. And he has to have a big dick. Like a dick that knows how to go to places, you know. Places not every dick can go."

"I think I get it," she replied, cutting off my tirade. "You want a big cock."

"Ah," I sighed softly, holding my heart. "Do you even know how happy it makes my heart to hear you say 'big cock'. I feel like you've grown so much. And I don't just want a big dick, Olive. I want a killer dick. There is a difference. I'd like to have a thick one, not too long, though, because I don't wanna be poked in all the wrong places. My dear vagina needs to be able to take it all in and hug. I want a killer dick, like it needs to put me into a coma after sex."

She laughed and got off the bed. "Got it. We'll order you a killer dick online. A pink one. And what are you even talking about? Have you even read my book? I say cock and dick plenty of times. I say even more…stuff."

"But writing it and saying it are two very different things. I bet Jason gets a boner every time you say cock." I grinned. "Do you try out scenes with him? Like when you get horny while you're writing a specific scene, do you call him to say, 'Come home and do me, Jason'? Does he have a killer dick, Olive?"

Trying her best to ignore me, she got off the bed to look at the other dresses that were hanging on the rack the stylist had left behind, as if she could escape me. "How about this one?" she asked, holding up another beautiful dress that was powder pink with almost nonexistent straps and a plunging neckline.

"First of all, you suck at changing the subject; we need to work on that."

She huffed and turned her back to me again as she fumbled with the remaining dresses.

"Second, there is nothing wrong with wanting a big dick that can please my vagina. And last but not least, why are you so intent on letting my boobs out to play tonight?"

"Because I don't want to stick out."

"Oh, I think it's too late for that. You wrote the book and they turned it into a movie. Not sticking out is out of the question, I believe, and I'm not sure my boobs would be of any help in that matter anyway. Do you think they have magic or something?"

"Fine. Try this one," she ordered, pushing the powder pink dress into my hands.

"Fine," I said, walking around her to get to the rack. "Then you're trying this one."

Olive looked at the white dress in my hands: it had a low dip in the back and it would fall all the way down to the floor on her. She was going to look mesmerizing.

"White?" she asked.

"Yes. White. Go change." I gave her a little push and a pat on her ass, then she disappeared into the bathroom.

The only reason we weren't getting naked in front of each other was because we wanted to make a grand entrance each time we tried a new one, build up some excitement.

"So…" she yelled from the bathroom as I sat my ass down on their bed.

"So?"

"So…how was it with Adam Connor? Every time I start mentioning him you tell me you hate him and then change the subject, and unfortunately for me you are good at that."

"And what makes you think I won't change it now?"

"Because you'll pity me? Because all you said when you jumped over the wall to this side after Aiden went to sleep was how much you disliked Adam, and that's not fair. Because how can you not talk about him to me when you spent…what four, five nights at his house? By the way, I have no idea how you got him to agree to that considering the way you met each other."

"Maybe I'm not talking about him because I signed an NDA?"

"Don't give me that crap, Lucy. You know I'm not asking about any private conversations you happened to overhear. I'm just asking what he is like. Like, what did you guys talk about?

Did he smile at you? Did you wake up at night and take a peek in his room? Does he sleep naked? Half-naked?"

I snorted and reached for Olive's phone. "I wonder who sounds like the psycho here."

"I'm just asking because those are the things I'd expect you to do."

"Thanks, Olive. I can answer one of the questions you have."

"Please tell me he walks around naked."

"I think I need to have a talk with Jason. Doesn't sound like you're getting it on the regular." I opened the Internet browser on her phone.

"I am getting it every day, thank you very much."

My lips twitched. I loved pushing Olive's buttons.

"I'm just curious. Call it research if you will."

"Sure. Just research," I drawled, laughing. "What the heck are you doing in there?" I yelled. "Get out here so I can have a look."

She opened the door and stepped out. "I had to pee first."

"Whoa." I exhaled, my eyes bugging out. "Holy shit, that looks good on you." She looked down at herself and pursed her lips as if she wasn't sure. "You don't even have to try anything else, Olive. I'm telling you, that's *the* dress for you."

"You think so?" She walked over to the mirror, looking over her shoulder to see the back. "I love how light it feels on my skin, but it's pretty low in the back."

"It's perfect. I'm not letting you wear anything else. Jason is going to flip."

Her lips tipped up, and she smoothed the dress down as she kept her eyes on the mirror. "I think I like it too."

"Trust me, it'll drive him crazy every time he puts his hand on your back."

"Okay. I'm sold."

"And," I said, waiting for her to look at me. "It looks beautiful on you. It's going to be an amazing night, Olive. You have nothing to worry about."

She took a deep breath and exhaled. "How do you know I'm worrying?"

I quirked an eyebrow at her and patted the spot next to me. "Because I happen to know you very well."

She smiled a little shakily and sat down. "Is it too obvious that I don't like this part all that much? I'd much rather see the movie for the first time with just Jason and you—not with all the cameras and all these other people I don't even know. It's something very special to me and they don't even know me."

"You can ignore everyone, Olive. This is your night with Jason, try to think of it like that. No matter what, it'll be a beautiful night. Everyone will talk about you. You should be proud of yourself."

"I wish my parents could've come, but they don't want to have all the lights and cameras on them. We'll go out there with Jason next week and watch it with them. You being with me tonight helps calm me a little, which is a shocker, but I'm still all jittery."

"You're telling me." I shook my head. "You hate it when *I* wake you up early, yet this morning you woke me up at five AM. I think that was my first clue as to how nervous you were."

She gave me a sheepish smile and dropped on her back. "Going to other galas with Jason was okay, but this feels different. I don't want the focus on me, but Megan said I'd have to do interviews with Jason. I'm gonna screw up."

Megan was Jason's publicist, and she was a badass.

"You're gonna be just fine. I'll be there. Jason will be there. After you get over the first part, the interviews, and all the flashing cameras, it'll be amazing. The movie will be amazing."

She nodded and closed her eyes. "Okay."

I reached for her phone and lay next to her. "Here, let me

show you something. I wanna scream and jump up and down, but I'm afraid that'll just freak you out more."

"Is it something bad? If it is, forget about it, I don't want to know."

I unlocked her phone and pulled up Amazon's website. "Do I scream and jump up and down when it's something bad?"

"One can never know what you'll do."

"Har har. Here, look at this." I held the phone up between us so she could see.

"Oh."

"Yeah. Oh." She was back to being number one on the Amazon charts, and quite possibly all the other platforms, too. I dropped the phone on the bed, and we stared up at the ceiling in silence. "You're a killer author, Olive, and I'm proud of you."

"Like a killer dick?" she asked, amusement evident in her tone.

"Exactly."

"Okay, I can live with that. Can we talk about Adam Connor for a bit? Please. I'm sure it'll calm me down."

"You're not fooling anyone, Olive," I said. "And I don't like the guy, what more can I say? I adore the kid, though. He's pretty awesome."

"And you were spending your days watching him because you didn't like the guy, is that it?"

"That was then, this is now. He might have a fantastic body, and a good sized bulge—"

"Don't forget the killer smile," she reminded me.

"He never smiles at me, so I wouldn't know that, but…"

"But what?"

"But…nothing. He is an asshole who sends innocent people to jail, and I hate him."

"Here we go again," Olive murmured.

You're thinking the same thing, aren't you? Maybe rolling

your eyes? Don't do it. Don't get me wrong, the guy was lickable, a tree I wouldn't have minded climbing. After all, how could I not think so after seeing him so close up? But that was before I saw his true nature.

I hated him and that was it.

"Soooo," Olive started after a short moment. "Do you want to talk about Jameson?"

I groaned.

———

WE MADE it to the premiere in one piece, and I was wearing the powder pinkish-nude dress with the plunging neckline as my boobs said hi to everyone glancing my way. I wasn't complaining, not really. I looked good after all. Olive, though…Olive looked phenomenal in Jason's arms. She wasn't the leading actress in the movie, but that was how the media was portraying her, and she definitely got more attention than the actual leading actress. It was Jason and Olive. The night was theirs. I was so happy for her, so freaking happy that she'd found what she was looking for.

Me? There was no sign of my killer dick, yet. I was hopeful, though; I'd keep looking.

I stood at the end of the red carpet where Olive and Jason were answering questions for the reporters. As soon as we'd exited the car, Jason had secured her hand in his and from what I could see, he still hadn't let go of her. I smiled and was actually thinking about sneaking inside where I'd heard I could find an open bar when someone spoke behind me.

"What are you doing here?"

That voice. I stiffened, but unfortunately couldn't stop the goose bumps from making an appearance. Slowly I turned around.

Adam *freaking* Connor.

Dear God…

He looked good enough to fuck out in the open. I could've had so much fun with him if only he weren't such a bastard.

"What are *you* doing here?" I asked instead of answering him.

His eyes dropped to my boobs, and he frowned. I frowned too and looked down to make sure nothing was wrong. When I couldn't find anything wrong, I put my hands on my boobs and lifted my eyes back to his. He was still looking.

Smiling sweetly, I tilted my head and asked, "Would you like to touch them?"

His eyes flew up to mine and his frown deepened. "What?" He shook his head. "Never mind. What are you doing here?"

"What do you *think* I'm doing here?" I asked back, dropping my fake smile. You'd think he would be at least a little nicer after I looked after his son, right? But nope, not this one.

He closed his eyes and sighed. "Ah. Right. You came with Jason and Olive."

"Bingo. You win the smartest guy award," I deadpanned.

"I'm sorry, when I saw you here, I thought…"

"Don't tell me you thought I was stalking you." He stayed silent, so I frowned. Forcing myself to soften my gaze, I leaned forward and whispered, "Fuck you, okay?" His gaze hardened, and I leaned back. "You're hot and all, I'll give you that much, but I don't like you enough to stalk you. Now, if you were Henry Cavill…that would change things."

"Good to know you gave up on stalking me and moved on to Henry."

And back to the start… "Who the hell do you think you are? I wasn't stalking you," I said through gritted teeth as someone bumped into me; Adam caught me by my arms before I could lose my balance and tackle him. I froze. My hands might have been splayed on his chest, but I would not admit to copping a feel.

"Are you okay?" he asked, dipping his head to look at my face.

Was I okay? Well, he smelled nice, so that was okay. His chest was hard under my hands too.

"No thanks to you," I mumbled, looking anywhere but his eyes.

Exactly at that moment, Jason and Olive decided to join us. "Hey, guys," Jason said as we broke apart.

"Hi," Olive added, smiling big at Adam. Jason pulled her closer to his side.

"I wasn't expecting to see you tonight," Jason said to Adam as Olive gave me a questioning look. I looked away. It was such a beautiful night.

The Giant—Adam's bodyguard—appeared out of nowhere. "Adam, she's posing. You'll have to catch her before she goes in."

Adam nodded and looked at Jason. "It was a last minute decision. If you'll excuse me, I have to talk to Adeline." He stepped away then looked back at Olive with a small smile on his face. "You look beautiful, Olive, congratulations on your success."

Olive blushed, and Adam left. I rolled my eyes and grumbled under my breath. "Suck up."

"It's as if I'm not the lead actor at all," Jason said, looking down at Olive. "You're stealing all the spotlight, little one. Should I be worried?" Olive smiled up at him, and Jason must've taken that as an invite 'cause he leaned down and gently kissed her on her lips. I leaned back a little and sure enough, his hand was pressed against the small of her back. The dress was a success.

When Jason's publicist came over with the private security hired by the studio in tow, the lovebirds had to break apart. Megan swept Jason away so he could do the last few interviews with his costar as Olive and I waited for him on the sidelines.

"What did Adam Connor want from you?" Olive asked as soon as Jason left.

"Nothing," I said distractedly as I moved my gaze over to the paparazzi and the mass of fans lined up behind the red ropes. "I think I'm ready to go in," I continued. "I'm starting to get anxious with all these people around.

"Don't even try to change the subject on me now. What do you mean nothing? What were you talking about?"

I glanced back at Olive and noticed the security coming toward us. "He thought I was stalking him, so I said fuck you. That's the gist of it. Happy now?"

"Why don't you try and be nice to him so you two can get married and be my neighbor?"

I snorted. "Please. I'd die before I married that guy."

"Mrs. Thorn," the blond security guy said as he stopped next to us. He didn't look that bad at all. Bulky arms, a white button-down, black slacks, slightly noticeable bulge...I didn't go for blonds that often, but what better time to change things around, right? "We need you to get inside, please," he added, holding his hand to his earpiece. Well, that was definitely sexy.

"What? Why?" Olive asked immediately, her eyes searching for Jason.

"What's wrong?" I asked and the guy turned his attention to me. I tried to give him my best smile.

"Ma'am, we need to clear the area so the..."

He was still talking, but I completely tuned him out. *Ma'am?*
Are you frickin' kidding me?
Are you frickin' kidding me?!

Olive pulled me by my arm toward the entrance of the build-ing. "Did you hear that?" I asked her in a loud voice as I kept looking over my shoulder. "He freaking ma'amed me! Did you hear him? Did you hear what he said?"

"I did," she replied, laughing under her breath.

"Don't laugh! This isn't funny, Olive! This is all because of him," I hissed. "He did this!"

"Who are you talking about? Jameson?"

"What?" I looked at her and shook my head. "No. It's Adam Connor. He is bad luck. Whenever he is around, something bad happens. I hate him."

"Here we go again…"

————

THE MOVIE WAS AMAZING. I had been the first one to read the book when Olive finished her manuscript, and sitting in a movie theater watching it all come alive was something I'd never forget. When it was over, I stood up and hugged my best friend, and we cried again. Then we laughed. Jason kissed Olive on her forehead, and I cried some more. And then we made it to the after party where there was music and hot guys and more celebrities. Surely one of them would have a killer dick, right?

I didn't even get to look for my killer dick.

Soon after we made it to the industrial loft where the after party was being held, I got a text message from Jameson.

I was too scared to read it straight away.

Even though I tried my best to act like he had never existed around Olive, sometimes he would pop into my head out of nowhere and disrupt my day. This was the first time he'd actually contacted me after his departure.

Dropping my phone back into my purse, I broke away from Olive and Jason, leaving them chatting with a group of people, and found myself a dark corner so I could close my eyes and slow down my heartbeat.

Isn't it the worst thing when your ex gets in touch with you when you're starting to move on with your life? Isn't it so inconsiderate of them?

I leaned my back against the brick wall and imagined myself on an empty road. I ignored the music roaring to life and quieted my mind. A sunny day, a gentle wind. A breath of fresh air. I forced myself to imagine Jameson standing at the end of the road. I still had feelings for him. Just a little more than a month before, I had thought he was mine, that I was different from my family. That my ending would be different than theirs. And I'd wanted that for myself. I'd wanted that for myself because Jameson had showed me it was possible, that it was okay to want that.

Standing in the middle of that imaginary road, I turned my back to Jameson and took one step after another. I left him behind.

I opened my eyes and I was back at the after party. I wanted to find Olive and have her read the text, but I thought better of it. This was her night. She would be angry at me for not telling her, but I'd make it up to her.

I took a much needed breath and unlocked my phone.

Jameson: *I miss you, Lucy.*

I could've easily smashed the phone on his head if he were somewhere reachable, but fortunately for him, he wasn't. Who the hell sends 'I miss you' to someone they've dumped? And why the hell would they write it anyway? If it was to torture, then mission accomplished.

My hand shaking, I dropped the phone back into my purse and walked toward the open bar.

When I had two tequila shots in me, I found Olive and, with Jason's help, convinced her to go on stage with me so we could get out a few songs with the band the studio had hired for the night. It took a lot of begging, but as soon as we started our signature song "Let's Marvin Gaye", the song Jason admitted had made him start falling in love with her, she relaxed and managed to forget about the audience, which consisted of a lot of celebrities and other industry people. As always, we sang to each other, not to them, and we danced ourselves silly, having the best time. After another tequila shot, provided by Jason Thorn, I sweet-talked Olive into singing "Lovefool" by The Cardigans. It wasn't a surprise that Jason couldn't help himself and kissed her silly on stage. Again.

It was the best interruption.

And I was finally forgetting about Jameson. Again. Kinda.

Olive and Jason by my side, I talked to a lot of people. I smiled, laughed. Even Jameson couldn't ruin such an important night.

———

A FEW HOURS LATER—OR maybe just an hour—I found myself getting pawed by some guy as I left the bathroom after splashing some water to my face. Was I drunk? Maybe a little. I blinked a few times and tried to remember where I was.

Olive's after party.

I had left their side to use the restroom.

Right.

"Hey," I mumbled, trying to push his shoulders back.

The mysterious guy licked my neck, and I shivered.

Shit.

That kinda felt nice.

Did I know him? Had he even given me his name before assaulting me with his tongue? For the life of me, I couldn't remember. As he was busy lavishing attention on my neck, I squinted and looked around—at least as much as I could in the dark. I was backed against a high wall in a narrow hallway, next to the unisex restrooms. I remembered chatting with a group of people with Jason and Olive, but I couldn't remember if this guy had been in that group. He wore a dark gray button-up and from what I could tell, he was built like a brick house.

He really knew what he was doing with his mouth too, but I wanted to put a face to that tongue, so I tried to push him back again. "Umm, hi," I repeated when pushing didn't work out quite that well. Instead of answering me or even acknowledging me, the guy's hands tightened around my waist, and he pulled me toward a small alcove.

"Whoa," I mumbled, my head spinning. His back hit something with a thud, then he spun me and this time it was my back that hit the steel door, knocking the air out of me. I winced, but he didn't seem to notice.

"Hey! Ease off," I said, slurring only a little.

"Shhh. I'll make it okay," the guy whispered into my ear, rubbing my shoulders. Then suddenly his hands started traveling downward, his hands squeezing my flesh.

"What…what are you doing?" I lifted my knee to shove him off, but my dress hit me right below my knees, so it was a useless attempt. I might as well have been moving under water. I raised my voice. "I said get off me!"

Suddenly there was a hand gripping my cheeks and pushing the back of my head against the door. I was having trouble breathing.

"I said shhh," he whispered into my ear and bit on my earlobe.

If he wasn't hurting me to the point that I was sure his fingers would leave their mark on my face, it would've been sexy.

Or maybe not.

But he was hurting me, and I'd made it perfectly clear I wasn't into what he was doing.

One of his hands found the edge of my dress and started hiking it up. "I said stop," I yelled as much as I could with his fingers pressing into my cheeks. The low bass of the music was drowning my voice anyway.

He bit on my neck and his lips found mine.

I squeezed my eyes shut and tried to turn my face away from his grip.

"I love it when girls like you play hard to get. I'm always up for a challenge."

Oh, hell no.

I tried to slow down my heartbeat and jerked my knee up; since he'd lifted my dress up, it was easier this time and hit the bull's eye. He grunted and let go of my face, doubling in front of me, his hands covering his useless jewels. I pushed my hair out of my face and opened and closed my mouth to relieve the ache.

"You son of a bitch, what the hell do you think you're doing?" I hissed at him. When he straightened up, I noticed he looked familiar, but I couldn't place him. Had I given him permission to paw me? I couldn't remember doing something like that, definitely not on such a special night for Olive. That being said, I did remember some harmless, playful flirting with a few guys, but it had all been in fun. After Jameson's text, I'd just needed that little self-esteem boost. I wasn't looking to get laid.

I hurriedly pulled my dress down and glared at the guy. His face had reddened, but he was sporting a big grin on his face.

Great…

"Look," I said slowly. "I'm sorry about your balls." I huffed a breath and continued. "Actually, I take it back. I'm not. You deserved it. I'm just gonna leave, okay?"

He lifted an eyebrow and kept grinning creepily. I started scooting away and lifted my hands, palms out. "I'm leaving. No harm done."

He licked his lower lip and stalked toward me. I tried to run past him, but he was too strong for me and slammed me against the door, yet again. This time he kept me in place with his shoulders. With quick hands, he had my dress almost up to my waist when I started screaming in his ear.

It's frightening how fast you can sober up.

And how fast you can turn homicidal.

The music was really loud, but I was sure somebody would hear me.

I squirmed, kicked, and screamed, but he still managed to push one of his hands up my dress and was squeezing the shit out of my breast. I was going to bruise for sure. However, considering what was happening, a bruise or two was the least of my worries.

"Fight me," he said. "Make me work for it."

That's when I started to panic.

He was crazy.

When my screams got too loud for him, he cupped my mouth with his hand and continued his assault on my body. I still thought he would stop.

I still thought it was a nightmare.

I still screamed against his hand.

When his fingers edged closer to my underwear, I stilled. Completely.

I stopped breathing.

My eyes welled with tears, and I swallowed.

Stupid stupid tears.

Oh, he was definitely going to die as soon as…

"Oh, you like that, don't you?" he whispered as his fingertips traveled over my panties.

The world stopped spinning.

He pulled his hand away from my mouth, and I screamed bloody murder with everything I had left in me.

CHAPTER TEN

ADAM

After my argument with Adeline, I headed toward the back door of the venue so I could escape and go home. I had known going there wouldn't change anything, but I had still needed to talk to her. Taking her to court for full custody of Aiden was the last thing I wanted to do, but Adeline...she was forcing my hand. She had no business being Aiden's mom.

The paparazzi were lying in wait at the front of the venue, so leaving that way was out of the question. It was already bad that they had taken shots of me and Adeline in a heated conversation —God knew how they would spin those shots—and the last thing I wanted was them capturing me storming out of the place.

I headed toward the back of the loft, rounded the corner, and found a couple going at it at the mouth of the hallway. Keeping my head down, I walked past them. Turning right, I pushed open the steel doors and felt the fresh air on my face. Right as I took my first step out, I heard someone scream.

My head snapped back, and I saw another couple in a compromising position. The way the guy was towering over the girl, I couldn't see anything, but I thought I saw *something*...

I glanced outside. Maybe I had just misinterpreted the

scream? Adeline wasn't a screamer in bed; she barely moved under me. Maybe I'd forgotten what a pleasure-filled scream sounded like?

Still, my feet took me toward the couple, and the closer I got to their cozy little hidden spot, the more I felt like a creeper intruding on something.

I saw a flash of a nude fabric, similar to the one Lucy had on when I had last seen her then another muffled scream and my steps quickened.

"Hey," I yelled so I could be heard over the music, and the guy looked at me over his shoulder, giving me a glassy stare. I frowned and my gaze strayed to the girl trapped between him and the door.

The first thing I noticed was the tears; then I realized it was Lucy with her stormy gray eyes, the blue completely gone. Her fear-stricken eyes lifted up to mine and something loosened inside me.

Call it a release of anger; it was to be expected after the night I'd had.

"Adam Connor," the guy said with a big smile. "Welcome to our private little party. Care to join in on the fun?" It was Jake Callum, an up-and-coming actor, a douche who thought he was *the* shit just because one of his movies had done okay at the box offices.

I noticed Lucy trying to push him off and my scowl deepened.

Prying him off her by gripping the back of his shirt, I slammed him against the wall.

"Easy, dude." He laughed, lifting his hands up between us. "I have a contract. Take it easy."

I looked down at his pants and sighed in relief when I saw he was all buttoned up, but then I noticed Lucy trying to wipe off her tears at the same time she was pulling down her skirt and my anger came back tenfold.

"Care to tell me what was going on here?" I asked, getting in his face and pushing at him.

Jake shrugged with a smirk. "Just having a good time with the lady, dude. Relax." His eyes slid to Lucy, and I tightened my hand on his shirt to get his attention.

"Don't look at her! I asked you—"

I didn't have time to finish my sentence because the little pain in my ass who was dressed as every guy's wet dream was pushing on *me* to move away. I looked down at her over my shoulder. When I didn't budge, her frown deepened, and she gave it another try. "What the hell are you doing?" I asked, glaring at her.

She quit trying to push me away. "Get out of my way," she growled.

"I'm trying to help you, for fuck's sake!" I bit out.

"I said," she growled. "Get. Out. Of. My. Way."

Well, I thought, *she's already proven she's a lunatic, so maybe I misunderstood the situation?* Maybe they were in the middle of a lover's quarrel? Apparently I knew nothing anymore.

I let go of Jake and took a step back. "My mistake then. Excuse me for interrupting." Lucy's eyes narrowed on me, but as soon as I was out of her way, her focus was on Jake. My eyes dropped to her chest, just momentarily, and I saw how sharp her breathing was.

I nodded at her, raked my hand through my hair, and reluctantly took a step back as she leaned toward Jake and crooked her finger at him as if she was about to whisper something in his ear. Why did that simple move make me even angrier? I was about to turn around and leave when out of nowhere her little fist flew in the air and landed squarely on Jake's nose. Cupping his nose, he groaned in pain.

"You bitch!"

Without any pause, Lucy kneed him in the balls.

I winced. *Ouch.*

She was about to get in another punch when I caught her hand before it could land.

"Whooaa, easy there."

It was a stupid move on my part. Never get in the way of Lucy Meyer. Ever. She stepped on my foot.

With her heel.

Very hard.

"Jesus, woman!" I yelled, momentarily dropping her arm.

"You little piece of shit!" she screamed at Jake before landing another punch on his shoulder.

"You crazy bitch," Jake hissed back, letting go of his nose so he could capture her wrist. Lucy stopped with her tirade, and he started twisting her hand. At a loss for words, I wrapped my hand around Jake's throat as I tried to keep Lucy away with the other.

"Drop it," I said to him as calmly as I could manage. What had I gotten myself into?

Jake's eyes hardened, and he twisted her wrist farther, causing her to gasp and twist her body to lessen the pain. I tightened my hand around his throat and pushed his head back into the wall until his face started to turn red and he was having trouble breathing. "I won't repeat it, Callum. Let her go!"

He shoved her hand away and a second later, Lucy was on him again, screaming obscenities, cursing him all to hell. I let Jake go and turned my back to him as he kept coughing.

"Stop it," I said to Lucy and got a light punch on my shoulder for all my troubles.

Jesus.

Did the woman listen to me? Of course not. I doubted she ever listened to anyone.

"I'm gonna kill him," she kept yelling while trying to hit Jake by reaching around me.

I glanced at the end of the hall to see if I could spot Jason, but there was no one near us, not even the couple who had been in a kissing frenzy just a few minutes before.

Her eyes were focused on Jake. "Who do you think you are!" she screamed again, pushing and pulling at me to get to him. "You little bastard! How dare you!"

"You either get her out of my face or we're gonna have a problem here, Connor," Jake croaked from behind me, his voice fucked up. Maybe I'd squeezed a little harder than necessary—not that I felt sorry for the guy.

"Shut the fuck up," I growled at him and finally caught Lucy's flailing arms.

"Let me go, Connor," she screamed and lifted her foot again. She must've been exhausted because she was starting to move much slower, and I knew her game, so I managed to move my foot away before she could find her target. I twisted her body as gently as I could and held her back against my chest, trapping her arms.

How nobody had heard the whole mess, I had no idea.

I braced my chin on her shoulder and whispered to her, "Calm down, Lucy. Calm down." She smelled of pink roses and a subtle hint of citrus, soft and sharp at the same time. I shook my head to clear my mind.

After a slight hesitation, she started squirming against me. "Don't tell me to calm down, goddammit! I'm gonna kill him. Let go of me."

"No. I need you to calm down for me, Lucy. Can you do that? Please, sweetheart. Calm down and tell me what's going on here."

Her chest falling and rising rapidly, she curled her hands around my arm. I was expecting her to try something on me, or simply push me away, but she surprised me by just holding on to me. "I told you…" she said slowly "…not to call me sweetheart."

"If you promise to calm down, I'll never call you sweetheart again. Will that make you happy?"

She took a deep breath with difficulty and nodded. Her hands were still gripping my arms, but I didn't think she'd appreciate me pointing that out.

Jake chose that moment to slither away from the wall and walk away from us. He faced us and kept walking backward. When he shot Lucy a quick salute and grin...Lucy went rigid in my arms for a second then let out a frustrated scream and tried to go after him.

I sighed and lifted her legs off the ground. "That's it. We're leaving." Carrying a kicking and screaming Lucy, I walked outside.

The moment I let her go, she tried to run past me and back inside again. I cut her off before she could manage that.

"Why would you do that?" she screamed, her chest heaving. Apparently it was time to attack me again.

"I save you and that's how you say thank you?" I asked, blocking the door so she wouldn't try something.

A security guard came running toward us. "Is everything okay here?"

Lucy turned her murderous eye on the guy and growled, "Yes!"

The guy ignored her and turned to me. "Everything good, Mr. Connor?"

She stepped in front of him and waved her hands. "Hello? Why are you even asking him? Maybe I'm the one having a problem with *him*?"

Ignoring Lucy yet again, he waited for an answer. I rubbed my neck and nodded. What was I even supposed to say? As soon as he left, Lucy whirled on me.

I raised my hand to stop her before she could start all over again. "Shut it." I was seconds away from getting in her face and yelling right back at her, but I made the mistake of noticing her shaky hands and all the fight I had left in me drained away.

"Look." I closed my eyes and tried to find the right words to say to her. "Look, it seems like neither one of us is having the best night here. I'm just trying to make sure you're all right, nothing more. Then I'm leaving, and you can go kill whoever you want to, okay?" I took a deep breath to give her some time. "If you don't want my help, that's fine. Just calm down a little so we can both go on our way."

Surprisingly, she nodded and turned her back to me. I won't lie, it was tempting to wait a few more minutes in silence and then just leave when she was feeling more like herself, but when she hugged her elbows to hide the fact that her body was starting to shake uncontrollably, I knew I couldn't leave her there.

Shit!

I thought about putting my hands on her shoulders and... consoling her? Warming her up? Just something to ease her, but I didn't think she'd appreciate that, so instead I faced her and tilted her chin up with my fingertips.

"Lucy?"

She opened her eyes and what I saw broke my heart: a single tear that followed an almost straight line down to her chin. Instinctively, I wiped it away. I didn't know shit about this woman, about who she really was inside, but from what I'd seen so far, I knew something was seriously wrong.

"I'm not crying," she announced.

"Of course not," I said softly.

"I'm not." She wiped at her cheeks with the back of her hand and looked up at me. "These are just angry tears."

"Of course," I repeated. "I wouldn't expect anything else from someone like you."

Her face flushed and her posture stiffened even more. "And what is that supposed to mean? Someone like me?"

Of course she'd twist my words. How else could she manage

to start another fight? If I didn't know any better, I'd say she fed on making me miserable.

I shook my head. "I'm not doing this with you. Good night and have fun, Lucy." I turned around to leave, but she put her hand on my arm and stopped me.

"Just wait a minute. What—"

"I meant someone as stubborn, strong, and willful as you, Lucy," I explained, cutting her off. "I'm not looking to start a fight with you. Not tonight."

She took her hand off my arm. "Oh."

"Yeah."

"Well then, I'm sorry."

"How unexpected of you. Was that the very first time those words have ever left your mouth?"

"Don't push it."

My gaze dropped to my arm, specifically to her hand that was keeping me from moving. "I'd like to leave now, if that's okay with you?"

She followed my gaze then seemed surprised to find her hand on me. Taking a few steps back, she said, "Of course. I didn't mean to touch you. Hopefully you won't call the authorities on me."

The way she said it...*God*, she infuriated me.

"Like I said, have a nice evening, Lucy."

I walked away from her. I walked away and it didn't feel right.

You must really be itching for a fight, Adam, I thought to myself as my steps slowed down. As if the first round with Adeline hadn't been enough, I was going to spend some more time with this crazy one. In a car. Where I couldn't escape.

When I looked back, Lucy was exactly where I'd left her. Her face was tilted up to the sky, her eyes closed. Moonlight looked good on her. Her features looked soft, her slightly pink lips inviting. My feet took me back to her.

"Do you want me to go in and get your friends?"

She opened one eye and gave me a defiant look. "No."

I tilted my head and waited for an explanation that never came.

"Okay then. Would you—"

"You can leave, I'm fine."

"Would *you* like to leave with me?"

Both of her eyes opened, and she seemed to consider my offer for a moment. "Yes," she said finally. "Yes, please."

"Would you like me to drop you off at Jason's place or somewhere else?"

"Jason's. If it won't be too much trouble for you, I'd appreciate that." The fight seemed to have left her and her shoulders dropped a little. I wanted to put my arms around her…close my eyes, put my arms around her, and just breathe.

I shook my head. "You want me to wait while you let your friends know you're leaving?"

"I don't want to bother them. I'll text Olive on the way."

"My car is this way," I said, motioning to the row of cars with my head. She followed me without a word.

I managed to avoid the paparazzi by taking the long way back home. A shot of a strange woman in my car would've given them too much ammunition.

The car ride was unexpectedly silent. I kept glancing at Lucy, but she kept her focus on the road. I noticed her rubbing the back of her hand on her dress, so I reached out and grabbed it to have a look.

"Hey," she protested, trying to pull her hand from my grasp. "What are you doing?"

"Keep still for a second." Her knuckles were all red. "You need to put ice on this." We stopped at a red light. Unconsciously,

I ran my thumb over the bruised part. "Where did you learn to hit like that?"

She grunted. "It wasn't a good hit. I didn't even break his nose."

"Oh, so that's what you were aiming for."

"Well, yeah. Why else would you hit someone? I wanted to see some blood."

On top of everything else, she was bloodthirsty too. Strangely, it suited her.

I let go of her hand and forced myself to put it back on the wheel. "Are you ready to tell me what was going on in there?" I asked. "Things got out of hand with Jake?"

"Jake? His name is Jake? You know him?"

"Jake Callum." I frowned and glanced at her as the light turned green. "You don't know him?"

"Oh yeah, I let him force his tongue down my throat *because* he was Jake Callum. Did it look like I knew him to you?" She angrily smoothed down her dress and then mumbled to herself, "I knew I recognized him from somewhere."

"How should I know whether you care to ask for a name before you start making out with a guy?"

Her head snapped to me, and I felt her eyes boring into the side of my face.

I sighed. "I'm sorry, that was wrong of me to say." Her answer had angered me; it shouldn't have.

"Apology not accepted." She looked back at the road again. The streets were empty.

After a few moments of silence, she spoke up, "Not that you need to know, but for your information, I don't even remember talking to the guy. When I got out of the restroom he was just there and on me."

I pulled my foot from the gas. "What are you saying?"

"You have trouble hearing?"

I pulled the car to the side and turned to face her. "What do you mean he was on you?"

"If you're not gonna get me home, I can find my own way." Before she could even touch the handle, I locked the doors.

"Are you saying he forced himself on you?" I said through gritted teeth.

Her face was flushed with anger when she looked at me. "What did you think was going on?"

I processed that for a second, then nodded at her.

"Can we go now?"

"No," I said shortly. After checking the mirrors, I made a quick U turn.

"Whoa!" she gasped, holding on to the window and her seat. "Where are you going?"

I didn't answer.

"Adam?"

We would be back at the loft in ten minutes.

She raised her voice. "Adam!"

I gave her a quick look. "We're going back to find Callum."

"No, we're not," she argued, her brows drawing together.

I ignored her.

"Hey." She hit my arm, trying to get my attention. "I already kicked his ass, what else could you possibly do? Or what? Are you going back there to thank him for putting me in my place? Just when I think I can't possibly hate you more than I already do—"

I hit the brakes so hard Lucy flew forward, slamming her hand on the dashboard to catch herself.

"Put your fucking seat belt on," I snapped at her.

"Are you *fucking* crazy?" She looked at me like I was the one who had lost his mind, but the yelling worked, and she obediently did what I asked without another peep. Thank God there were no cars behind us.

"If you *ever* tell me anything like that again, I'll make you sorry, Lucy. I won't even care that you don't know anything about me."

"What are you gonna do? Spank my ass?"

"Don't go and give me any ideas now."

Her eyebrows rose, and she opened and closed her mouth a few times.

"What did you think was happening there?" she asked in a calmer voice when I started driving again.

I clenched my jaw. "I thought you wanted him to slow down. I didn't think he was full-on trying to rape you, for fuck's sake!"

With the speed I was going, I'd be back at the loft in just a few minutes. Then I could smash the bastard's head in. If I'd realized what he was doing to her, the extent of it, I wouldn't have held her back.

I barely heard Lucy mumbling next to me. "Okay. Okay. Adam, I need you to take me home now."

"No."

"Adam?" Something had changed in her voice, so I gave her a quick glance.

She had paled and was looking at me with those big gray eyes.

Fuck.

Fuck!

"I want to go home now," she repeated, keeping her eyes on me. "Please."

I slowed down and pulled over carefully.

"Please," she repeated again.

I looked at the road then back at her. "We're almost there, Lucy."

"You're not hearing me. Either take me home or unlock the doors so I can find my own way."

I gave her a long look, studied every little expression on her face. The way her lips were pressing together, the way she was trying her hardest not to blink too many times. That little vein that popped up on the side of her forehead when she was angry, frustrated, or anxious. I didn't like the fact that I knew about that vein.

I shouldn't have noticed it.

I should've ignored it.

As our wills battled, she lifted her chin ever so slightly and ordered me to unlock the doors.

When I didn't, she started pushing all the buttons, trying to find the right one.

"Okay. Fine." I reached for her hand and touched her, curling my hand over her cold one. When she didn't punch me, I placed it back on her thigh. "We're going home. I'll take you home."

The rest of the ride was…long. Long and quiet and painful. The city was surprisingly quiet that night. I still kept my hand on hers, hoping she'd warm soon enough and stop shaking. The fact that she didn't push me away…

I stopped the car in front of Jason's gate and hesitated before I unlocked the doors.

Lucy waited with her hand on the handle, ready to flee.

"Is there anything I can do?" I asked into the heavy silence.

"I'd like to get out now."

I could understand that. I unlocked the doors and watched her shimmy down from the car. Before she shut the door, she mumbled a thank you and walked away.

How could a night out go so wrong?

I waited for her to get inside. Just to make sure, I told myself, nothing more. Instead of entering the code for the gate, she hiked her dress up a little and sat her ass down at the curb.

What I should've done was look away and go home. She'd call her friend, get the code, and go wait in the backyard or do whatever the hell she wanted to do. She had been nothing but trouble since the day I'd found her dripping wet in my backyard. She was the last thing my life needed. Quite aware of all that, I turned the engine off to go and join her on the curb.

Neither one of us spoke for a few minutes as we sat next to each other. It was a chilly night, barely any clouds in the dark sky.

"Let's go home and put some ice on that hand," I said, tiredly.

She sounded equally tired, if not more, when she said, "I don't have a home."

"Tonight you do."

———

I WOKE up to the sound of laughter ringing through the house. A woman's laughter and a kid's—my kid's, to be more specific. But Aiden was supposed to be with Adeline; it was her weekend. Had she brought him back? Frowning, I got up to find out what was going on.

The night before had ended abruptly after I'd helped Lucy ice her hand. One second I was holding her fragile hand in my palm, getting used to its weight in my hand as we stood almost nose to nose, and the next she was scrambling away from me. The moment she could, she'd fled to her room. Knowing there was nothing more I could do, I'd gone to bed, too, but I couldn't fall sleep. Apart from worrying about what I was going to do about Adeline, I'd worried about Lucy too because she'd managed to work her way into my life somehow.

Getting out of bed, I had spent some time in the kitchen, thinking maybe she'd join me. I'd seen the light coming from under her door, so I knew she was having trouble sleeping too.

She hadn't come out, so after a while I'd gone back to bed, and I thought it was for the best.

I made it to the living room and spotted Dan watching Lucy and Aiden with a fleeting smile on his face.

Aiden and Lucy? They were laughing uncontrollably, completely oblivious to their surroundings.

They didn't even notice me walking up to Dan. "What's going on here?" I asked.

His lips quirked up even more and to hide it he took a sip from the coffee cup he had in his hand. "They are practicing their laughter. Lucy thought Aiden's needed a little more kick."

"Is that so?"

"Yup." He gave me a quick glance. "He was feeling sorry for himself, so she said she wasn't feeling all that great either and thought it was the perfect time to practice how to laugh better."

I smiled. That sounded exactly like something Lucy would do.

"And what's Aiden doing here?"

"The little bugger tricked me."

I didn't have time to ask how he'd been tricked because Aiden finally noticed me and jumped off the couch, running toward me.

"Daddy!"

"Got you," I grunted, lifting him up in my arms.

"I missed you like crazy. You missed me too?" he asked into my neck, his thin arms holding on tight. I hugged him even tighter and dropped a kiss on his head.

"I missed you too, little man. What are you doing here?"

His head came out of my neck, and he held my face between his hands.

"Checking on things. You haven't shaved?"

I laughed. "What things are you checking on exactly?"

"You."

"Me?"

"I don't like you being all alone here. I think about it so much that sometimes I can't sleep at night. I know you miss me, so I came to check on things. Since I worry about you so much, maybe I shouldn't leave you alone here?"

"I thought you said you forgot to take your favorite book with you and that was why we came here, little guy," Dan said, grabbing Aiden's attention.

As he was weaving more tales to Dan, I glanced at Lucy, who was off the couch and watching us quietly. I tried to figure out her mood, but she was good at not giving away too much. She still had a smile on her face, but other than that, I couldn't even begin to guess what she was thinking.

"And then I said to myself, Dan is protecting Daddy, so he'd want to check things out too." Aiden was still talking.

"Oh, so that's what you said to yourself."

"Uh-huh. I knew you wouldn't say it because you're a big guy and big guys don't worry, so I said it for you. And now that Lucy lives here, we have to protect them both." He put his hand on my cheek again and turned my face so I'd look at him. "You wanted to see me too, right? Tell Dan I did good."

"You didn't do good, Aiden," I corrected him, trying to keep a straight face. "You can't lie to have your own way."

"But I didn't lie. I came to check on things!"

Dan's phone pinged with a new message.

"Okay, little liar, your mom texted. Grab your things, we need to go."

"But, Dan, we need to—"

"You don't need to do anything, buddy," I said, interrupting him. "You don't want to worry your mom, do you?"

His face fell. "No, but—"

"No buts, Aiden. You can't lie to Dan, okay?"

"Am I in big trouble, Daddy?" He averted his eyes and his hand started to draw shapes on my skin, a new nervous habit he'd picked up.

"Not this time."

He lifted his eyes and smiled a brilliant, wide smile. "You're happy I came to check on things, aren't you? You aren't angry with me."

I smiled back at him. "I'm always happy to see you, buddy."

He looked back at Lucy over his shoulder then back at me again. "Lucy said she was happy to see me too."

I shot her a quick glance then slowly lowered Aiden down.

"It looked like she was very happy to see you."

He nodded. "I think she likes me."

Even though he was trying to be very careful and talk quietly, I knew Lucy could hear everything he was saying. I could see her smile slowly widen, and it made me happy to see she could still smile after the day before. It made me happy that Aiden was there to make her laugh. I only wished I could've woken up earlier to see more of that.

"I agree," I said. "I think she likes you very much."

"Can you protect her for me? She isn't feeling well, and I want her to be safe."

My eyes shot back to Lucy. Had she told Aiden something?

"Of course," I replied to Aiden roughly. He was growing up, worrying about others. Then I looked at Lucy so she could see I meant the words. "I want her safe, too."

I saw her roll her eyes and knew she'd be okay.

Turned out, Aiden really had forgotten to take his favorite book with him, so after he ran off to get it from his room, he left with Dan, leaving me alone with Lucy.

I headed toward the kitchen to brew some coffee, and she followed me. I knew she had something to say.

"I can protect myself, you know. You didn't have to promise your son you'd protect me."

"Of course you can. I just thought it would be easier to give him my word than to explain that you wouldn't want my help because you hate me."

"Yes, I hate you." She nodded as if she was convincing herself. Her eyes roamed my chest and then she looked away. She was standing on the other side of the kitchen island, tapping the marble with her fingers.

I added water to the coffee machine, pressed the start button, and calmly waited for her to say whatever was eating at her.

"You should wear a shirt," she said finally.

I decided to tease her to make her smile. She had laughed with my son, so it was only fair if she gave me some smiles too. "What?" I asked her, peering down at myself. "You don't like me naked from this close? Every one of those photos in your phone was of me naked *and* zoomed in."

"That was then. Now"—she gave me another look, and I caught her swallow—"not that attractive, I guess."

"Ah, right. Not after I sent you to prison, right?"

She squinted at me. "Are you making fun of me?"

"Of course not. I wouldn't dare."

Satisfied, she nodded. "Good. Be scared of me. That's smart of you."

I nodded and rounded the kitchen island to stand in front of her. She followed me with her eyes.

"What are you doing?"

"I assume there is something you want to tell me, so I'm getting closer so I can hear you better."

"And you couldn't hear me from there because…?"

"Because I want you to know that I'm taking you very seriously."

"Go take me seriously from over there, buddy."

She put a hand on my chest to stop me from moving closer to her. I stopped and looked down at her small hand that was planted on my chest. I liked how she felt on me, her skin on mine. She looked down at it too and seemed surprised by it. I didn't even try to hide my smile.

"And I wanted to thank you," I explained. When she looked confused, I continued. "For making Aiden laugh like that. As I'm sure you've already noticed, he's having a hard time with the divorce." I placed my hand over hers, which made her frown deepen. "So thank you."

She pulled her hand away and rubbed it on her thigh. "Well, someone has to make him laugh. Since you're not doing the job…" She shrugged, and I laughed.

"Thank you for that too."

"You're welcome. Now go put on a shirt." She waved at me with her hand. "I shouldn't have to look at your naked…bare… unclothed…muscular chest. You're ruining my view."

I tilted my head to the side a little to capture her eyes. "It's my home. You're free to look away, Lucy," I suggested softly. When she met my gaze, her eyes lit up.

She put her hand on the island and slightly leaned forward. "Are we playing a game, Adam Connor? Because I love games."

I raised an eyebrow, but otherwise stayed silent.

"Oh, poor Adam." She made a sad face and my lips twitched. "You don't know me at all, do you?" She took a step forward and placed her hand on my chest again, making a big show out of it.

Little minx.

When I didn't object, she started moving a finger downward, her touch as light as a feather.

Our eyes stayed locked.

This time, *I* took a step toward her, raising the stakes. I wanted to see where she was going with the act.

"Does it feel good?"

She frowned at my question and her hand halted on my abs.

"Does it feel exactly like you imagined it or better? Too soft?" I flexed my muscles and leaned closer to her. "Too hard?"

She curled her fingers and lightly grazed my skin with her nails. I couldn't be sure if it was involuntary or if she was still playing, but with the way her chest was rising and falling rapidly…I could see I was affecting her.

She blinked. Twice. Other than that, her expression didn't waver. Then she licked her bottom lip and gently dragged her fingertips up and down my stomach, tracing my muscles, stopping when she reached the band of my sweatpants.

I dropped my eyes to her hand, just for the briefest second, and missed the moment she decided to rise up on her toes to whisper in my ear. I kept my head down and waited to hear what she would say.

"You're right," she whispered, a little too close to my ear to be accidental. Oh, she was good. Not quite as good an actor as me, but she was holding her own. "I did spend some time by myself, imagining how you'd feel under my hands." She rested her palm on my chest, and I closed my eyes so I could focus on her voice, focus on how good she sounded when she wasn't yelling at me. "Between my legs." My lips quirked up, my dick pulsing with need. I liked this Lucy much better.

"Do you think…" She paused. "Can I touch you?" Another short pause. "To see if it's hard? And big…"

I opened my eyes. If she thought I'd call her bluff, she was quite mistaken.

She leaned back, heated eyes meeting mine. I grabbed her hand and lowered it for her, making sure her palm stayed flat against my skin all the way down.

When our connected hands reached my sweatpants, I stopped.

She waited to see what I would do with an eager look on her face. She thought she had me.

Think again, my little stalker.

I walked into her and forced her back against the island. She wasn't expecting *that*, so she had no choice but to follow my movement. I dropped her hand and placed my arms on the counter, trapping her in. She could escape if she wanted to, our bodies weren't touching, but she didn't look as confident as she had just seconds before either.

I lowered my head, ripped a page from her book, and whispered into her ear, "It's big, Lucy. And hard." I gently touched her skin with the tip of my nose and inhaled her fresh scent. She was all soft, nothing sharp about her. "Touch me."

While I waited for her next move, I felt the urge to touch her chest, to slow her frantic heartbeat down, to take it…and maybe taste that inviting pulse on her neck.

A pretty pink flush took over her skin, and I smiled to myself. Granted, I wasn't sure if she'd go ahead and dive into my sweatpants, but even if she was brazen enough, she'd find exactly what I'd said she would find.

A moment passed. Then another.

I leaned back and met her eyes. She was pissed. I could see it in her eyes. She was planning a murder in her mind. A bloody one. I remembered why I found it so sexy when she was all fired up.

Trying her best to look nonchalant, she shrugged her tense shoulders. "I doubt it's anything *that* big, so I'll keep my illusions, thank you very much."

I didn't say anything, and she didn't look away.

The coffee machine pinged, breaking the thick silence.

"And now you'll never know," I said, backing away. I poured myself a cup of coffee and watched her out of the corner of my eye. She was still plastered to the island. "Coffee?"

She turned to look at me. "What?"

I raised my eyebrow, barely holding back my smile. "Would you like some coffee?" I repeated, lifting my mug.

"No." Her eyes dropped to my chest for a second then she shook her head. "I wanted to tell you something."

"Before this goes any further, I should tell you something."

We said at the same time.

She huffed. "You first. Nothing is going anywhere, by the way."

She could believe that as much as she wanted.

"Those first few days you looked after Aiden after school?"

"Yes. What about it?"

"There was a listening device in his toy so Dan could listen to what was going on."

She seemed to process it for a while. Her eyes slightly narrowing.

"Because..."

"Because you were a stranger. You didn't expect me to do nothing, did you? As much as I'd trust Jason looking after him, all I knew about you was that you enjoy climbing walls to watch other people." I took a sip from my coffee, keeping my eyes on hers. "Dan enjoyed himself immensely during the singing parts."

Her eyes seemed to narrow further. "You know what. I should be pissed. Hell, I'm pissed, but I get where you're coming from. I guess I would do the same thing if I were in your shoes. You're not the worst dad after all. So, there you go. You can stop feeling guilty about how wrong you were about me."

"I didn't say I was feeling guilty. I just wanted you to know."

"Now I know."

We stared at each other some more then Lucy was the first one to look away.

"Your turn. I'm listening."

"Now you can hear me from all the way over there?"

"Would you like me to come closer? Because I can."

Her eyes sparkled. "No."

"I didn't think so."

"You know what? Forget about it." She stormed out of the kitchen.

I put my mug down and caught up to her as she stepped out into the backyard.

My tone was gentle when I asked, "What is it, Lucy?"

I didn't think she would stop or even answer, but she did both.

"I want to press charges."

I stilled. She wanted to press charges against me?

"You know, for assault. I know nothing will come out of it and he'll just shrug it off, or the cops will think I'm just one of his groupies or something, but at least—" Her forehead furrowed. "Why are you looking at me like that?"

"He?" I managed to ask.

"Jake Callum." Her expression hardened. "Don't tell me he is your friend and you don't want me to go to the cops."

How could she even think that?

"Did it look like I was his friend when I wrapped my hand around his throat?" I growled at her.

"I didn't think so, but…you never know."

"I'm not his friend, Lucy. And yes, press charges. I'm your witness."

She pushed her hands into her pockets and looked at my face, not quite into my eyes.

"You'd do that?"

I wanted to go to her, embrace her, but I stopped myself. "Of course I would do that," I replied gruffly. "In fact, I'm going to call Dan, and you'll go down to the station with him. If they want me to make a statement too…" I checked my watch. "I have to be on set in two hours, but I'll drop by before I come home. It's our last day of shooting, otherwise I'd come with you, but—"

"That's okay," she interrupted me. "I wasn't asking you to come with me, and I don't need your bodyguard either, but…but thank you. And I know they won't do anything about it, nothing happened after all and…and maybe I'd had too much to drink. They'll think I'm lying." She bounced on her toes and looked away from my gaze. "I just want them to have something on file or whatever. In case he really does something to someone else. So they'll see it's not his first try."

At that moment, with those words, I fell for her a little.

"And," she started, her hand gingerly touching her breast. "He kinda gave me a bruise, so maybe that'll help."

I was surprised at how hard it was for me to actually stay in place and not go to her side to make sure she was okay.

"He left a bruise?" I asked, or more like growled. My words were barely audible.

She shrugged like it wasn't a big deal, her expression closing up. "I'm fine." She looked over her shoulder, toward Jason's place.

"Did you tell them?" I asked, almost certain she hadn't.

"Not yet." She lifted her chin, standing strong. "And you won't either."

"Only if you take Dan with you. Believe me, he'll help."

"They'll take me more seriously, you mean."

I didn't reply, but she already knew the answer anyway.

She seemed to think about it for a minute then let out a long sigh, averting her eyes from mine. "Fine."

The New Post-Divorce Adam Connor

*If you haven't been living under a rock, you must've already seen
the pictures of Jake Callum with a broken, bloody nose making
the rounds all over the Internet. Now, don't get us wrong, even
though he is new in the industry, we welcomed him with open
arms and promptly fell in love with his charming smile. Even so,
we have to admit, a broken nose is not a good look for the new
actor. Granted, he wasn't aware he was being photographed as
the shots show him speeding away from the studio lot where he
was supposed to start filming this week, but still...*

*Now let's get to the juicy stuff. At the time the candid shots had
gone viral, no one knew how he happened to sport a broken nose,
but after a little diggin' we found out that the new actor had a
violent altercation with none other than the newly divorced Adam
Connor.*

*Unfortunately, at this moment we have no idea how or why the
fight started between the actors in the first place. What we do
know is that Adam Connor is filming the last scenes of his movie
at the same lot as Jake Callum.*

*To say that we are shocked would be an understatement at this
point. Adam Connor grew up in front of the cameras, and as far
as we know has never been involved in an altercation like this
before. If it had happened, trust us, we'd know.*

An eyewitness that happened to be near Jake's trailer claimed Adam was already livid when he approached the actor. "There wasn't even enough time for the fight to accelerate. Jake was just coming back from a table read, and Adam stopped him before he could go into his trailer. I couldn't hear their exchange, but as soon as Adam was close enough, he threw the first punch, which must've broken Jake's nose. The next thing I knew, Adam had Jake up against the trailer door. After they exchanged heated words, Adam let him go and just left. It was the weirdest thing."

The rumor out there is that Adam's ex-wife, Adeline, was having a fling with Jake, and Adam snapped when he heard about it. You should also know that Adam was photographed having a heated conversation with Adeline at the premiere of Soul Ache *just the day before. While this sounds believable and it wouldn't be the first time it had ever happened, we're not so sure that was the case here. First of all, ever since the divorce, Adam has stayed away from everything involving Adeline. No press conferences, no interviews, no photo ops. Plus, there were rumors circulating about Adeline and her involvement with the celebrity trainer Mike Trevor, and Adam's only comment has been "I wish her the best." Now, does that sound like someone who is pining after his ex-wife to you? For all we know, he is quite happy about the divorce. No, we think something else was going on with these hot hunks, and we'll try our best to find out more for you.*

CHAPTER ELEVEN

LUCY

As I expected, the cops couldn't do much about my little altercation with Jake Callum. Truth be told, I went there already knowing that, but, hell, I wasn't expecting them to suggest that maybe I'd had too much to drink and wasn't remembering everything that had happened.

You'd know if you gave some sleazeball who thought he was the king of the world permission to put his tongue in your mouth after you hadn't kissed someone for weeks, wouldn't you? According to them, I wouldn't.

As if that wasn't enough, they said sometimes "parties like that" could get out of hand.

That was when Dan the Man stepped forward and took over. In the end, they promised they'd follow up and would talk to Adam and Jake, but couldn't make any promises that something would come out of it.

While it wasn't the best outcome, at least they'd have a police report on Jake Callum and if he ever crossed that line with someone else—though I hoped he wouldn't—they could come back to the police report and know it wasn't his first rodeo.

And you know what? Dan the Man wasn't the worst human

being after all. He even laughed at my jokes a few times, and by laugh I mean his lips twitched and he shook his head. In my book, that counted as a laugh.

"What are you thinking?" Olive asked, bringing me out of my thoughts.

"Nothing important." I swirled my wine glass and watched the red liquid spin around. "I'm not sure if I'm a huge fan of wine."

She looked at me over her laptop. "That is your second glass; you *are* a huge fan of it."

It was a Friday night, and we were working on Olive's next novel, plotting and taking notes. It was a glamorous night for us. It reminded me of old times, like our second year in college, the first time she had sent me a chapter and had me begging for the next one.

"That's it though. I had two, but I'm not convinced yet. I mean, it's classy, but is it me? And sure it's giving me a buzz, but the taste? Not sure about that either. I don't think I'm feeling all that great."

"Then stop drinking."

"Then what will I do? I think we're out of beer. Did you write down the next scene? Let me see it."

"Not yet. Let me read it again and see if it's any good. If you want beer, why don't you ask our neighbor?" she added casually. "Maybe he'll give it to you."

"Oh, the things your neighbor could give me," I mumbled to myself, my eyes still following the wine.

Olive sat up straighter but kept her face hidden behind the screen. "What?" As if she could trick me by acting all mellow.

"Catherine called again," I mentioned casually, ignoring her question.

When I didn't continue on about Adam, she slumped back in her seat. "What did she want this time?" she mumbled.

"I didn't answer." I shrugged, sniffing my glass and then

taking another sip. "She was probably calling to ask why I skipped the job interview she so graciously set up for me."

"You should've answered and told her you were my agent now." She got up, put the laptop on the coffee table, and headed for the kitchen. "I'm getting water, you want?"

"No to water, and I'm your *temporary* agent," I corrected her. "I'm still looking for a job, but I'm not gonna take anything else from her." I reached out for the laptop. "And I'm reading the scene."

"No," she shouted, slamming the fridge door closed. "I'm not done yet!"

I drew my hand back and looked at her over my shoulder. "Do you know how long it's been since I've read anything you wrote? I'm having withdrawals here. Have a heart."

She came back with a water bottle in her hand. "The new one is almost ready. As soon as Jasmine is done reading it, I'll send it to you."

Slowly, I uncurled my legs from under me and leaned forward to put my wine glass on the coaster. Clearing my throat, I asked, "Excuse me? Can you repeat that to me again? Jasmine? Who the hell is Jasmine and why the hell is she reading it before me?"

After drinking half of her bottled water, she gave me a smug look. "She is my beta reader—or maybe I should call her my alpha."

I slid forward in my seat and gave all my attention to her. "She is your what?"

"You know, beta reader, the lovely person who reads the book after it's done and points out things you should fix, or leaves encouraging notes. I do love my encouraging notes."

Was she fucking with me?

"Is this a joke?" She gave me a questioning look. "I know what a beta reader is, Olive. I was your one and only beta reader, remember those days? How could you betray me like this?"

"I guess you do know what it is," she said as if it meant nothing to her.

It was the worst betrayal in my book. How could she let someone else read it before me?

"I'm speechless. I've been waiting to read it for two months. How dare you?"

"Do you also know what a best friend is? Sister from another mister?"

I narrowed my eyes at her. "I could ask you the same question right now, my little green Olive."

"It doesn't feel all that great, does it?" she asked, giving me a side-glance. "I assume it wouldn't, because it sucks when you don't tell me stuff."

I huffed and leaned back against the couch. So that was what this was about. How had the sneaky little Olive managed to turn the subject back to me again? She picked up the laptop and continued with her little speech.

"First, I hear about the breakup a week later when I can do nothing about it."

"And what exactly were you planning to do if you knew about it earlier? Cry your eyes out?" I asked, but she ignored me.

"And then some stupid entitled jerk son of a bitch attacks you—"

"He didn't attack me, Olive. Let's not blow it out of proportion."

"And you tell me about it the next day. After you go to the cops. Cops, Lucy! And he did attack you. I don't care what those cops say, he assaulted you." She started squeezing the bottle in her hand, so I carefully reached out and took it from her murderous grip.

"Let's just say he was overly eager, and I did punch him after all, so one could say I attacked him back and it was all good. The only reason I didn't tell you about it as soon as it happened was because I wanted you to have the best night. You were having fun. You've been waiting for so long for that movie; I didn't want to mess that up."

She raised a brow and gave me a hard look. "It was all good only because Adam took care of it."

A party full of people and he had to be the one to save me, hadn't he? My freaking luck. Not that I wasn't grateful he happened to be there, but couldn't it have been someone else?

The killer dick I was waiting to find, maybe?

"Took care of it?" I balked at her. "Whose side are you on anyway? He sent me to prison, for God's sake, *the least* he could do was help me kick Callum's ass. And I can take care of myself, thank you very much."

"And no one should help you, right?"

"I didn't say that."

"You didn't need to."

I tried to stand up, but Olive grabbed my hand and roughly pulled me back down. "Jesus!" I exclaimed, half mortified and half amused. "I was just going to the kitchen to get rid of the bottle. A little feisty tonight, aren't you?"

She gave me her *don't try me* signature look, and I closed my mouth. Maybe she was right...just a little bit. I'd grown up expecting nothing from Catherine, not love, not kindness, not respect, just a whole lot of nothing. Even my own mother had decided to move on with her life without me, so I'd learned to take care of myself and not expect anything from others.

"I asked you if I could come and live with you guys for a while, didn't I? That should count as asking for help."

Olive was my exception; I *sometimes* didn't mind asking for her help.

"It does count." She nodded and snatched the bottle from my hand to put it on the coffee table. "But it's not enough. And because it's not, you're gonna answer my questions right now. After that I'll send you the book."

That got my attention. "So you lied? You didn't send it to someone else before me?" Was it so lame that I was hopeful?

"No, I did send it to Jasmine, this morning, and I was planning on sending it to you tonight, after we plotted the next one."

I rolled my eyes. "Fine. As long as this Jasmine chick knows I'm the alpha beta reader or whatever the heck it is called, I'm okay with her reading it too."

"Thank you for the permission," she said sarcastically.

I gave her a big smile. "You're welcome, my green Olive." She shook her head, but I saw the small twitch of her lips. "Should we hug? I could use the softness of your boobies," I asked, already leaning toward her.

"No, you don't deserve a hug, not yet."

"Ouch."

"Let's start with Jameson."

I groaned and leaned back again. "What about that jackass?"

"Did you text him back? No, wait. I don't trust you anymore. Give me your phone, I'm gonna check."

"You should start writing again, stat," I said, but still rose up to go get my phone for her. "You're starting to act all weird."

"No, I'm acting like a good friend." She took the phone from my hands and thoroughly checked my recent messages and calls.

"Happy now?" I asked, holding my hand open.

She slapped the phone into my palm and nodded. "I am. Don't text him. He can go to hell."

"My sentiments exactly. Okay, next question."

She twisted her body and faced me. "Tell me about Adam Connor. Are you sleeping with him?"

A laugh escaped my lips. "What? I don't even like the guy. What are you talking about?"

"You stayed at his place after the incident with Jake."

"And?" I waited to hear the rest of it, but she didn't say anything more, just waited for my answer. "In case you missed it the first time, or the hundredth time I said it, I'll repeat: I don't even like the guy. He was there, so I asked him for a ride, or he offered one, I don't even remember. And then since you guys were still at the party and I didn't have a key, he invited me to stay at his place. It's not like I haven't stayed there before."

"But this time around Aiden wasn't there, was he?"

"Yeah, so, what does that have to do with anything?"

"Fine." She sighed. "Be difficult about this."

"I'm not being difficult. I'm telling you, he put some ice on my hand, and I went to bed."

"Aha! He iced your hand? Now we're getting somewhere." She hugged a pillow to her chest and waited to hear more details. Unfortunately, I had none.

I started to tell her exactly that, but her phone started ringing and interrupted us. She held up her finger and ordered me to stay put as she talked to Jason.

Of course I got up and walked toward the sliding doors. It was a little over eighty outside and the weather was beautiful.

"I haven't started yet. Did you want something specific? Wait a second, I'll ask her," Olive said into her phone and turned to me.

"Jason is going to have Alvin grab some Chinese. What do you want?"

I loved Chinese, but at that moment, I couldn't even stomach the thought of it. Apparently I wasn't a wine girl or I was still feeling off. She frowned at me then kept talking to Jason. When she was off the phone, she was on me again.

"Where were we?"

"Nowhere, because there is nothing more to tell."

"You like him."

"I don't like him."

"You *like* him like him."

"Does it change the fact that I don't like him when you say it twice?"

"You like him more than you want to sleep with him."

"Please," I huffed, offended. "I'd happily fuck his brains out, but I don't even like him that much. Every time he talks I want to smack him upside his head." Actually, I would've fucked him any hour of any day. If you heard that sweet, thick, deep voice of his, you'd jump in his bed too, or on any flat surface really; I could go at it with him anywhere.

Forget about the voice; if he could just shut up and stand there, you'd still jump in his bed, begging him to take you. Besides, it wasn't my fault that I had woman parts; there was nothing I could do about that. His penis would fit perfectly into my vagina, and I had come so close to touching it. Come to think of it, I should have, even if it was just to see what his reaction would be. Too bad I'd chickened out because I was afraid of what he'd do next.

Long story short, Adam Connor was still a bastard in my book, but he was a hot DILF. But sleep with him? Nah, he was too tempting, especially when he was around Aiden. When I watched him interact with his son, the way he smiled at him or simply carried him to bed to tuck him in…boy, did it made me purr and melt faster than snow. Worst of it all, it made my battered heart skip a beat, which I did *not* like at all.

Olive closed her eyes and sighed a happy sigh. "I can already picture you two together. You're kissing. Passionately. It's a quick one because Aiden is there. But you are happy. Like crazy. And you love Aiden just as much as you love Adam. Adam definitely notices that and loves you all the more for it."

"Okay, crazy lady," I said, snapping my fingers to wake her up from her dream. "I'll leave you with your dreams and slowly back away." And I did exactly that; I opened the sliding doors and walked out, only to have Olive follow me.

"Come back here, I'm not finished."

I headed toward the ladder.

"Where are you going? Lucy, you can't run away from your dreams."

I faced her, but kept backing away. "My dreams? Those were all yours. I never dreamed about the guy. Dreaming about him fucking me six ways to Sunday? Sure, I admit I did dream about that, but all of it was *before* I met him." My back hit the infamous bush, and I turned around so I could climb up the wall. "And for your information, I'm going over to say hi to Aiden."

Olive leaned against the tree and smiled at me, showing me her full set of teeth. "Keep telling yourself that, little Lucy."

I straddled the wall and looked down at her. "You've officially lost your mind. Go write down a few words so your brain can start to function again."

"Lucy, close your eyes and imagine yourself sitting next to a waterfall. A waterfall where Adam Connor appears out of nowhere. Naked. Or half-naked. You're a calm little—"

I flipped her the bird and climbed down the rest of the way.

Shame on her for making fun of my relaxing tactics.

"Should I wait up for you, or are you planning on spending the night in Adam's bed? Because if you do, you know you're gonna have to give me details. I want the answers to everything you asked me about Jason. The size. The size is important. Measure the penis so I can picture everything in my mind."

"You keep calling it a penis and I won't tell you a thing. Bye, Olive!"

It was a good thing Adam hadn't thought of moving the ladder away yet. Until he did, I'd feel okay with invading his privacy. It wasn't like I was going to visit *him* or anything. I'd just missed the little guy and was hoping to catch him before his bedtime.

When I got close enough to the house, I could hear music. The doors seemed to be closed, but the sound was leaking outside. Rich people and their surround sound…

I stopped moving so I could listen and a few seconds later I recognized the unmistakable sound of Frank Sinatra's voice.

Huh, so my jerk had taste. Well, not *my* jerk of course, but you know what I mean.

I stood on the side where I couldn't be seen and spotted Adam near the bar cart. Had Aiden already gone to bed? I thought about knocking on the window to get his attention before he got his manly panties in a twist and accused me of invading his privacy again, but it was hard to take my eyes away from him. He was so damn handsome, the kind of handsome that made you start panting like a dog when you looked at him for more than a few seconds.

So I silently watched him pour himself a drink and read through the papers he had in his hands. He looked occupied—not in an *I'm reading some documents* kind of way, but an *I have a million things on my mind* kind of way.

I wondered what was making him look so miserable.

Truth be told, since he'd asked me to look after Aiden for a few days, I was seeing him in a different light. Sure, I hated him.

A little.

Kind of.

Strongly disliked him.

For the way he treated me that day and because I still wanted to jump his bones after what he did for me. But other than that, my heart melted a little bit every time I saw him— when he wasn't being a bastard that is, like he'd been the other day.

Who gives people permission to touch their junk? If you asked me, I'd say it was a great idea because him talking into my ear like that…and giving me permission to touch him? Silly, silly boy. He knew nothing about me at all. If I'd touched him, I would've ended up fucking his brains out and for reasons even unknown to me, I didn't want that.

Now, don't be all like, *but, Lucy, how could you hate such a fine specimen of the male form...* The biggest reason I had to keep hating him was because of the way I'd felt when he had touched me the other night, when he wanted to put ice on my hand. I'd felt those annoying butterflies in my stomach that Olive had always said she'd felt when she first saw Jason, and it scared the crap out of me. While I'd felt different kinds of butterflies in my lady parts when I was going after Jameson, these had taken flight in my stomach and they were deadly to me, like an allergy that could kill me unexpectedly.

After watching him for a few more minutes, I stepped forward and knocked on the glass. His head came up from the papers in his hand, and he spotted me. He seemed to hesitate before he got up from the couch and came to open the glass doors.

"Hi," I said when he was standing in front of me without a barrier.

He turned down the volume of Frank Sinatra with the help of a small remote control before he said, "I see you are creeping around in my backyard again." He had a small smile on his lips, so I didn't think he minded having me creeping around.

"If you don't want me creeping around, as you so rudely put it, you should move the ladder away."

"How can I help you, Lucy?"

"I'm good, thank you so much. And how are you doing tonight?"

He sighed and invited me in with a sweep of his hand.

"How nice of you to invite me in," I commented as I stepped inside and he closed the door.

"Is there anything I can do for you, or did you just come over to get in your daily amount of—"

I cut him off before he could finish his sentence. "Before you say anything you'll have to apologize for later, I'll let you know I came to say hi to Aiden. I missed him this week."

Adam looked at me for a long moment as if he was trying to figure out if I was lying to him or not. When he was satisfied with whatever he saw in my eyes, he ran a hand through his hair and motioned for me to sit down.

Wondering what was going on, I did as he asked and sat my ass down.

"So?" I asked when he didn't say anything for several long seconds.

"Adeline didn't drop him off, so I sent Dan over to see what was wrong." He checked his watch. "He should be here soon. You're welcome to wait if you want."

I drew my legs up and got comfortable in my seat. "You're not going to kick me out?"

"Aiden asks me about you on every phone call. I assume he'll be happy to see you here and that way I'll be saved from all the questions he'd ask if he didn't see you immediately."

That made me smile. "He loves me."

Adam smiled back. "Weird, isn't it?"

I frowned at him. "You're weird. I love the little guy too. He is way cooler than his dad could ever be."

Sporting a small smile, he shook his head and headed for the bar cart. I'd never seen him drink before that night.

"Something on your mind?" I asked, just to make conversation until Aiden got there.

"Too much."

I grunted and reached for my phone when I felt it vibrate in my pocket.

Jameson: *I wish you'd come with me.*

You didn't even ask me, you little shit!

It wasn't the first time I'd heard from Jameson since I'd gotten his *I miss you* text at the premiere. He'd been texting random things the entire week. I drew a long breath and uncurled my legs from under me.

"I think I should go," I mumbled, standing up.

Adam turned around with two drinks in his hands, whiskey from the looks of it.

"What's wrong with you?" He ignored my words and handed me the alcohol. Even the heavy smell made me nauseous. I scrunched up my nose and shook my head.

"No, thank you. I'm not feeling so great, so…I'll just see him some other time." I put my phone back in my pocket and placed the whiskey on a coaster. His eyes were still on me.

"Sit," he ordered as he sat down on the far corner of the couch. "He'll be here soon enough."

I looked outside and weighed my options: sit down and wait for Aiden or go back to Olive so she could question me more about my nonexistent feelings for Adam.

Spending some more time with the enemy it was.

"What's wrong with you?" he asked for the second time just before he took a sip of his whiskey.

I sat down and had trouble looking away from his clear, alluring eyes.

"Nothing specific, just feeling off."

"How's your hand?"

I lifted it up and checked my knuckles. There was still a redness and they were kind of sore. It was a good kind of sore, though; knowing I had hurt the douchebag, I didn't mind the reminder. And that reminded me…

"I should ask you the same question." I dropped my hand and motioned to his with my chin. "What went down with you and Jake? Did he really have something going on with your ex?"

He lifted an eyebrow, but otherwise stayed silent.

I'd been curious about it ever since I'd read the story online. Was what they were saying true, or had he punched him because of what had happened the night before? According to Olive, he had gone after Jake for me, but I had my doubts. Olive was a romantic at heart, and she wanted me to fall in love again; of course she'd think like that.

Feeling all hot and flustered under his scrutinizing gaze, I snapped at him. "What's wrong with you?"

"What do you mean?" He put his drink down.

"Why are you looking at me like that?"

That annoying eyebrow went up again. "Like what?"

"You know what, never mind." I looked away from him and did my best to ignore him for the next five minutes or so until he got up to get himself another drink.

I was thinking about Jameson when a water bottle appeared in front of my face.

"Thank you," I said sincerely and took it from his hand.

"You're welcome. You look subdued, maybe you should see a doctor," he suggested as he sat down closer to where I was sitting.

"I'm fine."

"Suit yourself."

I uncapped the bottle and took a big gulp of cold water. Then I closed my eyes and imagined myself some place else...maybe in the woods, or at a lake house where trees and calm waters surrounded me. I could sit on the deck, close to the water, and read Olive's new book. I smiled to myself. I could fall in love with as many men as possible and the curse couldn't even touch me. There was something special about falling in love with fictional characters through words. On that deck, with the birds fluttering around and the wind moving my hair, I'd be happy.

"What are you doing?" Adam asked quietly.

I didn't open my eyes when I answered, "Dreaming."

A long moment passed before he spoke again. "Where are you?"

"Lake house. Reading Olive's new book. There is a soft wind. I like wind; it makes me happy for some reason. Feeling that soft touch on my skin, in my hair. The sun is peeking through the trees, so it's not cold. The water looks beautiful. Calm and peaceful."

"Is there an empty chair beside you?"

"You'd annoy me, so no." I opened my eyes and looked at him. "No hard feelings."

He smiled and reached for the papers he had put down when I came in. "No hard feelings, Lucy."

Feeling a little better, I looked around at his home and sighed. It was getting closer to Aiden's bedtime.

"Do you do that a lot?" Adam asked, his eyes on the papers in his hand.

"Do I do what a lot?"

"Go some place else."

I shrugged. "You're welcome to think I'm crazy."

"I didn't say that. Actually..." He stopped talking, threw the papers on the coffee table, and rubbed the bridge of his nose.

Curious, I asked, "Actually...? Actually what? Don't be one of those people, finish your sentence."

He shut his eyes and leaned his head back. "At the risk of sounding like a Hollywood brat...I used to lie in my bed and imagine I had a simpler life. Instead of being dragged around to parties where drugs and booze were lying around on glass tables, where I had to look after Vicky, my sister, so she didn't accidently play with white powders thinking it was makeup or flour, so she didn't reach for one of those wine glasses thinking it was her juice...I used to wish for normal parents. I wished I could have friends over without worrying about how my parents would act depending on their moods. Don't give me that look," he warned when he opened his eyes and found me looking at him.

I ran my hands up and down my arms and kept silent.

"I know what you're thinking," he continued, misunder-standing my look. "They gave me a good life. A good education. Opportunities I maybe wouldn't have had if they weren't my parents. I'm not saying my life was miserable or anything, but back then I wanted to be a normal teenager. With normal parents. Just a normal life, you know, without the paparazzi, without the bullshit of Hollywood." His eyes hardened and he added, "You might think you know everything about someone because they're in the public eye, but you can never know what's going on behind closed doors."

"I understand," I said in a barely audible voice.

"Do you?"

I looked away from him. "I have to give you the backstory first. I don't know who my father is," I started, surprising myself. Was I actually going to tell him about myself? The words just wanted out, so I guessed I was. "According to Catherine, my grandma, my mom was completely in love with him. They were living together, but when he learned that she was pregnant with me, he packed his stuff and left. Apparently he'd already told her he never wanted to have kids, so he saw it as a betrayal. After I was born, apparently my mom decided she didn't want to have me either and dumped me on Catherine. And Catherine...well, she took me in, but she is a very difficult woman."

I glanced at Adam to see if he was even listening to me. When our eyes met, he lowered his head in a small gesture. "Go on."

I huffed; it would've been easier to stop talking if he was just ignoring me. "Catherine...now Catherine never married either, but she was living with the love of her life and then they had my mom, so it was all sunshine and rainbows for a good long while, I guess. But when my mom was two years old, dear old Grandpa started cheating on Catherine and then left her for the other woman, actually getting married to her a month or so later. Catherine returned home, which wasn't the best thing apparently because her own parents—who were not married, by the way—treated her like shit. Still, she raised my mom as best as she could, but turned very bitter in time. When my mom dumped me on her, they weren't even talking to each other, so obviously the women in our family are pretty fucked up and there are no men in sight."

I gave him another glance and found him waiting for me to continue. "So we're cursed. And Catherine...well, she took care of me when my mom left, but like I said, she is very controlling and difficult. To everyone looking in from the outside, it looks like she is an angel for taking me in, but that's not how it was. She wanted me to be a version of her. Nothing I did was right. There was only her way and when you didn't follow her rules or do what she wanted you to do, she knew how to throw everything she ever did for you in your face. I don't think she is mentally stable, actually, but she did take care of me instead of kicking me to the curb, so I do owe her, I guess."

There was a moment of silence.

"Cursed?" he repeated my earlier statement. "Is that why you said you don't do love the other day?"

"I said that?"

He nodded.

Me and my big mouth.

And he remembered?

"Huh...I don't remember saying that to you, but yes. I don't want to end up being a bitter woman like them. And it doesn't look like we have any luck with love as a family, does it? So why force it? I'd rather be single and happy than fall in love with someone, pop out a kid...and then have him cheat on me or leave me when things get rough only to go and marry some other chick." I shook my head and hugged my knees. "The women in our family don't get marriage proposals. So, no, thank you. I'm much happier when I watch other people fall in love, makes me happier without all the heartache."

"You've never fallen in love with someone?" he asked, as if that was the most ridiculous thing he'd ever heard.

"I didn't judge you for wanting a normal life, now, did I?"

He leaned forward and put his elbows on his thighs, dangling those sexy forearms in front of me as his eyes pierced my own. "I wasn't judging you, Lucy."

Why did I have to get all flustered when he was looking at me like that? I reached for the water bottle and took another sip to pass time. "Well, it sounded like you did." I gave a small shrug. "Anyway, with a woman like Catherine, I needed the escape. When I was in bed at night, I used to close my eyes and imagine being somewhere else." I gave him a quick glance. "I didn't imagine a different life, or someone coming to my rescue, but I enjoy closing my eyes and going somewhere far away. It calms me. Or sometimes I imagine I'm a waterfall, or the wind, or the sun. Essentially, by dreaming, I created my own sunshine for the days I needed it. It was my escape. I know it makes me sound like a crazy person, but it helps me calm down, so fuck you if you think I'm crazy."

He let out a loud laugh, and I slowly got up from my seat. See, I had plenty of reasons to hate him. I knew it made me sound like a crazy person, I knew it, but that didn't mean it didn't hurt to see him laughing at me. I gently threw the water bottle on his couch and headed for the glass doors. Maybe Olive would let me cuddle up to her for a while. I was feeling a little sick after all. She wouldn't be so cruel as to turn me down.

Before I could open the doors and step outside, Adam caught me by my wrist again—I swear the guy had a fetish of some sort. I looked back at him over my shoulder and tried to shrug him off, along with the tingles his closeness and touch were sending down my spine. I wasn't angry or anything, just tired and, well, yeah, maybe a little hurt. "I'm glad to be your amusement for the night, but I think it's time for me to leave."

"Don't," he said, his thumb gently moving over the sensitive skin on my wrist. My brows drew together, and I looked down at where he was touching me, but his finger had already stopped moving, as if it'd never happened. "I wasn't laughing at you, Lucy," he said in a soft tone, and my head jerked up. We were standing a bit too close. He must've come to the same conclusion because he let me go and backed off.

I didn't sway toward him at all. Not me.

He put a hand on the small of my back, and geez he had big hands—all the better to hold me with, I guess—and gave me a gentle push back toward the couch.

I sat on the edge and watched him grab his phone from nearby.

"Let me call Dan and see what the holdup is." He glanced up at me from his phone and added, "You've waited this long, he'll be sad if he hears he missed you."

He looked genuine, so I decided to stay. "Fine." I scooted back into my seat and grabbed a pillow to hug.

Dan didn't pick up, and I could see the frustration in Adam's face. Pacing in front of me, he tried another number. When that didn't work either, he let out a long sigh and rubbed the back of his neck.

"I don't like this," he said finally, his hands working on his phone.

"Did you try your ex?"

"She isn't answering. Neither is Dan. Adeline might be on set, but Aiden was supposed to be at home with his nanny."

"Maybe they're on their way?" I suggested, a little worry creeping into my voice.

"They must be," he mumbled, putting away his phone. "I'll

give them a little more time. Sometimes Aiden takes a lot of time to get ready."

We sat in tense silence as we listened to the soft murmurings of Frank Sinatra. The longer there was no little human running through the front door, the more anger seemed to emanate from Adam. The more I stayed, the more I felt like I was intruding on another family moment, which was a weird feeling after I'd already intruded on them on multiple occasions.

"So, what are those?" I asked, motioning toward the papers when I couldn't take the silence any longer.

"New scripts."

"Come on, I'm sure you can give me more than that."

He glanced back at the front door once again, then turned around to reach for the papers. "New offer. I have a contract with the studio and I owe them one more movie. They sent over two scripts for me to choose from, but I'm not so sure about either of them."

"Can I see?" I held out my hand and waited.

"This is one of those things you can't mention anywhere else, Lucy."

I rolled my eyes and wiggled my fingers. "Give it to me."

He handed them over, reluctantly. I had better things to do than go around and spread rumors about the new movie Adam Connor would star in.

"How's the agent thing going?" he asked as I looked through the first script.

I answered him without lifting my eyes from the pages in my hands. "I'm almost there. I narrowed it down to two publishers, and I'm waiting to hear back from them. I also pursued other deals—audiobook, etc. What's this one about?"

He scooted until he was sitting very, I repeat, *very* close to me. I willed my heartbeat to slow down, because what the hell, heart? *What's wrong with you? We're not supposed to like the guy, remember?* No need to do cartwheels just because he is within touching distance.

His arm brushed my shoulder when he took the script from my hands, and I happened to inhale at the very same moment. What a coincidence, right?

I took a deep breath and felt a tingle on my arm where his skin had made contact with mine. First of all, stupid skin and stupid tingle. Second, he smelled like whiskey and something warm, wild, and deliciously masculine. It was the perfect invitation to nuzzle his neck and get lost in his scent and body…which was a very, very bad idea. I closed my eyes to ignore him, but that only intensified his scent and how close he was sitting to me. He smelled good enough to attack right then and there. If it had been someone else, I wouldn't have even thought twice before I did exactly that, but with Adam, I forced myself to stay still.

You might think maybe scooting away from him could've solved the problem, but I was not a pussy; I would never shy away from a guy just because I wanted him. Screw that. If he wanted to play with me, I'd play him right back.

Trying my best to breathe from my mouth without looking like a weirdo, I leaned toward him and let my arm rest against his as he checked the script in his hands. He seemed so relaxed, which angered me even more.

There I was trying my best not to act like he was affecting me, and he didn't even notice that I was having a mental breakdown from his proximity. Hell, I was seconds away from letting my inner singer out to play and singing him "Pillowtalk" by Zayn.

How fun it would be to piss off the neighbors with Adam Connor, indeed—especially when those neighbors were Olive and Jason.

My mind millions of miles away, naked in a king bed with Adam, I had trouble focusing on his words when he started talking.

"In this one I'm supposed to be a devoted husband to a socialite only to end up killing her and running away as a dedicated detective tries to catch me."

"Boring," I managed to say.

"Yea, that got a no from me too."

"Shouldn't your agent get something better for you?"

"He should, which is why I'm getting rid of him."

I lifted an eyebrow and gave him a side-glance. "From what I hear, you're getting rid of an awful lot of people. Is it true what they're saying? That you are lashing out at people who work for you because of the divorce?" I made the mistake of looking into his eyes, and he held my gaze with a hard expression on his face.

"Looks like spying on someone isn't enough for you, you also keep track of them through the tabloids."

"Please, why would I even keep track of what's going on in your life? I just happened to read about it when I was looking through Olive and Jason's premiere photos. One link took me to another and then another…I wasn't checking up on you, trust me. I lived in your house for a week, remember? There is nothing about you that's exciting. Hell, even Dan has a more colorful life than you."

He tossed the script away with unnecessary force and it landed on the floor. I gave him a quizzical look, but he pretty much ignored me, already focused on the next script.

"Is that the winner?"

"How did you come to know about Dan's *colorful* life?" The question was harmless enough, but the way he was holding himself so still as if the answer mattered felt strange.

"Because we talked? He doesn't hate me as much as he did when he first found me in your backyard. Can't say for sure if he loves me or not, but at least he is engaging in conversation now. I even made him laugh a few times. We're becoming friends, I think. I'm wearing him down."

"When did you guys have time to talk this thoroughly?"

"When you sent him to the station with me. What's wrong with you?"

"Nothing." He shrugged my question off. "This one is about a brother and sister. They are con artists and work with this small group of people. My character is supposed to fall in love with his mark and then end up killing his sister when she goes after his love."

"That sounds a bit more interesting," I conceded.

He grunted and turned a few pages, handing the script to me when he was done. "The dialogue isn't strong enough. The sister should be a stronger character if she is going after his love interest. She is made out to be this unstable person, which takes away from the character. Someone else has to go over it and change things around."

I looked at it and couldn't see anything jump at me. "Change what?"

He leaned closer to me and our legs touched.

Good Lord! He was practically abusing me at that point.

"Let's do a read-through, you'll see what I mean."

"Read-through?"

"Read the lines to me, Lucy."

"Who am I? Laurel?" I pointed at the name and looked at Adam.

"You're Laurel, my sister. And I'm Damon."

"Okay. You start."

At the top of the script it said, *Ext. The Cemetery – Night* then said Laurel was walking over to Damon with a suspicious look on her face as he waited for her next to their father's grave.

Suddenly he got up and offered me his hand. "Let's stand up so you can get into your role."

I snorted, but still took his outstretched hand to stand up. "I'm not going to be your costar. I don't need to get into my role."

"Come on, humor me."

"You want me to do this because you think I'm unstable too, is that it? I'll make the character more believable for you?"

"Don't be so suspicious, Lucy. Just read the damn lines."

The scene was just two siblings talking. What could be the harm, right? Who would skip the chance to read lines with freakin' Adam Connor—especially lines that might very well end up on the silver screen.

"What are you going to read?" I asked, looking around to see if there was another copy.

"I already read through it twice. I'm good with that scene. Just start reading."

The script in one hand, I smoothed down my shirt, shook out my shoulders, and read the damn lines.

"Why did you ask me to meet you here, Damon?"

Adam reached out and lifted my chin with his fingertips, short-circuiting my brain.

In the background Frank Sinatra was singing "Fly Me To The Moon".

"You're supposed to look at me when you're speaking. And put a little more emotion into it. The scene is set; read through the lines to get a sense of what the script gives you."

I willed my heart and a few lady parts to calm down then looked straight into his bottomless green eyes. "I'm not an actress…be happy with the amount of emotion you're getting."

Greedy bastard.

I looked down at the script, memorized the next few lines, and this time said them without looking down.

"Why did you ask me to meet you here, Damon?"

"I thought it would be fitting," Adam continued on with his acting.

"They thought siblings meeting at the cemetery would be fitting?" I asked, giving the papers in my hand a skeptical look.

"And what the hell does this mean?" I pointed at the writing between the lines.

"I thought it would be fitting," he repeated, looking at me pointedly.

Jesus, what the hell is your problem, dude?

I rolled my eyes and continued. "We haven't been here for what? Fifteen years? Why now?"

"We sat by his tombstone and made a promise to each other, do you remember?"

"This is where our life started; of course I remember, Damon."

He nodded solemnly and finally looked away from my eyes. "And now we're at the end of another road."

"What are you talking about, Damon?" I glanced at the script then back up at him.

He released a deep breath, ran his hand through his hair, and took a step forward, getting a bit too close for my comfort again. "I can't do this anymore, Laurel. I can't be a ghost in the night, I can't pretend like I'm someone else. I want more for us."

I hardened my voice as much as I could and read the next lines. "This is all about her, isn't it, Damon? This is all about Jessie. She is nothing more than a mark, or did you forget that already?"

Adam reached out and took the script from my hands for a quick glance then handed it back to me. I parted my lips to make a snarky comment about how much he sucked as an actor, but he pressed his finger to my lips.

Again with the touching.

Frank was still killing it in the background.

I frowned, but kept quiet.

"You can't tell me you're not tired of all the lies, Laurel. When is it gonna be enough?"

Breaking out of character, I sighed. "Are they talking to each other like this for the entire scene? Face to face?" Adam tilted his head so I got the message and went on with my reading.

"Not yet, Damon. Not when we're so close to getting everything we wanted from the very beginning."

He sighed and looked away again. "She's pregnant, Laurel. Jessie is pregnant."

And the plot thickens.

I read the next lines and snorted. "How can you be sure it's yours? You knew she was dating that Jake guy up until a few months ago."

When Adam looked at me, his features were tight. "It's mine."

I quirked an eyebrow. "Take care of it. Make her get rid of it. You can't let this ruin our plan. We waited a long time for this."

"Laurel is quite the bitch, apparently," I mumbled under my breath as I turned another page on the script. Suddenly Adam's hands were on my cheeks, and he was pressing a kiss to my forehead.

"What the hell?" I mumbled, looking up at him as I tried to scramble away.

Danger! Danger!

Abort!

He gestured to the script. "Read."

And of course, right there at the top, it said, *Damon kisses her on the forehead*

Putting my game face back on, I tried to keep my cool.

He kissed me again, his lips surprisingly soft on my forehead, and I tried to stay as still as possible with his face so close to mine.

Then he forced me to meet his eyes. Yes, he forced me...I was pretty sure there was some sort of magic involved because I was barely able to breathe with his hands cradling my face and his eyes pulling my soul closer to him.

Asshole.

I swallowed, then cleared my throat for good measure.

"You're my sister, Laurel. I love you," he said with a soft smile on his lips. "I love you, but I'm done. Don't make me choose. I can't do this anymore, not when I have so much to lose."

I glanced down at the script as my brain was having difficulty functioning properly. "What about me, Damon? What do you expect me to do? Go on with my life? Act like her family never ruined ours?"

Adam's thumb caressed my cheekbone and my entire body started to burn up. Was that in the fucking script? Then his head was coming toward me, and I was bracing myself for a kiss on the nose or something equally innocent like that.

Weird sibling relationship, but whatever, right?

Our eyes locked and, never breaking eye contact, his lips softly touched mine. I froze.

Me. Lucy Meyer, the girl who would have loved nothing more than to kiss Adam Connor just a month before froze with that same Adam Connor's lips on her lips. My traitorous body took a step toward him to keep the connection.

Definitely weird siblings.

For a few dangerously long seconds, he let me feel his lips on mine as they moved ever so slowly. Then there was a gentle nip on my lower lip and before I knew what was happening, he was kissing me for real, coaxing me to open my mouth.

Gently.

But I felt his tongue. I swear to you, I did.

I inhaled sharply and before I could react in any way, he was pulling back.

Let's get this straight. I did not follow his lips. Neither did I sway toward him like a love-struck teenager. Nah, I'm not that girl. It was just a trick of the eye.

As soon as he let me go, I ducked my head and started turning pages like a madwoman. When I couldn't find what I was looking for, I simply raised my hand and slapped him. Hard.

For a long moment, neither one of us moved. Frank was ending another song like a boss, and other than my heavy breathing, he was the only thing we could hear.

Finally, Adam asked, "What was that for?"

"What do you think?" I managed to croak out. Even though I'd been standing in the same exact spot for the last few minutes, I felt like I'd run a marathon—and that was from a small kiss where I didn't even get to taste him properly. I cleared my throat. "You just kissed your sister." I pointed a finger at him. "And don't try to tell me that was a peck either. How do you think she'll react?"

The record player started playing Frank Sinatra's "It Was A Very Good Year", my favorite, and Adam gripped my chin with his fingers and tilted my face up. It wasn't a gentle chin grip either. His big, warm hand practically engulfed the lower half of my face.

It was definitely a panty-melting moment. Who doesn't love a man—especially a man who looked like Adam Connor—taking control of your body—in a sexy way, of course.

"I didn't kiss my sister, Lucy," he murmured, leaned in, and then kissed me. Again. Like full-on kissed me. His fingers holding my face in place, he tilted his head and sneaked his tongue inside my mouth.

That kind of kissing.

So that's what he tasted like. Warmth. Silk. Addiction. Sex. Danger. Insanity.

The script in my hand fluttered to the floor.

My brain was a complete mess, giving me all kinds of danger warnings.

He tilted my head to the right and practically ruined me with the way he was kissing me.

It was a kiss wrapped up in another kiss.

Does that make sense? No? It didn't make sense to me at the time either.

Yes, Lucy! Yes!

No, Lucy! No!

It was like I'd had multiple personalities living inside my head all this time and they'd been waiting to get out of their hidey hole just for this special occasion.

But then again, Adam Connor was kissing me...what the hell was a girl supposed to do when faced with such a problem? Hate or not, you'd go for it too. You'd give it your all and you'd make sure you gave it to him good.

My hands empty, I grabbed his shirt and pulled him closer, returning his kiss with fervor. I could've written a poem about how good it felt to have him tower over me, and I wasn't even the writer.

His grip on my chin tightened to the point that it came danger- ously close to hurting me, but I was loving it. I hated him, but I was loving the way he was controlling the kiss. Controlling me. How could his touch feel so different than that asshole Jake Callum's?

I was loving the way his breathing was getting out of control —just like mine. I was loving that he had sneaked his left hand around my waist and was pulling me toward his body.

Our tongues were in a battle, and I didn't care who came out on top at the end as long as he kept his lips against mine.

I wanted him to lose his shirt so I could feel his skin under my touch, but that would have required breaking apart from his lips, and I wasn't too fired up to do that. The earth beneath my feet could've cracked, and I still wouldn't have let go of him. He turned his head the other way and deepened the kiss, forcing me to arch into him.

I was starting to think it was okay to not be kissed for more than a month if the kiss you'd get at the end of that drought was like this one. I was okay with anything that man would do to me.

And holy hell, he was devouring me as if he was quenching his thirst. I was seconds away from climbing him and trying my best to fuck him standing up. It would require a lot of maneuvering, but I could give it my best shot.

Unable to hold it back any longer, I moaned, and he slowed us down, giving my lips a few nips as I tried my best not to hyperventilate in front of him. His hand let go of my face and gently pushed my short hair behind my ear.

Just when I thought the torture of my senses was over, he leaned in and kissed my cheek, then a little higher, heading toward my ear. My head, acting on its own, tilted to the side to give him more space to work with, and he chose that moment to run his tongue along the shell of my ear, making me groan even louder.

All I could do was hold on to him. I was *that* gone. Can you imagine? My vagina was very happy, though.

"Lucy," he whispered, and all the little hairs on my body stood up. Why did my name have to sound so damn good coming from his lips?

His nose in my neck, he was breathing me in, and my body was practically melting away in his hands. I felt like I was coming to life. Or floating out of my body. Or all of the above.

"Call me crazy, my little stalker, but I think I like you," he murmured against my skin, his hot breath warming me from top to toe as he nipped at my skin.

"And I think I don't like you at all," I whispered back when I could think long enough to form words again.

"Hmm," he hummed next to my ear, causing my eyes to flutter closed. What was he playing at? "Then you won't kiss me back if I try to kiss you again, I assume?"

It was a stupid declaration. All kinds of kisses were welcome as long as they involved those lips touching parts of my body, and the asshole knew that, of course.

I tried to pull away, thinking he was itching for another slap, but his big hands rounded my waist and before I knew what he was planning to do—I'm not ashamed to say I was hoping for another one of those hard kisses—he started walking backward and taking me with him.

He fell onto the couch, and I magically climbed onto his lap. Again, I didn't want to, of course, so I was blaming his big, strong hands. If he hadn't been touching my waist, I would've totally walked out on him. However, since his hands were still on me, urging me closer, instead of walking away, I started to lean into him to have another taste of those lips.

Go big or go home, right?

With one of his hands still on my waist, he slid the other one around to my back and into my shirt.

I gripped the back of the couch with one hand and put the other one on his chest. It made me giddy to feel his frantic heartbeat under my touch. I had no right to feel giddy about his heartbeat. I should've gotten off his lap and run away.

What did I do? I stayed for more.

He rested his hand in between my shoulder blades. Skin on skin. Hot skin on burning skin. Making sure I was standing on my knees the entire time, I pressed my boobs against his broad chest and dove in for another brain-scrambling kiss.

He let out a long, satisfied groan that scrambled my brain even more so and ruined my panties. Then he moved his hand higher up so he could grip my neck, hold me to his lips. Controlling me. It was sexy as hell, and somehow sweet. Protective. It could've been even more sexy if he were about to feed his cock into me.

The visual made me release an even louder moan than before.

The lady beast in me was off its leash, and it was looking to devour the man who was between my legs.

He drew me back from his lips and gave my neck a squeeze to get my attention. My eyelids were dead weight, but I managed to open them enough to see his expressive eyes looking straight into my soul.

"You're not as good as I thought you'd be." The words just spilled from my mouth, taking me by surprise.

His lips parted, his eyes unreadable. Before he could get a word out, the front door opened and someone slammed it shut.

Aiden.

It was enough of a jolt to move me into action. I scrambled to my feet and wiped my mouth with the back of my hand. My shirt fell down, covering my back again, and I silently cursed Adam for making me feel naked without his hand on me.

He was still sitting on that damn couch and looking at me like he was seeing me for the first time.

"Adam, we have a problem. You're not going to like this," a voice announced, and then Dan the Giant Man stepped in from the hallway.

"I'll just go to my room," I mumbled before walking away quickly.

Dan was frowning down at me as I passed him, but thankfully didn't utter a word. Halfway to the room, I realized I wasn't staying there anymore. I could hear Dan and Adam talking in hushed voices. Face palming myself, I groaned and walked back out into the living room.

"Funny story," I started, walking around them then just continuing out to the backyard without finishing my sentence.

I was over that wall and in front of Olive's sliding doors in mere seconds. The doors were locked.

"What the hell?" I murmured and started banging. The lights were still on inside, so I knew they were up.

"Olive!" I shouted, getting closer to the glass to look inside.

Suddenly the thin beige curtains moved, and Olive jumped out of nowhere.

"Holy fuck," I screamed, scrambling back. "Have you lost your mind? You scared the shit out of me."

"I'm not letting you in," she said, standing on the other side of the glass doors. I caught the satisfied quirk of her lips.

"What? Why the hell not?"

She crossed her arms over her chest and lifted an eyebrow. "Spill."

"Spill what?"

Her eyes narrowed on me, and she leaned in closer to the glass, studying my face, I assumed. Then her eyes widened, and she gasped. "You kissed him! Your lips are all puffed up. You kissed him and you weren't going to tell me!"

"Excuse me? I'm standing right here trying to get in so I can tell you about it!"

"You're lying."

"I'm not, Olive."

"Then tell me what you did."

"I didn't do anything."

She gave me a disbelieving look.

"Are you really going to talk to me through the glass?"

"I'm waiting."

"Fine. Jesus. I never forced you to tell me something like this."

She let out a loud laugh. "Are you sure? Think more thoroughly. You did way worse to me. I still remember you texting Jason on my behalf, saying I was single. One hundred percent."

"You should thank me. You ended up marrying the guy, didn't you?"

"Don't change the subject, Lucy. Tell me what happened over there or I'm not letting you in, and I'm definitely not sending you a copy of my book. You should hear what Jasmine is saying about it. She thinks it's fantastic."

"I think you've been hanging out with me for far too long; you're starting to act like me."

"Spill. It."

I held my hands up. "All right. All right. Calm your tits, woman. I thought Aiden would be there, but he wasn't home yet, so Adam offered to let me wait for him to get there."

"You're doing good, keep going."

Despite the situation, I laughed and got closer to the glass.

"Fine. He kissed me," I whispered, just loud enough so she could hear me. "Then I slapped him because he was kissing his sister."

Olive's eyes widened.

"Then he kissed the shit out of me again. And I kissed him back. Then just when I was about to lower myself on his lap and feel the size of his dick before I could die from curiosity, Dan the Man came in."

"You suck, Lucy. I have no idea what the hell any of this means. He kissed you and his sister, and you slapped him?"

I nodded, feeling proud of myself. "Well, close enough. He kissed me after I told him about Catherine and my curse."

She moved closer, pressing her forehead against the glass, shock all over her face. "You told him about the curse?"

Another quick nod. "After the slap, he kissed me again, and, meh…" I paused for a beat and then shrugged. "It was better, I guess. At least he wasn't gentle. The slap must've helped."

"I hate you," she said.

"And that's exactly what I told him, too. He said he thinks he likes me, so I told him I hate him."

A big smile stretched across Olive's lips. "Adam Connor loooves you."

I gave her a bored stare. "I didn't say that, now, did I?"

"And you're totally falling in love with him."

I snickered and shook my head. "If you say so, crazy. Now open the door, I told you everything."

She turned her back to me and leaned against the glass door, giving me a coy look over her shoulder. "I'm going to write a book about your love with Adam. It's going to be epic."

"I'm not falling in love with him, for God's sake."

"You will. And I'm gonna love every second of it."

"I'm cursed, remember, Olive? Quit playing and open the door, it's getting cold out here."

"Please, we are in LA, it's September, how cold could it get? And I'm sure Adam already warmed you up. Maybe I should text him. Where is your phone?"

"Olive! I swear to God..." I banged on the glass. "Open the damn door! You're becoming a mini me, and I'm not liking it. There can only be one of us. You should be the calm, sensible one, not the one who leaves her friend out in the cold for coyotes to eat just so she can learn what's going on! That's what I'd do!"

"I learned from the best."

I was stuck between feeling like a proud mama and an annoyed one.

Her eyes were sparkling with amusement. "I'm doing research for my next book. Since I'll be writing about you, I better get into character." Then her face sobered, and she sighed. "Why do you do this to yourself? Go have fun with him." She tilted her head, gesturing to Adam's house. "You're not cursed, Lucy. If he kissed you, it means he is interested even after everything you did.

"Excuse me? Um, weren't you with me on that wall that first day? If I'm a stalker, so are you."

"I didn't get caught, now, did I?"

"Nice. What a great excuse. Now, open the door."

"Tell me why?"

"Why what?"

"Why won't you go back there and give it a try. See where it goes."

Since she wasn't opening the damn doors, I turned my back to her and sat down in front of the door.

"Lucy?" she prompted.

I looked up at the sky. "Because if I fall in love with him I won't survive that fall."

Adeline Young Lost Her Son at the Airport

These exclusive photos of Aiden Connor (5) crying at the airport while surrounded by paparazzi went viral in no time. Adeline Young arrived at LAX around six PM and as soon as she got out of her car with her team, she rushed into the airport, as you can clearly see for yourselves in the pictures.

So far, this sounds like just another celebrity spotting, right? Wrong. Before we go on with the story, we want you to know that as a team we had a discussion about these photos, about whether or not we should share them with you, and in the end, even though we think they are heartbreaking, we thought since every other news outlet was running with the story and you'd be able to see it everywhere online, it wouldn't change a thing if we just skipped posting them. So after that disclaimer, we should also tell you that we won't keep these photos up for long because what you see in these photos is never okay. Shoving a gigantic camera in a kid's face while you're screaming to get his attention and scaring him to death is never okay. We don't care whose kid he/she is.

All of that being said, are the paparazzi who took the photos the only party to blame here? That's a big no.

When Adeline Young arrived at LAX so she could board her flight to New York, she had her publicist Neil Germont, the right hand to Michel Lewis, and two of her assistants with her. As the group rushed into the airport to catch their flight, you can see another assistant getting out of the car and rushing behind them. That's where things go wrong. The next shot is of Aiden Connor climbing out of the SUV on his own, clearly searching for his mother. The panic on his face speaks volumes, if you ask us.

You would think someone would come out and get him, right? That's what we were expecting, because how is it possible to forget a kid in the car with so many assistants around?

The next snap of Aiden is the one that went viral last night. You can see him crying as the paparazzi surround him, and we're not talking about two or three people taking pictures of you from afar here. If you look at the background of the photo, you can get an idea of the number of people surrounding him and pushing their big cameras in his face. Now if it were any of us in the same situation, even we would start panicking, but for a five-year-old, we can't even imagine what a scary experience that must've been —having a large group of people you've never seen in your life yelling your name right in your face while you're searching for your mother.

We're even more sad to say that none of the photographers helped Aiden get to his mom. According to our source, Adeline's assistant came back to get him when they realized he was not with them, and the whole ordeal only lasted for about a minute or two, but for a kid that age, it must have felt like an eternity. What rubs us —and many others—the wrong way is that it wasn't even his mother, Adeline, who came to little Aiden's rescue. It was an assistant.

We all know that ever since her divorce, Adeline Young has been a very busy woman as she is trying her best to get back in the game and score a movie deal while all eyes are on her, but busy or not, we are certain she will receive a fair amount of backlash for this incident.

We are still trying to reach Adam Connor's new PR team for a comment. It's not likely we'll get any comment at this point, but we can't wait to see what his next move will be.

CHAPTER TWELVE

ADAM

"File it today. I don't care what you have to do, I want you to get it done by the end of the day."

On the other end of the line was my lawyer, Laura Corey. "Give me a second, Adam."

I closed my eyes and waited.

"Okay. We're filing for sole custody of Aiden, then. It's not gonna be an easy process. Are you ready for it?"

"I want my son, Laura." There was no question about it anymore; no reason to give Adeline time to come to her senses.

"Okay, Adam. Okay. We'll start the process today. Do you want me to get in touch with your new PR team and discuss how we are going to move forward with this new development? I have to be honest with you, I'd recommend you to talk to a news outlet you trust or at least release a press statement. It's better if you get ahead of everything and give a short explanation instead of letting them run wild with it."

"I'm not looking to make a big production out of this, Laura."

"And I'm not saying you should. Just think about it. In these situations, it's better to offer an explanation instead of staying silent and letting the press run wild with it. And after last night's photos, trust me, they will run wild with it."

"Which reminds me," I started, something heavy taking residence in my stomach. "I want Aiden's photos off the Internet, and I need the names of those photographers. They knew what they were doing was illegal. It shouldn't have happened."

She sighed, the sound making me even more agitated. "You're right, it is illegal, but it's hard to implement the law. I'll have my investigator try and get the names of the photographers, but you know they protect each other. It'll be a long shot."

"I still want you to try."

"Of course I will. We'll talk again."

She ended the call. With the phone still in my hand, I walked out to the patio and called Adeline. Again. The night before when Dan had come back from Adeline's place without Aiden and let me know that she had left the city with him, without giving me any notice even though she knew it was my day to take him, I'd called her repeatedly until she answered her phone. It hadn't been a fun phone conversation. When she tried to explain to me why she'd had to take him with her, I was speechless.

She answered the call on the fifth ring. "Adam. Hello."

"Adeline. Where are you?"

"We just landed at LAX."

"Are you heading home? I'll send Dan to get Aiden. Then you and me...we need to talk."

"Adam." She sighed. "I know I messed up. You have every right to be mad at me, but I'm perfectly capable of dropping Aiden off myself."

"And I'm telling you, you don't have to."

"I want to, Adam. Please give me a chance to explain. I want to apologize to you face to face, and I think it'll be good for Aiden to see us together."

I didn't want her apology, and I didn't want to see her, especially after seeing the photos of Aiden crying as he stood in the middle of a paparazzi frenzy. As far as I was concerned, we were done. In every way.

After I ended my conversation with Adeline, I had another talk with my new PR team and set up everything that needed to be dealt with. As much as I wanted to keep everything private and didn't agree with my lawyer, I knew it would spill out; at least this way I'd have control over how much and what had to spill.

An hour later, Adeline walked in holding Aiden's hand. The night before when I'd called Adeline, she'd said he was tuckered out and sleeping, so I couldn't talk to him about what had happened and how he was doing.

Every time I dropped him off at Adeline's place, he'd get quiet and look at me as if I was betraying him. The look he was giving me when he walked in was the exact same look and it pierced something in my chest.

Not knowing what I was dealing with, I knelt in front of him to get a hug. He was having none of it. He stood completely immobile against me as I rounded my arms around him.

With my arms still around Aiden, I glanced up at Adeline. She pursed her lips and mouthed a quick *sorry*.

I sighed and let go of my son.

"Hey, buddy. I missed you."

He muttered a low *hi* under his breath.

"Did you have fun in New York with your mom?"

Another non-answer in the form of a mumble.

"Aiden," Adeline murmured gently as she let go of his hand and fixed his hair. "Can you give your dad and me a few minutes?"

"Okay."

Without meeting my eyes, he skirted around me and headed toward his room, only to stop midway.

His eyes met mine fleetingly as I slowly rose up. "I've been good, so can I ask for something?"

"Of course," I answered. He'd get pretty much whatever he wanted from me at that moment if it meant he'd look me in the eye.

"Can I ask for Lucy?"

"He's been asking for her ever since we landed," Adeline added.

Of course he'd ask for Lucy. I'd want her too if I were him. Matter of fact, *I* wanted her too. That was another matter I hadn't had time to handle…not that you could ever make the mistake of trying to 'handle' Lucy, but we needed to talk about that kiss. As much as it made me sound like a pussy, after the night before… we needed to talk, and after that, I needed to kiss her again—most likely to shut her up.

"We can call her, buddy, but I don't know if she's busy."

"Can we call her now? If we call her now, we can ask her if she missed me. 'Cause if she did, she'll come for me, I know it."

I faced Adeline. "Can you wait while I call her?"

"Of course, Adam," she replied with a gentle smile, touching my arm for a brief moment before heading toward the living room as I reached for my phone.

Aiden took a few small steps toward me, but he was still being distant. I hoped seeing Lucy would help. I dialed her number, and she answered on the third ring.

Her opening line was, "Are you calling to get a few pointers?"

Who knew what she was talking about. "Pointers on what?"

"Kissing, of course. I mean, you weren't the worst, I guess, but…I don't know, I think you could use a few pointers, and if I think that, that means you can *really* use a few pointers."

Even though Adeline was sitting just a few feet away and Aiden was looking at me with hopeful eyes, my lips twitched.

"Because you've done such a good job of it yourself?"

There was a short moment of silence. "What's that supposed to mean?"

"I'm just saying, I happen to think you could use a few pointers yourself. I don't want to break your heart, but…"

When she spoke her voice was high-pitched. "But…? But what?"

"I'm afraid this is not a good time. We'll have to discuss it some other time."

She growled. "I'm the best kisser you could've ever had, you asshole."

"If you say so, Lucy."

"If I say so? *If I say so?* Who do you even think you are?"

The small twitch turned into a full smile. If she had been standing next to me, I would have loved to show her who I was, but unfortunately for us, she wasn't. Instead, my son was pulling on my shirt, trying to get my attention.

"Can I talk to her? I think she missed me. I think I should be the one to talk to her."

I nodded at Aiden and held up my finger.

"There is someone here who wants to talk to you, Lucy. Do you have a moment?"

"Now you ask me if I have a moment? After you ruined my afternoon? And who wants to talk? Is it Dan? I just talked to him this morning."

She was talking to Dan? The question came to the tip of my tongue, but I held it back.

"No, not Dan," I said curtly. Without any further explanation, I handed the phone to Aiden.

"Don't push her, okay?" I said gently. "If she is busy, you can always see her some other time."

"Hello? Lucy? Is it you?" He held the phone with both hands and focused his gaze on his shoes. "I'm Aiden. Do you remember me?"

I glanced at Adeline to see what she was doing and found her eyes on us. She gave a small nod and looked away. Having her in my house felt strange, like she didn't belong in my life. So much had changed in so little time.

"Did you miss me? If you miss me you can come see me now."

"Aiden, don't push her," I reminded him quietly, giving him my attention. He didn't even spare me a glance.

"Okay. Can you bring Olive, too? She must have missed me too. Uh-huh. When will she come then? Okay. I'm waiting for you, so you can't be late."

Whatever she said on the other end of the line, Aiden smiled and nodded to himself. "Five minutes, Lucy. Don't be late, okay?"

Quickly, he handed the phone back to me and ran to his room.

"Aiden, be careful," I yelled after him, but I was still being ignored.

After making sure Lucy wasn't still on the line, I put away my phone and made my way back to Adeline. Halfway over there, I remembered Lucy's fondness for that wall and instead decided to stay close to the glass doors so I could unlock the door for her when she came over with murder on her mind. I leaned against the glass and met Adeline's eyes.

For a beat we both watched each other in silence and just took each other in.

"How are you doing?" she asked.

"Up until yesterday, I was doing fine, Adeline."

"You can't possibly be blaming me, Adam."

"And who am I supposed to blame, Adeline? Should I blame Aiden for wandering out of the car on his own?"

Adeline sighed and pushed her long blond hair behind her ear. "He shouldn't have gotten out of the car until someone came to take him, but you're right, he is not the one to blame."

"How nice of you to agree with me on something."

Hurt flashed across her eyes, but she covered it up pretty quickly.

She got up from the couch. Her white jeans were hugging her long legs while the gray shirt she was wearing was relatively loose on her breasts. Still, I could see that she wasn't wearing anything underneath. Whether it was a tactic or not, I had no idea, but I wasn't falling for anything—especially not into bed with her.

As she started to make her way toward me, her phone started ringing in her purse, and she looked back at it. Then she moved back to the couch to take the call.

"I'm waiting on a call from the director in New York, Adam. Do you mind if I take it?"

She didn't wait for my answer.

At that exact moment, someone banged on the glass doors, and I jolted out of my thoughts about how much I should tell Adeline of my plans. I turned my head and was met with Lucy's angry eyes. I smiled. I was starting to acknowledge the fact that I loved seeing her all worked up and ready to spit fire at me.

My little warrior.

She lifted her hand, and before she could break the glass with her pounding, I unlocked the door so she could get in.

"Asshole," she muttered as she was passing behind me.

"Excuse me?" I asked as I raised an eyebrow at her.

"Ass-hole," she repeated, louder this time. "When was the last time you kissed someone anyway?" she asked, looking up at me. "That was awful. Such a big disappointment."

I leaned in and held back a smile when I saw her body do a little sway toward me. My lips grazed her ear, and I whispered, "Are you trying to make me kiss you again, Lucy? Is this your way of asking me without having to ask me? You think I'll fall for it?"

She made a low growl in her throat and this time I did nothing to hide my smile. "Because if it is, it's working. I'd love nothing more than to kiss you senseless again and watch you cling to me for dear life."

I caught the shiver that ran through her body, the slight bend of her neck that brought my lips closer to her skin. It was sexy as hell and just as tempting. Catching the reflection of Adeline on her phone with her back to us, I made sure my nose gently bumped her skin and took a deep breath. "But this time...this time I'd like to finish what you started. I'd like to peel off your clothes. Touch you." I pressed a quick, small kiss on her neck. "Kiss you...and kiss you...and kiss you...I'll kiss you as long as you want, sweetheart. And I'll still be kissing you while you're coming on my fingers." I leaned in a little farther, making sure my lips were right next to her ear. Out of the corner of my eye, I noticed her tongue darting out of her mouth as she secretly tried to lick her lower lip. "And on my cock," I added, my voice coming out raspier than I wanted. "I'll look into your eyes and kiss you until your lips are all red and swollen. I bet you'd love that."

When I leaned back, her body had gone completely still, but her eyes...ah, those gray eyes were melting. They were melting for me in a way I would've loved to watch were she under me, over me, or wrapped up around me.

"I...I..."

"Yes, Lucy?" I prompted.

Her eyes slowly narrowed into slits. When she crooked her finger for me to get closer and opened her mouth to speak again, she was trying her best to cover her reaction to me with her sharp words.

"I wouldn't touch your lips with a ten-foot pole, Adam Connor," she whispered as her chest rose and fell rapidly. "And I seriously doubt you can fuck me like I like to be fucked with a four-inch dick."

I leaned back and smiled down at her. "You think I'm four inches?"

"Adam?" Adeline called; I saw Lucy's body tense further.

I took a step back from her and turned my body toward Adeline.

"This is our famous Lucy." I let her know.

Her eyes found Lucy and a smile spread across her lips as she came forward to greet my firecracker.

She was our Lucy, Aiden's and mine.

I caught Lucy's eyes as she glanced between me and Adeline, but she didn't say anything. When Adeline reached her, I backed up and watched her kiss Lucy on the cheek.

"It's so nice to finally meet you," Adeline said genuinely.

"Ah." Lucy glanced at me, her eyes probing, but when she couldn't get a read on me, she focused on Adeline instead. "Hi. It's nice to meet you too."

"You should see how Aiden's eyes light up whenever he talks about you."

"He mentioned me?" Lucy asked as a sweet smile formed on those lips I was starting to become very interested in.

Adeline shook her head and touched her arm. "He talks about you nonstop. You're his new favorite thing. I'm so glad I caught you today. I've been meaning to tell Adam to bring you around one day so we could meet."

His new favorite *thing*…Adeline and her words. And why in the world would she want me to bring Lucy around?

"Oh?" Lucy asked, just as confused as me.

Adeline glanced at me over her shoulder. "Adam mentioned that he had to let go of Anne, the nanny before you." She faced Lucy before I could interrupt. "He didn't explain why, of course, but Anne was a little too interested in what was going on around here if you ask me, so I'm happy he found a new nanny instead."

"Huh? That's weird," Lucy said, eyeing me over Adeline's shoulder. I shook my head and kept silent.

"Lucy is not a nanny," I corrected her.

Adeline turned back to me again. "But Aiden said she is looking after him."

"She is, but she isn't his nanny. She was kind enough to spend time with him last week because I couldn't find anyone."

Adeline kept glancing between Lucy and me.

"I live next door," Lucy piped in. "Temporarily," she added. "I'm Olive's friend. Olive Thorn? Jason Thorn's wife? I'm sure you've heard of her." Lucy's eyes slid to me.

You're on your own, sweetheart.

Adeline's face lit up as I watched the awkward interaction between them. I could've helped, I suppose, but where was the fun in that?

"The writer? That's the Olive Aiden keeps mentioning?" Adeline turned to me. "I knew they were your neighbors, but I didn't think they were your *next-door* neighbors."

"What difference does it make?"

Adeline rolled her eyes and pulled Lucy farther into the living room. "Come on, we need to sit down for this."

Lucy's confused eyes met mine as they passed me, and I smiled down at her.

"I adored her book, and I heard the opening numbers for the movie were huge. I'd love to meet her too," Adeline continued as soon as they were sitting down.

"She'll be happy to hear that," Lucy replied.

"I hope you don't think this is awkward, Lucy. Since you're spending time with Aiden, I'd like to get to know you a little more. I know he loves you, but…"

I shook my head. *So that's where she is going.*

"Aiden," I yelled, and a few seconds later we all heard his running feet coming toward us. When he saw Lucy, he changed course and ran toward her. Lucy got up, and Aiden threw himself to her and hugged her legs. She grunted with the force, and the laugh that came after the grunt was beautiful.

"Hey, little human," she said affectionately.

Aiden tilted his head back and looked up at her with such pleasure.

"You came!"

"Of course I did. How could I miss seeing you?"

"You were almost late, though, so you'll have to stay longer."

Aiden dropped his arms down and waited for her answer, his eyes scheming.

Seeing him so happy eased the worry in my chest. Maybe he wasn't that scared anymore, now that he had his Lucy. For a brief second I wondered what Lucy would've done if she had been in that car with him. Would she have left him behind and trusted the assistants to take care of him? Or would she have even forgotten about him in the first place?

I seriously doubted it.

Lucy made a show of checking her nonexistent watch. "Ah, I can't tell, how late was I?"

Aiden grabbed her wrist and stared at it for a while. "You were an hour late, Lucy! Now you'll have to stay for an hour."

"Huh, look at that. And here I thought it was only five minutes. I guess I'm staying for an hour then."

Aiden jumped up and raised his fist. "Yes!"

"Aiden," I called to get his attention, and he looked at me. He had that sweet smile only a child can have when they've tricked their favorite person into spending time with them. "I still have to talk to your mom, so maybe you can take Lucy into the backyard and tell her what you were up to in New York?"

"Okay," he answered readily, his eyes still shining with excitement. Grabbing Lucy's hand, he dragged her out to the backyard.

"Ah, Adam," Lucy mumbled before I could slide the door closed. Aiden let go of her hand and raced toward the pool.

"Aiden, slow down," I yelled after him.

After shooting a quick glance at Adeline, Lucy smiled and quietly whispered, "She doesn't know why you fired the nanny?"

"She does."

"Then she doesn't know you had me arrested?"

"She knows that, too."

Her brows drew together, and she gave me a long look before walking away to join Aiden as she muttered under her breath, her voice too low for me to hear.

Adeline's eyes were following them as Aiden ran back to meet Lucy so he could drag her again.

"She is babysitting him?"

"If she isn't busy, she comes over for a few hours until I come back. Or Dan watches him."

"You trust her after the Anne incident?"

"You mean the incident where our son almost drowned?"

Adeline knew about the 'pool' incident, but not so surprisingly she showed no signs of worry for Aiden.

She rolled her eyes. "You don't have to say it like that. We wouldn't want anyone to hear what happened."

Of course she wouldn't. I shook my head and tried to let it go.

"So you trust her? How about Jason and Olive?"

I didn't even need to think about the answer to that question. "I wouldn't leave him with her if I didn't. Plus, he enjoys spending time with Jason and Olive, too." I glanced outside and saw the duo sitting on the lounge chairs as Aiden chatted animatedly. "From what I can see and hear from Jason, so do they." She wasn't asking about Jason and Olive for Aiden's sake.

I didn't feel the need to mention to her that we had put a

listening device on Aiden's toy to make sure everything was okay. Come to think of it, I didn't feel the need to explain anything to Adeline anymore.

Sitting across from her, I let go of her a bit more. A bit more of what she was to me. What she'd been to me.

"How are you doing?" she asked when I stayed silent.

"Good, Adeline."

"Are you sure? I know you took a break with Michel, too. I'm here if you want to talk, Adam."

I raised my brows, and she had the decency to look away from me.

"I never meant to mess up your life, Adam."

"My life is not messed up, Adeline. In fact, I'm very happy with how things turned out, and I didn't take a break with Michel, I fired him. You and me…we are not heading in the same direction anymore. It didn't make sense to keep him on."

"It doesn't have to be that way, you know that."

I shook my head and relaxed into my seat. "I don't have a problem with how things are with you and me, Adeline. You made your choice, and I'm okay with that. I moved on. You moved on. Our problem right now, and what I would like to talk about, is Aiden."

"I don't see him as a problem, Adam."

"Oh, but you do, Adeline. He was the reason you wanted a divorce, remember?"

She sighed and got up from her seat to stare outside into the yard where Lucy and Aiden were in sight. "Do you think we made a mistake?"

"A mistake?" I asked, not following her.

She turned to face me, clutched her hands at her back, and leaned against the window. Looking at her, I searched for the feelings I'd had for a girl who was nothing but pure sweetness, but I couldn't find what I was looking for. It was truly over for us. And not only that Adeline, the Adeline I'd known, was nowhere to be found either. Sure, she was still sweet and considerate when she wanted to be, but she wasn't the same girl I'd met on set and fallen for.

Maybe she had adapted to Hollywood, and I was the one who had changed—drastically.

"With Aiden. Do you think it was a mistake?"

Shocked at the question, I just stared at her. "How can you say that, Adeline?" I managed to force out after some time. Thinking back on it, I thought that was the moment that solidified my decision about taking Aiden away from her.

"I'm not saying having him was a mistake, Adam. Don't take it like that. I love him."

I could sense a but coming, and she didn't disappoint.

"But do you think our *decision* was a mistake?"

To me it sounded like she was asking the same damn question.

"After you learned about the pregnancy, you made all the plans, Adeline. It was your decision."

"But then it wasn't."

"Yes." I nodded, giving her that much. "After I saw him, it became our decision."

She left her spot next to the window and sat down next to me. Close.

"Would things be different for us, do you think? If Aiden hadn't happened. Do you think we would've still ended up here or made different decisions along the way?"

I looked into her eyes and saw that she was being genuine. I exhaled. "I don't know, Adeline. I *can't* know. If you're asking if we would've ended up getting married either way...I think we would have. I loved you. Maybe it wouldn't have happened so fast, but yes, I think we would have still ended up together."

"I loved you, too, Adam," she whispered. "So much that I couldn't imagine waking up without you sleeping next to me..."

"But now you can," I finished for her.

She looked away.

"I think I *did* make a mistake by forcing Aiden and me on you. And he changed you. He changed *us*."

"Of course he changed me. The problem is he couldn't change you and *that* is what ended up changing us. I don't see why we're having this conversation again, Adeline. We went over all this when you gave me your 'I want a divorce' speech. I have other things to talk to you about. I don't have time to listen to you talk about how our *son* was a mistake for you."

"Our son," she repeated, meeting my eyes. "I'm sorry. Things have been hard for me lately."

"What? You didn't get the green light from the director?"

"Actually, no, I didn't get the green light. I already told you I had to take Aiden with me because the director wanted to see me around Aiden. The role is a mother who tries to protect her son from an abusive husband, so when the tabloids ran with the story that I forgot Aiden in the car…it must've affected his decision."

"Must have…" I shook my head. "He is not a purse you can take wherever you want to show him off, Adeline. Just because you're spending time with my mother doesn't mean you have to act like her, too." She pursed her lips. "I wanted us to talk so I could tell you that I'm filing for sole custody of Aiden. I didn't want you to hear it from a press release or see it in the tabloids."

She put her hand on my arm and leaned into me.

"You knew it was coming, and I think after what happened yesterday, it's high time we do it," I said before she could have a chance to protest.

"Adam, you can't do that to me. Not now, not after what happened. And you have to think about Aiden, too. We talked about this before. Forget about me, do you know what he'll think? What everyone else will think?"

I twisted my body so I could see her face. Her hand gently squeezed my arm.

"What will he think, Adeline?"

She released a long breath. "He'll think I don't want him, and so will everyone else."

"Do you want him?"

"Yes, Adam. Of course. This is working out great for him. One week with me, one week with you. And this way, I have time to focus on my career. I'm finally going back to doing what I love."

"I never stopped you from doing what you love, Adeline. Like everything else, taking a break was your decision, too. You thought if you left him with nannies and went back to shooting people would judge. In the end, you always did what you wanted to do, so don't even try to dump this on me."

"Adam," she started again and my temper flared up. I stood up and looked down at her sad face.

"What happened yesterday, Adeline? Did you forget he was in the car with you?"

She scowled at me. "Of course not."

"Then what happened?" I repeated my question through gritted teeth.

"Rita was supposed to have him. It was her fault."

"Rita, your assistant. You're gonna sit there and blame *an assistant* for not taking care of *your* son?"

She remained silent.

Her phone buzzed on the couch across from her and her eyes slid that way. To my surprise, she didn't go for it.

"I saw the photos," I explained. "I saw the photos, and I never saw you come back to rescue him. He stood there, Adeline. He stood there and cried until another one of your assistants came out to take him in."

She stood up and met my eyes, her voice rising. "He should've waited in the car, Adam."

"He is five years old, Adeline. He was going after his mom."

Her phone stopped buzzing then started to go off again.

"Take it," I said. "I'll send Aiden in so he can say goodbye— if you have time for that, of course. If not, I'm going out to spend time with him so he can start looking into my face again instead of at my feet and then I'm meeting with my lawyer. I suggest you do the same. You'll still have your weeks with him until the judge makes a decision."

I walked away from her, but her voice stopped me before I could step outside.

"I won't give up on him that easily, Adam," she said, her voice harder than it had been seconds before. "I won't let everyone think I'm okay with you taking him away from his mother."

"Of course you can't, Adeline," I agreed with her. "How would that make you look in the public eye? A woman who doesn't care about her kid..." I shook my head. "You'll have a much harder time getting auditions that way, I imagine, with the bad press and everything. You'll fight for it, I know. Me, on the other hand...I don't care what they think at all. All I care about right now is what that kid"—I gestured with my thumb over my shoulder—"thinks of me. And if I never hear him beg me not to send him away again, I think that will be enough to make me happy."

CHAPTER THIRTEEN

LUCY

"You're a dog," I said to Aiden, and he giggled, covering his mouth with his hand.

"I'm not a dog, Lucy," he managed to sputter in between giggles. I smiled at him.

We were sitting out in the backyard, lounging as his daddy talked to his mommy. Geez, but I had acted like a complete weirdo when I saw her. I mean, she was an actress, even though she didn't actually act in many movies, but still, she was. More than anything, she was known as Adam Connor's wife.

So after the things the clever asshole had murmured into my ear, lifting my head and seeing his wife—ex-wife—had messed with my mind for a second there.

"Okay," I gave in. "You're more like a cute puppy."

"If I'm a puppy what are you? A cat?" he asked, his eyes dancing with mischief.

"Why does everyone think I'm a cat? No, today I'm gonna be a bird. Now close your eyes."

"But I wanna be a bird too."

"You do?" I looked at him with one eye half-open. "Okay, then we are both birds today."

He nodded enthusiastically and closed his eyes.

"Now, what would you do if you were a bird?"

"I'd fly away!"

"Where do you wanna fly?"

"You're weird, Lucy," Aiden announced.

"Good weird or bad weird?"

A moment of hesitation on his part.

"Good weird. I like you."

"That's good," I said with a smile. "I like you, too."

"Aiden," Adam called out; I peered at him over the chair.

Handsome bastard.

He walked toward us with easy steps and my eyes took in everything that was Adam Connor. He looked at me, so of course I looked away, but damn those eyes of his.

He kneeled between our lounge chairs, his fingers holding on to the chair mere inches away from my face. He focused on Aiden.

"Dan is on his way over here. Is it okay with you if I leave you with him for a few hours?"

Aiden shrugged.

Well, well, well...isn't that interesting?

"I need you to look at me, Aiden," Adam said with a sigh.

Aiden's eyes lifted up to his father, but I could see it was the last thing he wanted to do.

"I need to go and see my lawyer. Will you be okay with Dan?"

"Why can't I stay with Lucy?" Aiden asked.

Adam's gaze found mine.

I raised an eyebrow at him.

"Because," he started, looking back at Aiden again. "I'm sure Lucy has other things to do. I'll be back as soon as I can, then I want to talk to you about what happened and how it's never going to happen again, okay?"

Ah, so that was why the little human was giving him the cold shoulder.

Aiden shrugged again. "What are we gonna talk about? You didn't want me, so Mom took me away to fly."

My eyes flew to Adam, and I saw his entire body tighten in a scary way. "Is that what your mom told you, Aiden?"

Aiden's answer was reluctant. "No."

"Get up," Adam ordered, and I realized I was intruding on another private moment, but heck, at that point it wasn't my fault anymore. They should've stopped having those moments around me. So I stayed.

Aiden uncurled his body from the lounge and stood in front of his dad. His eyes dropped down to his shoes as he twisted and twisted those little fingers.

Adam gently lifted his chin up so he could look into his eyes. "I know you're confused with everything that's been going on, the back and forth between your mom and—"

Aiden scrunched up his face. "I'm not confused. You don't wanna kiss and squish Mom anymore, so you got yourself a divorce."

My lips twitched, but I kept it under control. Adam, on the other hand…Adam didn't look all that amused, but, God, did he look sexy with that scowl on his face.

"We both wanted the divorce, Aiden. It wasn't just me."

Another shrug.

"So you still want to kiss and squish Mom?"

"I didn't say that."

Boy, was he screwing this up.

"I think your dad loves you very much, Aiden," I jumped in. It wasn't my place to say anything, but the sexy dad was taking too damn long to get to the point. Both the father's and son's gazes turned to me and it was my turn to shrug. "I know how upset he gets when you leave to spend time with your mom. I saw it myself. He sits around and cries all day." I scrunched up my nose. "It's pathetic, really."

"No, he doesn't," Aiden said with bright a smile.

"Oh, he does, little bug. I saw it myself."

He cocked his head. "Were you watching him over the wall again, Lucy?"

"Yep."

He turned to his dad and threw his arms around his neck. "I don't want you to cry, Daddy. I won't leave you and go to fly again. I promise."

Adam met my eyes as he held on to his son. "No, you won't leave me. I'm not letting you go. Not anymore."

I will not swoon.

I will not swoon.

I will not swoon.

"DID you put the note on the door?" Aiden whispered from his hiding place under the wood table.

I was hiding behind the couch. "I did. Don't worry, he'll see it."

"You put the gun where he can see it too?"

"Yup."

He giggled. "Do you think he'll be angry?"

"Angry? Psshhh, he'll have the best time of his life. He'll thank us, trust me."

After Adam left, I stayed with Aiden. An hour later when Dan the Man joined us, we convinced him to go out on a scavenger hunt for us. You know, so he could get the necessary things for a fun movie night: pizza, candy, snacks, M&Ms, burgers...the list went on and on. As soon as he was out the door—and I swear I saw a small smile playing on his lips—we hatched a plan to get back at Adam for letting Adeline take him away to New York. I knew he'd had nothing to do with it, but still, we were out for revenge—and a little bit of fun—so it was as good an excuse as any in our book. More importantly, it put the biggest smile on Aiden's face when I first came up with it.

We called to find out when Adam would be home and left a note on the door.

Are you ready to cry all the tears, Adam Connor?
Catch us if you can!
PS. Just because we felt sorry for you, you can use the gun. It's
loaded.

Right under the note, there was the smallest size Nerf Super Soaker gun you can find. Aiden and I had the bigger ones. In fact, they were so big that Aiden kept having trouble holding his up.

We heard the door open and then Adam's voice trickled in.

"Aiden?"

I held my finger up to my mouth and warned Aiden to stay quiet. He nodded, but couldn't hold back the small giggle that escaped his lips. He looked so damn happy. I grinned at him and got ready to blast Adam with freezing cold water.

I tilted my head slightly up, only enough that my eyes and forehead were visible, and saw him walk into the big opening between the kitchen and the living room where we were hiding as quietly as we could.

"Dan? Anybody home?"

Another giggle from Aiden.

I checked again and saw that he hadn't taken our game seriously: the gun was just hanging in his hand with the note we had attached to the door. So be it. We had warned him.

He walked farther into the room, closer to us.

I got Aiden's attention and held up one finger—our signal. Then I opened my palm and mouthed *Go*.

We stood up at the same time, exactly when Adam was standing in between us, and blasted him with water from both sides. As the first stream of cold water hit his shirt, he opened his mouth in shock. I started laughing and pumping the gun to hit him with more water.

Aiden's giggling was uncontrollable as he hit his dad's stomach with more water.

Adam's shocked eyes jumped between his son and me, then he lifted his little gun—no pun intended—and started shooting water at his son as he advanced on him. Aiden squealed when the first hit found its target and ran outside. There was another loaded gun waiting for him near the lounge chairs. That left me alone with his father.

He lowered his gun and turned to face me.

Big mistake.

"What is this?" he asked as his hand smoothed his wet T-shirt. He lifted his hand and shook off some of the water. We'd gotten him good. My eyes followed his hand because, oh Lord, I could see the outline of his abs and those pecs...Jesus. What a glorious view. He took a step forward, and I took a step back.

"Don't come any closer." I raised the gun.

He stopped, the expression on his face making my lady parts purr. Those eyes...goddamnit, those eyes!

"We're cheering Aiden up," I explained as I backed away from him since it didn't look like he intended to stop.

"We? Looks to me like I'm the one doing all the work."

"Well, you *are* the one who made him sad after all. It's just a little water, Mr. Hotshot Movie Star, you won't melt away."

"I think you will—"

I didn't let him finish and blasted him with more water, right on his crotch.

He stopped speaking and looked down at his now wet pants. When he glanced up at me with a raised eyebrow, I braced the gun at my hip and shrugged.

"Run, Lucy. Run for your life," he murmured and then lunged at me. I saw him throw away his gun and before he could get to me, I turned around and *ran*.

"Incoming!" I yelled, letting Aiden know his dad was coming out. Another blast of water hit Adam's face just before he could catch me. His fingers touched my arm, but with my ninja skills, I squealed and managed to slip away from him and the tingles his hand caused every freaking time he touched me.

Since my gun was empty, I reached for the fifth gun we'd hidden in the backyard and hit Adam from the other side.

Adam advanced toward Aiden, and he jumped up and ran away, laughing and screaming.

"Daddy, you can't catch us!"

"Oh, trust me, I will."

"You're all wet now! We got you!"

"When I get my hands on you two, you'll be singing a different tune."

Adam pretended to catch Aiden, but then let him skirt away from him.

"You're not catching Lucy! Catch Lucy!" Aiden screamed as he eyed his father to guess which way he'd run next.

"Hey now!" I yelled, but it was too late, my water gun jammed—the stupid thing. Before I could figure out what was wrong with it and fix it quickly, Adam quickened his steps and almost caught me.

Dropping the gun, I twisted away from him, but I was too slow. His arm sneaked around my waist, and he caught me just as I'd started running away. His chest cushioned my fall and I grunted with the force he drew me to himself. He circled his arms around me and whispered into my ear.

"Thank you for making him laugh, Lucy. But…"

I didn't melt, nor did my heart quicken. Not at all. Zilch. I didn't like him very much after all.

"I'm afraid I have to take you down. Aiden!" he shouted, and Aiden appeared in front of us, holding his weapon high.

"Aiden! Man down! Help me, little human!" I shouted.

"Let her go, Daddy!"

"Come and get her if you want her so much," Adam replied, and his arms gave me a light squeeze as he leaned down and secretly pressed his lips against my neck.

The son of a bitch!

"I'll save you, Lucy!"

Feeling free, safe, and happy, I dropped my head back on Adam's shoulder and our eyes met. The smile that was stretching my lips slowly disappeared when I saw the look in his eyes.

Shit.

Shit.

Shit!

"You can't look at me like that," I whispered as he slowly backed us up. Despite all the cold water I'd shot at him, his body was surprisingly warm against my back. And firm. And mouth-watering. And heart-quickening.

"Why not?"

"Because I'm not supposed to like you."

The smile he gave me was soft and then suddenly his fingers were laced with mine against my chest. "But I like you very much, Lucy."

And just like that, before I could curse him, there was cold water all over my face.

"Aiden!" I sputtered as Adam's chest shook with laughter.

"I'm shooting at him, Lucy! You're in my way!"

"Aim at his face!" I yelled back.

"He got you!"

"He is right," Adam repeated his son's words. "I think I got you."

"Think again," I muttered and gave him a pitiful push with my elbow. And then another. I was pretty sure I hurt myself more than I did him. Pathetic, I know...

He pulled me and we were falling back, and darn it, but I was still in his arms and couldn't find it in me to complain.

We fell back into the pool with a big splash, and Adam let go of me. I swam back to the surface and gasped for air. As soon as Adam's head was above the water, Aiden started spraying him with more water. I joined his son and splashed him as much as I could.

Adam lifted his arm and wiped the water off his eyes. After a mock growl, he yelled, "I'm coming for you, Aiden."

I looked behind me to see Aiden squealing and running back inside the house. It was a good thing he'd remained fairly dry; I would've bet the hardwood floors and all those soft carpets had cost Adam some good money. When I turned my head back and saw Adam slowly swimming toward me, I panicked and tried my best to get away from him until my back hit the edge of the pool.

Adam dropped a little under water until all I could see were those glittering green eyes. Then before I could control my heavy breathing and give my heart a good shake so it could get itself together, he was on me. His arms held on to the edge and trapped me in between his body and the tiled wall of the pool.

"First, you," he said and my eyes dropped to his mouth. He wasn't breathing as hard as I was, but he didn't look all that calm either. "You have anything to say? Maybe an apology so I'll take it easier on you?" he asked and my eyes jumped up to his.

"Why would I apologize?"

"For ambushing me."

I tilted my head and tapped at my lips a few times with my index finger. "Nope."

"Good."

And just like that his lips were on mine. I grunted and tried to push his chest off me, but then his hands grabbed one of mine from between us and laced our fingers again.

Damn him.

Damn him and his skillful tongue that had just pushed its way into my mouth.

I stopped struggling and kissed him back just as hard because who was I kidding? He was a freaking good kisser. He growled deep in his throat as if the contact wasn't enough and he was dying to have more. Letting go of my hand, he grabbed me by the backs of my thighs and secured my legs around his waist. My arms rounded his neck as I got more into the kiss and then…

Then I felt his cock.

Holy shit!

His cock was most definitely not a small gun. Actually, it was nowhere near four inches. He felt thick; a cock that was that thick couldn't be short. It would be more than disappointing if that was the case; it would be a lie! Not that I had really thought it would be four inches anyway, but it would've made my life so much easier.

Just when I tightened my legs around him—you know, so I could try and measure how long he actually was by rubbing myself all over him—he pushed my legs off and stopped kissing me.

Have I told you lately how much of an asshole he was?

Slowly I opened my eyes and met his hypnotizing green ones, which was very hard to do considering I was feeling more than a little dizzy. My only saving grace was that he was breathing just as hard as me.

We both heard Aiden's excited voice at the same time, and I looked over my shoulder toward the house. He was nowhere in sight, and I hoped he'd listened to me and hidden in one of the kitchen cupboards just like I'd told him to do if things went sideways.

"Daddy, you can't find me! I'm that good!"

I looked back at Adam.

He hesitated for a second, but then his eyes moved away from mine, and I swallowed.

Phew! It had been a close call. The fact that I hadn't ripped off his wet clothes or licked any part of his body—*especially* a specific part of his body—was a big personal victory for me.

"If you don't stay here tonight, Lucy, I'm breaking into Jason's house," he warned me, his eyes finding mine again.

My spine tingled. Hell, my whole body tingled…especially my heart.

I took a shaky breath and finally spoke, "I'd love to watch you try."

He leaned in and pressed his mouth against my skin where my shoulder met my neck. I felt the soft touch of his lips, his warm breath as he softly exhaled on my damp skin.

Danger, Lucy. Run. Hide your heart.

Did anyone ever blow on your wet skin with their warm breath? No? Try it, it does amazing things to your ovaries.

"Stay here tonight, and I promise I'll give you better things to watch."

He pushed away from the edge of the pool and me, and got out of the pool to get to his son.

CHAPTER FOURTEEN

ADAM

She didn't listen to me. Of course she didn't.

I opened the door and entered Lucy's room. She was sitting cross-legged right in the middle of the bed. To be honest, I wasn't all that surprised to see her waiting for me; it would be just like her to wait and see if I really did do what I said I'd do. When she saw me, her eyes widened and a small smile played on her lips.

"You son of a bitch!" she whispered in awe. "You did it. You actually broke into their house!"

I hadn't. However, I didn't see the need to correct her. I'd called Jason and asked if he could let me in so I could talk to Lucy, and he was kind enough not to question my odd request—although he did murmur, "Good luck," after pointing out Lucy's room to me.

Instead of mentioning my encounter with Jason, I leaned my back against the door and asked, "Why did you sneak out when I went to put Aiden in bed?"

We had watched "Happy Feet" per Aiden's request and had a few slices of pizza each while he chatted with Lucy all throughout the movie, up until he fell asleep on the couch.

"Dan said he'd leave in a few, so I thought you could use some alone time with your bodyguard and your son." She shrugged then drew in a deep breath. "Don't just stand there, come on in then."

"You know damn well Aiden was already asleep when I carried him away, Lucy. And I specifically told you to stay with us when we were in the pool."

"The pool, right."

We stared into each other's eyes for a short heartbeat then she dropped onto her back, stretched out her legs, and opened her arms as if she was getting ready to be tied down.

"You can do it," she said with a suffering sigh.

Confused, I asked, "I can do what?"

"Well," she began, her eyes trained on the ceiling. "You broke in, so now I *have* to sleep with you. I mean, if I didn't, it would be cruel of me. After all, you deserve it."

When I didn't say anything—because I was trying very hard to follow her logic—she propped herself up on her elbows and looked up at me.

"Didn't you come here to fuck me? What are you waiting for? Come in and take me. I shall endure the process."

I had to stop myself from laughing.

"To fuck you? You shall endure?"

She let out a dramatic sigh, and I smiled before she could catch me.

"You know, have sex, bump uglies, thread the needle, the lust and thrust, the horizontal hula, dip your four-inch wick, burry your four-inch bone, the grand slam—although with a four-inch tool, I'm not sure how grand it'd be, but…I'm curious and ready, so let's do it."

I walked farther into the room and sat down on the edge of the bed, right next to her hip.

She followed my movements all the way to her side. As much

as she was trying her best to look like a virgin sacrificing herself for God knows what, I'd caught the way she looked at me on more than a few occasions. More than that, she must have forgotten that I already knew that her body practically vibrated every time I touched her, that she couldn't stop herself from pressing her body against mine whenever I kissed her. If we did end up having sex, it'd be no sacrifice for her.

"You really have a thing for four-inch dicks, don't you?"

She raised an eyebrow. "I prefer bigger ones, though I'm sure yours looks cute on you."

I smiled.

She gave me a tentative smile back.

"So you want me to bump uglies with you, huh?"

Her brows drew in together. "That's why you said to stay at your place, isn't it? I mean, that's why you broke in here."

"Actually, I asked you to stay over so we could talk, and so I could thank you for what you did for Aiden. What you keep doing for Aiden and me. We, both him and I, really needed today. I can't say being blasted with cold water would have been my first choice, but…"

For a brief moment, disappointment flashed across her beautiful features, but she was quick to hide it.

My little liar.

"Oh," she murmured. "When you kissed me like that back in the pool, I thought you wanted me to stay so you could do me. And you're welcome, I love seeing the little guy laugh."

"You're making me dizzy with all this romantic talk."

"I don't do romance, Adam Connor."

"The curse, right?"

She nodded, her eyes daring me to make fun of her.

My eyes dropped to her parted lips, and I couldn't help myself. I reached out and gently ran a knuckle across her lower lip. She stopped breathing.

"You like how I kiss you?"

"You're an awful kisser," she forced out in a whisper as she shook her head.

"That bad?"

"The worst."

"You'd never kiss me again, then?"

"Never."

I leaned in and softly kissed her lips...first the top one, then the bottom. Her eyes fluttered closed, and I saw her hands tightly grip the sheets. Keeping my eyes on her face, I drew back and licked my bottom lip. "Even *that* is bad?"

"Worst ever," she whispered, her eyes cracking open.

"I don't want to be your worst, Lucy."

She licked her lips and stayed quiet.

"You want me to do you?" I asked, letting my eyes wander over her body.

She shifted in place. She was still in the same clothes: black leggings and a Superman T-shirt. The gray shirt did nothing to hide the fact that she wasn't wearing a bra.

"No. I don't want it. Becau—"

"Because you don't like me," I guessed, forcing my eyes to look away from the outline of her nipples.

She nodded. "*But,* since you broke in here, I feel obligated, like you earned doing me. Think of it as your prize for being adventurous and giving breaking and entering a try."

I glanced away and tried to appear like I was thinking it over. I stretched my legs out on the bed and leaned against the headboard.

"Excuse me? What are you doing?" she asked with a small frown on her face.

"Getting comfortable. Come on, lie back down."

"I'm fine, thanks. Why don't you go and get comfortable in

your own bed, your own house?" Suddenly she straightened up, giving me a harsh look. "You didn't."

I arched an eyebrow. "I didn't what?"

"You didn't leave Aiden alone in the house."

"Is that a question or fact?"

"Question."

I rested my head on the headboard and closed my eyes. "That's why I like you, Lucy Meyer. Of course I didn't leave him alone. Dan is at the house."

She grunted. "What exactly are you doing here if we're not gonna have sex?"

"Like I said, I came to thank you, maybe steal another kiss while we're at it." I opened my eyes and turned my face to her. "Since you keep telling me I'm a bad kisser, I'm trying to improve myself."

"And I'm your guinea pig?"

"Since you're the only one who's been complaining…"

"Well, go try your moves on someone else. I'm done kissing you."

"I'll think about it."

"Did you come here to irritate me?"

I closed my eyes again. "Did you see the articles that have been floating around? The photos of Aiden?"

I felt her hesitation, then felt the bed dip. When I looked down, I saw her lying down again, her head in line with my waist.

"Yeah. Hard to miss."

"I'm filing for sole custody. I never want that to happen again and as long as he is with her, I know it will happen. Maybe not next month or the next, but eventually it will happen again. I still have to send him to her until the judge decides, but I think they'll be on my side."

"And Aiden? Have you thought about Aiden?"

"What about him?"

She turned to me and looked into my eyes. "It's his mother, you know. He loves her. We talked, and he said he only jumped out of the car even though he knew he wasn't supposed to because he thought she forgot about him and would be sad if she couldn't see him anymore. Do you think he'll be okay with only seeing her every now and then? He is just a kid, Adam. He needs his mom."

"Do you think, even for one second, that she spends any time with him? That she is a good mom? Oh, she was. In the beginning, Aiden was her world, but then the magic disappeared. She said she couldn't bond with him like she thought she would. She realized it wasn't what she wanted, wasn't who she wanted. The only reason she was on that plane to New York with Aiden was because she needed to show him off to a director so she could get a role, Lucy—which she didn't get, by the way. I won't let her use my son."

My son.

He was only mine.

He'd always been only mine.

"Not having a mother sucks," Lucy said quietly, breaking into my thoughts. "It's not my place to say anything. I *know* it's not my place to say anything, but…just before you do anything, be sure that you're doing the right thing for Aiden, not for yourself."

"He'll still see her whenever he wants. I'm not trying to stop him from being with her. I just want to make sure he is safe while he is doing that."

"You should talk about this with Aiden, not me. Ask what he'd think about staying with you full time."

"He is five years old, not twelve." I needed to change the subject. "I found someone to look after him. Meredith Shay. She is forty-two years old, has good credentials, and she seems like a happy person. She smiles a lot, and I like that. I think it'll work this time, but I know Aiden would still love to see you."

A small smile played on her lips as she looked up at the ceiling. "So I'm getting fired from the nanny job."

"You never accepted any money, so technically it wasn't a job."

She grunted and dropped back on the bed. "If you're okay with it, I'd still love to see him too."

"You love him," I pointed out. "I watch how you are around him. I watch you, and I can't take my eyes off that girl, Lucy. I'm glad you're not worried about your curse with him."

"Now who's the stalker, Mr. Connor?"

I waited for her to make a snarky comment about what I'd just said, but instead we shared a heavy silence.

"I do love him," she confirmed without hesitation. "He is just a kid. He deserves all the love he can get. And the curse doesn't work that way. I'm allowed to love my friends and be loved by them, and Aiden is my best friend at the moment because Olive is pissing me off. Kinda. But not really." She sighed. "I just can't fall in love with someone who has a dick. As long as I don't care about a guy too much, I'll be fine. I'll be different from them. I won't be like them. The curse will end with me."

Them being her grandmother and mom. *Bullshit*, I thought to myself. She was as unique as it could get, and with every passing day, with every smile and unabashed laugh, every smirk and scowl thrown my way, I was starting to like her even more.

"I think your heart is broken, Lucy," I said, something I was sure she already knew and tried her very best to hide from everyone around her. Or maybe she wasn't even aware of it after all this time.

She didn't look at me, but I caught the sudden rigidity to her body. I'd struck a nerve; that was good. "I think they broke your heart a very long time ago, and you've been walking around, not sure what to do with it, not sure who you can trust to take care of it, ever since you were a little kid."

Very carefully she rested her arms against her stomach and clasped her hands together tightly.

"And I think it's time for you to get the hell out."

She had a beauty mark just below her right eye, so close to her lashes. I'd seen it that first day I'd grabbed her wrist and held her close to my body. Like everything else about her, even that small, inconspicuous dot intrigued me. My eyes found it, and I stifled the urge to reach out and feel it with the tip of my finger.

"I'm not saying it to make you upset, Lucy," I said softly.

"You're not making me upset, *Adam*," she retorted.

"That's good then," I said when it was clear she was shutting down on me.

I dropped my legs down, ready to leave her to her thoughts and get back to Aiden so Dan could leave for the night. Then my eyes focused on hers, and I changed my mind. Mind you, she wasn't looking at me or anything. Her eyes were still focused on the ceiling, and I realized I didn't like that. I didn't like that I was the one who had caused that stiffness in her body when I wanted nothing more than to melt that same body under my hands. But she wasn't ready for it. Not yet. She would be. But not yet.

So, instead of getting up and leaving, I twisted my body so I could get close to her, placed my hand next to her shoulder, leaned down, and stopped when my lips were close enough that she could easily feel my hot breath against her skin. She didn't move a muscle, but more importantly, she didn't stop me.

I sighed and reached out to touch the beauty mark under her eye. She had more of them, one on the tip of her nose, one close to her lip, one right under it hidden by the shadow her lip casted...just like she was hiding her heart.

"What did you wrap around your heart to protect yourself, beautiful girl?" I asked, letting my fingertip trail down from her cheek to her chin. Her eyes cut to mine, and I knew I had her attention. "I see you unwrap it, whatever it is you have around your heart, so I know it's there. You change when you are with your friends, with Aiden, but as soon as you can, you wrap it back up. I hope it's not a steel cage, Lucy. I hope you're being gentle with your heart, taking care of it for me."

She lifted herself up and leaned back on her hands, successfully pushing me away from her face. Her scowl melted into a smirk, but her eyes looked vulnerable. "Was that line from one of your movies?"

"Are you just a character, Lucy? A character that is written by others?" I asked. "Or are you a real person?"

The scowl came back. "Of course I'm real."

"Then don't ask me stupid questions. I don't need to use movie lines to impress someone I'm starting to care about."

"So you think you impressed me? You think I'm that girl who'd melt at your feet just because you said something someone else wrote?"

Instead of answering, I kept at her. "I'm a pretty straightforward guy, Lucy. I don't play games. Not that I can't or don't enjoy certain ones, but this kind of game"—I gestured between us —"I don't want to play. We have one shot at this life, so I'm not gonna spend my time playing games with anybody. I'm not about that. What you see is what you get with me, and the more I look at you, the more I'm around you, the more I like what I see. It's not just your face, your smile, or your beautiful eyes that tell me all kinds of stories every time I look into them long enough. I like how you are with my son, how you actually enjoy spending time with him, how you enjoy the banter between us. I like how you are trying your hardest to protect your heart from me at the same time you're trying not to show how hard it is to do so. I'm telling you that I'm going to give you what you want from me, what you wanted from me from that first day you watched me over that damn wall. I'm going to sleep with you, Lucy Meyer, and I'm going to kiss you, my unexpected stalker. I'm going to kiss you without having to trick you," I announced. Her confused eyes slid back to me. "I'm only telling you because I know you need to prepare yourself for it."

"I don't sleep with guys. I fuck them or let them fuck me and then I ask them to leave. And thanks for the pity sex offer, but I'm not in the mood anymore."

"That's good, because I didn't mean now. I'm not planning on sleeping with you until you admit that you like me too. I'm not expecting a declaration of love from you, but it'd be nice to hear something other than 'I hate you' coming from your lips."

She opened her mouth to speak, but I got there before her.

"Yes, Lucy, even though I sent you to 'prison', you still like me. I'm sure it's eating at you, too." I smiled a little when anger sparked in those beautiful eyes.

I reached up to touch the beauty mark closest to her lip, and she slapped my hand away. I chuckled. It wasn't a hard slap. With us, it was pretty much foreplay at that point.

"But when it happens—'it' being you acknowledging the fact that you like me—I need you to unwrap that protective shield around your heart. I won't...*bump uglies* with you while you're so busy trying to protect your heart that you're missing what's happening around you."

"Nothing is happening, Adam. Whether we do the grand slam or not, nothing will ever happen. I don't even think I want to bump uglies with you anymore. I feel like I'd have better luck finding someone to get me off on Tinder. If you think you can make me fall in love with you, you have another thing coming. I suggest you get over yourself."

She turned her face away and attempted to get up from the bed, but I caught her chin between my thumb and index finger, and she stilled, half of her body facing away from me.

"I have a son," I told her, stating something she of course already knew. "I don't fuck around. If we get into bed, it won't be a one-time thing. I'm not that guy. If something happens between us, I'll be a different guy for you."

"You were married; you didn't have enough time to fuck around yet. And fucking around is fun. Be a guy, go have fun."

"It's been a while since I separated from Adeline, Lucy." I let her chin go, and she settled down. "I had plenty of time and a lot of opportunities. But, like I said, I have a son. I'm not planning to parade a long line of women in front of him. I'm not going to be that parent who leaves him with the assistants and the nannies while I'm off shooting a movie, having the time of my life in another country. And even if there were no Aiden, I've never been that guy. I'm not the life of the party; that never interested me. You're not the only one who doesn't want to end up like their parents."

"What do you mean?" It took her a second to get what I meant and when she did, her eyes bugged out. "Your dad cheated on your mom? The great Nathan Connor cheated on his Helena? And you knew about it?"

"They both had sex with other people, Lucy. I don't think they'd call it cheating. Their idea of love and marriage is different from other people. They worked hard and believed they had the right to play hard, too." I shrugged. "Their choice. Doesn't mean I want to follow in their footsteps. If I wanted to do that, I wouldn't have married Adeline."

"So they had an open marriage."

"Something like that."

"Huh. Didn't see that coming. Color me surprised."

I relaxed. "Do you want to know what a director told me one day?"

"I guess I have time."

I smiled and shook my head at her. She was full of it. "It was my first time working with him. Douglas Trent." I lay down next to her and our arms touched. She didn't pull away. "I think I was eighteen when we started shooting the movie. It was one of the biggest roles I'd gotten so far, and I was working my ass off to prove to everyone on set that I'd auditioned and gotten that role because I'd deserved it, not because of who my parents were."

"You're talking about the movie *The First Day*?"

"Yes. Great cast. Big names. My first day, I was late to the set. My sister...something came up, and I couldn't leave her alone at the house. When I finally made it to set, Douglas met with me in my trailer and laid it out to me. I remember his no-bullshit attitude and it impressed me. Before him, everyone tried their best around me because of my parents and their influence in the industry, so I knew nobody would've minded if I was an hour late for my scenes. He told me that before I set foot on his set, I'd have to decide what mattered to me, what would matter to me in ten years. Did I want to become a Connor, or did I want to become Adam Connor. There is a big distinction between those two, and I was shocked into silence that he could see that after meeting with me only twice. I was impressed because people seeing the difference between those two things is important to me. Don't get me wrong, my parents were great actors, they still are, but...that's another story for another time."

"What else did the director say?" Lucy asked.

"He told me a lot of things. There was one big name among the actors that didn't think I could shoulder the role and keep up with them. We had a lot of scenes together, and he didn't think I was the right choice, and when I was late, I just proved him right. So Douglas asked if I could handle it: the hours, the work, everything. He asked me what mattered to me. Was it the interviews, the fans, the public attention, the women, the money? I told him it was the energy that filled me when I heard the words action, it was the camera, the director, the cast, the script. It was the crew, the preparation for a role. Those were the things that mattered to me. Sure, I'd take the money and the fans and the interviews—all that came with being an actor, but that's just it: those are the things that come *with* being an actor. They are not what matters. They are not the reason I do this. I do this for myself because I seem to have the talent and it is what I want to do. So," I said finally as I turned my head to glance at her. "What matters to you, Lucy? Where do you see yourself in ten years? Will you be busy making sure no one touches your heart again just so you won't end up like your mom and grandmother? Or will you be living your own life on your own terms? Is your life about not being like them or is it your own story?"

"You do know I just broke up with someone, right? It's not like I'm not capable of love. I'm just practical. I know what will happen, so why step off the cliff if I know I'm just gonna fall into the ocean? And like I just said, I did step off that cliff just a few months ago and look what happened."

"I never said you aren't capable of love. And what happened exactly? So you jumped off the cliff and told the guy you loved him. Then you fell into the ocean, and what? Did you love him so much that you will never ever fall in love again?"

She let out a frustrated sigh and sent me an annoyed look. "It's not that. Of course I walked out of the ocean. Just because a guy cast me aside doesn't mean I'm gonna wallow in my tears and secretly love him for the rest of my life."

I pulled her down and under me, causing her to release a sound between a gasp and squeak.

"What do you think you're doing?" she asked.

"I really, really like you, Lucy Meyer. So I'm doing some thinking," I replied, keeping my gaze on her face.

"About what?"

"About how long I'll have to wait until you get over your hang-ups and I get to touch you like I want to touch you."

She gave me a lazy smile and before I could take my eyes away from her smiling lips, she somehow managed to surprise me enough to push me onto my back and maneuver herself over me. The next thing I knew she was straddling me—not all the way down, she made sure our bodies weren't touching, but she was close. *We* were close. I lay there, completely shocked, completely hard, and utterly pleased with her. I'd let her do whatever she was planning to do until I had to stop her. I wasn't interested in playing with her, not like she wanted to. Or maybe that was wrong. I was *very* interested in playing with her, exactly like she wanted to, but not on her terms. Not a quick fuck. Not when every word out of her mouth turned me on beyond any reason.

She placed her hands on either side of me on the bed, leaned down with her body, causing her boobs to press against my chest, and stopped when her lips were only inches away from mine. My hands found her hips, and I lightly held her above me. "You're so sure of yourself, aren't you?" she whispered. "Probably always had girls throwing themselves at you since you were what, four-teen, fifteen? Well, newsflash, Hot Dad, I'm not your fan, not anymore."

She lifted her boobs, cast her eyes down, and looked in between our bodies. I didn't have to follow her eyes to see that my hard-on was noticeable. She had no idea what she was getting herself into.

I tightened my grip on her hips and pulled her slightly forward. She lifted her eyes back to mine, and I watched her throat work as she swallowed. She must have realized she was pressing her boobs against my chest because suddenly she jerked her body upward and did her best to avoid touching my body.

"Why don't you have a seat, Lucy," I suggested, fighting the urge to rip her pants off and guide her down onto me. "Get comfortable."

She pressed her lips together and kept hovering over me.

Just when I thought she was about to climb off me… "Do you know what I like, Adam Connor?" she asked and kept talking instead of waiting for an answer. "I like tattoos; I find them to be very sexy on men. Like, I give you permission to rip my clothes off and take me right where we are standing kinda sexy. I also like a big cock because it feels amazing when a guy knows how to use it." She leaned in farther. "You have no idea...no idea whatsoever how much I love a big, hard cock that can give a good, rough fuck, Adam. The way it feels when I come on them, around them...like it's too much, but not enough at the same time." Her lips stopped next to my ear, and she released a small moan that came from deep in her throat and reached right down to my dick. "And believe me, they make me come *very* hard," she added.

I closed my eyes and smiled before she could catch it. She lifted her head and kept talking, not realizing that she was digging herself deeper into me. There was nothing, *nothing* that could ever be sexier than a woman who knew what she wanted from a man in bed, who didn't have any issues with sharing what got her off, or how she wanted to get off. And Lucy Meyer was already dangerously sexy in my book.

Right at that moment, Lucy Meyer was pushing herself under my skin without even realizing it, and I was about to push myself right under hers, even deeper than I already had.

"I like a man who knows what he can do with his tongue, his hands, *and* his cock. I like a man who makes me beg for more, who makes me burn for him, over and over." She kept going. "He'll have to know how to take everything from me." She patted my chest with her hand and her tone changed as she backed off. "You're not that guy, Adam Connor. You look like you could be that man, but no, you're not."

"You really think I'm not that man?"

She nodded. "I'll even give you an explanation free of charge. First of all, you're not a good kisser. You make me feel nothing at all. We learned that the hard way. And we also established the fact that you have a small cock. Small for me," she corrected hastily. "I'm sure some girls would be into that since you're a movie star and all. And hands…" She licked her lips. "Okay. You have big hands. I'll give you that much. But I'm doubtful you know how to use them properly." Standing on her knees, she straightened up. "So, as you can see, we don't match. You're a good actor and all, but I need more than good acting in bed."

She lifted her knee to get off me, and I used that moment to take back the bit of control I'd let her have.

She dropped to her back with a shocked gasp and this time it was me hovering over her, inches away from her lips.

"You want to hear what I'd like to do to you, Lucy? What I'm going to do to you when you stop with all the acting?"

"Goody. Can't wait to hear it." Her words came out breathlessly.

I nudged the side of her nose with my own and gently forced her to bare her neck to me. Then quietly and unhurriedly, against her throat, I said, "First, I'm going to kiss you until you forget your very own name, Lucy Meyer. I don't care if it takes hours to taste every inch of this beautiful mouth, I won't stop kissing you until you're a dripping mess for me and your heart is beating out of your chest with excitement about my kiss." I curved my hand right under her neck and let my thumb gently caress the soft skin. Her eyes glazed over with lust. "While I'm still kissing you, Lucy…" I whispered, ghosting my mouth right over hers. Her lips parted, and I realized her eyes had already closed on their own. *You're not that guy, my ass.*

"I'm going to undress you so I can touch every inch of your body. With my lips, my hands…" I kissed a path down from the edge of her lips to the neckline of her T-shirt and let my hand travel down to her waist. When I reached the hem, I ordered my cock to ignore her harsh intake of breath and reached under her shirt to touch her skin. "So soft," I murmured as I pressed my lips right underneath her ear and let my palm wander upward, slowly heading toward her breasts.

Her breathing quickened, and she opened her eyes.

Storms. Two beautiful storms looking right into my soul.

She was angry, I could see that much, but she also looked hungry, so I gave in and gently kissed her lips. My hand tightened around her waist when she started shifting her hips under me. Her tongue came out to wet her bottom lip, and I softly bit into it, pulling a low moan from her.

"Just a small taste," I said. "Just to hold you over." Her scowl came back in full force. "Maybe I'll put my cock right in here and let you have a taste before I do anything else. Or maybe I won't. Maybe I won't be able to stop myself from going deep inside you before I make a mess in your mouth and watch you swallow it all."

"Who said I'd swallow?" she asked as her hands made little fists.

I grinned—I couldn't help it—and watched her eyes flick over to my mouth. "Oh, you can't wait to swallow it all up, can you, Lucy? Just like how I can't wait to lick every inch of your pussy."

Seconds ticked by as we stared at each other.

Finally, she swallowed. "What else would you do? Not that you'll get a chance, just curious…"

"Oh, I'll do a lot of things to you, Lucy. I'll definitely let you do a lot of stuff to me, too, because I know you'll enjoy getting your hands on me." I looked down at her body where my hand had pulled her shirt up, and I could see the bare skin of her stomach. Don't ask me how I managed to stop my hand from going higher, but I did, and covered her up again.

"Too bad I can't just tear off your clothes and show you how many things I can make you feel if only you let me, how loud I can make you cry out when I overwhelm you in the best possible way as your pretty little pussy contracts around me," I murmured, looking into her eyes. "I bet you have a greedy pussy. I bet you'd beg me to give you more." If I thought seeing and touching her bare skin was too much temptation, the look I saw in her eyes was the killing blow. "Too bad I need to leave and can't have you to myself all night."

She cocked her head and pulled herself up on her elbows as I leaned away from her. And then she was pushing against my chest and climbing up on me again.

"You should stop doing that," I mumbled as I reached up to hold her hair away from her face, away from those beautiful eyes I couldn't seem to look away from. Seeing her cheeks slightly flushed and her chest rising and falling with deep breaths made my already hard dick jump in my pants.

"Are you ready to admit how much you like me?"

She shook her head. "Every time I tell myself maybe I don't hate the guy, you go and do something to show me that I actually hate you very much."

Surprised, I asked, "What did I do now to earn your hate?"

"You're speaking. And touching me. And whispering. And leaning in too close. And looking into my eyes. You're making your voice go all throaty. Stop it. When I tell you we can't have sex, you talk about my heart and all this stuff that isn't your concern."

I let go of her hair and raised my hands up in surrender.

"I didn't know you wanted to have sex with me that bad, Lucy."

She groaned. "I don't! That's my point. But you made me talk about big cocks that know what they're doing and..." Unexpectedly, she grabbed my wrist and pushed my hand right in her pants.

I could've stopped her. I could've pulled her down on me and told her to behave right before I took her lips in a crushing kiss. I could've done a lot of things instead of curving my fingers and letting them slip into her slick heat, but she was too intriguing, and I was too damn curious to see how she would explain her dripping wetness while insisting she felt nothing when I put my hands and lips on her.

"So this happened," she explained lamely in a breathy voice.

"Look at that," I murmured, softly playing with her pussy lips and clit, spreading her wetness all over her. "This happened because I made you talk about cocks?"

She nodded eagerly, and my eyes fell down to her hands, which were still gripping my wrist in an effort to keep my hand in place.

"I guess I should apologize for this," I relented, pushing my middle finger a little deeper until it passed through her tight muscles. "For making you this wet, I mean."

She tipped her head back, just slightly, and her hips jerked, pulling my finger in deeper.

"You didn't make me wet," she whispered, releasing a small moan when I swirled my finger inside her and then roughly pushed all the way in. The way her body came alive right in front of my eyes, the way she bit her bottom lip as a small gasp escaped her lips...every little thing she did was pulling me right to the edge of insanity.

"I didn't?" I pulled my finger out of her tight pussy and ran my finger over and around her sensitive clit. "That's too bad then." Before I could take my hand out of her panties, she stopped me.

"Wait! Wait!"

"Yes?"

She scowled at me and let out a frustrated sigh. "This is why I don't like you."

I pulled my hand out.

"Wait! Goddamnit!" Determined, she grabbed my wrist and pushed it back in. God, her eyes really did something to me, that determined but unfocused look combined with that stormy color.

She was a storm all on her own. Hell, she'd been a hurricane ever since she had tumbled into my life.

"Fine. Fine, your voice did me in," she admitted finally.

"Hmmm," I murmured, gently pushing my finger back into her pussy. "You like my voice, and my hand. For a girl who claims she hates me, you seem to like a lot of things about me."

"Just your hand and your voice. Everything else about you…I hate it."

Pressing my free hand against her back, I flipped her under me again.

"Hate is a very strong emotion, Lucy. And you know what they say about love and hate: it'd be so easy for you to tip over that edge into love."

She opened her legs to me willingly and then got in my face. "Keep dreaming."

I smiled at her.

"We'll see."

Widening her legs a bit more, I pushed another finger inside her burning heat and watched her eyes lose focus again.

"I think—"

Sneaking my free hand under her neck, I held her mouth to mine and kissed the words out of her mouth while I enjoyed her arousal soaking my fingers. Every time I kissed her, I could hear the blood humming in my veins. And more than that, I could feel her trembling under me, her body vibrating with the need she was trying her best to conceal.

Even though I knew it would piss her off, I had to take my raging hard-on and leave. So I pulled my fingers out of her pussy, gripped her chin, and deepened the gentle kiss I was giving her just before I let her lips go and got up from the bed to saunter to the door.

"What?" she mumbled, looking up at me in confusion. "What are you doing?"

Damn those beautiful boobs of hers. The way I could see those perfect nipples moving up and down as her chest moved with her labored breaths was pushing my cock's patience to its limits. "Good night, Lucy."

Her face sobered, and she gave me a blank look. "You're leaving? Now?"

"I'd love nothing more than to listen to you moan under me all night as I bury my cock in a certain part of your body, but you don't even like me, remember? Tell me you like me and maybe I'll change my mind."

"I don't like you."

I nodded. "That's what I thought. Besides, I need to get back to Aiden."

When she heard Aiden's name, her shoulders seemed to relax a bit, and she pulled her knees up to hug them against her chest. "So you weren't planning on staying even if I lied and said I liked you. Nice. What a standup guy."

I shrugged and opened the door. "Maybe not. But I would've definitely taken you with me."

"I wouldn't have come."

Stepping out of her room, I looked back at her and smiled. "I think you would've, my little stalker. Actually, I think you would have come more times than you ever did with any other guy."

Her eyes narrowed, and she paused as if she wasn't sure if she should speak the next words, but it didn't take long before she did. I found myself wondering if she ever held anything back. "Thank you for stopping before I could make a big mistake."

Damn it, but with every word out of her mouth she issued a new challenge I just couldn't not accept. And *that* was the biggest turn on for me—after her beautiful face, those stormy eyes, and those nipples, of course…and I guess it wouldn't be fair to leave out her perfect ass.

"You're welcome," I agreed readily. "You might be onto

something. I wasn't sure you could keep up with me or satisfy me enough, anyway. I'd hate to try and fake it just to protect your delicate feelings."

I heard her little growl and closed the door before the pillow she threw could hit me in the face.

I couldn't wait to watch those beautiful eyes of hers roll back in her head.

CHAPTER FIFTEEN

"Olive."

"Olive, wake up."

Nothing. Not even a groan.

"Olive. Olive. Olive."

Finally a groan. "Go away, Lucy."

"You have to wake up," I said as I started pushing both of my hands on the bed to make her bounce on it.

"Give me a good reason and I'll consider opening my eyes," she mumbled, turning away from me and hugging the pillow tighter to herself.

"Because I woke up."

"Yeah. I don't think so. Nice try, now go away."

"Olive."

"Lucy."

I sighed and got on the bed. "Olive, wake up."

"Lucy, go away."

This time it was me who groaned.

"That's not how we play the game, Olive. I come to your room to wake you up and you wake up. And I can't even lie on your boobies and get comfortable because you're lying on top of them. Squishing them. Killing them. Have a heart, woman!"

"What did you do to Jason?"

"What did *I* do to him? Were you dreaming of us having a threesome?" I gave her a gentle push and settled down to lie next to her. "I'm flattered that you chose me to play a role in your fantasies, my green Olive. Give me all the details."

She released a long sigh. "You're not going away, are you?"

"Umm…" I pulled one of her pillows from under her head. "Nope."

"That's what I thought. Okay." She accepted the inevitable and plopped onto her back, hitting the covers a little too enthusiastically for my taste. "What time is it?"

"Nine something."

"Really? Well, that's a first. You usually wake me up at a more ungodly hour."

"See?" I bumped her shoulder with mine. "I can be nice. I'm a good friend."

"Okay. Now that I'm awake…why am I awake again?"

"Because I have news."

"Good news or bad news?" Olive asked as she lifted the covers so I could get under them. As much as she acted like she hated when I woke her up early, I knew she loved my visits to her bedroom just as much as I did.

Okay, maybe not as much as I did, clearly, but she loved them nonetheless.

I thought about the things I wanted to share with her and couldn't decide if they were bad news or good news. Definitely a few good ones, but maybe a colossal bad one that would eclipse all the good news? I wasn't going to think about that one until I was forced to.

"A few good ones, maybe a few bad ones, too?" I ventured without committing to anything.

"Okay. Hit me."

"Which one do you want first?"

"Give me all the good ones first."

I nodded. Good choice. "The best one among all the good ones is that I got you..." I drew out the word and paused just to build up more tension.

"Yes...you got me...?"

"I got you...a freaking AUDIOBOOK deal for *Soul Ache*!"

She sat up in bed and looked at me with big eyes. "We have a deal?"

"Yup. We got one. And that's not even the best part about it." Having trouble containing my energy, I sat up and crossed my legs.

"Tell me already!"

"You're going to be the narrator!"

Her face fell. "What? The narrator? Why would I be the narrator?"

"Because who would read your book better than you?"

"Lucy. No."

I pushed at her shoulder, and she staggered back. "Olive. Yes."

Shaking her head, she got out of the bed. "No way. I'm not doing that."

I watched her pace the length of the bed and let out a long breath. "Yes, you will. And you wanna know why you'll do it with the biggest smile on your face, my green Olive?"

"Oh, please, enlighten me."

"Because your freaking husband is your co-narrator, that's why."

The pacing stopped, and I had trouble containing my giddy smile.

"Jason? He'll read with me? You talked to him about this?"

"Of course I did. As much as I think I should have the right, since I practically gave you to him wrapped up in a pretty little package, I can't make decisions like that in his name. So I talked to him a few days ago and considering the size of that smile he gave me, he really, and I mean *really* liked that idea. The publisher loved it too, sooo...it's a go!"

She climbed on the bed again, sitting on her heels and wearing the cutest grin on her face. "You're a genius, Lucy. I love that idea. I don't like the fact that I'm gonna be reading it, but me and Jason...I love it."

I smiled back at her. "You're welcome, my little green Olive. At first they were concerned about paying Jason, but he doesn't want anything, so the deal is only for the audio rights for *Soul Ache*. You're getting a very big chunk of an advance for it. I made sure of that."

"So that means you're getting a big chunk of commission, too."

I furrowed my brows. "Uh, no. I'm just helping you. And I actually like having the title of temporary agent, so I'm keeping that, but yeah, I'm not taking your money."

"Yes, you are. Why the hell would you spend so much time talking to so many publishing companies?"

"Because I'm helping you."

"Yes. Because you're good at this stuff. With numbers, with getting people to do what you want them to do. And you care about my work. You care about my characters and you want the best for me. I don't think there is a better agent than you for me, so I'm keeping you and you're keeping your commission."

I narrowed my eyes at her and considered her words. I mean, I did need a job, that was already an established fact, but taking money from my best friend...I didn't care for that idea all that much. She was my best friend, my sister from another mister. I'd help her as much as I could and truly enjoyed helping her with anything she needed, but when—

Olive snapped her fingers in my face, breaking into my thoughts. "There is nothing for you to think about. I asked you to be my agent. Agents get paid. You got a deal for me, which makes you officially my agent. Not a temporary one. I didn't even ask you to get me an audiobook deal, yet you still did. You're my agent, Lucy. And you get twenty-five percent."

"Twenty-five percent? Are you crazy? Do you even know how much of an advance you're getting?"

Was I really considering taking money from my friend? And that amount of money? I didn't think so.

"That's around what agents take. Every book deal, audio deal, foreign rights, or whatever you get in front of me to sign, you'll get twenty-five percent of it, both from the advance *and* the royalties."

Feeling uncomfortable, I shook my head and shifted in place. "No way." No *freaking* way, that was too much money. "Twenty-five is too much. Don't give that much of your money to *anyone*."

She shrugged as if I was the one who was talking nonsense. "You're my agent. You'll look out for me and get me the best deals possible. You already did it. I don't know why we're still talking about this. I would never even think of suggesting that I could narrate the book with Jason. Even if I did think of that, I could hardly get them to say yes on it. Also, Jason already played Isaac, are you sure his contract wouldn't be a problem?"

"Way ahead of you. I already talked about that with his agent. Tom said it would be a good promotion for the movie when it's out on DVD. And he checked the contract to make sure, too. Everything is okay on that front."

"See?" She pushed my shoulder with her index finger—a little too hard. "You already thought of everything. You're my agent."

"Yeah," I relented and rubbed the spot she had just poked. "I'm an agent who doesn't even have an ARC of your next book. What an agent. Maybe you should ask Jasmine to be your agent."

Was I still a little jealous about that? Yeah, maybe. So what?

Olive extended her hand and gestured with her chin for me to take it. So I took it.

"Twenty-five percent."

I sighed. "Ten percent."

She gave me a bored look. "Twenty-four percent."

I think you can guess how long it took us to agree on a number, but in case you're not sure, a long, long time. There was a lot of handshaking along with nodding and some more head-shaking. At the end of it, we agreed on fifteen percent and that was it.

"Now can we go to sleep?" she asked with a hopeful look. "Maybe a short nap?"

I tackle-hugged her, and we fell onto the pillows. "We're working together."

She laughed. "Yes. I can already hear the distant sound of you cracking the whip."

I let out another long sigh. "Always thinking the worst of me. I'm being very nice to all the publishers."

"I love it when you crack the whip, so it's all good. Wouldn't want anyone else to be my agent. You know what you should do?"

"What?"

"You should call Catherine and let her know you got a job."

I gazed at the ceiling, my stomach turning. "I don't think she'd be happy to hear that at all. She really wanted me to take that accounting job."

Feeling Olive's eyes on me, I did my best to look unaffected, but she knew me enough to see through it.

"Okay. I shouldn't have even brought her up. My bad."

I made a noncommittal sound and tried not to think about any of the bad stuff. "All right, are you ready for the second piece of good news?"

"No napping, then? Fine. Hit me."

"No napping because we're going out to celebrate the audio-book deal."

"Mimosas?"

Alcohol…I wasn't sure I could do that. I wanted to drink all the alcohol, all the tequila I could get my hands on, but I was very afraid that I wasn't going to be able to do that for quite some time. I nodded anyway and thanked all my stars that Olive didn't question my silence and left it at that.

"Now before a celebratory breakfast, the second piece of good news is that I have a much, much bigger, like a humongous-ly big deal I'm trying to finalize before I tell you about it, and the third piece of good news is that I found an apartment!"

Olive propped herself up on her elbow and looked at me with a pouty mouth, looking all sad and heartbroken. "What? You're leaving?"

I turned onto my side to face her. "Did you hear what I said about the humongous-ly big deal? No?"

She kept staring at me, so I rolled my eyes.

"I've been here for weeks, Olive, and I've been looking for a small apartment since the day I got here, I just hadn't found anything."

"And now you have. Where?"

"Closer to our old apartment. You remember the tea shop that closed? The one where you dumped a cup of tea over my head and got us kicked out? Two blocks from that. It's still close to USC, so I think I'm gonna look into getting a roommate."

She eyed me sharply. "I didn't dump it over your head. I tripped and fell."

"Yes. You fell on me. When you had a hot cup of tea in your hand."

"It wasn't hot. It had cold milk in it. Anyway, you survived.

And you shouldn't leave now. Not when you're getting closer to Adam and Aiden."

I snorted and let out a not-so-ladylike laugh. "Getting closer to Adam Connor? Are you kidding me? I hate him even more than I did a few days ago."

"Why? Because he isn't doing those pushups anymore?"

Jesus! Even my own friend was taking that self-absorbed bastard's side. I sank back into the bed.

"So disappointed in you right now, my green Olive. I bet you won't feel all lovey-dovey toward him when you hear that he broke into your house last night."

Hmmm, maybe I could convince Olive to press charges against the Hotshot Movie Star. Now, wouldn't that be a great plot twist! And such great revenge, too. However, Olive was quick to kill those beautiful dreams.

"He didn't break in. He called Jason, and he let him in. And I was right on the other side of your door after he sneaked into your room because I had to listen and learn why he was here, but Jason pulled me away, and I couldn't hear a damn thing. So spill already. Did he rock your world?"

"We didn't have sex," I mumbled under my breath.

"Not for your lack of trying, I assume?"

Ignoring Olive, I reached for her phone on the bedside table and checked the time.

"Look at that, we need to head out. I don't want to be stuck in traffic until lunchtime. My stomach is grumbling; I need food, maybe waffles, maybe eggs, maybe croissants, maybe all of the above. I also need coffee. Then I'll probably need dessert. Come on, lazy head." I jumped out of bed and smacked her with one of the pillows. "We're going out to celebrate."

"I'll never understand your enthusiasm for mornings, Lucy." She pulled the pillow out of my hand when I was about to smack her—lightly, of course—again and pushed her hair out of her face.

Just as she was rolling out of the bed, she stopped and turned to me with a frown. "You said you had good news *and* bad news. You never told me the bad news."

I avoided eye contact and played with the edge of the covers to have something to occupy myself with. "Let's just say we have to swing by Target to get something. I'll tell you all about it after the celebratory breakfast. I'm dying from hunger, come on." I threw the cover at her face. "Stop torturing me and get up."

"Jesus. Fine." She flung the covers and hopped down from the bed after a long stretch and yawn. "What time is it?"

"Maybe around…eight-ish," I said over my shoulder as I walked toward the door with quick steps—everyone needs a head start when they are running away from an angry female.

As I reached the doorframe, she dropped her hands, very slowly, and looked at me with murder in her eyes. So, obviously I smiled at her. Big. "It's called breakfast for a reason, it has to happen very early, Olive. Don't be mad at me."

"If I were you, I'd start running."

A Father Fighting for His Son: Another Custody Battle?

Remember the last time we mentioned we were hearing rumors circling around about the possibility of a custody battle between Adam Connor and Adeline Young? Well, the day has come, folks. The battle has begun.

Now, usually when a celebrity couple goes through a custody battle, we rely on sources close to the couple to spill about what goes on behind those closed doors, because who doesn't like a healthy dose of drama when it comes to the lives of their favorite celebrities? But in this case, we think the reason behind this new development is pretty obvious, wouldn't you agree?

Yesterday, Adam Connor released a statement saying he had nothing against the mother of his child, but to ensure his son's safety in light of recent events, he was filing papers to request primary custody of his son, Aiden Connor. The only comment that addressed the paparazzi mess in the statement was made in one single sentence: "Understandably, Aiden is still uneasy about what happened, but he is doing better."

Hollywood's hottest dad also pointed out that he wasn't trying to sever the relationship between the mother and son, that he was okay with Adeline Young having visitation rights. To top it all off, even though Adam Connor stressed that he wasn't doing this to hurt Adeline and was only thinking about what his son needed at this point in his life, we think Adeline will be plenty pissed when she gets the call from her lawyer.

What are your thoughts on this? After Adeline got slammed by the media outlets and diehard Connor fans because of the way she handled everything after the incident, we are thinking this might not have been her first clash with Adam on how she is raising their son—or not raising, in her case. Do you think she'll fight this?

If you were a fan of the couple and were rooting for them to get back together…we'd say it's time to say goodbye to those dreams. When we tried to reach Adeline's reps for a comment on Adam's statement, but the only thing we heard was crickets. No doubt they'll release a statement on their own when they've had enough time to regroup, so we'll make sure to keep you in the loop on future updates.

We'll leave you with the best part of Adam's statement.

"My son means everything to me. I have to know he is safe. I have to make sure he isn't worrying about things he shouldn't even think about or know about at his age—like being scared about whether a man with a camera will jump out from behind the bushes when he is playing in his own backyard. The only way to do that is if he is in my care and I know where he is and whom he is with at all times. Again, I have nothing against Adeline. We still talk, we still spend time together, and I wish her nothing but the best. This is not about us. It is about what's best for Aiden. While I get that this may be front-page news for some people, I'm asking you to respect our privacy going forward. Please don't make this out to be something it isn't. This isn't Adam Connor fighting with Adeline Young. This is a father fighting for what's best for his son."

CHAPTER SIXTEEN

LUCY

Sometimes it takes years for your life to change. In some cases, a lifetime. You wake up one morning, look around, and suddenly realize that everything has changed. The people you thought were your friends, loved ones…they are long gone. Your life isn't the same. Time has slipped away and you didn't even notice a thing.

However, sometimes…sometimes it can change right in front of your eyes.

All it takes is the blink of an eye.

One moment you think you can handle anything life throws at you…and the next moment…well, to put it nicely…you're screwed.

While I was sitting all by my lonesome in Olive's backyard, those were the thoughts that were crossing my mind. That I was screwed. That I had fucked up.

Royally.

I had left Olive and Jason inside after telling them the news and had come out because 'it was such a beautiful night and I had to do some stargazing'…which actually meant I needed to get some fresh air and try my best to assure myself that everything would be okay and that I should just breathe. Just close my eyes and breathe. When Olive got up to join me, from the corner of my eye I saw Jason gently grabbing her hand and shaking his head.

I didn't think he'd be able to keep her inside for long, but I appreciated him trying all the same.

Having successfully breathed for at least a few minutes without having a sudden heart attack, I looked over my shoulder to see if Olive and Jason were still up.

They were. And they were dancing.

With no music.

I still don't know what about that scene struck my heart so strongly, but I remember the raw pain I felt in my chest.

Don't get me wrong, it wasn't jealousy. I wanted nothing but happiness for them, but maybe it was the first time I'd wanted someone to hold me that closely, to look at me just like Jason was looking at Olive. His fingers were playing with her hair as Olive's head rested against his chest. Eyes closed.

There was no music.

Nothing but the two of them in the world.

So, for a brief moment, I wanted the same for myself.

The feeling of security that someone was there to hold you up when gravity was too much to handle on your own, that you had someone you could trust enough to let go.

Just for a moment, I wanted someone to hold me up and tell me everything would be okay, that my fears were uncalled for.

When I heard music drifting over from nearby, I hesitated only for a moment before I hauled my ass up from the ground and carefully climbed over the wall that stood between Adam Connor and me.

As I followed the stone pathway, I stopped moving when I saw him standing in front of the glass windows watching me. It was a slightly different version of the Adam Connor I'd seen that first night with Olive: button-up shirt, rolled up sleeves, black slacks…the only difference was that he didn't look like he was trying to figure something out. The opposite, actually. As we stared at each other, he looked like he'd figured everything out.

He was everything a girl could ever want.

Not to mention the hottest DILF.

Feeling a sudden chill in my bones, I hugged my arms and kept walking toward him.

He never looked away from my eyes as he opened the door for me.

Before he could say anything, I took a step forward, leaned up, and kissed him. It wasn't an 'I want to fuck your brains out' type of kiss, even though I wouldn't have minded doing just that. It was…a different kind. A kind I didn't want to name.

Oh, hell. Fine. It was a sweet kiss. The kind of kiss I avoided.

He didn't stop me. He stood there, his lips moving so softly against mine as I did my best to quiet my screaming heart.

When his arm gently touched my waist, either to push me away or pull me in—I couldn't take the chance—I pulled back from his lips and started hearing the music again.

"Lucy…" Adam murmured, his hot breath against my wet lips.

"I don't know this song," I murmured back and finally looked into his eyes. "I know it's George Michael, but I don't know the song."

He was silent for a moment as he searched for something in my eyes.

"It's called 'Jesus to A Child'," he said after an awkward silence.

I nodded, but said nothing more.

"You came over to ask about the song?"

"I've never heard of it. It's a beautiful song."

"It's old and it *is* a beautiful song."

Those vivid green eyes that were looking at me with such intensity were also gentle. Could he see what I needed even though *I* had no idea what that was anymore? I forced a smile on my lips, trying my hardest not to show how much I was shaking inside as I stood in front of him.

You shouldn't have climbed over that wall to get to him, my brain screamed at me. *You shouldn't have listened to your stupid heart.*

"Do you like dancing?" I asked, ignoring common sense.

"No."

"Oh," I said, surprised. "Okay."

"Ask me anyway," he countered.

I hesitated.

"Will you dance with me?"

"Yes."

He took my hand in his warm, big one and pulled me inside. As soon as he closed the door and turned to me, I walked up to him, put my hand on his heart, and rested my head next to it. His body froze for a moment, but then he circled one of his arms around my waist and pulled my body closer to his.

I released the breath I was holding and something eased in my heart.

Something eased in my *stupid* heart, I should say.

He didn't ask me what was wrong, though I knew he would eventually. All he did was gently push my hair behind my ear and rest his chin on the top of my head.

My *fucking* stupid heart shivered.

Then he lifted his left hand and pulled my hand away from his heart. That was a little disappointing, but I knew I was taking it too far.

As I dropped my hand, he caught it midway and started

linking our fingers together. My eyes opened, and I watched the pad of his thumb lightly caress the sensitive skin between my thumb and index finger as my fingers fit perfectly in between his.

I curled my fingers around his hand and held on.

Never lifting my head up from his chest, I glanced at him through my lashes, only to see his sole focus was on our hands. He looked...he looked different. Thoughtful. Worried? Then he blinked and brought my hand back to rest against his chest, his own hand covering mine.

The nerve...I know.

I was the one who was trying to seduce him out of his pants; he had no right, *no right* whatsoever to try and seduce my heart.

But...I let him hold my hand anyway. It was comfortable.

Standing like that with him was comfortable. Hearing his steady heartbeat. His warmth against my body.

The hand splayed on my back was just as comforting as his hand holding mine. It tethered me to the world.

Or maybe just to him.

It was all so easy on my heart.

And it was all so scary.

I still let him. Don't judge me. If you were me, by now you would've melted away; at least I was still standing upright. I win, you lose.

So I let him hold my heart in his hands. It was only for a moment anyway.

Suddenly the song ended and the silence that filled the room was somehow louder than George Michael had been. It only lasted for a few seconds as the same song started back again.

But...for those few seconds, Adam had kept us moving in a gentle sway and I'd gotten my wish. I'd danced with no music. Even if it was for a fleeting moment, I'd had what Olive and Jason had.

And that should've scared me shitless...but it didn't.

Did I mention what a stupid heart I possessed?

I closed my eyes again and let Adam dictate our moves as I absorbed the painful words. It wasn't just the words either. You could tell he was in pain too—George Michael, I mean.

He was in pain for the love he had lost, and I was lost searching for the love I knew I could never have.

"Is it true? What he is saying?" I asked, my voice low.

"Which part?"

"Does love really hold bliss?"

"You tell me. You were the one with the boyfriend."

"And you were the one with the wife. With Jameson…I loved him…but it wasn't like that. I never had that."

"What do you mean?"

"He was…we were…we were great in bed, I'll tell you that much, but out of it…I don't know, I never trusted him like Olive trusts Jason. He was a flirt. He wasn't serious about it, but it still hurt to see that he wasn't all that different with other people than he was with me. When I catch Jason looking at Olive, even when she is doing something mundane like drinking water or generally acting like a crazy person, I see his lips tipping up. If I'm feeling extra mushy and look hard enough, I can actually see his love for her. Again, mushy, I know, but it looks beautiful on them. Love looks beautiful on them. It looks right. Before I came here…" I hesitated, not sure if I should share or not. "They were dancing with no music. In the middle of their living room, they danced with no music."

"Ah," he muttered, his hand moving a few inches up and down on my back—a gentle, soothing caress I wasn't expecting. "That's where the dance invitation came from."

"No," I denied quickly…a little too quickly, maybe. "No. I wasn't jealous of them or anything like that," I repeated. "The song. I liked the song. I came for…the song."

"I like the song too, Lucy," he murmured so softly I almost didn't catch it.

Were we even talking about the song anymore? It didn't sound like he was talking about the song.

When he didn't continue, I closed my eyes and focused on the damn song and the lyrics again. I liked the song. Heck, I think I loved the song. I *didn't* like Adam Connor, though. He wasn't the reason I had come over. I certainly wasn't falling for him or anything stupid like that. It didn't matter what my heart was saying, it didn't matter how my body lit up every time his skin was on mine. It *didn't*.

Maybe.

"Relax, Lucy," Adam muttered, and I noticed we had stopped moving. I took a deep breath and let everything out.

The song ended and started up again.

It was a really good song.

A few minutes into the song...or maybe it was only a few seconds in, I took a deep breath. In Adam's arms, feeling unattached yet connected to something I couldn't name, I had lost track of time, the world, and the situation I had put myself in. Suddenly, Adam let go of my arm, and I thought about fighting him for his hand, to have him hold it just for a few more seconds, just until the song ended, just until...but I didn't want to be *that* girl who asked for something she knew she wouldn't get.

Snap out of it, Lucy!

His fingertips touched my chin, and he tilted my head back and away from his chest.

I looked deep into his green eyes and found out that I didn't want to look away. I didn't want to interrupt whatever he was doing to my heart.

Witchcraft maybe?

His lips parted as his brows furrowed. Was that anger I saw in his eyes?

"Why are you crying?" he asked in a hard voice. "What happened?"

I frowned at him and touched my face. When I looked down, I could see wetness on my fingers. I was crying? When? How?

"I…" I started, but couldn't find the words, didn't know how to finish the thought as the tears kept coming. *This must be what they call hormones.* I already didn't like it.

"Lucy…"

He tilted my head up again and his thumb wiped away my tears.

The tears didn't stop coming. His hand on my back tightened, and I lost myself a little more, felt myself falling a little further. Despite having his hard body pressed against mine, his hand holding me in place, I could feel my body start to shake, the hopelessness of the day finally catching up to me.

I put my hands on his chest and tried to push him away, but it was like trying to push away a lion that didn't want to move. He somehow managed to pull me closer, and I let him.

"Lucy," he warned, his voice gravelly. "Tell me what's wrong."

We stared into each other's eyes for so long.

"I'm pregnant," I admitted in a broken voice. Adam let go of me.

It was the lowest moment of my life. Not that being pregnant was anything bad because for someone else, someone who wanted to have a baby, someone who was looking forward to having a baby…it was everything. For me…being pregnant was the confirmation I'd never wanted to receive.

I really was cursed.

"I did it," I said, curling my arms around my stomach. "I'm just like them. I'll be just like them. Bitter. Unhappy. Angry." I lifted my eyes up to meet his. "Not at the baby. Never at the baby.

I'll always be angry at myself, and I'll end up being angry at the world. I should've never said 'I love you' to Jameson. He was a flirt, yet I still said I loved him. I knew it would never work, but I still said those stupid words. And now I'm being punished. I should've...I shouldn't—"

Why the hell was I still crying?

"I'm not crying because I'm sad," I tried to explain, my voice rising. I was such a disgrace to womankind. "I'm angry. These are stupid angry tears. Or hormone tears, I don't know! I don't wanna cry!"

Then his lips were on mine and my words got lost between us with my gasp. His fingers tangled in my hair as I pushed myself up on my tiptoes to put my arms around his neck and pull him down to me. This one wasn't a sweet kiss or a lazy one. This one was full of life, full of pain, pleasure, hate, anger, even a little bit of hope and love.

I took a deep breath through my nose.

Shit! The smell. The smell of his skin.

Don't breathe, Lucy. Don't breathe. He's toxic. Don't do it.

The hell with it! I moaned and breathed in his scent. His fingers tightened in my hair, and I let his tongue surround mine, licking, sucking, pulling, pushing as he slanted his head in every possible angle.

I was done for.

This was the end of me.

With a guttural groan, he tilted my head with his hands and went in deeper, took more from me. I grabbed at his collar, clawed at his neck, pushed my fingers into his hair, pulling on it. Hard. The hiss of pain he whispered into my mouth was beyond satisfying to hear, to feel vibrate through my body.

He tilted his head the other way and kissed me into oblivion. His body was towering over me, forcing me to move a couple steps back. It was perfect. It might have been the best moment of my life. At the very least, top five.

Hell, it was the only kiss that actually deserved to be called a kiss. The way his hand moved, his fingers threading into my hair, his palm cupping the back of my head with the perfect amount of gentleness and roughness, holding me just where he wanted me…the way I could almost hear his wild heartbeat…the way I pulled at his hair, clawed at his neck to get him closer so I could drown myself in him…

The way my entire body was begging for him, trembling to feel his hot skin on mine, every one of our movements jerky and frantic.

It was a beautiful mess.

It was the perfect mess.

My heart…my own frantic heartbeat drowned out every other noise but him.

Everything but him was just white noise.

Holy hell!

My body burning brighter and trembling harder in his arms, I let out a soundless protest when he took his lips away from mine. With my eyes still closed, I leaned forward to take them back, but his whispered words forced me to come back down to earth.

"Stop, Lucy. Stop."

Wasn't he aching just as much as I was? Didn't he want me?

I wanted him. I wanted him inside me.

Oh God, I wanted to have his cock inside me. I wanted him to never stop kissing me. I never wanted that connection I'd just felt to break. That warmth. That tremble he gave me. That high I felt when his lips stopped my world.

"Look at me," he whispered in a low voice, and I had to force my eyes to blink open so I could actually *see* him.

God, he looked so good. Those fucking eyes of his were killing me. I'd never look at that shade of green the same way again. Still breathless and unsettled, I let go of his hair and rested my hands on top of his shoulders. Jesus, his hair looked like he'd just had the best fuck of his life. I lived for kisses like that; the ones that made you feel like you'd been fucked good and well without even having a cock in your vagina.

"That was…holy hell, that was a good kiss, Adam Connor." I cleared my throat and patted his shoulder. "You're learning. Glad to help."

"It was the only way to stop you from spewing bullshit and crying."

I stopped breathing and my body turned rigid in his arms.

"What? You kissed me so I'd stop crying on you? You…you jerk!" I pulled away from him, but he caught my wrist in midair and roughly pulled me against his chest.

"Let me go," I said through gritted teeth.

"Shut up," he said hoarsely, his fingers loosening around my wrist. "Please, just shut up for a second."

I didn't move.

"How?" he asked after almost a full minute of looking into each other's eyes, breathing in each other's air. "Lucy, how are you pregnant?"

Oh, right…

I did my best to get my breathing under control and pushed my hair away from my face with my free hand. It was unsettling to have all of his attention on me, those eyes piercing my well-constructed walls as fast as I tried to build them up. Also I could still smell his goddamned cologne, which did stupid things to my poor, neglected vagina…and maybe my heart.

"When a penis enters a vagina and then—"

His eyes still open, he slanted his lips over mine and kissed me until my shoulders relaxed, and I melted in his arms again. Then he took them away from me.

How many times have I already told you that he was a bastard?

"For a second, just be honest with me, Lucy. Be yourself and tell me what's going on."

"What the hell do you think I'm doing?"

He started to lower his head again.

"Fine. Stop. Stop. Enough. Okay? Enough."

"Tell me what's going on without all the bullshit. You told me Callum hadn't—"

Callum? As in Jake Callum? What the hell was he talking about?

"Jake Callum? What does he have to do with anything?"

He visibly relaxed in front of my eyes. "So it isn't him?"

"I have no idea what you're talking about." I shook my head. "The baby is…" I touched my stomach again, looking down at it as if I could actually see the life growing inside me. "Jameson. My ex."

"You're sure? You're sure you are pregnant then? You went to a doctor?"

"I took a pregnancy test today. Those are pretty accurate from what I hear."

Now he was the one shaking his head. "You have to go to a doctor. Have you told him yet? Your ex?"

"Not yet. And I know. Of course I have to go to a doctor, but I missed my period and have been feeling off lately, so I took the test and…" I opened my arms. "Tada…a baby." My throat was dry, and I didn't think I sounded cheerful at all. "The apple doesn't fall far from the tree, right? And you were making fun of me when I said my family was cursed." I gave him a dry laugh and it died out as quickly as it had started. "Who's laughing now?"

He didn't laugh. Not even a smile. I was losing my edge.

I took a deep breath and backed away from him. Dropping my head in my hands, I massaged my temple.

Why had I come over here again? Oh! Yes. I thought I could seduce Adam Connor because he owed me that much after teasing me the night before.

Nice job, Lucy. Awesome job...

"Are you going to call him...your ex? Will he come back here?" Adam's voice was gentle, as if he were talking to a skittish horse.

I looked up at him and sighed. "I just found out a few hours ago. I didn't really think about what I want to do."

His eyebrows rose. "You're not going to tell him."

Was that a question?

Bristling, I grumbled, "What do you take me for?" I looked behind me to make sure the couch was there and sat my ass down before my legs decided it was time to play the damsel in distress. "This isn't a book or a movie. There is no romantic story here, no arc in the plot, no happy ending. I'm not gonna hide the pregnancy from him and then pop back into his life when I can't take the guilt and say 'surprise' after the kid is a few years old. Of course I'm going to call him; he won't get off that easily, and he better help me through this."

The couch dipped, and Adam sat down next to me, our arms touching. Did he have to sit that close? Really?

And was I still interested in seducing him?

After that kiss? Hell yes, I was.

"I've decided you're going to make love to me," I announced, looking straight ahead.

"Excuse me?"

"You heard me."

"No, I don't think I did. Could you repeat that?"

"You're going to make love to me."

"Is that an order?"

"No, just a…fact. You've been married, so you must know how to make love. And if not, you're a sort of, kind of good actor. Act."

"And you don't?"

"As you can imagine, I know how to do the grand slam, bumping uglies, and all that stuff. I…" I turned my head and glanced at him. "I don't think I've ever made love to anyone."

"Your ex?" he asked, his disbelieving eyes on me. "I thought you said you loved him."

"I thought I did. I mean, I did. But he had a giant thing in between his legs and as I already told you, I have a thing for those, as in I like my fucks to be good and hard." I shrugged and looked away. Was that heat I was feeling on my face?

What the hell, Lucy?

"And how do you think making love works exactly?"

I gave him a quick glance and saw that his lips were twitching. I could deal with amusement. I twisted my body, pulled my leg up on the couch, and faced him.

"I believe it requires looking into each other's eyes at all times. A slow entry. A little gasp and a little moan here and there. We'll skip whispering I love yous to each other, of course. Other than that, I believe it's a slow thing. Maybe an orgasm? If you can manage, but no pressure, of course. Just because your kiss improved, I'm not gonna assume—"

"And you want me to make love to you why? You don't think I can fuck you?"

"Who knows. I'm sure you have your moves, but I want you to make love to me because I assumed, being an actor and all, you could give a good performance, so I could have that at least once in my life."

He tilted his head, looking all confused and sexy. "Once in your life?"

"The curse?" I prompted. "I'm having a baby. I did exactly

what my mom did. I'm not saying I love you to anyone ever again, hence not making love to anyone again."

His eyes roamed my face, and he shook his head like I was being ridiculous and he didn't know what to do with me. "Lucy...I..."

I held my breath and waited for his words. If nothing else, I wanted his lips on mine again. I'd settle for that, too, if this offer didn't work out.

He touched my cheek with the back of his hand, then my still swollen lips with his fingertips. "Do you remember what I asked you last night? Nothing changed. Admit that you like me and I'll show you how to make love."

"I'm reduced to bargaining for a 'maybe' orgasm."

"I don't think I'm asking for too much, do you?"

"Okay. I'll give you a thirty-two."

"And that means...?"

"Out of a hundred, I'm giving you a thirty-two. That's how much I like you."

He seemed to think on it for a few beats then smiled at me.

"I can live with that. You are forty-nine for me."

Dumbfounded, I widened my eyes and, without even realizing what I was doing, scooted back from him. "No."

He raised an eyebrow. "No?"

My heart pounding in my chest, I said, "Fifty is like edging toward love. Take it back. Give me a thirty-five or something." His fingertips reached for me again, and I scrambled back as far as I could go. "Take it back."

There could be no talk of love between us; I wouldn't fall for that again, like I had with Jameson.

After studying me for what seemed like an hour, he rose up from his seat and leaned down to rest his lips against my ear. "I will always be honest with you, Lucy. My son is in love with you. Who knows, maybe I'm falling for you too? Is it too hard to believe that I like what I see when I look at you? That I like talking to you, arguing with you, watching you laugh with my son, watching *you* smile. Maybe after I make love to you, I'll fall a little more. So, I think forty-nine is a good number. Ask me again in the morning, I'll let you know how you did."

I leaned away, my back arching against the arm of the couch. He was becoming dangerous. His mouth, his eyes, his body... everything about him was getting too dangerous to stay close to him. Was it enough to deter me from having him inside me? Well, not really. Not yet.

Like I'd said before, for once and for all, I was ready to make love, and my vagina seemed to have chosen him as its victim. I was okay with that choice.

"No answer? No objection?"

I shrugged and tried to relax into the couch. "I don't believe you, so it's okay. You are free to say whatever you wish to say. I'm not someone who falls for flowery words."

His eyes bored into mine, and I swallowed the thick lump in my throat. Even though I didn't believe him, that didn't mean it wasn't affecting me.

He straightened and fixed the cuffs of his shirt, drawing my eyes to his hands.

"Stay right where you are," he ordered and started to walk away.

For a brief second, the fog in my brain cleared up enough that I remembered Aiden. Jolting up from the couch, I blurted, "Aiden? Where is Aiden?"

Adam stopped in his tracks toward the hallway. "We are leaving for Paris tomorrow, Dan, Aiden, and I. He is spending the night with his best friend." He paused, his lips stretching into an unexpected smile. "One of his best friends, I suspect. He is at a sleepover, Lucy. You're all mine."

"He is with Henry? That British actress' kid?"

"You know his best friend's name?"

"Of course I know his name."

"Don't be so surprised, Lucy. Not everyone cares about those things. Certainly not his own mother."

With that, he walked away.

Now what did that mean? And what about making love?

"What about the sex?" I shouted after him since there was no one else but us in the house. Plopping back down, I pulled my legs up, laid my head on the arm of the couch, and muttered to myself, "What about my lovemaking?"

Hesitantly, I raised my hand and rested it on my stomach. Why didn't I feel different? Wasn't I supposed to feel different? Shutting my eyes, I took a deep breath and just let myself be still.

Before I could let my thoughts pull me to a place I didn't want to go, I heard Adam's footsteps. A second later, his fingertips trailed over my lips, and I parted my mouth.

I opened my eyes to see him standing over me. He looked just as hot when he was upside down.

"Are we doing it or not?" I asked, keeping my tone neutral. My eyes took notice of how his shirt wasn't tucked into his pants anymore, and I almost, *almost* squirmed on the couch. I was about to have sex with Adam Connor. I couldn't show him how much I was ready to get rid of my stupid pants. "If not, I have a—"

"Always the romantic," he murmured, almost to himself. When I saw him lowering his head, I shut my mouth and let him kiss me upside down. As much as I adored that scene in Spider Man, it was weird being kissed upside down. Our teeth crashed, he bit down on my lower lip then slid his tongue in my mouth, and fuck me if the way he was kissing me didn't make my toes curl. When he was about to pull back, I groaned softly, put my hands on his cheeks, and arched into the kiss.

Just a little more.

Surprisingly, he didn't stop the kiss, but slowed it down. I guessed we were getting into the making love part. Nice and easy was practically the slogan for it, wasn't it? I felt his hand on my stomach and my eyes opened. He must have sensed it, or my body had made it apparent I was surprised to have his hands on me, because his lips stopped moving, and he pulled back to meet my eyes. Breathless, I waited to see what he was going to do.

His hand slid down farther. Intrigued, I raised an eyebrow at him before I looked down to watch his big, beautiful hand. And that forearm…it was right in front of me, begging to be stroked.

Shit!

Why do you even have a thing for forearms, Lucy?

Thanks to the way I was lounging on his couch, I had a perfect view of his hand. I clutched at the cushion under me and watched his fingertips lift my shirt and go straight under my leggings.

This…this territory was what I knew.

I squirmed in place and felt Adam's breath right next to my ear. Then his hand cupped my pussy, and he pushed two of his thick fingers inside me without even hesitating.

"So wet and ready for me, Lucy," he muttered, his tongue coming out to leave a wet trail on my neck.

I let out a soft moan as I arched my neck. Almost shaking with excitement, I circled my hips, managing to draw those skillful fingers deeper inside me.

"You're soaked, Lucy. My cock will slide right into you."

"That's exactly what I want," I said dreamily.

He pulled his fingers out, and I let go of the cushions to clutch his arm.

He froze over me, and I waited to see what he'd do. Sure, I wanted his cock, but just in case he couldn't manage to make me come, I wanted his fingers to do the job. He started stroking me. At first, softly, barely touching, his slick fingers ghosting over and around my clit. Then he dipped his fingers down and inside me, giving me a few deep thrusts as I practically hugged his arm like a koala. Then he took them out and repeated the torture.

"You're playing with me," I gasped out when he withdrew his fingers for the fifth time. "I don't like it."

I felt his teeth against my neck, my earlobe. "Oh? I thought you wanted me to play with you." Another swirl around my clit and then three fingers entered me.

I groaned and let my legs fall open. "Is torture a part of making love? Either make me come or let's skip to the good stuff."

"You don't get to make all the rules, Lucy. Either we do this my way or we don't do it at all."

"And you say this after you make me burn?"

"Your choice."

He was crazy; it was the only explanation, and that was why I didn't like him. I wanted him though, and it felt like I wanted him more than I had ever wanted anything in my life. Hell, even my vagina had readied itself as if it were going to have sex with Henry Cavill.

"Fine." I huffed and moaned loudly when he pressed hard on my clit and made my eyes roll back in my head.

That unbelievably sexy arm of his? It was still in my hands, and I was stroking it up and down, trying to rile him up just as much as he was riling me up, ghosting my fingers over the hairs on his arms, clawing at him when he got me a little too close to the edge.

"Please, make me come," I begged, beyond crazy for the hot and heavy release that was dancing right at the tip of his fingers.

Despite all my objections, he pulled his fingers out of me and trailed my wetness on my stomach, dragging my shirt with it until it rested under my boobs. Then he pulled his arm out of my grasp and moved to my side.

My eyes followed his every move, and I did my best to keep my eyes away from his crotch area.

Wordlessly, he pulled me up from the couch and took off my shirt. My heart beating wildly, I let him take off every piece of clothing on me. When I was completely naked, his gaze moved over me and my entire body trembled from the inside just from the expression on his face alone.

"You have one minute."

Without waiting for another offer, I walked the two steps that separated us and started to unbutton his shirt. It was the very thing I'd wanted to do when I was spying on him over the wall that first time. He lifted his arms up for me, and I unrolled the cuffs layer by layer. Before I pushed the shirt off him, our eyes met and a chill moved down my spine.

So annoyingly handsome. Hungry. Powerful.

Then I moved my hands over his broad chest and those strong shoulders. "You should work out more. You're not quite there yet," I said, the edge of my lip tipping up. He didn't need to work out at all. He was perfect just the way he was, and it was annoying as hell.

"Every word out of your mouth…" He shook his head.

He reached out and twisted my nipple as an answer, making me groan. When those amazing lips went for my neck, sucking and biting as he played with my boobs, I finally went for his pants and undid the button. My hands were already shaking, too excited about what I'd find in there.

I trailed a fingertip down the zipper and felt something hard. That was all the time I had to feel though because he was lifting me up and dumping me on the couch.

"Time's up," he said through clenched teeth.

I didn't have it in me to pout; I was more interested in getting him inside me.

I made a point of closing my eyes and not looking at his body when he took off his pants and climbed onto the couch. His big hands pushed my knees open.

"Can you make love on a couch?" I asked, a little breathless already. "Isn't that against the rules?"

I'd probably die before the whole thing was over. Now that we were actually naked, just like I'd wanted for quite some time, I was starting to freak out for no apparent reason.

"Where would you want to make love?" he asked, his hands moving down from my thighs toward my very excited vagina.

"I don't know." I squirmed in place when he pulled my pussy lips open with his thumbs. "Isn't it supposed to be in bed?"

"I had a few fantasies of fucking you right here; couch will do."

Then I was suddenly pulled down, and I squealed, goose bumps rising on my entire body. I was scared shitless to open my eyes and look down.

"You're not going to open your eyes?" He took my breast in his mouth, his tongue swirling around my hard nipple, then sucking and biting.

"Shit!"

I arched my neck, practically melting under his mouth's assault on my poor boob. His other hand cupped the lonely one and tweaked my nipple.

"Answer me."

"I don't want to be disappointed just yet."

"The four-inch thing again?" A not-so-gentle bite had me hissing and pretty much dripping under him.

"Yeah."

"Open your eyes, Lucy."

I didn't hesitate.

Wow.

My eyes met his and he was all I could see. That determined face. Those round shoulders.

I was lying right under Adam Connor, and I didn't mind one bit that I was giving the control over to him.

"I told you I don't play games, Lucy. Are you sure this is okay?"

Whatever the hell did that mean?

"Does it look like I'm not okay with anything? Come on." I arched up and reached up, moaning when he attacked my lips with the same amount of greed. I lowered my voice. "I want your cock in me, Adam."

"You want it?"

"Yes." I smiled. "All four inches of it."

He laughed, a low, throaty sound that vibrated through my body. I smiled back.

"Okay, Lucy. Close your eyes."

I closed them and then curved my arms around the arm of the couch. I was nothing but a trembling wreck when I felt his lips next to my ear.

"I'm going to un-break your heart, Lucy," he promised in a low voice.

I couldn't stop my body from shivering.

"My heart isn't broken, Adam," I whispered back just as quietly.

His hand moved down from my breast.

Lower.

Lower.

Leaving a burning path in its wake.

A finger teased my opening.

"It is," he whispered, leaving open-mouthed kisses along my neck.

Was this making love? Torturing each other until one of you lost your mind?

"It is," he repeated right before he took my nipple between his teeth and pulled. I wanted to close my legs, or touch myself, or hell, hump the couch. "And I'm going to make it whole again. I'm going to heal it so you can feel what you do to me."

I'd never been so ready, so slick, so *scared.*

Then I felt him move away from me and heard the sound of foil ripping open.

I counted. It took him around seven seconds to put it on. Was that good news? Had I counted right?

I was breathing hard and still holding on to the cushion under me as if my life depended on it.

"Is it in?"

I mean, I thought I was feeling fingers moving in and out of me, but maybe it was his cock? Maybe life was *that* cruel?

"Lucy…if nothing else, just because of that comment I'm about to ruin you for any other man."

My lips quirked up. "Oh? You wanted me to lie and say your dick is the *biggest* gift to humanity?"

"Let's see if your smart mouth will be able to do anything but scream and moan in a few seconds."

It didn't even take a few seconds for me to release my first groan. He pushed his cock into me, stretching me wide open. When my hips started sliding up, his hands grabbed my legs and adjusted them around his back.

"Oh, shit," I cursed when the move only pushed him deeper into me. "Oh, shit."

I opened my eyes and found him looking straight into mine. I swallowed and held his gaze. He pulled his hips back, hands still holding my thighs, and gave a little more of himself.

I bit back my groan.

"More?"

I nodded.

Fuck, yes!

He looked down at where we were connected and watched his cock pull out of me, which made my brain go all mushy. Then his thumb found my clit, pushing, circling, stroking, and yet he still pushed in deeper.

"You're creaming all around me, Lucy. Dare I say you like my cock?"

I might have whimpered. He might have groaned. I can't remember a few seconds of it.

I let one of my legs fall down from his back and lifted the other one so I could throw it over the couch.

"Is that your way of saying you want more?"

I couldn't laugh; something was lodged in my heart, making it hard to do much of anything.

"I doubt you have more to give."

My answer was a deep fucking thrust that had my toes curling with the exquisiteness of it.

I gasped and smiled. I let go of the cushion so I could run my hand all over his chest and scratch his burning skin, leave a mark, my mark.

"Oh, Lucy," he rasped. "Oh, what am I gonna do with you?"

He put one of his hands next to my waist, the other one on the arm of the couch.

He drew out that monster cock of his then pushed it back in farther as he settled over me.

I was lost. Gone. Completely and utterly shattered.

He was so deep in me, filling me to the brim. I was trying my best to stay still so I could get used to his size and not lose it in two seconds flat. I wanted to watch him work. I wanted to see how he made love.

"Ready?" he asked, his body as tight as a rubber band.

"Do your worst," I replied.

And he did. Oh, he did. The thrust...that delicious thrust deep into me.

"Holy fuck," I muttered, my eyes rolling back in my head.

His next thrust had me scrambling to hold on to him. Every

time he pushed harder into me, jarring my bones with pleasure, I clawed at his body. To push him away or pull him in deeper, I had no idea.

I had to admit, he was kind of huge. Okay, fine, he was absolutely huge. But, hell, the thickness, that was what was killing me in the most perfect way.

"Jesus, Lucy," he rasped out, going back to more shallow thrusts. His body still covering mine, moving against mine like hot liquid, he looked at me. There was something happening behind his eyes, but before I could put my finger on it, he pressed his mouth against mine and kissed me.

I ran my hands up his back and threaded my fingers through his hair, groaning my pleasure into his mouth.

"Big enough for you?" he asked when we broke apart so we could breathe.

"Just," I answered, my body a shivering mess under him.

His lips latched onto my nipple and it pulled at something right between my legs. My muscles clenched around Adam, and he cursed.

"Do you feel my cock?" he murmured, his eyes as dark as the night outside.

"Yes," I moaned, trying to open my legs wider so I could take him deeper into me.

He pushed his hand between the couch cushion and my waist and lifted his body up from mine.

"Does it feel good?"

I bit my lip and nodded. He was thrusting into me so slow, dragging my nerves all over the place.

His lips parted, and he whispered, "Good. Now you'll never forget how it feels to have all of me inside you."

I wasn't ready for the way he started driving into me, his hand holding my waist in place as he pushed his cock all the way in only to pull it back and work it into me again.

He was hitting me so deep, so hard, there was no way I could hold back my screams and groans, nor did I want to.

I started to feel myself tighten around him, his own moans and groans a distant sound to my ears. My toes curled and something started to grow inside me, building right in my core. Adam kept fucking me at a relentless pace, his hips grinding into me every time he went in too deep. The sound...oh, the sound of our thighs slapping together, my wetness...

"That's it, Lucy. That's it."

I grabbed on to Adam's hard-as-stone biceps and started to shake with my orgasm. Oh, when this was over, I was going to kill him.

"Come on, Lucy," he murmured through clenched teeth. "That's the best you've got? Give me more. Give me everything you have."

Just when I thought the pleasure rippling through my body was about to stop, he changed his angle and hit a different spot in me and it all started again.

"Holy shit! Holy shit! Holy shit!" I kept chanting and threw my hand back in the hopes of grabbing on to the arm of the couch. What my hand connected with wasn't the couch; it was the lamp shade on the side table just next to the couch.

My body burning up with my release from the inside out, I ignored the crashing sound and tried to calm my body down instead. He was *not* going to give me a heart attack! My body still shaking, I pulled at Adam's hair.

"You have to stop," I gasped, my words barely making any sense. "Something's wrong. Adam, stop."

He slowed down his thrusts, but they were still too deep, making my boobs bounce at every thrust. The tip of his cock was still touching that perfect spot. I was feeling too damn much.

My legs were still shaking, my body still on fire. "You

bastard," I managed to say. "You said you'd make love to me, not fuck me out of my mind."

His eyes followed mine and saw that I was trying to keep my legs steady with my hand. Leaning back, he pushed his arm under one of my legs, holding it up and straight against his chest.

"There are no rules, Lucy. This is how I make love to you."

"Oh, you stupid, handsome asshole. You broke my vagina."

He pulled out until only the head was in, curved my leg behind his back, and then slowly slid all the way back inside. He had me moaning under him in seconds.

"Your pussy feels perfectly fine to me," he murmured and took my lips again.

He was pushing into me so slowly, playing with my nerves.

Since it was all shot to hell, I held his face in my hands and stared at him. "Make me come again, Adam. I want to come on your cock again." If this was my one night with him, I wanted to come around him and on him as many times as possible.

"Fuck, Lucy, you're still pulsing around me. Don't worry, I'll make you come around me all night."

I let go of his face and arched my back, pulling him inside me again. He licked my nipple and the wetness, the warmth of his tongue made my entire body shudder under him.

"I love seeing you tremble under me."

I arched an eyebrow and stayed quiet. My entire focus was on arching my back and moving my hips so I could meet his thrusts and take his cock deeper into me, where it needed to be. "And this pussy…" He pulled out completely, giving me my first look at his hard, thick cock as he held it in his hand.

God! I really liked his cock. I really, really liked his cock.

Then two of his fingers were pushing into me, and he was swirling my wetness all over my stomach. "Look how wet it is for me. Look how much it loves my cock."

Oh, he had no idea.

While his eyes were taking in every inch of my body and how I glistened with my own juices spread out all over me, my eyes were on his cock and that thick vein I could see through the condom.

I promised myself I would take him into my mouth before the night ended, with the sole purpose of making him just as crazy as he was making me.

CHAPTER SEVENTEEN

ADAM

My heart thumping in my chest, my cock as hard as a rock in my hand, I took in the expression on her face. When I'd dropped Aiden off at his friend's house, I wasn't expecting a visit from Lucy. I didn't think she'd come anywhere near me, at least for a few days while her anger burned out.

But she'd come. She'd managed to clear my head of my troubling thoughts and dropped a bomb right at my feet.

Pregnant. She was pregnant.

And she had ordered me to make love to her.

How could anyone say no to that? More importantly, to her. I certainly couldn't, not when she looked at me as if her world would crumble if I turned her down. Even more importantly, I didn't want to say no to her.

The pregnancy...it didn't change how I felt toward her. It didn't change the fact that I still wanted her. But where did it put me? What did it mean for her? Would she get back with her ex? Move away?

Instead of getting answers to those questions, I decided to give her something she wouldn't forget, something she couldn't just push away with the back of her hand.

Standing over her with my cock in my hand, I gave myself a few lazy strokes as she watched me intently.

After having a taste of her tight pussy, my hand wasn't doing it for me. But for her, for that look in her eyes, I didn't mind giving her a little show.

I let go of my cock and let it rest for a moment.

Getting up, I took Lucy's hand and pulled her up.

"Hold on to the back of the couch."

She arched an eyebrow, but didn't question me. In seconds she was on her knees, arching her back and giving me the best fucking view of her ass.

"What the hell is that?" she asked. I followed her eyes to the couch cushion.

Reaching for one perfect ass cheek, I gently stroked and then pulled it apart so I could see her pink, wet pussy. I pushed my hand between her legs and heard her whimper when two of my fingers entered her.

"Sore?" I asked.

"I'm okay. You didn't answer me. Did you come?"

I looked at the wet spot on the couch and got closer to her so I could push my cock against the soft, soft skin of her perfect ass.

"Did it feel like I came? That's all you."

Her head whipped back, and she gave me a shocked look. "What?" she whispered.

I pushed my fingers deeper into her and her back arched to take more. I couldn't look away from her red lips, those teeth pulling on the swollen skin.

Pulling my fingers out of her, I found her clit and gave it a gentle squeeze.

"All you, Lucy," I repeated. "I told you, your pussy is very happy with my four-inch cock."

She gave me a small smile over her shoulder, her fingers white knuckled as she held on to the couch. "Thank God you're not four inches. It would be so disappointing and I'd feel so very sorry for you."

I pushed my cock in between her legs and gave her a gentle thrust so she could feel it slide against her sensitive clit.

That wiped the smile off her face, and I was fascinated with the small scowl that replaced it.

I held her hips in place and asked, "Ready for your third orgasm?"

"Second."

"Lucy." I nodded toward the wet spot. "You almost squirted for me. You came for the second time before the first one was done. That's two."

She pursed her lips and stayed quiet.

I rested my hips against her ass and pulled at her hair until her back was resting against my front.

"I asked if you are ready."

Her small hand found my cock, and she squeezed the head. My body shuddered with pleasure, and I bit her neck, drinking up her moans.

"I'll take that as a yes."

I pushed her front down, grabbed my cock, and after a few hard strokes, slowly pushed into her in one slow movement, not stopping until she had every inch of me inside her.

Hearing her exhale in one big rush and seeing her widen her legs stiffened my cock even farther inside her, so when she tried to move forward and away, I squeezed one ass cheek in my palm as a silent order for her to stay still and took a step closer to her.

"Shit," she groaned when I gave her the last bit again. "You're so deep," she muttered almost to herself, her head hanging.

"Look at your ass," I whispered huskily, my voice sounding too thick to my own ears. I massaged her flesh, stroking, admiring. "Look at that beautiful ass."

As my cock was throbbing inside her, I was unable to stop

myself from gently massaging her tight little hole. Would she let me in?

My fingers still slick with her wetness, I gently pushed in a finger, and she groaned, her head falling, her body trying to pull away from the intrusion. "Maybe not today," I said, yet still pushed in farther until she looked at me over her shoulder.

"You're not that lucky, Connor."

I pulled out and pushed in again, making sure I was moving my cock in and out of her slick heat too. Her head lolled down again, and she released another groan.

"Maybe not today," I relented. I grabbed her hips and let her have it for a full minute. Shallow thrusts mixed in with deep, hard ones.

"Yes, yes, Adam, fuck, right there, right there."

Her cries of pleasure fueled me to give her more as my hands tightened on her hips. Pulling her, pushing her...pounding her with everything in me.

I let one of my hands slide up her back, caressing the hot skin between her shoulder blades. She looked so beautiful, so open at that moment. To my cock. To me. But she was too far away, her lips, her skin...I wanted her eyes holding mine.

I rounded my hand on her throat and pulled her back up against my chest again. I saw goose bumps on her arms, the pulse on her neck erratic, her breathing shaky.

I could have her like this every day, I thought to myself. *I could have her like this every day and it still wouldn't be enough.*

"Look at you," I whispered next to her ear, my hand still around her throat, my cock still moving in and out of her.

She pushed her ass back, and I closed my eyes.

"So beautiful," I said reverently. "So fucking beautiful. Does my cock feel good, Lucy?" I asked and felt her body tremble.

I pulled back and drove into her. Hard.

She gasped, her hand coming up to rest on my hand that was on her throat, fingers curling around my wrist.

"So fucking good," she whispered huskily. "Will you pound into me? Make it hurt?"

I let my other hand move up from her hips and palmed her breast. "You want me to hurt you?"

"It hurts so good when you're—"

Opening my legs wider behind her, I thrust up and groaned when her muscles clenched around me. Her breath hitched, her lips lazily stretching into a smile.

I could see my sweat dripping onto her skin as she creamed around my cock.

Roughly gripping her chin, I turned her head so she could meet my eyes, nothing but raw pleasure and deep hunger in those stormy eyes.

"You want me to go deep on you." It wasn't a question. "Did it feel good when you came all over my cock, Lucy? You liked how that felt, huh?"

Biting her lip, she nodded.

Holding her body flush against mine, I started pumping into her, our skin slapping.

She closed her eyes and that little frown appeared again.

"Kiss me," I ordered. "Kiss me and I'll give it to you again."

To my surprise her eyes looked bewildered when she opened them. Didn't she see what was going on with me?

"Kiss me, Lucy," I said, gentler this time. I grabbed her arms and placed them around my neck. I nibbled on her chin, my hips moving too slow for either one of us to lose it and come. "Kiss me, baby, so I can make you come all over my cock again. Don't you want that, Lucy? I really need to feel this sweet pussy tighten around me. Will you give that to me? Will you let me come inside you?" I found her clit with my fingertips and tenderly stroked her, causing her muscles to ripple around me.

She moaned and let me have her lips. Holding her chin in one hand and her hips in the other, I worked my cock into her with steady, fast thrusts. For a second her mouth parted from mine, and she moaned deep from her throat as her head dropped back against my chest.

I kissed her and swallowed every sound she made as I picked up my pace. Her hands tightened around my neck, her fingers grabbing my hair, pulling and pulling and pulling until I had to close my eyes and focus on anything other than how she was pushing me into complete madness. I groaned into her mouth, sucking her sweet tongue.

She broke apart from my lips and bent over the couch, letting me watch her ass pushing back to take more of me inside her.

"Oh, God, Adam. Oh, God."

I wiped away the sweat from my forehead and grabbed her hips so I could pound harder into her.

"Yes. Yes. Harder. Right there, Adam. Yes!"

"Widen your legs, Lucy."

I could see her legs shaking, her arms barely holding on, but she still opened them wider.

"You're so thick. So deep. I love that," she murmured, and it was all I could do not to puff out my chest as I listened to her moan in pleasure. "Please, don't stop. So close, Adam. So close."

My hands holding on to her small waist, I drove into her with everything I had. I'd never felt so big in my entire life as I watched her pussy take my cock, my balls slapping against her skin. I'd never felt so full and complete and right.

So fucking right.

A perfect pair.

"Talk to me, Adam. I'm so close, please talk to me."

I sucked in a breath, barely holding onto my sanity. She was right on the edge, seconds away from taking me down with her.

She was a ball of pleasure waiting to burst wide open right under my hands, right around my cock.

"Come on, Lucy," I whispered breathlessly, splaying my hand on her back and stroking softly. "Squeeze me. Do you feel how hard I am for you?" I leaned over her body, slightly changing my angle, and it hit her. "That's it, Lucy. That's it. Come on my cock, sweetheart."

She sucked in her breath and silently broke apart right in front of my eyes. Her whole back erupted with goose bumps, her pussy squeezing my cock to death, her body shivering. Not wanting to hurt her by being too rough—rougher than I'd already been—I ground into her, barely holding my own release back.

When she pushed back against my cock and let out a loud moan, it was my undoing. I ground deeper into her and let myself go as she kept shaking under me. Her arms gave up and she rested her face against the couch, letting me push deep into her as I came with hard throbs inside her.

As her walls kept milking me, I almost collapsed onto her body.

Instead, I took a deep breath and tried to slow down my wild heartbeat. She was never getting away from me, not after this night, not after what she'd just given me.

"Lucy," I murmured softly. My hands shaking, I stroked her back, and she flinched, her skin too sensitive. She was drenched in sweat just as much as I was. I ran my hand up and down her warm skin, gently massaging the base of her neck as I slowly pulled out of her to take care of the condom.

"I have to…" I started, but the rest didn't come since I chose to listen to her harsh intake of breath as I severed our connection. I tied the end and threw it on the floor.

Still on her knees, Lucy straightened up, and I saw her hand disappear between her legs.

"Shit."

"What?" I asked, standing behind her again.

"Nothing."

Ignoring her protests, I dipped my hand in between her slick folds and caressed her swollen flesh. She twitched in my arms. "What's wrong?"

"Too wet," she replied, sounding almost annoyed.

"There is no such thing." I dipped my fingers inside her, barely getting in, and then licked my fingers clean of her as she watched me over her shoulder with her mouth parted.

"I hate you so much," she whispered, her eyes focused on my lips.

I kissed her. There was nothing else I could do when she was so close, so naked.

So mine.

I gripped her chin and kissed her harder.

"I have to leave."

Of course she'd want that.

"You're not leaving this house tonight."

"Try to stop me."

"We haven't tasted each other, yet, Lucy." I grabbed her hand and put it around my half-hard cock. She stroked me and stopped at the base, squeezing.

"Gentle," I whispered, kissing her neck.

"I just watched you taste me."

"That's not enough. I want to eat you out. And you haven't tasted me yet."

"Are you offering a sixty-nine, Adam Connor?"

"I'm offering everything," I said, nudging her with my nose right behind her ear.

She stopped breathing for a few seconds, and I was afraid I was going to have to carry her to my bedroom and lock the door on us, but then she said, "Sixty-nine is a good offer, and I do want to take that gorgeous cock into my mouth."

"Good," I murmured, running my hand up and down on her stomach.

I helped her off the couch and took her reluctant hand in mine. She looked down at her clothes and bent down to pick them up.

Hugging her from her behind, I pulled her up.

"Don't," I whispered near her ear. "Don't. I want to see you on my bed, legs spread wide open."

Did she think I couldn't feel her body shiver against mine? How long did she think she could hide herself from me?

She laughed softly. "It won't make me hate you less."

"I believe it's too late for that, Lucy. You already like me too much," I said in a thick voice. "Maybe even more than you liked having my cock in your body."

I dug my fingers into the soft skin around her hips, wishing nothing more than to imprint myself on her so she would remember, so she would know who had touched her, who had held her trembling, begging body in his arms when she needed to be held by someone who cared.

It didn't surprise me that I wanted to be that for her—though I knew she'd yell at me for even suggesting she needed someone to hold her up. I guess that was what had drawn me to her since that first day I held her body against mine, our eyes showing nothing but hatred for each other minutes before I had the cops walk her off my property.

The more I watched her, the more I listened to her, *heard* what she was saying without even moving her lips, the deeper she pulled me in.

Adam Connor Caught at the Airport with His Son: Kidnapping?

The photos below show Adam Connor carrying his five-year-old son through the doors of LAX as they are rushing to catch their flight to France. The fact that Aiden Connor was hiding his face in his father's neck as the cameras snapped photos of them hurrying through the gates shows how much he was affected by what happened the last time he was at the same airport. The father and son were flying to Paris to attend the birthday party of Victoria Connor, who's been living in France for almost six years. Helena and Nathan Connor left the city hand in hand just days before to attend the same birthday party. We're not sure if Aiden's mom was invited or not, but we know she hasn't left the city since her return from New York.

Apart from feeling bad about little Aiden Connor, could the quiet movie star get any hotter? We don't know about you, but the protective father thing is really working for us at the moment. If you don't think the photos capturing the father and son are enough of an answer, we have no idea what will be. Since the news about Adam Connor filing for sole custody of Aiden Connor hit the media, this is the first time the pair has been seen in public. Adeline Young, however, has remained quiet as far as we know. And trust us, we know plenty about these two.

We can almost hear you asking what else we can share about

Adam Connor and Adeline Young. We know there are rumors circling around that Adam Connor has started dating again (yes, we were just as shocked), and that this new development was one of the main reasons (other than the airport incident, of course) he decided to change the custody agreement. From what we've heard from numerous sources close to the movie star, his new woman isn't happy about Adam having constant contact with his ex-wife, whether it is about their son or any other issue. Apparently she was a great influence on the Academy Award-winning movie star when he decided to go ahead with the custody battle.

On the other side of the ring, Adeline Young was seen with the famous director Jonathan Cameron as they were leaving a restaurant opening just this week. While they could have been having a meeting about a future project, we have statements from multiple onlookers that Adeline was showing signs of distress while Jonathan was trying to calm her. Could this be Adeline Young's new boyfriend? To be honest with you, it wouldn't surprise us; we knew it was coming. The couple left the building together and drove away in Jonathan's car, neither of them answering the questions thrown at them upon their exit.

Do you think they are both moving on with their lives? Moving on to other people?

We are still hoping the news about Adam Connor dating isn't true so we can keep dreaming about becoming the famous actor's new love interest. It could happen. You never know.

CHAPTER EIGHTEEN

LUCY

I woke up in Adam Connor's arms before the sunrise, before the stars could fully disappear. He'd made me come more times than I'd ever come before in one single night. He had well and truly broken my vagina, and I couldn't find it in me to be angry with him. I didn't remember going to sleep holding his hand, but as soon as I became aware of where I was, I let go of it immediately.

I moved my fingers, opening and closing my hand to get rid of the alien feeling. The warmth. The sudden emptiness.

I was deliciously sore, something I would've celebrated by embarrassing Olive if it were any other time, but I was too angry at myself for falling asleep in Adam's bed to even think about running to Olive to wake her up.

Sliding off the bed, I allowed myself one last look at the near perfection that was lying in the middle of the bed.

That chest.

That cock.

Those fingers.

Oh, those *lips*.

Those dirty, dirty lips that had whispered even dirtier things to me the entire night.

Without making a sound, I found my way back to the living room, put on my clothes, and walked out of his home.

———

"GOOD MORNING, LUCY," Jason greeted me as he trailed behind Olive.

Olive was quiet, her eyes trained on me in deep concentration.

"Good morning. I made pancakes." I pushed the plate holding a stack of twenty pancakes forward and flipped another one on the pan. "Get a good night's sleep?"

"You didn't wake me up."

I glanced at Olive over my shoulder and opened the fridge to take out the apple juice.

"Good morning to you, too, sunshine. And you're welcome."

"Why didn't you wake me up?"

"Because you hit anyone who tries to wake you up."

"You really do," Jason murmured as he kissed Olive's temple and reached to take a pancake.

With Jason's help, Olive climbed up to sit on one of the barstools and kept a watching eye on me.

I handed Jason the maple syrup and took out the plate of fruit I had cut up before starting the pancakes.

Sliding the hot pancake onto Olive's plate, I started on another one. "I'm gonna go check out the apartment I told you about. You'll come with me?"

"Because that's the most important thing we should do right now, right? Find you an apartment."

Jason's hand stopped midair as he was about to reach for a piece of banana.

I sighed and flipped the pancake.

"I'll leave you girls alone to talk," Jason muttered before dropping a kiss on Olive's neck. Rounding the island, he took out a bottle of water from the fridge and surprised me by wrapping a hand around my arm and pulling me against his chest.

"Be nice to our adopted daughter, Olive," he said with care, his hand stroking my arm.

I smiled and wiggled my eyebrows at Olive.

As an answer, she gave Jason the evil eye and asked me, "Why are you walking funny?"

My smile stretched bigger. "Because Adam Connor fucked me for hours."

"Ohhh-kay. I'm going to take a shower before I meet up with Tom. Play nice," he reminded us as he left the kitchen.

"You didn't come home last night."

I turned off the stove and leaned on the island. "That's true, Mom."

She nodded and started playing with the coffee mug in front of her.

"Do you want coffee?"

"No."

"Apple juice?"

A slight hesitation…then, "Yes."

I poured two glasses of apple juice and handed her one. It was a favorite for both of us.

"Did you talk to Jameson?"

"Not yet. I wanted you to be next to me when I made that call."

Her shoulders relaxed, and I knew I'd given her the right answer.

She took a sip of her juice then reached for a piece of mango. I did the same and then reached for my first pancake.

"Are we going to have a baby, Lucy?"

I poured a good amount of maple syrup on my pancake and took a few bites before I could answer. "We're having a baby."

Olive put another pancake and a few pieces of fruit on her plate. "We should make an appointment with a doctor. Be sure."

"Yes. Do you remember Karla?"

She nodded.

"I got in touch with her the other day to see if she'd want to be my roommate because I knew she was having trouble with hers." Olive's shoulders tensed up again. "Anyway, her dad is a doctor, so I thought we could get his help."

"Will you call Jameson before or after the doctor?"

I shrugged and finished my pancake.

"You okay?"

"Nothing else I can do now, my green Olive."

For a while we ate in silence. We didn't manage to finish all the pancakes, but definitely put a dent in the stack.

"And Adam?"

How to answer that loaded question…

"You're smiling," Olive commented, averting her gaze when my head snapped up. "Even though you're too stubborn to admit it, I can see that you like him."

I parted my lips to make a joke of it, but she cut me off. "I'm glad, Lucy. I'm glad it went well with him last night. You deserve to be happy, even if it's just for a night when it could be for longer than that."

She finished her apple juice and jumped off the barstool. "Oh, and yes. I'd like to come to look at your apartment…if you're still thinking of getting one, of course."

With those cryptic last words, she left me standing in the kitchen.

A few minutes later Jason was back.

"You okay, daughter of mine?"

"Is she angry with me?"

He sighed. "She isn't angry with you. It's just…last night she realized you might move to Pittsburgh."

"Oh, for God's sake! Move to Pittsburgh? To be with Jameson?"

"For the baby…"

I pushed the remaining pancakes toward Jason and dumped some maple syrup on them.

"I have a meeting with Tom, Lucy. I don't have time—"

"Eat," I ordered. "I'm a pregnant lady now. Don't upset me. I slaved over the stove to feed you two. Eat."

Dutifully, he took a bite.

Leaving him in the kitchen, I called out, "Olive! My little green Olive! You still haven't asked about Adam's cock size. I think he is thicker than Jason!"

I heard Jason choking on his pancakes as I headed toward Olive's room. "And I have to tell you about what he did to me with that cock on his couch, against the wall, *and* on his bed!"

———

Adam: *Answer your phone, Lucy.*
Lucy: *Go away.*
Adam: *You can't leave my bed like that again.*
Lucy: *I won't be in your bed again.*
Adam: *I will be back from Paris in two days with Aiden. Make no mistake, Lucy. We will talk. And trust me…you will come to my bed again.*
Lucy: *In your dreams.*
Adam: *And yours.*

THE BASTARD.

———

"HELLO? LUCY?"

"Hi, Jameson. How are you?"

A deep sigh came through the line. "I didn't think you'd call me, not after ignoring my texts."

Olive was sitting next to me in her car, and we were finally calling Jameson. Olive pressed her ear on the other side of the phone and gave me an innocent smile when I frowned at her. Sighing, I put the call on speaker.

I shifted the phone to my other hand and shook the left one, trying to steady the shaking. I was turning into a complete chicken shit.

"I didn't ignore them," I replied when Jameson called my name again.

"You didn't answer them, Lucy."

"There wasn't anything left to say."

"You're wrong. We still have things to say. I miss you."

I glanced at Olive. "Well, yes. Now we do have things to say. That's why I called you."

"You missed me too," he said in that silky, seductive tone of his.

I kept silent and listened to my heart just for a second…and realized that it didn't tremble when it heard that familiar voice it used to like so much. It wasn't right, didn't hold that teasing tone my heart was favoring these days.

"I'm sorry, Jameson, but that's not the reason I called. I-I-I… I'm going to call you back."

I ended the call and dropped my head back on the headrest.

"What are you doing?" Olive asked.

I turned the radio on, thinking maybe some music would help quiet my mind.

Olive turned it off. "What's going on?"

"Do I have to tell him? I mean now? Do I have to tell him

TO HATE ADAM CONNOR   303

now? We are about to enter the doctor's office. Can't we call him after we get the results?"

Somehow Olive was much calmer than I was; usually it was the other way around.

She grabbed my hand and gave it a squeeze. "Breathe, Lucy."

I took a deep breath.

"Do you want to be the wind today?"

I smiled.

"What will you be? A bird flying with me?"

"If that's what you want."

"You'd be a cute bird. Being the wind, I'll knock you down, and Jason can come and rescue you then you can have bird sex and—"

"Again. Breathe, Lucy."

I exhaled.

"Oh, God, Olive," I groaned and looked at her understanding eyes. "What did I do?"

"Nothing. You did nothing. It just happened. And that's okay. It'll be okay. Whatever the results are, you got this. So we'll have a baby. It'll be the luckiest kid to have you as a mother, and she or he will have a kickass aunt."

"I really don't think so. The curse should've ended with me. Now—"

"Now, nothing. You're not cursed, Lucy." Another squeeze around my hand. "Call him back. Tell him what's going on and then that's it. We'll walk out of the car and go into the doctor's office together. Just one step at a time."

She was right. I knew she was right and there was no point of freaking out, but then why was my heart beating in my stomach? *Is that the baby?*

"Okay, I'm freaking out," I pointed out the obvious.

"Do you want me to tell him?"

"No. No." I took a few deep breaths and called Jameson back.

"Lucy? Are you okay?"

It didn't escape my notice—or Olive's—that he hadn't called me back as soon as I'd ended the call. If he missed me like he kept saying, wouldn't he have called back? Jason would've called Olive back in a heartbeat just to make sure she was okay. So Jameson was my mistake.

"I'm sorry," I said into the phone. "I'm sorry, I freaked out."

His tone was sharper when he demanded to know what was going on.

I gave him the news as straight as I could. "I thought you'd want to know," I began. "I took a pregnancy test." Complete silence. I closed my eyes. "It was positive, but they are not always accurate, so I have an appointment with a doctor in a few minutes and I'll let you know what I learn from those results."

Still complete silence.

"Jameson? Are you there?"

I glanced at Olive and saw that she was biting her lip, anxiously waiting for Jameson to say something. Anything. She raised her eyebrows. I brought the phone closer to my lips. "James—"

"Yes. Yes. I'm here. I'm sorry. So you're pregnant. With a baby. My baby to be specific. I wasn't expecting that."

I chose to believe he wasn't trying to imply that the baby might not be his. "Yeah. Me neither."

"You were on the pill." There was no accusation in his tone.

"I was."

"Wow. Lucy…wow."

The corner of my mouth tipped up, and I touched my stomach. "Yeah."

"What will you do? What did you decide to do? With the baby, I mean."

Nice, I thought. *Very nice.* That pretty much wiped the smile off my face. A quick look at Olive and I saw she was seconds away from speaking up.

"Right," I said quickly. "I'll let you know after the results. I have to go now. Goodbye, Jameson."

"The bastard," Olive spat out as soon as I'd ended the call.

"Can't say I don't agree."

"I didn't think I could hate him any more. Give me the phone, I'm gonna call him back."

I held my phone tighter in my hand and moved it away from Olive. "And do what exactly?" I shook my head and undid my seat belt. "Let's just go up and…and…go pee in a cup or whatever."

"I decided that when I'm writing your story, I'm going to kill Jameson. I'm going to make you marry Adam Connor and then kill Jameson off."

I patted her arm. "That's the spirit."

CHAPTER NINETEEN

ADAM

Our trip to Paris changed nothing. Every year, we took Aiden with us, despite Adeline's objections, and every year I asked the same questions, scared out of my mind that the answers would change. Other than the fact that Adeline hadn't joined us on our trip, nothing had changed. Not the answers. Not the city. Not the people in it. Not anything.

"Daddy? Can I go see my friend first? I know they missed me."

"You just talked to Henry a few hours ago, Aiden. I'm sure he'll manage for a day until you see him in class."

"But it's not just Henry or Isabel."

Isabel, right. How could I have forgotten about Isabel?

"You FaceTimed Isabel just yesterday, I believe."

"Yes, but it's not just them. I have more friends, you know. What about Lucy? What about Olive? Even Jason must've missed me. We were gone for *days*. Tell him Dan."

I met Dan's eyes in the rearview mirror, and he shook his head.

"Tell him," Aiden pressed.

"I'm sure they missed you, buddy."

"See, Daddy? Even Dan missed me when he didn't see me for a whole day. Dan got to see me, we should let them see me too."

"Aren't you forgetting someone else?"

He looked at me silently, eyes still begging.

"Your mom? She missed you too, buddy."

"She did?"

Such an innocent question.

I caught Dan's eyes again as he took a left turn, getting closer to Adeline's house.

"Of course, little man," I replied to Aiden.

He nodded solemnly and turned his head to look outside, hugging his iPad to his chest.

"I'll stay with Aiden," Dan interrupted my bleak thoughts. "You take the car and go to your meeting with the agent. I'll drive Adeline wherever she wants to go in her car."

"Thank you. I'm sure she'll appreciate that."

"When will you come back to take me?" Aiden asked, his fingers swiping the screen of his iPad even though the thing was out of battery.

I ruffled his hair. "Your mom gets to have you for one week, buddy, remember? Then I'll come and take you home."

Nothing but a quick nod.

Everything was set in motion, but it would take time to get full custody, which was why I had to adhere to the rules we had set before, after the divorce. Until it happened, until Aiden stayed with me full time, I'd come and check on him more often. If that meant I had to come face to face with Adeline more, or share a dinner or two in that timeframe, I'd be okay with that.

After dropping Aiden and Dan off at Adeline's and watching her give Aiden a quick hug, for the life of me I couldn't understand how she couldn't bond with him like a mother was supposed to bond with their kid. At the time she had wanted him more than I did. She fought for him more than I did. He was the perfect boy.

He was perfect, and he was mine.

Adam: *Why are you hiding from me?*
Lucy: *Who says I'm hiding?*
Adam: *You don't take my calls.*
Lucy: *I'm texting back, aren't I? Maybe I don't want to hear your voice. Maybe I don't like it. Be a little humble.*
Adam: *You love my voice, Lucy. You loved it when you were begging me to talk to you so you could come around my cock. And you came so gloriously.*
Lucy: *I hate you.*
Adam: *We need to talk.*

"HOW IS SHE DOING?" I asked Jason as he met me in their backyard. It was late at night, the lights in their pool dim, the house completely dark.

"She is okay," he said after a moment of hesitation. "She is handling everything okay. But, that's Lucy for you. She won't cry and scream about it."

I was starting to realize the same.

"She asleep?"

He nodded and crossed his arms over his chest.

"I heard you've been talking to Tom. Jumping ship?"

"Last movie is in production and I'm itching to start something new. Bob Dunham has been good to me, but I don't think we're seeing eye to eye anymore."

"I've heard you're contracted for one more movie with Sun Down Pictures. How is that going?"

I shook my head and looked back at their house. "I don't like it. That was his first mistake. They change their people too much. I'm not a big fan of the writers they have right now. I still have time until the end of 2018. I'll decide on something. Until then, I think it will work out with Tom."

"You're in good hands. He is excited to take you on. Since you're the family type, he's over the moon that he'll have no problems with you in the media."

I chuckled. "Not much of a family left."

"Still. I don't believe you have any sort of sex tape hidden away, do you?" Jason arched his brow as he waited for an answer.

"I don't believe I do."

"Then you're golden. After the scares I've given him for years, I don't think he can go through it all over again. Other than this latest news frenzy about your divorce and ex-wife, I rarely see you on any of the tabloid covers—unless it's a family photo, that is. You're Tom's dream actor. He'll have fun working with you."

Tired, I rubbed the back of my neck. "We had a good meeting the other day. He said he might have something I'd be interested in. We'll see how it goes." Thinking I'd heard a door open, I looked over my shoulder.

Jason laughed, the sound low and warm. "It's a little late to pay her a visit, don't you think? But if you want to see if she is okay or not with your own eyes, I can't fault you for that."

"If you don't mind."

His mouth still curved up at the edges, he dropped his arms and gestured for me to walk ahead of him. "If she attacks you, it's on you."

"I'll take my chances," I muttered. I figured she was probably going to make a scene, but maybe I'd get lucky and slip out of her room without waking her.

Stopping in front of Lucy's room, Jason whispered, "We care about her, Connor. I hope you know what you're doing."

Without making any further comment, I ducked my head and entered Lucy's room.

Just like her personality, she slept all wild and free: legs tangled in the sheets, face buried in her pillows, her body sprawled right in the middle of the bed. It was too dark to notice anything other than her beautiful silhouette.

From where I stood, she looked peaceful, yet my feet still took me closer to make sure. I pushed a few strands of her hair out of her face and watched her sleep.

She hiccupped.

I smiled and found myself getting in bed with her. I'd been out all night. Rushing to a meeting with my lawyers. Having dinner with the director as we discussed the production process for the movie. Talking to my new publicist. Talking with the production company about which shows I'd have to appear on for the promotion of the new movie. I'd talked and talked and talked.

Now I just wanted to listen to Lucy breathe.

I curled my arm around her stomach and slowly pushed my hand under her T-shirt, stroking her soft, warm skin.

She released a soft groan, and I felt my dick come to life.

I sighed against her skin, resting my nose against her neck. My hand stilled on her stomach, and I listened to her soft breathing.

She hiccupped again.

I laughed and ran my hands down her arms as gently as possible.

She stirred in her sleep. "Olive?"

"Shhh, it's me," I murmured, kissing her neck.

She shivered under my lips.

"Adam?"

Leaning forward, she reached for the light.

"Don't."

"What's going on?" she asked in a low voice still laced with sleep. It was sexy as hell. "Breaking and entering again?"

I took her hand in mine and kissed her wrist as she turned to face me.

"Don't hide from me, Lucy," I said, surprising myself. I hadn't come into her room to tell her that. "Don't ignore me."

"I have no idea what you're talking about, Adam. What time is it?"

"Past midnight."

For a little while we lay silently on our sides, doing nothing but staring into each other's eyes. The light coming from under the door wasn't enough to let me see her beauty mark, or those stormy eyes that pulled at something in my chest, but I was content; what I could see of her was enough to settle my heart.

"The doctor?"

"I have an appointment for tomorrow."

"Your ex?"

She shook her head, glancing up at the ceiling. "I talked to him, but I don't want to talk about it."

I didn't push. I wasn't itching to talk about her ex either.

"How was your vacation?"

"It wasn't a vacation. I...I have to fly to Paris every year."

She moved a little, getting comfortable. "Your sister's birthday, right?"

I smiled a little. "Stalking me online again, I see."

She snorted. "You keep calling me a stalker, I might as well earn my nickname."

Would I share my secrets with her one day?

"You're not trying to kick me out or slapping me for getting in bed with you...you sure you're okay?"

Propping her hands under her head, she took a deep breath.

"I'm scared, Adam."

For her to admit that to me, someone as strong as her, was huge. The worry in my chest lessened. She was letting me have a piece of her heart without even knowing what she was doing.

"Come here," I muttered and pulled her closer. She didn't put up a fight. She didn't ask what I was doing or why I was doing it. She simply lifted her head and let me slide my arm under her neck so she could rest more comfortably.

Playing with her hair, I closed my eyes and let my forehead rest against hers.

"It'll be okay, Lucy."

"It won't be. It can't be. And I'm so fucking scared because I'm not ready to have a baby by myself, Adam. I know nothing about babies."

"I do. We'll make it okay, Lucy. I'm here for you. I have no intentions of letting you hide yourself from me."

"You don't understand," she insisted, her body pulling away.

I put my hand on her back and pulled her flush against my chest, our noses inches apart, her breath becoming mine.

"Don't hide from me, Lucy. Don't pull away."

"I'm so tired," she whispered, her body still alert, still ready to put distance between us. "I'm so tired of trying to hold everything up and just messing things up even further. I talked to Catherine." She sighed and dropped her forehead to my chin, her hands curling into her chest in between us. "I don't even know why I did it. That's not true, I know why I did it. I thought…maybe, you know. Maybe she'd be there for me. Maybe she'd do something and everything would be okay. She is family after all; that's what family does. That's what Olive does for me."

"I take it that didn't go well."

A humorless laugh. "Yeah, you could say that. Every time I

talk to her, happy or sad, she has a way of killing something inside me."

"I'll hold you up, Lucy. You can trust me. I see who you are. I see who you are, and I want you to choose me. I want you to open your eyes and look at me so you can see that I have what it takes, that I can take care of your heart for you."

"I don't hate you anymore." Her fingers moved on my chin, on my neck, her touch a searing mark on my heart.

I wanted this girl...this strong, beautiful girl. I wanted her to be mine. To hold her hand and walk on the street. To smile with her. Do simple things. Things other people took for granted. I wanted to laugh with her.

I wanted to sneak into her heart just as I'd sneaked into her bedroom.

"I don't hate you anymore, Adam Connor, but I can't love you. I can't fall for you like that. I don't want to break like them."

"Lucy," I murmured. "Do you think even for one second that you'd let anyone break you? Don't you see who you are when you look in the mirror? If someone's heart is breaking, you'll be doing all the damage."

"You would. You and your son would break me."

"Aiden loves you."

"And I love him. But when you break my heart, I'll lose him, too. Because of you...being an asshole," she said with the first signs of amusement in her tone. "I'd lose both of you."

"So you're sure it'd be my fault. Something I'd cause."

"Have you looked at me? I'm an angel."

I tilted her head back and pressed a soft, quick kiss on her lips. "Let's not play games, Lucy. I want your heart, and I will have it. Let's not play, let's skip those parts."

"Hmm." Her lips moved against mine, and she cupped my chin in her hands. "Brat."

Coming from her lips, it didn't sting. "Just because you are who you are, do you think you can take anything you want?"

Her finger parted my lips and pushed into my mouth. I grazed her skin with my teeth then gently sucked on it. She moved closer.

"I don't want much, Lucy. You should've seen that by now."

"Yet you still want my heart."

"I want a *chance* to have your heart. I'll do the rest. Just forget about your stupid curse and trust me. That's all I want."

With her palm on my cheek, her lips pressed against mine.

Time stood still as she kissed me like she'd never kissed me before.

"You wouldn't be good to my heart, Adam Connor," she whispered against my lips. "You're already making it hurt."

I wove my hand through her hair and held her head still as I took over her lips. She let me. She moaned so sweetly, so ready for me already.

Did she know her hand was shaking as it lay on my cheek? That she was falling for me even as I kissed her like she was already mine? Did she know how much she was ruining me?

I moved my lips over hers more firmly. I moved my arm from under her and held her beautiful face in my palms. With every moan, with every gasp, I took a little bit more from her. I took everything inside me and told myself that this would be it. That my nights and days and everything in between would be filled with this woman. That I wouldn't let her go. I'd be her home. I'd give her a family. I'd *be* her family. Her heart.

In that bed, her lips against mine, her hands holding on to my wrists, I promised her without words that I'd take everything I could take from her and in return give her the world.

I'd be that wind she loved to feel on her skin so much, the wind that put that peaceful smile on her lips.

I'd be her love.

The one who broke the curse she believed in so strongly.

If she had a baby, I'd give it my world. In return, all I'd take from her would be the battered yet still strong heart in her chest.

She let go of my wrist and one of her hands moved on my chest, sliding lower and lower. Her hips were restless, her body constantly moving against mine. I let go of her lips and pulled my shirt off so I could feel her hands on me.

Breathless from my kiss, she didn't even hesitate before taking off her own.

"Lucy," I growled softly as I took her in my arms again, her nipples hard against my chest.

"I want you," she whispered. "I want your cock inside me again. Stretch me wide open, Adam."

Her dirty, dirty mouth...

"You can have me, anything you want, Lucy."

"Now," she whispered, her hand sneaking in between us, her legs tangling with mine as if she wanted to make sure I'd stay.

She quickly worked my pants open and her hand was on my hot flesh, pulling my dick out. Stroking. Moving.

"I'm seriously in love with your cock," she murmured, her eyes closed, her teeth biting on her own lip. "You're not even in me and my legs are already shaking."

"Good," I managed to say roughly. "Mine is the only one you'll have for quite some time as far as I'm concerned."

She laughed, a beautiful sound. "Always so sure of yourself. You've barely learned how to kiss. I wouldn't be so sure of myself if I were you."

My hips moving on their own, I let her play with me, pet me. She tilted her head down and watched her hand move on me as I closed my eyes. It was dark, but I knew she could see enough. My cock pulsed in her hands, growing and hardening. When she swiped her thumb around the head, I leaked onto her fingers, more than ready to get inside her tight, wet pussy. I roughly pulled her head up and kissed her until she was out of breath again. Her hand tightened around me, her fingers not quite closing around the girth as I growled into her mouth, kissing her harder.

When she was drunk on my lips, I pulled away and bit her chin. "I thought you wanted to take me inside you. Are you done playing with me?"

She let me go and reached down, sliding off her underwear. As soon as she was done, I reached for her leg and pulled it over my thigh.

I palmed the curve of her ass, closing my eyes and memorizing the feel of her under my hands.

"Adam," she groaned impatiently.

I dropped my head against her chest.

"Lucy. I didn't plan for this. I don't have a condom with me."

Her groan caused my dick to twitch.

"Are you...clean?" she asked.

"Of course."

"Well...I am too. If you want to...that is...because...I want to..."

My forehead resting against her chest, I pulled on her hips and pushed the head of my cock into her.

"Christ," I groaned, feeling her hot flesh ripple around me without any barriers between us.

"Yes..." she moaned, her head falling on the pillow with a soft thud. "Yes."

She was so tight. One of her legs was still flush against my thigh, so I made sure to lift the other one higher to slide in more easily. I was tempted to slide another finger in her ass again, just like the last time, but didn't want to push my luck. This...taking her bare, skin to skin...it was more than enough.

Swallowing thickly, I buried myself deeper into her, inch by inch. Before I could go all the way, she pulled my head up by my hair and kissed me in a frenzy.

Returning her kiss with fervor, I pulled out of her wetness and thrust back in, my grip on her ass tight.

"Adam…" I was a whisper on her lips. The sweetest whisper.

"You're not gonna ask me if it's in or not again, are you?"

A strangled laugh escaped her lips.

"No. It's in there all right."

"Good," I murmured and thrust back in. "You want it all?"

She nodded and bit her lip as she rested her forehead against mine. "Do it."

I moved my hips up at the same time I pulled hers down on me.

She groaned, her back arching, her muscles contracting around me. "It's in. It's in."

I laughed, trying to keep it as low as possible. "And you're soaked. Again."

"Yeah." Her hand moved up and down on my arm, fingers twitching at the slightest move of my hips.

I pulled out and slammed back again, starting us in a slow but steady rhythm.

Closing my eyes, I listened to her shaky breathing.

"I won't last long," she whispered like she was in pain.

I stopped moving. "Am I hurting you?"

She laughed softly. "Yeah, but you make it hurt so good. I feel like I'm flying. I don't even care if I come or not, this is…" She groaned and gasped when I pounded into her a few times and then slowed down again. "This is perfect. I'm trying my best to keep quiet, but—" Her breath hitched when I started pumping into her harder and faster.

"You can take it," I growled into her ear.

"Yeah. Yeah. I can. Don't hold back." She held on to my shoulders and arched into me.

My hips pounding into her, I watched her bite her lip to quiet herself and my dick got harder in her tight pussy as her walls shook around me. Her fingers bit into my skin, and I was simply mesmerized by her.

"S-slow. Slow, Adam." Her palm pressed against my chest.

"Why?" I groaned into her neck. I was having trouble focusing on anything but the tight, soft flesh around my cock. She was so wet, so warm.

So unbelievably mine.

"If you keep driving into me like that, I'm gonna come, and I want you to stay inside me a little more. Just a little more."

I drove into her with lazy but deep strokes and pushed her hair away from her face. We were still on our sides, her ass still in my hands as I used it as leverage, pulling and pushing her on my cock. "I'll stay inside you as long as you want, Lucy. Don't hold yourself back. I'm not going anywhere."

Leaning down, I licked her nipple and groaned when her muscles squeezed me even tighter.

"Oh, God," she moaned. "Oh, shit!"

Desperate to give her more, I pulled her over me in one quick move and her eyes went wide open, her shock clear on her face.

She gasped loudly when my cock slid into the hilt.

Thank you, gravity.

I grabbed her wrists and pulled her down on my chest.

"Shhh," I whispered, sliding my hand around her neck. "You don't want to wake up your friends, do you?"

In reply, she ground her hips on me, moving them in a circle, driving me out of my mind.

"You love it, don't you? You love making me go crazy."

She put her hands on my chest, giving me a view of her beautiful, swollen breasts. I caressed her thighs, her skin burning hot under my hands.

"You are the one who makes me go crazy with your stupid cock," she whispered.

My hands moved up to her ass, and I made her sit up. Before

she could slide down on me, I lifted my knees up and started fucking her from underneath.

Her hands on my chest made tight little fists as I gave her every inch of my cock, slamming into her until she was a shaking mess over me, seconds away from tipping over. I pulled my cock out until all she had was the tip and then seated her back down, going in as deep as her body would let me.

I didn't think she was even expecting the orgasm that took over her body. I picked up my pace and fucked her harder as she barely managed to hold herself up. I was relentless, watching her breasts move with the power of my thrusts...I wanted her to give me everything, to let go.

When her breath hitched, she cupped her mouth with her hands and let out a loud groan, her hand barely muffling the sound. I sank into her over and over again until her body started swaying over me, her eyes rolling back into her head.

My jaw clenched. I hissed out a breath and slowed down my thrusts so she could take a breath and calm down. Her pussy was gripping me so tightly, making it almost impossible to move inside her.

When she opened her eyes and looked at me with that gorgeous smile on her lips, I was gone. Taking over for me, she moved on my cock, her inner muscles still twitching.

"You've ruined me," she said, that smirk still very much in place. "I love it. I fucking love the way you bump uglies with me, Adam."

My heart hammering in my chest, I laughed and let my hands roam over her stomach, her thighs, her breasts.

I wasn't going to last long.

"Where do you want me for your second one?" I asked in a raspy voice. "I'm too close. How do you want me to take you?"

She tilted her head and looked at me for a few silent seconds.

"In my mouth," she said finally and slid off my cock. I was

completely drenched with her juices. As she positioned herself between my legs, I stroked myself, loving the fact that I was the only one who could make her come so hard.

"Look at this mess," I mumbled, watching her lick her lips at the sight of me. "Are you going to clean it all up?"

She nodded and rounded both of her hands around the base of my cock before pulling up. Licking her lips, she got closer and licked the side of it from top to bottom.

"Come here, Lucy."

Letting go of me, she moved and gave me her lips before I could even ask for it. I kissed her and sucked her tongue into my mouth, loving her taste. Too soon, she pulled back and went back to my dick.

I opened my legs wider and watched her slowly pull the head into her mouth, her eyes locking with mine as she slowly took it deeper.

She sucked me into her mouth, making me groan and relax deeper into her bed.

With one hand, I gathered her hair so it wouldn't take away from my view as I watched her suck me off.

"You're perfect, Lucy. You're so perfect."

She moaned while I was still in her mouth and started sucking me harder, moving her hands up and down at the same time.

I loved to watch my dick disappear in her pussy, but watching her take me in her mouth and doing it with such pleasure...it sent tingles down my spine.

There was no way I was letting her go. I could spend a lifetime just watching those lips suck me off, kiss me, smile, sputter lies as she insisted on how much she hated me.

When her gag reflex kicked in, I eased her off me and caressed her cheek. "Easy, sweetheart. Nice and easy."

She nodded and swirled her tongue around me.

I was seconds away from making a mess on her face, not minutes.

"Suck on the head," I rasped out, barely enough strength left in me. Thank God she listened. "A little more. That's it. That's it, sweetheart. Take more of me."

Desperate to come, to have her in my arms, to feel her heartbeat against mine, I grabbed her under her arms and pulled her up next to me.

"What are you doing? You were so—"

I kissed her and pushed her hand on my cock again, rounding my own over hers.

"I want you closer," I said in a thick voice. "I want you on my lips when I come."

Giving me a soft kiss as if she understood what I meant, what I needed, she let me set the pace and in a few seconds I came all over our hands and my stomach, the warm liquid rushing out of me in waves.

Groaning into her mouth, I closed my eyes and let her hand softly stroke me down from my high.

For a few minutes, neither one of us spoke as our bodies calmed down. I grabbed the sheet and cleaned my stomach and our hands. When my heart rate was back to normal—or at least close to normal—I turned to Lucy and softly took her mouth.

She melted in my arms.

When she gently stroked my cheek, I stopped kissing her and just breathed in her scent.

"I want you, Lucy."

"You're not coming anywhere near my vagina right now. Every time you get in there, my legs start to shake uncontrollably."

I laughed softly. "Lucy, don't you know? If your legs aren't shaking at the end of it, you haven't been fucked good and well."

She laid her head on my chest, and I stroked her hair.

"Thank you," she said. "I didn't realize how much I needed you tonight. Thank you for coming to me."

Tipping my head down and seeing the look on her face...I shut my mouth and held her tighter against me.

She was mine and that was that. I didn't have to understand what was going on, I just had to accept it, and it was okay if she wasn't ready to accept that yet. I didn't mind waiting. She was worth it.

"I will be the one who speaks to your heart, Lucy Meyer, just like you seem to speak to mine," I murmured as my lips moved against her forehead, and she slowly fell asleep in my arms.

Breaking News: Adeline Young's Alleged Sex Tape

Yes, you read that right. There are rumors and, well...a hard copy of Adeline Young's sex tape being passed around. The thing that makes this unexpected news even more shocking is that the person who is trying to sell the twenty-minute video to the highest bidder claims that the video is dated to a time when Adeline was still married.

Have we actually seen this alleged sex tape? Are we sure Adeline Young is the star of the show? Yes, and yes. We've viewed certain parts of it and we're sorry to say that, yes, Adeline Young is indeed the star of this short movie. And what a movie it is...if you don't believe us, you can have a look at the stills that popped up online late last night.

Throughout their marriage, neither Adeline nor Adam was spotted with a stranger. When we first heard about the divorce, we kept repeating that fact, but if the reported date of this tape is true, it means Adeline Young did indeed cheat on her husband at least once that we know of.

We are still waiting to hear back on the identity of this mystery man, and as soon as we have a name we will share it with you. Then again, does it really matter? Will it affect Adam Connor any less if it's another actor or a random guy from the street? We don't think so.

We reached out to Adeline's publicist early this morning, and they profusely denied the sex tape claims, insisting that the stills taken from the tapes were altered. Since the young actress has been using every opportunity to get in front of the cameras since her divorce, we are expecting her to send out a press release out or show up in a live interview to try to get ahead of the claims. No word from Adam Connor's reps yet.

CHAPTER TWENTY

LUCY

Gently, I lowered the laptop onto the bed where I had fallen asleep in Adam's arms the night before then stood up.

Inhale and exhale, Lucy.

When I was calm enough to breathe like a normal person again, I walked into the living room where Olive was working on her manuscript.

"Olive," I sputtered, not knowing where to put my hands as I stood in front of her.

Her eyes widened when she saw that I was shaking like a leaf, and she jumped up from the couch she was half-buried in.

She rushed to my side. "Pregnancy. Baby. Doctor called. Results."

I shook my head and jumped up and down on my toes, my hands starting to shake in front me.

"You did it," I squealed and then put my fist in my mouth.

Inhale and exhale.

"I did what?" She put her hands on my arms to stop me from fidgeting in place. "Lucy, you're starting to scare me. I did what?"

Bubbling over with excitement, I gripped her hands and

leaned in closer so I could shout in her face. "You got yourself a deal for ten fucking million dollars!"

Her face went slack, and she whispered, "What?" And then came the shout, of course. "What?"

My heart beating in my throat, I released a deep, deep breath. "Olive," I started to explain as calmly as I could, which wasn't very calmly at all. "If you sign the contract they've sent over, you'll be the proud owner of...ten fucking million dollars!"

Right when she started to jump up and down with me, she stilled. "Oh, wait. Lucy, no. What did you do? Did you offer them my first unborn child or something?"

I laughed, my cheeks hurting from the amount of smiling that was happening on my face. "No. They want to republish *Soul Ache*, and they want three more books from you. You already finished one, so that leaves two more for you to write."

She covered her mouth with her hands, clearly still in shock. I hugged her, hard, and helped her jump with me.

"Oh my God, Lucy. Oh my God. Oh my God."

"That's exactly what I said when I started reading the contract an hour ago."

Her eyes were still big when I let her go and her gaze met mine. "That's why you went to your room? I thought you were... oh, hell. Did you say ten million dollars?"

"Yep," I nodded, barely keeping still.

This time it was Olive who crushed me in her arms. "You did it. You've officially become my agent, Lucy. We're working together. Oh my God!" She pulled back and smiled even bigger. "You're rich, too! You never have to call Catherine again! We're gonna have a baby and we're making money and we're selling books!"

We laughed for what seemed like hours and cried like the saps we were.

"I have to call Jason," Olive ranted. "I have to call my mom."

As we started the search for her phone, my own started ringing. As if it were a living, breathing monster that would bite my head off if I got too close, I hid my hands behind my back and leaned over the coffee table to see who was calling.

"Doctor's office," I whispered, looking at Olive with what I was sure were frightened eyes. "It's the doctor's office. What do I do?"

"Do you want me to answer?"

I swallowed the lump in my throat and grabbed the phone.

"I should be okay," I managed to get out before I swiped the screen and said hello to whoever was waiting to speak to me on the other end.

God, please don't let me have a heart attack. I promise, I'll be good from now on.

"Hello. Yes, I'm Lucy Meyer."

I blindly reached for Olive's hand, and she held it in her tight grasp.

"Yes. Yes, I'd like to know, please."

I heard the words. Thanked her. Ended the call. Gently placed my phone down, and just stood there.

"Lucy?"

Starting to feel nauseous, I walked over to the couch and sat down. Olive rushed into the kitchen and came back with a glass of water; I assumed I must've mumbled something about feeling nauseous.

Kneeling in front of me, she waited for me to speak.

I swallowed, cleared my throat, and then finally spoke as I looked into my friend's worried eyes.

"I'm not pregnant. I'm…" I flattened my palms against my stomach. "We're not having a baby."

"But your period…"

"I don't know. Maybe it decided to take a vacation?"

"Could be. You were stressed and sad about the break up."

Seconds ticked by in silence, then Olive got up from the floor and sat down next to me.

"What does it say about me that I'm relieved, Olive? Does that make me a bad person?"

"Oh, Lucy." She put her arm around me, and we fell back against the couch. "Of course it doesn't."

"I still feel like a bad person."

"Well, you aren't, so stop thinking like that."

"I just didn't want to make the same mistakes they did. That was the whole point."

"I know, Lucy, and that's okay. It's okay to want to be different even though you're already nothing like them."

Itching to change the subject, I said, "I'm not pregnant, and you're rich." I let that simmer for a while then glanced at my best friend, allowing myself a hint of a smile. "I think this calls for a celebration."

"Dance party?"

"With singing and everything."

"Jason is meeting with Tom and…Adam, so I think we should invite your future love interest and his adorable son, too."

I groaned and got up from the couch. *Wait a minute…* "Why is he meeting with Jason *and* Tom?"

"Tom has a script for the two of them. They might end up being costars. So, you see, now you *have* to marry him so we can travel together while they are shooting on location and even do interviews. We'll be like Kristen Bell and Mila Kunis."

"Only they are actresses and we're not," I pointed out.

"Well, yeah, but they are married to actors and they're all friends."

I thought about it—not the Kristen Bell-Mila Kunis part, of course, and not even the crazy marriage part, but the simple inviting Adam and Aiden part. I'd missed the little human after all, and…and it wouldn't hurt to have Adam Connor around either; he was good eye candy.

Especially when my stupid little heart pitter-pattered so happily when he was around.

"Fine," I grumbled. "Fine. Let's call him too."

Olive squealed and jumped up, fishing for her phone among the cushions.

Was my guard slipping? Was my heart making another mistake by starting to feel all happy and light around this amazing, hot as hell man who thought he was falling in love with me?

CHAPTER TWENTY-ONE

ADAM

My meeting with Tom had gone well. Actually, it had gone even better than just well. After we discussed my current situation with Sun Down Pictures, Jason joined us, and we further discussed the possibility of working together on a new project. Tom was definitely excited about it, and I thought Jason was too. After scrolling through the pages of the script, I promised them I'd finish reading it as soon as possible; from what I could see, it was going to be a good one.

Unfortunately, what happened after the meeting threw me off completely. We exited the café where we'd had the meeting and parted ways with Tom. After we agreed to meet back at Jason's house and see what Olive's surprise was, Jason got another call while we waited for our cars to be brought around.

Ending the call, he turned to me.

"Okay. Here is the deal." He ran his hand through his hair.

Intrigued, I waited for him to continue. Was I about to be uninvited after being invited by Olive? I wouldn't have been surprised, especially if it was Lucy's decision.

"I'm not gonna pretend I know what's going on between you and Lucy, but I'm assuming there *is* something going on."

He paused, waiting for any kind of acknowledgment from me. I nodded for him to go on.

"You know she is pregnant, and still you spent the night with her last night. Again, because of that, I'm going to assume there is something serious going on and she is somehow important to you."

"Exactly where are you going with this, Jason? Was that Lucy on the phone?"

"No. And to be honest I really don't want to meddle, but if Lucy leaves, Olive will—"

The valet brought our cars, and we were distracted for a minute or so. Before Jason could go on, my phone started ringing. "What do you mean if Lucy leaves?" Distracted, I checked the screen: my lawyer.

"If she leaves for Pittsburgh."

Slowly, I raised my eyes and met Jason's uncomfortable gaze.

"Pittsburgh? Lucy didn't say anything about leaving for Pittsburgh." For some reason, I didn't think she'd lie to me about something as important as moving away. She wouldn't just disappear.

"I'm not saying she is leaving, but that phone call..." He sighed and shook his head. "I have no idea if you'll do anything with this, but I'm just giving you a heads-up anyway. Her ex is waiting for me to pick him up." He raised his phone up. "The call was from him."

"And..." I prompted, my mind suddenly a very quiet and dangerous place to be in. "They are getting back together."

He shook his head. "I have no idea what's going on between them, but I don't think so. He is here about the pregnancy. I don't think he handled it that well when he heard it from Lucy, and I'm assuming he is here to make things right. I'm taking him up to the house."

"He wants her," I guessed.

Wincing, he rubbed the bridge of his nose. "From what I hear from Olive, yes. Yes, I think he wants her back."

"Give me a head start," I said immediately, rounding my car as Jason stood still in his spot. "Take the long way or something. Give me a head start."

When I jumped into my car and drove away, Jason was smiling.

————

AFTER I DROVE through the gates, Olive met me at the door.

"Oh," she mumbled, looking flustered. "Hi. I thought you were Jason." Leaning to her right, she looked behind me. "Aiden?"

"Aiden is still at school, and I'm afraid I won't be able to get him from Adeline, not today." Not when she was all the media were talking about. Beyond that, I didn't think she'd let me take Aiden when it wasn't my time after I pushed the sole custody thing on her.

"Oh, that's too bad. Come in, come in."

Closing the door behind me, I followed her inside.

"Can I speak to Lucy?"

"Of course. Uh, we were in her room, would you like me to get her?"

"Would you mind if I steal her from you for a bit? I only need a few minutes."

Giving me a curious look, she smiled softly. "Of course. She is yours to steal."

Frowning at her choice of words, I walked away.

When I reached Lucy's room, the door was wide open, so I went inside and closed it behind me.

"Adam? What are you doing here?" Lucy asked as she came out of the bathroom.

"Didn't you invite me?"

She came closer and smiled mischievously. "Yeah, well, it was Olive really, but I didn't object too strongly, so that should count for something."

I nodded. "I expected that much."

"I'll change my question then. Why are we holed up in here? I'd say you wanted to get in an afternoon quickie, but your face tells me something else is going on."

"We need to talk."

"We need to talk about…" She crossed her arms and waited for me to go on.

"I was going to give you time, Lucy. Instead of trying to knock down your walls, I was going to wait until you were ready to lower them on your own, but we just ran out of time."

She dropped her arms and straightened, her expression unreadable.

I took a step toward her, but still held my distance. "Something's going on here. There is something about you, something between us…I can't figure out what it is exactly, but I want you in my life. I know you—at least I feel like I know you, and I want you to give me more of yourself. I asked you to give me a chance to take care of your heart last night, and I'm afraid I need an answer now."

She was standing completely still in front of me, her eyes unreadable. As always, I had no idea what she was going to say, and I didn't like it. I didn't like that she was keeping me out.

"What's going on here?" she asked finally. "You just said you didn't want to push me, yet here you are, doing exactly that."

I stepped into her, and her back hit the wall. Keeping her gaze, I dropped my forehead on hers and breathed in her scent to try and calm my suddenly racing heart. She couldn't leave.

"Your ex is here. In LA. Jason is bringing him here."

She stepped back from me, her brows drawing in together in confusion. "Jameson? He's here?"

I nodded. "I can only assume he is here for the baby…and you."

"Adam, there is no—"

"No. I need you to give me an answer before you see him."

"I doubt he is here for me, Adam. You're being ridiculous. When I told him I was pregnant he asked me what I was planning to do with the baby. That's not a question someone who cares would ask."

"Lucy," I said softly, holding her chin between my fingers. "No guy would fly to another city for a girl they didn't care about."

I ran my finger down her jaw and watched her lips part for me. Leaning down, I stole a soft kiss. "You're gonna make me pull out the big guns, aren't you?"

"I have no idea what guns you're talking about, but sure, let's see them. Pull them out."

"I'm just a boy…standing in front of a girl, asking her to love him."

A wary smile surfaced on her lips.

"Quoting 'Notting Hill', huh? That is a big gun, you're right. You think that will get to me? That it will make my heart beat faster to hear you say that to me?"

She reached for my hand and pressed my palm against her heart where I could feel how fast her heart was beating for me.

We stared at each other for a long moment, standing just like that.

Skin to skin.

Heart to heart.

"I heard some girls melt away when they hear a guy quoting movie lines, so I thought I should give it a try on this girl."

Her hands dropped from mine, so I curled my hand around her neck, feeling her pulse beating.

"You make me crazy, Lucy."

Slowly, her smile disappeared. "You're scaring me, Adam."

"That's good. I don't mind scaring you if it'll make you accept that we're feeling something for each other."

"I can't love you," she returned before the words were even out of my mouth. "I can't give you those words. You may not believe me when I say I'm cursed, but that doesn't change the fact that I am."

I pulled her closer to me, her chest against mine.

"Lucy, tell me you hate me. I don't care. I'd rather have you lie and say you hate me than have someone else who lies by saying I love you."

"If I say I hate you, it really means I hate you. I'm not lying. And you do piss me off, so I really do hate you actually."

"Okay." I buried my nose in her neck and smiled. "You're mine then? He doesn't get to come back here and have you?"

The knock on the door interrupted us before Lucy could give me a real answer.

"Lucy? Uh...Jameson is here. He is waiting for you."

I looked down at her and found her looking up at me.

"I'll be there in a minute. Thank you, Olive."

Olive's voice was a low murmur on the other side of the door. "Of course."

I let my lips rest against hers and sighed.

"I'll let you have your way with me. Every night."

"Fine. Okay. I'll try."

"I knew bumping uglies would be the thing that would get to you. I'm contemplating if I should be worried about how much you love my cock."

She let out a small laugh and rested both her palms on my

chest as I curled my arms around her waist and forced her to get even closer to me.

"Well, I do love that thing. And you're not that bad with it. An okay kisser, but not so bad in bed."

Finally, I released a long breath and relaxed. This felt right. I smiled against her lips. "Good. I'll let you play with it as soon as we're alone."

I pulled back and after giving me a smile, she moved toward the door. "I think I should go out there."

I put her hand in mine. "We can do it together. If he is interested in being in the baby's life, it means I'll be seeing him around."

She snorted and shook her head. "You're so sure I'll keep you around for that long, huh?"

"I plan to be and don't worry, I won't be kicked out that easily. I know how to take care of what's mine. You won't want to lose me."

With her hand still on the doorknob, she gave me a long look.

"You want me *and* the baby? You're not even worried that I'll be pregnant and gigantic? Just asking to make sure."

"Baby or not, you're still the same, and I want you. I want you and everything else that comes with you—even your little curse."

Just as I'd promised her the night she'd come to me, I would heal her heart and be the one who broke her curse if that's what it would take for her to believe in me.

CHAPTER TWENTY-TWO

LUCY

So I said okay. So I broke my own rules and gave in to him. Rules are meant to be broken, aren't they? And this time I wouldn't say those words. I wouldn't show him how much I cared, how hard I was falling. I would pretend. He wouldn't see so he couldn't hurt me.

I was dating Adam freaking Connor.

My heart feeling restless and trapped in my chest, I walked out of my room with Adam right behind me.

I found Jameson standing in front of the open door, gazing outside. His hands were hidden in his pockets, his shoulders tensed.

I halted in my tracks and watched him stand there, Olive and Jason nowhere in sight. I looked behind me and saw Adam standing a few steps behind, giving me some space, I assumed. He gave me a reassuring smile and leaned against the wall, clearly telling me he had no intentions of leaving the room.

Before I could say anything, Jameson called my name, and I had to look away from Adam's hypnotizing eyes.

"Lucy." Jameson's voice was soft, and I thought I heard something else underneath it...regret? Or maybe he was just tired from the travel and I was reaching.

I took a deep breath and met him halfway.

Feeling Adam's eyes boring into the back of my head, I let Jameson press a soft kiss on my neck, just below my ear—his favorite spot, which had also been my favorite spot not that long ago.

For a brief moment, I closed my eyes and expected a rush of feeling from the touch, but it wasn't there. It never came.

Not love. Not even anger.

Surprised, I took a step back.

"What are you doing here, Jameson?" I asked, my voice a little hoarse.

"I'm sorry for what I said on the phone, Lucy." He released a deep breath and threaded his hand through his hair, looking lost. "I didn't know what to think, and I said the wrong words."

"It's okay."

Maybe if I really had been pregnant, I would've been pissed at him for his words, but since I wasn't, I didn't see the need to pretend.

"No." He grabbed my hands and tightened his hold. "No, it wasn't okay, and I've missed you, Lucy. I know—"

Jameson's eyes moved over my shoulder and his words halted. "Could you give us a minute, please?"

"I'm afraid I can't."

My hands still firmly in his, Jameson's eyes dropped to mine with a frown on his face.

Then I felt Adam's hand on the small of my back, and I tensed.

"You can let go of her now."

"Lucy?"

I cleared my throat and thought I might as well go ahead and introduce them. It would be a silly thing to do since both of them were obviously aware of who the other one was, but I couldn't think of anything else to say or do.

Gently, I pulled my hands out of Jameson's hold.

"Jameson, this is Adam Connor. He is…Olive and Jason's neighbor."

Adam dropped his hand and the room's temperature dropped pretty quickly after that.

"Adam…" I took a chance and glanced up and behind me, half-expecting to find him gone. But, no, he hadn't left. He was still there. His scent was still lingering on me, but not…his touch. There was no warmth.

Shit.

How would I introduce Jameson to him? 'My ex' sounded so…stupid.

"Adam, this is my friend Jameson."

There was no handshake, just heads nodding.

Awkward.

"I'll ask again, can you give us a minute?"

"And I'll answer again, I'm afraid I can't."

Oh, for God's sake…

Not giving Jameson a chance to reply, I grabbed his arm to get his attention.

His scowl shifted to me as soon as I touched him.

"Jameson, I'm not pregnant," I blurted out. I'd never been one to enjoy drama.

Aware that this would be news for Adam, too, I chose to keep my eyes on Jameson. I didn't mind having Adam in the room with us, but this was between me and Jameson. Even after the way he'd left me, I'd give him that much.

The scowl was still on his face when he asked, "What do you mean? But you said—"

"I said I was going to let you know after I got the results from the doctor's office."

"But you said you took one of those home tests."

"I did. But I only took one." I looked over my shoulder at Adam before I spoke again. "I was scared to take more than one. Apparently even those tests can be wrong."

"So you got the results from the doctor and…they are final."

I nodded. "Yes. Today. Just a few hours ago." I glanced behind to gauge Adam's expression, but he gave away nothing. The fact that he was not meeting my eyes didn't bode well.

"I was going to call. Though, to be honest, I didn't think you'd care…which is why I'm so surprised to see you standing here."

"I didn't come back just because of—uh, the pregnancy. I wanted you—"

Adam's arm slid around my waist, and I relaxed into his touch as he spoke.

"Lucy." My insides turned into complete mush every time he uttered my name with those lips, and I hated him for that a little bit. Just a tiny bit, really. "It makes no difference to me. Baby or no baby. I'm only glad because now you won't spend hours upon hours worrying about ending up like the females of your lovely family. And…"

He paused and shot a very quiet Jameson a quick look, to give his words a bit more punch, I guessed. "And you deserve better. You don't deserve to panic about something like this on your own. You don't deserve to be alone. You deserve so much better."

With those words, he leaned down and captured my lips. Right in front of Jameson. I didn't think it was to make him jealous, but maybe it was to make a point? What the hell did I know? His lips were on mine, and that was enough knowledge.

I didn't think he thought about it as staking his claim, but as soft as it had started—a soft, intimate reassurance, maybe—when it ended, it was as possessive as any of his other mind-scrambling kisses, dare I say almost as possessive as the ones he gave me when he was inside me, busy making me feel like I was walking on clouds?

His voice thick and smoky, he continued. "I have to go meet my lawyer. He's been calling me for an hour. I need to see if something's wrong."

Still a little delirious from his kiss, I nodded.

"Be ready at eight. We'll go out to dinner and talk, okay?"

Talk about what, I had no idea.

"I—" I cleared my throat. "Actually, we have something to celebrate, so we used Jason's name and made reservations for drinks and dinner. It's a pretty big thing."

"Am I invited?"

"Would it change anything if I said no?"

"No, it wouldn't."

I rolled my eyes, but I think he saw the twitch of my lips. "Then by all means, you can come too."

He gave me another kiss on my cheek, right at the edge of my lip actually, and my heart got excited all over again.

"Then we'll go home after dinner. Talk."

"Home, huh?" I said softly with a hint of a smile. He'd said the same thing the night he'd given me a ride after the Jake Callum disaster.

He nodded and caressed my cheekbone.

Not sure what I was trying to say, I met his gaze and admitted, "I don't like saying this, but you get a forty-nine from me right now, Adam Connor."

And now, on top of everything else, I had to start hating him for making me feel like he could be my home one day.

"I like forty-nine. That's a good number."

When Adam sent another look at Jameson and left, I knew I was completely screwed. With just a simple kiss, he'd managed to make me forget that we weren't alone in the room, that my ex was staring at us with the most terrible, heartbroken expression on his face.

"When did this happen, Lucy?" he asked into the silence.

There was no point in lying. "I'm not sure. Five minutes ago? A month ago?"

He walked away from me and sat down on the couch. Feeling awkward, I did the same and sat across from him.

"So you're not pregnant."

"No." It was hard to gauge what he was thinking.

He linked his hands together and leaned forward, his elbows resting on his thighs. After shooting me a quick look, he sighed and admitted, "I wanted you to come with me, you know. Before I left, I thought about a thousand ways to ask you, a thousand ways that would be the right way to ask you where you'd end up saying, 'Yes, Jameson. I want to come with you.' But I figured you'd never say that. You'd never take a risk that big. After all, you refused to sleep in the same bed as me for months; how could you even consider moving away with me? And then I thought, maybe it shouldn't be this hard to ask such a simple question. Maybe if it was right, if you'd wanted to come with me, you would have said something when you heard about the job offer. But you never did. So I left."

"So you left," I repeated his words when it became obvious he wasn't going to continue. Maybe he was waiting for me to confirm his suspicions. I couldn't do that. Even though I knew it would've made him feel better about his decisions, I couldn't—didn't *want* to lie to him. "If you'd asked, I would have come with you, Jameson." I gave him a rueful smile. "But maybe you're right. If it was so hard for you to ask me to come, if you had doubts about my feelings, feelings you knew were hard for me to admit, then it wouldn't have worked out anyway."

"I didn't handle it well when I heard you were pregnant."

"No, you didn't."

He nodded and looked out. Where had Olive and Jason disappeared to?

Then he smiled and rose up. "I'm not sure if I'm sad there is no baby or relieved."

I pushed myself up too. "Maybe this will sound heartless to you, but I'm relieved."

He looked surprised at my words.

"Neither one of us is ready to be a parent, Jameson. I'm not even sure if I'll ever be."

We shared a long moment of silence, then Jameson released a humorless laugh and rubbed his neck.

"What a mess. What a freaking mess. I thought if you ended up deciding to have the baby, I could persuade you to come to Pittsburgh with me. I thought it was a sign for me to try to ask you again…not that I did a bang-up job the first time. That's why I came here, and not only is there no baby, you're dating."

"I'm not dating," I bristled.

"What was that little show I saw then?" He gestured toward the door Adam had disappeared through.

I frowned. "It's not like that." But was it? What had I agreed to exactly? What did he want? Sleep in the same bed? Because even that was a big thing for me. Date? Could he even date? Be seen out in the public with me? Sex? What did 'You're mine then' mean? And could you even date a movie star? How?

"I see," Jameson murmured, and I remembered that I wasn't alone.

Walking over to me, he put his hand on my shoulder, his eyes holding mine. That's when I felt a trickle of emotion, something I could remember. Then without any hesitation he pushed his fingers into my hair and pressed a firm kiss on my lips. No tongue, just a last kiss filled with what ifs and apologies. It was such an unexpected move that I didn't know how to react. He pulled back from my lips only enough that the tips of our noses were almost touching, then closed his eyes and held me to him.

"Jameson..." I whispered, putting my hand on his tattooed wrist. He let go of my hair, but didn't back away.

"When you first told me you loved me, I felt like I'd scaled fucking mountains. He's a lucky son of a bitch. Make him work harder; he is right, you deserve better."

A quick kiss on my cheek, and he was gone.

CHAPTER TWENTY-THREE

ADAM

That evening as I drove through the colorful city to the restaurant after getting a short text from Jason telling me where I could meet them, I was still replaying the meeting I'd had with my lawyer in my mind.

The leaked sex tape—the *alleged* sex tape—was apparently real. Whoever was holding the hard copy in his or her hands was trying to get the best bid for it, and to entice the parties to bid higher, they were releasing stills from the video...stills that clearly showed Adeline half-naked with a cock in her hand as she was quite literally captured swallowing it. It wasn't the most perfect shot of her beautiful face, but it was most definitely the money shot that had all the media in a frenzy over who'd get the full video.

"We can use this," said Laura, my lawyer. She must have seen the look on my face because she didn't even pause before continuing. "It's a low blow, I know, but if you're serious about sole custody, we can use this to our advantage. Look at the time stamps; if this isn't altered, it means she was cheating. And if it happened once, we can most likely find others. Even if there are no sex tapes, we'll find something else. We should use this, Adam. It will make our jobs easier, trust me."

"No. I'm not looking to drag her through the mud. She'll have a hard enough time recovering from this as it is; I don't want to dig and find something else. I'm not doing this to destroy her, Laura; I want you to keep that in mind as you proceed forward. I just want my son with me. Find another way. Dig into something else, talk to her lawyers, find another way."

The shots weren't altered. She had cheated on me while we were still married. I knew that for a fact because in the photos you could see her hand, and I could see a small rash on her wrist, a redness caused by an unexpected irritation from a copper bracelet she wore for a shoot. The date matched when she had that rash.

Was I surprised when I heard there was a sex tape? Can't lie; yes, I was. Adeline…Adeline, for all her faults, had been loyal, or so I'd thought. But I was past the point of being angry about the existence of it. I couldn't go back and change the time, change the mistakes we'd made together. It didn't affect me anymore. *She* didn't factor into my life anymore. It was her mess, and only hers. I'd already instructed everyone on my publicity team to do their best to keep me out of the whole thing. There would be no comments coming from me. No quotes.

Still, I spent the entire day ignoring every single call that came from Adeline or her assistants. My mind filled with Aiden and what this new situation would mean to him, I left my car with the valet and entered the restaurant at exactly ten past seven. I was ten minutes late thanks to LA traffic.

At first, when I didn't see Lucy sitting next to Olive, I didn't think anything of it, but the closer I got to their partially hidden table toward the back, the possibility of her still being with that Jameson guy dawned on me.

Had I made a mistake by leaving her with him?

Had I lost my bright light?

Jason's head came up from Olive's neck, and he gestured to me with his hand. Olive noticed me too and offered me a shy smile. My steps faltered before I could get to their table and ask where Lucy was because Lucy emerged from the hallway a little to the right of where her friends were sitting. She sent a beautiful, unsure smile my way.

She looked stunning—as always. She wore black fuck-me heels with a black dress that hit her a little above her knee, and the neckline of her dress made it possible for me to see those delicious swells of her breasts. That was all I could take in as I changed my direction and headed toward her, my steps lighter now that I knew she was there.

With a small smirk plastered on her face, she rubbed her palms on her dress, subtly pulling it down in the process, and started toward me. A waitress walked up to the table that stood right between us, almost tripping me in the process.

Lucy smiled.

I laughed.

Steadying the waitress, I apologized to her and quickly rounded the table.

As soon as I was in front of Lucy, I captured her face in my hands and released a deep breath.

"You're here."

She snorted. "Did you think I'd let them celebrate without me? I don't think so." Her fingers curled around my wrists. "What's up with the face holding?"

I nudged her lips open with my own and kissed her until she was breathless in my arms. When I let go and brushed my thumb over her red bottom lip, she was holding on to my shirt.

I cleared my throat and smoothed her hair back just so I could keep touching her for another moment. "For a second there I thought the bastard tricked you into leaving with him."

One eyebrow shot up playfully. "Do I look trickable to you?"

I laughed and brushed another kiss on her lips. "No. You're anything but trickable, Lucy Meyer."

"Good. I'm glad you know that." Her eyes darted around. "Can we sit down already? People are staring, it's awkward."

I didn't give a fuck about what people thought—I was so used to feeling eyes on me all the time that I barely noticed it anymore —but still, I listened to her and grabbed her hand as we walked back to the table.

I kissed Olive's cheek, helped Lucy sit down, and greeted Jason.

"I guess we have more than one thing to celebrate tonight," Olive said with a big smile on her face.

"Olive…" Jason sighed.

"What?" She turned to face Jason, her eyes big and innocent. "I'm not doing anything."

As she was busy appealing to Jason, I brushed my fingertips over Lucy's wrist, watching the tiny hairs on her arm rise up under my touch as I murmured into her ear. "Everything okay with the ex?"

She gave me a small smile and nodded. "I think this time it's really over."

"It wasn't over already?"

What exactly had they talked about after I'd left?

She shook her head and reached for her water glass. "No, it was, but I think this was it, you know. Final. I don't think we'll ever see each other again."

"And are you okay with that?"

She took a small sip of her water and nodded, her eyes turning back to her friends.

I decided I could wait a few more hours until we were alone so we could talk. "I hear congratulations are in order," I said, interrupting Jason and Olive's quiet conversation.

"Oh, thank you," Olive replied, beaming at Lucy. "But I think congratulating Lucy would be more appropriate. I did absolutely nothing. She is the one who got the deal after all." She turned her eyes back to me. "And by doing so, she officially accepted the fact that she is my agent now."

"Congratulations," I repeated, reaching for Lucy's hand under the table. "To both of you."

They both gave me brilliant smiles.

After that, we gave our orders, and I discreetly asked our waiter if he could bring out a bottle of champagne. We fell into easy conversation as the night went on, and I discovered a different side of Lucy as I watched her interact with Olive. She looked free and happy with her. She didn't look troubled or worried. That was exactly how I wanted her to be when she was with me.

More than a few times, I found Jason looking at his wife with love as she laughed without abandon with Lucy. Despite everything that was going on with Adeline, I found myself laughing along with them.

When two fans who were having dinner at a nearby table came over and asked for autographs both from Jason and me, we quickly signed the napkins they were holding out and before we could object, they took a quick picture of the four us then hurriedly walked away.

Lucy's tense body leaned into me, and she whispered, "Aren't you gonna go after them?"

"To do what?"

"To take their phone and delete the picture?"

"Lucy." I sighed and pulled her chair a little closer to mine. "They weren't the only ones taking pictures tonight. Trust me, from what I saw, at least three other tables were secretly taking our picture."

"Is that okay? I mean, I know how these things work...what if they post it online? I guess that's a stupid question because they probably already have."

"So?" I asked, watching her intently, trying to understand what had her so worried.

"So?" she choked out. She leaned back and tilted her head, thinking something over. "Huh. It's like that, then. You were serious about what you said earlier."

"And you weren't?"

"I didn't know…"

"You didn't know what?" I prompted when she trailed off.

"I didn't know what you meant exactly. I thought we were gonna talk about what you said earlier today."

"What part was hard to understand? You're mine now. Don't know how to explain that further."

"Ha ha," she said without humor.

The waiter brought our desserts and another bottle of champagne for the ladies, cutting Lucy's little speech short. As soon as he left, she was back at it.

"You know exactly what I mean."

"Actually, I don't, but let me be more clear. You're mine means, from now on, you're mine and only mine."

She let out an exasperated sigh. "That's your idea of an explanation? That explains nothing. Does it mean we're having sex, exclusively? Does it mean we're dating? And if it does, can you even date? Are we in a relationship now? Do I have to sleep in the same bed with you all night? These are important questions, and I don't have the answers."

"Looks like you've been thinking about it a lot."

"I'd like to know what I'm getting into."

"How about you stop worrying about it?"

"How about you give me a hint?"

"Wasn't me telling you I'm falling for you a good hint? I thought that explained everything."

A small gasp had our heads turning.

"I'm sorry. I'm sorry. Please keep going," Olive whispered, looking amused.

"I hate to interrupt this, but I think it's time for us to leave," Jason said, his eyes aimed at the entrance.

I glanced back and saw the manager talking to a few people that kept pointing toward us; it appeared there was a sea of paparazzi waiting outside. Jason called out to our waiter and asked if we could walk through their kitchen and take the back door, something that was unfortunately not new to either one of us.

As soon as we got the okay, we were on our way with Olive and Lucy taking the lead as we were ushered toward the back door.

"I should've called Dan," I muttered to myself, shaking my head. "With everything that's been going on with Adeline, they're probably lying in wait in front of the house, too."

Jason glanced back at me as we reached the back door. "Call him now so he can come here and take care of your car. My driver will drop us off. You'll use the wall so they won't know you are home."

"Thank you. I think that's a good idea."

As we waited for Jason's driver to come around the back to pick us up, I gave Dan a quick call, asking him to pick up my car and then check up on Adeline and Aiden before he got back to the house. As much as I didn't mind ignoring her calls that day, it didn't mean I wasn't worried about how she was treating Aiden with all that'd been going on. She might still be angry at me for the upcoming custody battle and refuse to let me see Aiden whenever I wanted to when it was her week, but that didn't mean I'd just let her be.

"Is there something I can do to help?" Lucy asked once I was off the phone with Dan.

"Car is here, guys. Let's go before they think of posting a lookout back here too."

I gave Lucy what I hoped was a reassuring smile to let her know everything was okay—or at least would be—and guided her outside to the waiting car.

After we all piled in the car and drove away from the madness that was building up at the entrance of the restaurant, it was Lucy who took my hand in hers and made me feel like I had conquered the world.

CHAPTER TWENTY-FOUR

LUCY

Shockingly, the amount of people waiting in front of Adam's gate was even worse than what we'd seen downtown. Thankfully, not one single soul could see through Jason's black windows, and Adam went unnoticed as we drove through the gates and he walked into Jason and Olive's house with us.

As I held on to the back of the couch so I could take off my heels, I watched him pace back and forth like a trapped animal. Not exactly sure what to do or what to say in a situation like this, I stayed silent. Was part of his anger because of the cheating? Sensing my eyes on him, he turned to me.

"I'm sorry, Lucy. I know I said we'd talk, but I haven't heard from Dan yet, and I need to know how bad things are at Adeline's."

Shaking my head, I left the safety of the couch and walked up to him. "Are you crazy? That's not even on my mind right now. I'm worried about the little guy, too."

He sighed and rubbed his forehead.

Pretty much helpless, I met Olive's eyes.

"Jason?" she called out as her husband joined us in the living room. "Maybe the driver can take Adam to Adeline's place?"

"Yeah, he hasn't left yet, Adam. If things are this bad at your place, it can't be any better at Adeline's."

"That's what I'm afraid—"

Finally, his phone started ringing.

"Dan? What's going on?" He covered his eyes with his hand and released a suffering sigh. "Yes. Did they see him leave? Okay. Okay. That's fine, bring him through the gate. I'm at Jason's place. I'll be there in a few minutes."

Ending the call, he turned to us.

"He is bringing him here. Apparently things are even worse at Adeline's and when he offered to bring Aiden back here so she could take care of everything else, she didn't put up a fight."

I closed the distance between us and touched his arm. "That's good, right? Do you want me to come too, so I can distract Aiden from what's going on outside?"

He touched my face, his palm warm against my cheek. "Only if you promise to distract me too."

I couldn't help but smile at him; he made me do that a lot these days. "We might be able to work something out."

———

ADAM WALKED in with Aiden in his arms, Dan bringing up the rear with a ferocious scowl on his face.

"Look who is here to see you, big guy," Adam murmured to Aiden, whose face was buried in his neck as his little arms held on tight. The PJs he was wearing had adorable little blue cars on them.

"Hi, Aiden." I walked up to them, not sure what was going on exactly or how bad it was. Could the day have gone any worse, for God's sake? It had started out so promising only to turn into a complete mess.

Aiden came out from hiding and gave me a small wave. "Hello, Lucy. Did you come for me?"

My face brightened. "I did. Your dad asked me if I wanted to see you, and I jumped on it. How are you doing?"

"I had a tough day. Mommy was really sad. I didn't want to leave her, but she said I couldn't help."

Oh, dammit. I glanced at Adam and saw his jaw clench—and what a sexy jaw it was. I shook my head and focused on the anxious little boy.

"We all have tough days every now and then. Do you know what I do when I have a tough day?" His little hand holding on to his father's shirt, he just shook his head. "I have a little ice cream and watch *The Lion King* or *Zootopia* with my best friend." Those were his favorite movies to watch.

"You watch them with Olive?"

I nodded. "Yes. She loves them just as much as I do."

He blinked a few times, his eyes already sleepy. Dan must have taken him right out of his bed.

"I love them, too." He turned his eyes to his dad. "Daddy, can I watch them with Lucy now? I had a really tough day."

Adam forced a tight smile on his face and brushed away Aiden's hair. "It's past your bedtime, Aiden."

"Just a little, Daddy? Please?"

"How about we build a fort right here in the living room and watch the movies under it? Maybe if we invite your dad to watch with us, he won't say no."

Aiden's eyes got big and hopeful as he straightened in his dad's arms. Out of the corner of my eye, I saw Adam smile and Dan shake his head.

"But I don't know how to make a fort, Lucy. I've never made one before. Have you?"

"Of course I did, but I don't think I can quite do it without you. Would you help me?"

"Yes, I can do that." He touched his father's cheek to get his attention. "Can we build a tent, Daddy? You can watch with us, too. If Lucy starts crying again, you can help me hug her and tell her she is being silly again."

Adam laughed and nodded. "Okay. We'll do that then." He lowered Aiden down and the moment his little feet touched the ground, he started toward his bedroom.

"I'll bring my favorite pillow!"

"I'll get the sheets." As I was walking past Adam, he grabbed my wrist and stopped me. I raised my eyebrow and looked up at him. "Your fetish again?"

He leaned down and kissed me. The soft touch of his lips, the intimate thank you made my head spin when his tongue sneaked into my mouth. Before I knew what was happening, it was over.

"Thank you for being here, Lucy. Being with us." he said in a gruff voice. Aiden came running in with two pillows in his hand.

"I brought my other favorite pillow for you, Lucy."

"Thank you, little human," I said quietly. He carefully placed the pillows on the couch and reached for my hand.

"Come on, I'll show you where the sheets are." He pulled me away from his dad and stopped at the mouth of the hallway. "Daddy, are you gonna help us?"

"I have to talk to Dan before he leaves. I'll be with you right after that."

"You don't want to watch a movie with us, Dan?"

"I have to leave, big guy. You'll take care of your dad and Lucy for me, won't you?"

Aiden visibly puffed out his chest and nodded. "I will. I'll do a good job."

With that promise, he pulled me into his room so we could choose from his favorite sheets.

After rummaging through various sets, we decided on two light blue ones, one green that almost matched his eye color, one red, and one white with red and black trains on it. We also stole a few pillows from his dad's bed.

When we emerged with our loot, neither Adam nor Dan was in sight. Aiden dumped everything in his arms on the floor and helped me with mine.

"Can you get the cushions down? We'll stack them on the couch so we can make it higher. I'll go and check on your dad."

"Lucy…do you think he'd let us have ice cream?"

"Hmmm." I narrowed my eyes to appear like I was thinking very hard about it. "I'll ask, but I think he'd say it's a little late to have ice cream."

Aiden crossed his arms over his chest, mimicking my stance, and tilted his head to the side. "Yeah, I think you're right. But he wouldn't say no if we asked him tomorrow! And maybe Mom can come with us, too."

"Yes. You're right. We'll ask him tomorrow."

I helped him climb onto the couch so he could throw the cushions on the floor and headed toward the front door where I could hear Adam's voice slowly rising.

"Hey," I hissed, grabbing the attention of two very angry men. "He is worried as it is; how about you keep it down a little?"

Dan's scowl deepened, but he didn't say anything. Adam was on his phone and looked seconds away from losing it.

"What's going on?" I asked Dan quietly.

"Adeline," he grumbled, his tone communicating his opinion of Adam's ex quite clearly.

"Adeline, I'm not going to make a statement with you. I don't care how this affects your career at all. You should've thought about that before you decided it would be a good idea to cheat on me with a director to get a role."

I bugged my eyes out at Dan and swallowed the words threatening to spill out.

Oh, boy.

In the next breath, Adam's entire body tensed. I could practically see the vein throbbing in his neck. He closed his eyes to take a deep breath that didn't seem to relax him at all.

"You won't do that to Aiden. You won't make him go through that."

"Lucy!" Aiden shouted my name, and Adam's head snapped toward the noise.

"I'm sorry. I'll go," I murmured, and his eyes softened when they fell on me. I raced back to Aiden without saying anything else.

What the hell was going on?

CHAPTER TWENTY-FIVE

ADAM

"You either come tonight so they can get a shot of you entering my house with a smile or the statement I make tomorrow will be a different one, Adam."

Those were Adeline's last words as she hung up on me.

"What's going on?" Dan asked, trying to keep his voice down. I could hear Lucy's murmurings to Aiden as they started on the fort Lucy had promised. I checked the time: ten o'clock, way past Aiden's bedtime.

"She wants me to make a statement with her and basically hint that we are getting back together."

Dan's face hardened. "And if you don't?"

"If I don't, she'll talk about Aiden."

"Even she wouldn't do that," Dan countered as a frown appeared on his face. "Does she think it wouldn't backfire on her?"

My throat tightened as I tried my best to swallow down my anger when all I wanted to do was smash my phone against the wall and just go be with my son and Lucy.

I heard Lucy release a mock growl then Aiden's laugh filled the house. "I have to go," I said gruffly, looking into Dan's eyes as Lucy and Aiden's laughter rang in my ears. "She is trapped. She isn't thinking clearly, and I can't risk her making a mistake like that."

"I'll take you to her."

I nodded as Dan opened the door and stepped outside. "You start the car; I'll be right there."

I found Aiden standing in front of the TV and laughing at Lucy as she tried to save herself from the attack of the sheet over her head.

"I will get you, little human." She growled and moved toward Aiden, and he squealed and ran to hide behind my legs.

"Aiden, why don't you get the pillows in my bedroom, too?"

He tilted his head to look up at me. "We can take them all?"

"Of course. If we're gonna make a fort, it better be a comfortable one, don't you think?"

He nodded enthusiastically and ran away, and I turned to find Lucy staring at me with knowing eyes as she pulled Aiden's train sheet over her shoulders.

"You have to go."

I closed the distance between us and pulled her into my arms, breathing in her soft scent to calm myself down. The sheet slid down her shoulders, fluttering to the floor as she moved her hands over my chest, instinctively understanding what I needed from her.

"I have to talk to her. She is…if I don't, she's going to make a big mistake."

She pulled back and looked into my eyes for a few seconds. "I understand."

I smiled. She couldn't understand this. She couldn't understand how much it'd hurt Aiden if Adeline said something stupid in front of the cameras just to get the attention off herself.

"You can't, but I promise to explain everything one day."

The second the words left my mouth, I knew I'd said the

wrong thing, even before I saw the small flinch. She pulled back completely. "You said we'll talk, right. We'll do that one day."

"Lucy, no." I touched her face and took comfort in the fact that she didn't pull away. "This...whatever it is that's going on in Adeline's life changes nothing for us. You still don't get to run away from me."

Aiden came out with two pillows hugged to his chest, both of them larger than his small body, and I had to let go of Lucy.

Taking the pillows away from Aiden, I lifted him up in my arms and pressed a kiss on his forehead. "I have to go and check on your mom, but I'll be back as soon as I can. Would that be okay with you?"

"Lucy gets to stay?" His eyes flitted between me and Lucy.

"Yes. Lucy gets to stay with you. You two start the movie and I'll catch up with you, okay?"

"You'll take care of Mom so she won't cry anymore? I tried to give her a hug, but she didn't want it."

I hugged him a little tighter to myself. "I'll take care of your mom. You don't have to worry about a thing, buddy. Do we have a deal?"

He hugged my neck and nodded.

I mouthed a quick thank you to Lucy and lowered Aiden down so he could get back to building a fort with his friend.

Before she could turn away, I stole a quick kiss from Lucy that didn't last long enough and got out.

———

ADELINE WAS PACING in her living room where all the drapes had been pulled closed when her assistant let us in through the front door. I had been right: the street was littered with paparazzi that came to life as soon as they saw my car come around the corner.

"Leave us alone," Adeline ordered her assistant and Dan.

Even though Dan already knew everything there was to know about us, I preferred to have this conversation with Adeline alone.

"We have to make a statement," Adeline started as she lighted up a cigarette. "Don't look at me like that," she snapped before I could make any kind of comment. "It's just stress. I'm not starting up again."

I stayed silent. She could smoke herself to death for all I cared.

"We have to make statement," she repeated. "Together. I don't know what we'll say exactly, at least not yet, but you have to be in front of the cameras with me, holding my hand. Neil and your mom agree with me."

"My mom? You're still talking to her?"

She puffed out some smoke, and I found myself trying to pinpoint exactly when everything had started to go so wrong for us. Had it ever been right? "She said you're not answering her calls. This…this thing affects them too. They don't want the family name to be mentioned along with something like this."

"Did they forget that you're not family anymore?"

She pressed the cigarette into an ashtray with jerky movements and picked up another one as she tilted her head at me.

"Am I not Aiden's mom, Adam? Does that not make me your family forever? And you might prefer not to talk to them, but I still consider them my family."

Of course she did. She fit right in with them.

I clenched my fists and faced the windows that looked out at a small guesthouse and the backyard.

"I thought so too. Neil thinks the only reason they haven't mentioned who I'm with in the video is because his face was cut off. From the stills they're leaking it doesn't look like they have a better angle and we can use that. We can release a statement or have Neil interview us about it, or someone else if you want to.

He thinks the best way to go about this is to say it was shot without our knowledge and we knew nothing about it."

Somewhere in the middle she lost me. "Excuse me? What do you mean without our knowledge?"

"We have to say it's a video of us. The date matches. The only reason everyone is so obsessed with it is because they think I was cheating on you and that I'm the reason our marriage ended. If we tell them that it's you, everyone will lose interest. You coming here tonight…" She gestured outside with the cigarette between her fingers. "Them getting a picture as you pulled in, that will help. After all, if I had cheated on you, you wouldn't have come."

"But that's not the reason I'm here, is it?"

She took a deep drag of her cigarette and blew it toward the ceiling. "No, it isn't. And like I told you on the phone, I don't want to make a statement about Aiden, but if you force my hand, to save myself, my career, I will do exactly that. After the divorce, this is all I got, Adam. If you hadn't filed for custody maybe this would've just blown over, but everything came back to back. I can't let a sex tape ruin everything."

We stared at each other in the silence that followed her words.

I forced a smile on my lips and clapped at her performance. "And when you throw us under the bus, will you add that it was your idea from the beginning?"

She smiled, the tension melting away from her features and making her look soft and sweet. "Of course I will. You didn't want him after all. I was the one who had to talk you into it. You can't argue with that, can you?"

"What happened, Adeline? What happened to you?" I asked, already past the shock and disgust.

Putting out her cigarette, she walked up to me. "I love him. I love him, Adam. Please don't make me hurt him. Nothing ended up being what I wished for, but I did my best. I did my best as your wife, and I don't deserve this. All I'm asking for is your help. Nothing more. We can act like we're thinking of getting back together. We'll pretend as if this brought us back together, and when the waters settle down again and I start filming regularly, I'll let you have sole custody—"

The door to her living room slammed open, jolting both of us.

"Dan, what's go—"

"We need to leave. We need to leave right now."

CHAPTER TWENTY-SIX

LUCY

Lying next to Aiden as he slept, my own eyes started to close as I waited for Adam. I wasn't exactly sure if we'd end up talking about us when he got back, and quite frankly I was probably the last thing on his mind, but still, talk or no talk, I knew I'd feel much better when he was back with us.

Aiden had fallen asleep ten minutes into the movie after we built our impromptu fort that was only really big enough for the two of us. He snuggled closer to me in his sleep, and I smiled down at him. He was the perfect kid.

"Can you keep a secret, Lucy?" he had asked me just moments before his eyes had lost the fight and he had fallen asleep.

"Of course. I love secrets. Tell me."

He looked away from the TV and played with his pajama bottoms. "I cried today."

"What happened?" I whispered back just as quietly as he had.

He lifted his eyes up to meet mine, his fingers still twisting and pulling at the fabric. "You can't tell my dad, though. Okay?"

Nodding, I waited for him to continue. "My mom was on the

phone today and she was crying, so I thought I could give her a hug and make it okay, like I did with you when you cried over *Lion King*, but when I tried to get her attention, she yelled at me and told me to get back to my room. My nanny rushed after me and said my mom was just sad and didn't mean to yell at me, but I still cried a little because I don't want her to be sad. I just wanted to give her a hug."

The bitch!

"I'm sure she didn't mean to yell at you, Aiden. I think she was having a bad day today, which is why your dad left so he could help her. She'll be okay."

"I know," he murmured. "But it made me cry anyway. I always miss my dad when she yells at me because she never yells when daddy is there." I tried to find something to say but came up empty.

Shit.

"Love you, Lucy," Aiden murmured, his eyes already closed.

My heart melted in my chest, and I secretly plotted ways to kill the oh-so-put-together bitch. Maybe a heavy camera could fall on her face? That would be fun. Who'd yell at a kid when they offered to give you a hug just to make you feel better? Like who in the fucking world?

"I love you, too, little human," I murmured back and brushed a light kiss on his cheek.

I felt my eyes slowly start to close, so I scooted down and got a little more comfortable without waking Aiden up.

I wasn't sure if it was seconds or minutes later, but something woke me up. Groggy and not exactly sure what was going on, I looked around and listened to see if what I'd heard was Adam.

The door didn't open. There was no sound of a car. There was no Adam.

I'd muted the TV before I'd closed my eyes, but the light from the movie was enough that I could see around clearly.

When that weird feeling didn't go away, I rubbed my eyes and slowly sat up.

It was then I heard the sharp sound of a twig breaking. My heart beating heavily in my chest, I pulled back the sheets and peered out from our little hiding place, toward the backyard. It was dark outside, and more than that, the couch in front of the windows was making it impossible to see outside from my point of view.

On my hands and knees, I crawled out of the fort and waited.

Listened.

Nothing.

But then, something.

I saw someone walking past the window as his or her shadow fell on the wood flooring right in front of me.

Holding back my gasp, I crawled back and started to shake Aiden.

"Aiden. Aiden, you have to wake up." My voice was barely audible.

He moaned and blinked his eyes open.

"Aiden you have to get up for me, okay?"

"Is Daddy back?"

"Not yet, sweetheart, but I need you to get up now, okay?"

"Okay," he mumbled, letting me pull him into a sitting position.

I heard a clicking that sounded suspiciously like someone trying to open the door, but a second later it was all silent again.

Aiden kept rubbing his eyes, but I pulled his hands down to get his attention again. "Aiden, listen to me. I need you to—" *Holy shit!* I realized I'd left my phone in Adam's room when we were stealing more pillows from him. "Aiden, as soon as I say so, we will run to your dad's room, okay? Can you do that for me?"

"But why?"

"Because we need to hide, okay?"

"Is this an emergency?"

"Yes. Yes, it is. We need to hide so I can call your dad and tell him to come back here, okay?"

He scratched his head and gave me an adorably confused look, which would have been cute if the possibility of danger wasn't so imminent.

"But, if there is an emergency we are supposed to call nine-one-one and Dan. Daddy told me so."

"You're absolutely right, but first we need to get to your dad's room so I can get my phone, okay?"

He nodded as I helped him up to his feet and stayed on my knees. He was short enough that he couldn't be seen over the couch.

Taking a shaky breath, I crawled away from Aiden for a second. Holding on to the arm of the couch, I peered outside, and when I was sure there was no one lurking in front of the windows, I got up to my feet and told Aiden to run.

I can't tell you how grateful I was that he didn't make me say it twice and ran straight to his dad's room.

I was right behind him.

My hands shaking, I grabbed my phone from the top of the dresser and barely managed to find Dan's number in my contacts list.

"Everything all right, Lucy?"

"Dan," I whispered, relief filling me as soon as I heard his voice. "Dan, someone is out in the backyard. I think they're trying to get in. You need to come back now."

"Lucy." His voice was as steady as always, but unfortunately it did nothing to calm my racing heart. "I need you to take Aiden and hide. Can you do that? Can you get Aiden and hide in one of the rooms?"

"Look, this might be nothing," I said when he was done freaking me out even more. "Maybe it was just—"

Someone knocked on a window, the noise as clear as a bell, and I jumped, my heart in my throat.

"Talk to me," Dan ordered in a sharper voice.

"Okay. Okay, we need to hide and you need to get back here right now, Dan. They just knocked on the window. Get back here now!"

I ended the call and realized I was out of breath as if I had just run a freaking marathon in the last minute I was on the phone. Then I met the frightened eyes of a five-year-old who had heard every single word of what I had just said. Cursing at myself, I kneeled in front of him and before I could utter a word, he threw himself in my arms.

"I'm scared, Lucy."

"It's okay," I assured him in what I hoped was a strong voice. "It'll be okay, Aiden. I'm right here with you, and your dad and Dan will be here as soon as they can."

Then my worst nightmare happened: we heard the unmistakable sound of someone breaking a window.

As soon as Aiden started screaming, I put my hand on his mouth and muffled his screams. His tear-filled eyes met mine, and I shook my head. Tucking his legs around my waist, I got up from the floor and ran toward the adjoined room that was Adam's closet.

It was either the worst place to hide or the best. After looking around to find the best spot, I parted the row of pants, dropped back to my knees, and urged Aiden to crawl back to the narrow empty space between the clothes and the wall, hoping we'd be concealed. I crawled in right after him and pulled him back into my arms.

I could already feel his tears wetting my shirt as he cried silently.

Holding my breath, I tried to listen for footsteps, but couldn't hear a damn thing. Quickly dialing nine-one-one, I told the operator what was going on in a hushed whisper, gave him the address, and let him know that we were hiding.

He told me to stay on the line and that the cops were dispatched, but all I could hear was a man whispering Aiden's name as his footsteps got closer and closer.

"I can hear footsteps. I can't talk. I hear his footsteps," I mumbled to the guy that was trying his best to keep me calm. Shaking like a leaf, I put down the phone and gestured at Aiden to be quiet. Just to make sure, I put my hand over his mouth and whispered to him to close his eyes. I'm not ashamed to admit I did the same.

The house and our hiding place were completely dark, but the simple act of closing my eyes gave me a stupid sense of security that meant nothing if the guy found us.

If it were just me, if Aiden wasn't clinging to me as if his life depended on it—and maybe it did—I would've grabbed something sharp or heavy and…hell, I don't know, maybe I would've attacked him myself. I knew I couldn't do that, couldn't risk Aiden.

The footsteps stopped in front of Adam's room, or maybe he was in the room. I was seconds away from passing out and the only thing that stopped me was the little boy in my arms who was shaking even harder than me. Then a chill went down my spine when another whisper came as he called out Aiden's name again.

"Aiden. I'm here to take you home. You can come out, your mom sent me to get you."

I held the kid tighter to myself and rested my head against his, my hand still very much covering his mouth. The amount of pressure I was putting on my body to keep both of us still was colossal. And yet, if he stepped into the room, I was pretty sure he'd spot us in a heartbeat.

The footsteps retreated without any other sound, and I swallowed down my scream.

We could hear him whisper Aiden's name as he searched every room for him.

Then I heard the sweet sounds of the police sirens and let the first teardrops fall from my eyes.

CHAPTER TWENTY-SEVEN

ADAM

There was a sea of people in front of our house. I saw three police cruisers with their red and blue lights flashing and countless cameras trying to get a view inside the wide-open gates as two officers tried to hold them back.

We'd called nine-one-one on our way to the house and learned that Lucy was on the line with another operator. When they asked me for the gate codes as Lucy had stopped responding, I thought my heart had stopped beating.

Nothing, and I mean *nothing* could have prepared me for the mess that was waiting back at home.

"You need to stay calm," Dan instructed me. "There are cameras everywhere, Adam. If the guy is still here, you need to stay calm."

None of his words really penetrating the haze in my mind, I watched as the cameras pulled back from the gate as soon as they recognized the car. They swarmed around us, making it impossible to move farther.

Ignoring Dan's shouts, I pushed open the door, knocking a few cameras down in the process, and ran up to the gates.

The first thing I spotted was my son in Jason Thorn's arms

right outside our house next to another police cruiser. Something broke inside me—or maybe something mended...maybe both. I lost count of the seconds it took me to get past the cops who tried to block me and get to their side.

"He fell asleep," Jason murmured as he gently passed my son into my arms. I ran my hand over every inch of his body to convince myself that he was okay, that no harm had come to him, and crushed him to my chest as my breath shuddered out of me. All the ruckus going on just a few feet away didn't even faze him as his head fell on my shoulder and his tiny hands instinctively held on to my shirt.

I dropped my forehead on his shoulder and took a deep, calming breath.

When I lifted my head, all that mattered was finding Lucy... and she was right there, right there next to Olive, holding her friend's hand in a tight grip as tears ran down their faces.

"I fucking love you," I said in a growl, going for her. "I fucking love you, Lucy."

She held on to me just as tight as I was holding her to myself.

Her body shook against mine, and I heard her breath hitch. If I could have, if it had been possible, I would've held her closer, pulled her tighter.

"I love you," I whispered into her neck before brushing a kiss on her skin. "I love you. I love you."

I closed my eyes and ignored all the shouts and the flashes.

I kissed her lips countless times as I tasted her tears.

I kissed her neck, her throat, her nose. Everywhere. Every inch.

I thanked her again and again for being there for my son for the second time.

I held her in my arms for long minutes.

I ignored the entire world around us.

It was at that moment, that specific moment where everyone

around us disappeared and it was just the three of us, where she trusted me enough to hold her up, trusted me enough to let me whisper my love to her, that made me sure I would do everything in my power—even if it meant fighting with her—to make her understand that I was the one who would make her happy for the rest of our lives, that I was the one who had already broken her curse.

A Terrifying Night for the Connor Family

What a day, folks. What a freaking day…
The day started with Adeline Young refusing to comment or answer questions about the sex tape rumors and somehow progressed into a nightmare when an alleged stalker of Adeline broke into Adam Connor's house in Bel Air. However, that wasn't how the night ended for the Academy Award-winning actor. The night's big ending was him being photographed with another woman in his arms as they kissed in front of the cameras. It took some time, but we finally identified the lucky woman as Olive Thorn's literary agent, Lucy Meyer. The couple was also photographed having dinner with Jason and Olive Thorn the night before.
Before we cry buckets of tears for missing our opportunity with Adam Connor, let's get back to the terrifying night his son and his new girlfriend had.
The alleged stalker J.D. is apparently one of Adeline Young's number one fans who took things more than a little bit too far. After he was arrested in the actor's house for stalking and breaking and entering, J.D. admitted that he had been stalking Adeline for days now. He admitted to breaking into the house and said he "meant to harm Adam Connor for upsetting Adeline,"

who he believed was his future wife. "I couldn't sit back and watch her cry while Adam Connor took her son away from her." In the video below, you can hear the tearful nine-one-one call the new girlfriend made, and it intensifies the chilling night they had as they hid in the closet until the police entered the home and apprehended the intruder. As far as we know, J.D. wasn't armed when he was arrested, but none of us want to even imagine how he would have reacted if he had found Aiden Connor and Lucy Meyer in their hiding place, as he believed he was there to save the little boy from his father and return him to his mother.

An hour before the emergency call was made, Adam Connor had been photographed entering his ex-wife's home. From what our sources say, he raced home as soon as he heard something was wrong back at his place. The photos below show him running up to his house as he takes his sleeping son from his neighbor Jason Thorn's arms and holds on to his crying girlfriend.

We're so relieved no one was harmed and that Aiden Connor is spending the night safe in his father's arms.

We're also working tirelessly to find out more about the new girlfriend.

CHAPTER TWENTY-EIGHT

ADAM

After the cops left with the intruder in cuffs, Jason and Olive went back to their home with promises to come back in the morning and help with whatever we needed. After everything was said and done, it was only the four of us left behind.

With Aiden still sleeping in my arms, I grabbed Lucy's hand, guided us to my bedroom, and closed the door behind me. I needed to be alone with them for the night, knowing Dan would be busy making calls and taking care of things for me. Morning wasn't too far away anyway; I'd deal with everything in just a few hours. But for the night, at least for the remaining hours, I was where I wanted to be.

Lucy helped me tuck Aiden in and sat with me for a few silent minutes as I watched my son sleep peacefully, his hands tucked under his head, his mouth slightly open. I brushed his hair away from his forehead and smiled when he kicked my leg with his feet. If I hadn't known he'd always been a very heavy sleeper, I would've been worried about his ability to sleep through all the commotion. When I was sure he was okay and safe, I pulled Lucy into the bathroom with me, ignoring her questioning look.

I heard the soft click indicating that the door was shut and just rested my forehead against the door until my head wasn't spinning anymore.

I felt Lucy's hand on my shoulder and back, stroking, caressing.

"He is okay, Adam. He is safe now."

I turned around and gripped her wrists in my hands, not hard enough to hurt her, but not loose enough that she'd think she could get away easily.

"You're safe, too. This is it, Lucy," I said thickly. "This is all the talk you'll get. Give me everything you got, tell me all the reasons why we can't be together, and I'll prove every one of them wrong. This is it. You won't get another chance. I won't let you go."

I forced my body to do the exact opposite and let go of her wrists. I waited, still standing in front of the door, blocking her. I didn't think she'd run away from me, but with Lucy you could never know; she always had a way of surprising you, and I wasn't about to take the risk.

"Okay," she said with a sigh. "Okay, Adam. You win."

I slipped my hand around her waist and pulled her closer. "I win what, exactly?"

"Apparently you win me." She gave me a tentative smile and raised her fist in the air. "Yay? Congrats? You got yourself a relationship. Enjoy."

"I'm blinded by your enthusiasm."

"You're welcome."

An unexpected laugh bubbled out of me, and I leaned down to kiss her, but she stopped me before I could taste her, before I could make her eyes go out of focus.

"Before you give me what I'm pretty sure will be an awful kiss, I want you to know that I know that this can't go anywhere."

I shook my head and exhaled. "You have to stop it with the enthusiasm, Lucy."

"I'm being serious. I need you to know that it's okay. When the time comes and this ends—"

"Because of the curse, right?"

"Yes. Make fun of me all you want, but when this comes to an end—"

I reached down and pulled her shirt off her, successfully shutting her up.

"What are you doing?" she asked calmly.

"Time to talk is over."

"I just wanted to tell you that it's ok—"

I pulled down her pants, lifting her feet one at a time to free them. Then I did the same with her underwear as she held on to my shoulders, and then I took off her bra. Reaching for her hair, I pulled out the hair tie and watched her hair fall down onto her bare shoulders.

"Okay, Adam. Okay."

Then it was her turn to slip her hands under my shirt and feel my hot skin under her fingertips. I was hard to her soft. When she pulled up my shirt, I stripped it off.

I watched her unbutton my pants and pull them down with my boxer briefs.

I was ready for her. Completely. Heart and body.

Her hand circled around my hard, warm cock, and I closed my eyes to enjoy the feel of her skin on mine, gently bringing me to the edge. Capturing her eyes with my own, I stared into the beauty of her and took her lips.

Letting my hands move down her body, I scooped her up as she let out a small gasp and wrapped her arms around my neck, her legs around my waist as I dropped her onto the counter.

We needed no words for this.

I leaned down and breathed in the unique scent of her I had come to love so much. She dropped her head back and moaned sweetly. I loved that I could do this to her, that I could soften her edges, soften her heart. Lifting her breast to my mouth, I circled my tongue around her nipple and kneaded her flesh in my hand until her breathing became heavy.

I kissed her when she asked me to, then stopped when she groaned and threw her head back as my fingers entered her. I absorbed every breath, every moan, every plea that fell from her lips. When it all became too much, I guided myself inside her soaking wet pussy and swallowed down her long groan as both of us watched me became one with her.

"Just you and me from now on, Lucy," I whispered into her skin. "Just you and me."

Dropping my forehead on her shoulder, I slid out when I was halfway in and gave her a little more when I knew she was ready to take all my length. Her fingers raked my shoulders, her back arching, her breasts pushing against my chest. I watched her bite her bottom lip as her brows drew in together when I was buried deep inside her.

I made love to her and it was no different than what we'd had before. It had been the best with her from the very first time. I basked in every gasp as I drove inside her and when she begged me for more, I gave her more.

I loved her harder.

Kissed her deeper.

Held her tighter to me so I could give more and more and more.

"I want everything, Adam." She panted into my ear as my thrusts shook her body and caused her to slide back. I put one hand on her lower back to keep her in place and slipped my arm under her knee to open her wider, go in deeper.

"You don't want just my cock, do you? That's not everything. You want *me* too."

Her fingers dug deeper into my skin, and she nodded. "I want you *and* your cock. I want it all with you."

"You'll have everything," I whispered as her muscles started twitching around me and she became rigid in my arms.

She bit my shoulder to keep herself quiet, and I picked up my thrusts, giving her everything just like she asked every time I was inside her. I continued until she relaxed in my arms and it was my turn to let it go. I came inside her with my own groan as she held my face in her hands and kissed me for what felt like days.

Even after I'd given her everything I had, I kept rocking into her gently. I could take her for hours if we had the time. I was still hard enough to keep going, but I knew I needed to hold my son in my arms just as much as I wanted to be inside the woman I loved.

I gave myself a few more minutes, took her slowly, and stroked myself in her heat, just until our breaths slowed down. I told myself, just another minute…when she surprised us both by coming around my cock again, a tingle went down my spine, and I came with her.

The only thing on my lips was the whisper of her name and the promise of us.

Adam Connor's New Love a Homewrecker?

Yesterday, just a few days after what went down at Adam Connor's house, Adeline Young sat down with Vanity Fair to speak about her marriage and what really went down between the once happy couple.

Amidst the alleged sex tape rumors—we're still waiting on the edge of our seats for that video to be released into the world, by the way—Adeline Young made an unexpected statement, and we're not sure what to think of it yet.

"I never wanted to talk about this, but after seeing the photos of them together, I didn't want this to be swept under the rug," said the Hollywood actress when she was shown the pictures of Adam Connor in an embrace with Lucy Meyer while he held their son in his arms. "No one called me to let me know what was going on, that my son was in danger. I read about it the next day and learned about the details as I answered the questions of the detectives who knocked on my door. I was blindsided. It shouldn't have been a nanny taking care of my son in a situation like this. He needed his mother, and I wasn't given the chance to be there for him."

According to the beautiful actress, Lucy Meyer started to work for Adam Connor as Aiden's nanny before she became Olive Thorn's literary agent. While this happened after the couple was already divorced, Adeline Young claims that they were talking about getting back together, giving it another shot. "I met her. I watched her play with my son. I was so blinded by the love and trust I had for my husband that I didn't see what she was trying to do. I didn't see her for who she is. I'll never stop fighting for my son."

She continues to claim that the sex tape was recorded with none other than the handsome actor himself. "We were young. We made a mistake. I'm afraid the only reason it resurfaced recently is because Adam didn't want me to come out and tell the world he had cheated on me with her in a time when I was so vulnerable and still so in love with him."

The interview continues in the same tone, and we are not exactly sure what to believe at this point.

Unexpectedly, as soon as the interview went live, Adam's reps released a short statement of their own, claiming there had never been a moment where Adeline and Adam discussed the possibility of getting back together and that the relationship between Adam Connor and Lucy Meyer started only very recently. They also added that Lucy Meyer had never worked as a nanny for Adam Connor, that they only had a friendship that bloomed into something more as they continued to spend time together.

We told you, you should've acted fast and bought yourself a shed close to Adam Connor's house so you could knock on his door and offer him baked goods or maybe ask for a cup of sugar. Now it seems like we're all too late.

CHAPTER TWENTY-NINE

LUCY

I read the interview. I read the interview again and again, trying to make some sense of it, but nope, my name was still there and I was accused—quite bluntly—of breaking up a marriage.

How could I have broken up something that wasn't even there? Were these people this stupid?

When I started reading it for the fifth time, Olive had to yank the tablet away from the death grip I had on it.

"What the hell?" I shouted, then lowered my voice when the other people turned around to give me the stink eye. I leaned forward in my seat and gripped the edges of the table to anchor myself. Then my phone started going off and my rage hit another level. "How did they even get my number?"

Olive sighed. "It's a mess."

"It's more than a mess. What the hell did I do to her?"

"You didn't do anything, Lucy. I suspect this is just to get the spotlight off her and onto Adam...or she is trying to get back at him; who knows. Ever since their divorce, she's been all over the place. You know the saying *There's no such thing as bad publicity*...I think she took that to heart."

We were downtown at our favorite café, waiting for Olive's

new publishing team to arrive so we could go over their plans for her next novel. More than that, it was a celebration of the deal. We learned about the interview from Megan, Jason's publicist, when she called to let Olive know there was a whole media frenzy surrounding it and that it was likely I'd be pestered by phone calls.

If I'd known how true that was, I would've never have left the house that morning. The moment we drove out of the gates, we were followed by paparazzi.

"Maybe she was hoping to get back with him. I mean, apparently she was, according to her. Maybe if I hadn't climbed that damn wall, they'd be back together by now. Adam never said anything about a reconciliation, but what do I know about their relationship, right? They were married for years and not only that, they have a kid together."

"Don't go there, Lucy. If they were meant to be together, it wouldn't have mattered how many walls you climbed."

I took a deep breath and exhaled.

"We can leave, you know. I'm sure if we called Jason or Adam they'd come and get you."

"Why do I have to run away, though? I didn't do anything. And I want to be in this meeting, dammit. I didn't do anything wrong that requires me to tuck my tail and run away from the vultures."

The table started vibrating again, so I grabbed my phone and turned it off completely; it was either that or drop it into the glass of water in front of me.

Before Olive could speak, her phone started to go off. I growled and dropped my head into my hands in frustration.

"No, wait, it's Adam. Do you want to answer?"

I thought about it. I shouldn't have felt the need to, but unfortunately, I did. "I don't think I can do that right now," I admitted finally. When Olive winced and eyed her phone, I added, "It's not him, Olive. I just don't want to talk about this right now. I want to act like it never happened for at least a few more hours and focus on the meeting."

"Okay, so we won't answer. You're right. He knows where you live anyway, so it's not like you can run away."

"These last few days I've been wondering whose side you're on, and this kinda gives me the answer, I guess."

She gave me a cheesy grin. "What can I say? I love that he made you fall in love with him so easily, and I think you've met your match; he won't let you go easily no matter what you do or say. I think you're curse-free, Lucy Meyer, and you don't know what to do with yourself."

"Please." I snorted. "I'll be curse-free the day I marry someone, wearing a white dress. That's the tipping point in our family. No one has quite made it there yet. And even then—"

Olive's gaze shifted, and she grabbed her water glass to hide an even bigger smile behind it.

"What's wrong with you? Why are you snickering?"

She gestured behind me with a quick chin lift, and I turned back to find freaking Adam Connor barreling toward us with quick, angry steps.

"Why is your phone off?" he asked as a greeting.

"What the hell are you doing here?"

He gripped my elbow and pulled me up. "You're coming with me. We have things to discuss."

As pissed as he looked, his grip on my arm wasn't firm, so I shrugged it off with a quick twist.

"Although everyone seems to think I'm a nanny these days, I'm actually an agent and have a meeting. I'm not going anywhere right now."

His frown deepened, and he turned to Olive. "Is it okay if she skips this one?"

Olive was listening to our exchange in fascination. "Oh, please," she piped up. "Take her away."

The next thing I knew I was being ushered out through a back door and into a waiting SUV.

———

THE RIDE back to Adam's house was dead quiet.

As soon as we walked through his door, I whirled on him. "That meeting was important to me, Adam."

"And you're important to me. Why did you ignore my calls?"

"I ignored *every* call, not just yours. And like I said, I was busy."

"I'm not gonna let you stew on something like this, Lucy. Not if I can help it."

"Okay then, talk." I crossed my arms over my chest and waited for him to go on.

After he watched me for a long minute, he offered me a seat, which I rejected.

"Okay, Lucy. Okay. Let's do it your way—as long as you don't run away from me. The interview...she says it's me in the sex tape, that it's us; it isn't."

"You brought me here just to say that? You were married, Adam. So you had sex and recorded it. So what? Do you think that's why paparazzi are hounding me? To ask what I think about it?"

The sex tape thing wasn't even on my radar. Would I have watched it? Absolutely not, but that part of the interview wasn't the issue. He walked closer to me, and I dropped my arms, ready to bolt.

"I bought the tape."

He took a step forward, and I backed away with a frown on my face.

"What?"

"This morning, I paid one million dollars to buy a sex tape that proves my ex-wife cheated on me while we were married, with a director…most likely so she could get a role in his movie —which she didn't."

"Why did you do that?"

"Because she is forcing my hand. I won't go in front of cameras or give interviews to fuel this stupid thing she started, but I could do this. So I did. Now, if she insists on coming after me— or you for that matter, she'll know I can prove her every word wrong."

It was time for me to take a seat. "You're gonna blackmail her?"

"Not exactly blackmailing. In theory, it is, actually, but she can't take the chance of it getting out, so I won't end up using the tape anyway. Now that's not what I need to talk you about. I just wanted you to know that interview is the only time she'll utter your name. If she keeps at this cheating thing, she'll have to deal with the consequences."

"If that's not it, then what did you want to talk to me about?" I leaned back and braced myself.

"I'm going to tell you a little story. Vicky, my sister…she was eighteen when she moved to Paris. Her friends here weren't exactly the best influence on her, and she got into drugs…not heavy stuff, but still drugs. As we discussed before, my parents threw a lot of parties and as much as I tried my best to keep her away from it all when she was younger…after she reached a certain age, my help wasn't needed. Long story short, she hooked up with the wrong people and…got pregnant."

I frowned, not sure where he was going, but listened carefully. Adam sat down on the other end of the couch and tightened his hands into fists.

"My dad and mom arranged for her to go to Paris to stay with my aunt who lives there. They couldn't risk a scandal like that. She was a month and a half pregnant when they sent her away. And Vicky...she was so young, Lucy." He glanced at me with a small smile and looked away. "I tried my best to shield her from my parents, but in the end she made her own choices. I guess sometimes no matter how much you want to save someone, you just have to accept the fact that you can't, not unless they let you." He shot me another look then got up and started walking around.

I didn't like where his story was going. I didn't like it at all.

"She didn't want to raise the baby, but she didn't want to have an abortion either. And, well..." He raked his fingers through his hair and let out a dry laugh. "I've never said this to anyone before. Feels weird."

He walked to the window and just stood there silently with his back to me. He had the same expression on his face he'd had the first night we had spied on him. The only difference was this time around there was no barrier between us, no walls, no glass windows. He was just a few feet away from me.

"My parents weren't so keen on the idea of giving the baby up for adoption," he continued. "They were sure it would end up coming back to them. While this whole thing was going on, I was with Adeline. She came to Paris with me when we visited Vicky. She only knew about the pregnancy because she was there when I got the news, and I was in love with her and why shouldn't you trust the person you love, right?"

Facing me, he waited for something, or maybe he was preparing himself.

"Aiden isn't your son," I said, pointing out the obvious to ease things for him in case that was what he was waiting for.

"He *is* my son, Lucy," he corrected me immediately. "The moment Vicky gave birth to him and I held him in my arms he became mine, and he will always be mine."

"But how?" I blurted. "I mean...I don't get it."

"Adeline's idea. Mind you, she didn't share it with me first. She told my parents, and they jumped on it."

"But how?" I repeated again. Did I feel stupid for asking the same thing over and over again? Sure…but I really wanted the answer. "I remember seeing her photos, Adeline's…I mean…she was pregnant."

"She wasn't. She spent a lot of time in Paris, with Vicky. The house wasn't in the city, so the possibility of them getting photographed was slim to none. When she was here, back in Los Angeles, she wore one of those fake pregnancy things. Same when she posted on social media. Trust me, it looks frighteningly real, and I was filming anyway, so neither one of us was spending a lot of time in the city anyway. Only a handful of people knew about Vicky's pregnancy, Dan being one of those few, so there was no one who could link everything."

"Wow." What else could I say?

"Adeline wanted to get married and what better time to tie the knot than when your girlfriend is expecting?"

"Again, wow."

And he just kept going.

"My parents thought it was the perfect solution to everything. Vicky was okay with it. To be honest, she didn't care that much. Everyone was happy."

"And you? Were you okay with it all? Were you happy about it? I get it, your sister was only eighteen and that's young to have a baby on your own—by the way, who was the father?"

Another forced smile. "She isn't sure. Convenient, isn't it?"

I continued, "Yeah, well, what I was trying to say is, she was young, okay, but you weren't that old either. You were what? Twenty-two?"

He gave a quick nod. "A baby would have been a big scandal when the mother was only eighteen *and* the daughter of the perfect Hollywood couple, not to mention an unknown father. It could have either been one of Vicky's friends, or hell, maybe dear Mom and Dad's. With the way Vicky was, it was impossible to guess. But *Adeline Young* having my baby and us getting married…that would be good news. Great news. And I loved Adeline. And I loved my sister. I thought maybe she'd said okay because if I kept the baby, she'd get to see him."

"She still lives in Paris, doesn't she?"

"Yes. She's been clean ever since she learned about the pregnancy, but yes, she doesn't want to come back here. So I go to her. I take Aiden with me, and I go to her, every year on her birthday."

"So she can see her son," I guessed quietly.

Adam nodded. "So she can see what a beautiful son she has, but she wants nothing to do with him."

"Adam…I don't even know what to…" I wanted to go to him, but I also wanted to hear everything he wanted say, so I stayed put and waited for the right time.

"She doesn't want Aiden to know about her, so Aiden will only know Adeline and me as his parents. I don't mind that anymore. This last time…when we were in Paris for Vicky's birthday, neither my parents nor Vicky spent more than a few minutes alone with Aiden. I never want him to feel unwanted, never want him to work so hard to gain someone's attention like that, so I don't think we'll be going back to Paris any time soon."

I didn't want Aiden to ever feel unwanted either. I'd never wish that on anyone, let alone a child.

"Well, fuck them. If they can't see what a gorgeous and smart kid he is…I'm sorry, I know they are your family, but fuck them."

"Up until the moment I held him in my arms, I wasn't sure I could do it. Sure, I didn't mind the getting married to Adeline part because I loved her, but a baby? Like you said, I was only twenty-two myself. What the hell would I know about raising a baby? But then they gave him to me, and I…"

He got up and walked away. This time I went after him, but stopped before I was too close.

Keeping his back to me, he kept explaining. "I touched his face, those little fingers, those cheeks." There was a smile in his voice. "He was born premature; he was so little, but so perfect. How could anyone want to give him away?"

He turned around and looked surprised to find me standing so close to him.

"But the papers? The birth certificate?"

He raised his hand and tucked a piece of hair behind my ear. "You have no idea what people with so much money and power like my parents can do...can buy. Our publicist, Michel, had his own fixer; that's one of the reasons he is such a good publicist."

I shook my head. "It all sounds so crazy."

"It is."

"So why did you tell me all of this?"

"There is more than one reason."

"And they are?"

"I wanted you to know everything because you scare me, Lucy Meyer."

What the hell?

Giving him a disbelieving look, I asked, "*I* scare you?"

A nod.

"The other reason is because I want you to know everything. I want you to know that I trust you. I want you to know that the night I had to leave you alone with Aiden, she was threatening to talk to the media and let them know Aiden wasn't our son. She thought it would be enough to eclipse the sex tape. That's why I left in a hurry."

"Why would she do that?"

"To save what is left of her career. To make me look bad. She is making one mistake after another. Up until you and me got photographed with Aiden, she had become the villain of our story. Now that you're literally in the picture…"

"She wants to make *me* look like the villain so she can be the good one and slink away into the night."

"Exactly. But now she can't. If she talks about Aiden to anyone, I'll release the video. If she utters one more word about you, I'll release the video. A blowjob wasn't the only thing on there, and even though she believes the other guy's face can't be seen, she is wrong on that. If the video doesn't do the job for her, I'll start giving my own interviews and she *really* wouldn't want that."

"Tell me all of this isn't happening because of me, Adam."

He cupped my cheek in his hands. "This isn't happening because of you, Lucy. If there weren't those pictures of us together, she'd find something else to get her way. She has no ties to Aiden. He was the reason she wanted a divorce, which is why I was always planning to get sole custody. None of this is happening because of you."

"Why do I scare you?" I wanted to get back to that because I didn't get it. I didn't get how I could scare him, of all people. He, however, was scaring the shit out of me at that moment, and to be honest, I was done talking about the wicked witch.

"Because I said I love you and you never said anything." His thumb caressed my cheekbone, and he kept his eyes firmly on mine. "I wasn't expecting to hear it back from you, at least not yet, and I'm okay with that, but you acted like I'd never said anything."

"I didn't mention it again because that was adrenaline talking, not you."

"Oh? Is that so?"

The way his eyes were moving around my face…it was so tender, so loving that a lump formed in my throat.

"You have nine beauty marks on your face. Did you know that?"

What?

"Um…no, I've never counted them."

"I have. My favorite is this one." With the tip of his fingertip he touched my skin, right below my eye, and then let his finger trail down to my jaw.

I did nothing but watch his eyes follow his finger as he stopped right at my chin and tipped my face up to his.

Holding my breath, I waited for his kiss, hoped for it, but he held it back from me. Then his eyes met mine.

"I love you, Lucy Meyer."

He wanted so much from me…yet he wanted nothing at all. First he had pushed for the relationship and just when I was getting used to *that* idea, now he wanted more. It might have been nothing for some, but it was everything for me.

Closing the distance between us, he whispered, "I know you're scared too, Lucy, and you know what…if there is one thing I've learned about love, it's that it *should* scare you. A little or a lot, it doesn't matter how much, but it should make you *feel*. And you, my beautiful, stubborn Lucy…" He brushed his lips against mine, just a quick touch, and pulled back. "You scare me—no, I promised to be honest with you: you terrify me, Lucy, and I love it. I will never take you for granted, and knowing that you won't let me…you're the one I want, Lucy Meyer. You're the one I fell in love with."

Every word sending an arrow to my heart, I just stood there, my body trembling slightly, my breath caught in my throat. I simply watched him watch me. He cupped my face gently with both of his strong hands and kissed my lips. My breath shuddered out of me in a rush. I was in so much trouble. Pulling back, he kissed my nose, my eyes, my forehead, and my lips again.

"Now you're going to kiss me, Lucy. I know you won't give

me the words, but I need you to give me your best kiss," he whispered, his lips moving against mine. "And then you're going to give me a chance, the same chance you gave Jameson. I deserve it, and you deserve me."

Oh, the asshole. He was going to get more than a kiss.

When I opened my mouth and invited him in, he didn't hesitate before taking everything from me. It was a slow kiss, our heads moving in sync with each other, our tongues gentle. When I understood what was happening, why I was feeling like I was on the verge of crying, I held on to his arms and let him take over. He took another step into me, our bodies resting against one another.

Safe with one another.

I knew I would remember this moment years later; I knew when I would look back, when I would think of Adam, I would feel his warm, strong hands cradling my face. I knew I would remember the truth of his words ringing in my ear, whether he was there or not.

When it was over, he simply rested his forehead against mine, and we just breathed in each other's air. I hoped it had been his best kiss. I hoped no one would ever kiss him like that again, that I would be it for him, that my lips would be it.

"Tell me I'm a good kisser, Lucy," he murmured, his eyes closed. "Tell me I'm your best."

A soft laugh escaped my lips. I slid my arms around his neck and held on to him just a little tighter as I stretched on my toes so I could trail my nose against his neck and get more drunk on him.

"I taught you well; of course you're good now."

He laughed and wrapped his arms around my waist, his steady heartbeat beating against mine.

I took a deep breath, closed my eyes, and stood still in the safety of his arms.

"I don't want you to be taken away from me, Adam."

He pressed his palm against my back, holding me as tight and as close as I was holding him.

"I won't let anyone take you away from me, Lucy. You can trust me on that."

A teardrop slid down my eye, and I burrowed into his neck.

The next thing I knew, his hands were moving down my body, and I was swept off my feet. My face still in his neck, I let him carry me into his bedroom.

Gently laying me down on his bed, he settled on top of me, his body not even close to touching mine. His arms were braced on the bed, his face inches away from mine.

"I lose track of time when I kiss you," I murmured, caressing his face. "You make me lose track of myself when you look into my eyes with such intensity, Adam Connor. You make me feel like I'm the only one."

He exhaled and his eyes closed as he moved his head into my hand.

"You're going to tell me you love me. Tell me and give me your heart, and I promise you, Lucy…I promise you I'll take care of it."

"You stole my heart, you jerk."

"Not quite the right words, try again."

I laughed softly. "I think I fell for you, Adam Connor."

He started to say something, but I held my finger up against his lips.

"I love you," I admitted softly. "You're right, I love you, and it scares the shit out of me, too."

His lips slowly stretched into a smile and my heart brightened with the beauty of it.

I haven't mentioned what an asshole he is for quite some time, have I?

"I'll take care of you."

"Yeah, you keep saying that."

"Because it's true. You'll never have to protect your heart again. It'll always be safe with me, Lucy. You'll always be safe with me."

I swallowed the thick lump in my throat and ignored the way my heart was fluttering in my chest as if the space wasn't enough, as if it was ready, eager, and willing to rest in the hands of Adam Connor.

Stupid, stupid heart.

Closing my eyes, I tried to remember how to form words and just breathe. Adam waited patiently.

"Adam…when I say I'm cursed, I'm not trying to be cute. I want you to know that, no matter when or how this ends between us, I will hold your secrets." I shook my head in amazement and stared right into his eyes. "What you did…you're an amazing person, an amazing father, though you obviously have questionable taste in women." His lips curved up again, and he sneaked in a kiss, getting my heart all excited again.

"Thank you, baby."

"That last one wasn't a compliment," I clarified.

He got in another stolen kiss that ended up causing me to pull him down on me so I could feel his weight press into me.

"Wait. Wait."

He stopped, his breathing already heavy, along with my own.

"I'm rooting for you," I whispered. "I never wished for a prince to save me, because I can save myself, thank you very much…but I'm wishing for it now, Adam Connor. I hope—and I can hope really really hard—that your kiss will break the curse. I hope it's you, Adam. I hope you're the hero of my story, because I deserve to be loved, goddammit. I deserve to have someone dance with me to no music." I stopped so I could breathe and watched Adam's eyes darken. "I deserve to have you to myself. I deserve to love you."

He watched me, just watched for several silent seconds as I

tried to quiet my screaming heart. Then without saying a single word, he reached to his back and slipped off his shirt, giving me a view of his ridiculously sexy upper body. Then he reached for my shirt, slowly, as if we had all the time in the world. I helped him by lifting my arms up, then when he went for my jeans, I lifted my hips, too. When it was all gone and I was completely naked in front of him—in more ways than one—he got rid of the rest of his own clothes, settled over me again, and pushed inside me without giving me any flowery words. I didn't need any; I just needed him.

He was already hard, ready to fill me.

I took a deep breath and widened my legs as he pushed and pulled until he settled deep inside me, bringing us together in the most magical way; every orgasm with Adam had been magical thus far.

This time it was me who cupped his face in my hands and looked into the green depths of his eyes. "Don't hurt me, Adam. Don't disappoint me."

"Never, Lucy."

He took me with slow, steady thrusts, imprinting his cock on me, making my entire body ache for him, for the release only he was able to give me. Then he made me come around him, with nothing but whispers and promises on my skin and of course that big, beautiful cock of his. When it was his turn, he pushed his face into my neck, his cock as deep as it could go, and let go with a groan. He let me hold him until our heart rates lowered back to normal.

Raising his head, he asked me to say the words again, so I gave them to him.

"I'm so in love with you, Adam."

Such beautiful words. Being in the same bed as him, looking into his eyes and admitting that I'd fallen for him, I hoped even harder that he'd be the one to break my curse.

EPILOGUE

Six months later

I believe in sex. Wholeheartedly.

I believe when you're having sex with the one you love—especially if he is wielding a big one—you experience something out of this world. It's hard to explain. It's not quite the same as having sex with someone you'll only know for one night, even if he happens to be a God in bed. Don't get me wrong, sex with that guy is good too because orgasms are usually pretty magical things, but what I'm talking about is different.

Hear me out.

Loving someone, having sex with someone who loves you with everything they are, who trusts you more than they trust anyone in the world...it's beautiful, humbling, earth-shattering, and to be honest, a little crazy.

But yeah, sex with a one-night stand versus sex with Adam... let's just say Adam hit it out of the park every single time.

Would you like to know what kind of sex I love the most? You know almost everything about me, so it's only fair that you know that too.

Sleepy sex. I *love* sleepy sex. I could have sex with sleepy sex, I love it that much.

Specifically, I should say, I love sleepy sex with Adam Connor. To be woken with his mouth on me, to gasp into his hand as he tries to keep me quiet so my moans and gasps won't be heard by the perfect little human down the hall...to be woken with a magical cock pushing inside me--Adam's magical cock, just in case you didn't get that... I approve of that kind of sex each and every time.

So since I love sleepy sex so much, it was the perfect wake-up call on the best day of my life. I woke up with a big hand around my breast, squeezing and pulling my nipple. I groaned, and he shushed me gently. His lips were against my neck, kissing and licking and biting.

"What are you doing?" I asked dazedly, a small shiver running through my body as he softly bit my skin. I was still somewhere in between dream world and the real one.

His hand traveled all the way down from my breast to my thigh, and he pulled my leg up and over his thigh. I smiled, eyes still closed, and helped him by sliding back until my very naked ass rested against his very hard abs.

My leg secured over his thigh, his hand covered my hip, and he pulled me down a little.

"Adam," I murmured sleepily as I felt his hard cock between my legs. My body was already tingling from the excitement of having that thing so close.

I rolled my hips, as much as I could manage with him behind me, and turned my head back so I could have my morning kiss.

The minute my lips were close enough he took my mouth in a slow, seducing kiss. I moaned and just let my body go soft in his arms when the warmth of him reached deep into my bones. Slowly everything faded away, and I felt nothing but the love between us.

Without his lips ever leaving mine, I felt his hand spread me open, and I could tell he was making sure I was ready to take him. Then he guided himself into me slowly, his hips moving so fucking slowly. When it was all too much to take in, I broke away from his kiss and held my breath. One last inch and he was all in.

Completely mine.

He slid his arm under mine and curled his fingers around my shoulder, holding me still for his lazy thrusts.

"Good morning, Lucy," he whispered as I let go of my breath as quietly as I could.

I wasn't quite ready to say anything. "Hmmm," was all I could manage.

He pulled out, leaving nothing but the thick head inside me, and then pushed it slowly back in as I scrambled to grab his bicep with my right hand.

"Ahhhh," I murmured, too gone for words.

"I love waking you up like this," he whispered into my ear, somehow managing to keep his thrusts steady. "You're so soft, so willing to do everything I say when you first wake up in the morning." He pressed a kiss on my shoulder and gave me a perfectly timed hard thrust.

Jesus!

"When have I ever not been willing to get in bed with you?" I shot back quietly.

"Never, but there is something different about you when I take you first thing in the morning. I think you love it, too."

I loved everything with him, period, but yeah, I loved watching him do all the work as he held me in his arms and let me watch him through sleepy eyes. Some mornings I did wake up before him, and if and when that happened, I always made sure he had a good start to his morning…a very good and relaxing start.

"I love your cock, period," I admitted. "It doesn't matter what time it is, I love having it in me any time of day."

I managed to open my legs wider and started to roll my hips downward, urging him to go faster.

"Always so greedy and impatient," he murmured before sucking my ear lobe into his mouth. "I love you, Lucy."

With his words, I contracted around him and smiled through his groan.

"I love you, Adam." There wasn't even a moment of hesitation anymore. "I especially love when I get to come on you first thing in the morning."

"You do? You want to come on my cock? Last night wasn't enough?"

"Last night it was just two times. You were tired, so I didn't want to press." I turned my face to him. "It's your fault," I whispered, my eyes finally catching his. "I don't feel satisfied unless you make me come three times in one go. It feels like there is something missing."

"Hmmm, so I have to make you come three times now?"

I smiled up at him and a small moan slipped out of my mouth when he changed his angle and hit my sweet spot. He knew all my angles, all my corners now.

"Shhh," he quieted me as he kept working his cock into me, pushing me toward something I wasn't quite ready for. "You don't want Aiden to hear you and come to your rescue, do you?"

I shook my head and grabbed his forearm, whatever I could reach. Those lazy strokes were long gone; now he was on a mission to make me come, and he knew exactly how he could get me there. I loved Aiden with all my heart, but him coming to rescue me from his father was the absolute last thing I wanted. I wanted his father to ruin me, though in reality, he already had.

He took me exactly where he wanted to take me by pushing deep into me and grinding deeper and deeper. Oh, it was everything. I grabbed his hand and pulled it over my mouth as I came around him, and he didn't stop working me until my leg started to shake, and he had to pull it down to keep it still. Even after that, he gently pushed me onto my stomach and positioned his legs on either side of my hips.

A new angle, a tighter fit, still slow yet deeper thrusts. He gave me his everything that morning, and I took it all.

"You make me crazy for you, Lucy," he murmured into my ear at some point while I was trying not to pass out from all the sensations. "You make me happy."

If you think those words didn't hit the deepest, darkest corner of my heart, think again.

He gave me four orgasms that morning, and I gave him two—because yes, I was that good, too.

With that extra one, I should've known something was up.

———

"Good morning."

"Arrgggh, nooo."

"Good morning, Aiden."

"No. Just a little more, Lucy."

"But you have to wake up."

"Why? Why? I'm really sleepy, Lucy. I don't feel like I have to wake up yet."

"But I really want some pancakes, Aiden. I asked your dad, but he won't help me. I thought you would, but…"

He turned over and opened those eyes that looked exactly like his father's. "He won't help?"

I shook my head and tried to look very sad.

"You really want pancakes? Like really really want them?"

I nodded. "I'm afraid so. I really really want some pancakes with maple syrup. Lots of maple syrup."

Aiden released a suffering sigh and hit his bed with his little hand. He had turned six just a month ago, but he was still so little in my eyes. It hadn't been pleasant having Adeline over when we had his birthday party, but she was Aiden's mom—at least as far as he knew. Seeing that big, big smile on his face when he saw his friends, all the balloons and toys, and the huge, colorful bounce house in the backyard…his joy made it worth being in the same room as her.

To be fair, after Adam made her release a statement basically apologizing to me, she didn't do anything that would piss me off too much. Since Adam had bought the sex tape—which I was curious to watch, but I knew he'd already destroyed it—she wasn't being all that bitchy. She even signed over the papers that gave sole custody to Adam.

Oh, Aiden still spent time with her, still spent some nights at her place, but he was always happier when his dad was around. Just like me.

"Daddy will owe me. Big time," he muttered as he swung his legs over and got down from the bed.

"You're gonna help?" I totally knew he was gonna help. He loved pancakes just as much as Olive and I did.

"You already woke me up, so I guess I should so I can eat pancakes. You always eat more than me and Daddy. How come you do that, Lucy? Girls aren't supposed to eat that much."

"Ah, excuse me. That happened only once, and I was starving."

Heading toward his bathroom, he looked at me over his shoulder and smiled brilliantly. "You're always starving, Lucy."

The little squirt.

So with my helper on my side, we made pancakes as his dad took a shower and got ready for his day on set. As per Aiden's request, we also invited the Thorns over for breakfast. Since Adam and Jason were costars, the five of us spent a lot of time together, on set and off. Luckily, their call time for that day was a few hours away.

Olive helped me set the dining table as Aiden and Jason protected the pancakes from us. Trust me, Olive was just as enraged as I'd been when Jason backed up Aiden on the subject of us eating too many pancakes.

Jason was smart enough to slide his arm around her waist and kiss Olive just after that declaration, and he was lucky Olive didn't see him quietly high five Aiden.

When Adam came out of his shower wearing a sleek black suit, I had to do a double take.

"What's the occasion?" I asked lightly as he raked his fingers through his damp hair.

"Something special." He caught me in his arms and gently kissed me on my lips. I put down the fruit plate in my hands and turned to him in surprise.

"What's that for?"

"It's been five months today," he declared.

I knew that one. It had been five months since I'd moved in with him and Aiden. There wasn't much moving involved because I'd never had the chance to rent that apartment I'd had my eye on. One day all my clothes were at Olive's place and the next day they weren't. I didn't exactly get a say in it, but I wasn't complaining either. Like I said, sleepy sex had turned out to be my favorite kind of sex.

And Aiden…his reaction to the whole '*your dad and I are in a serious relationship now, is that okay?*' talk was to give me a part sweet, part sly smile. He was so much like his father.

"Does that mean he will get to kiss you whenever he wants to?" he asked, his smile still in place.

"Yes, I guess that means he'll get to kiss me whenever he wants to. If I'm angry at him, he doesn't get to kiss me at all, though."

He giggled. "What else does it mean?"

It meant a lot of things his little ears couldn't—shouldn't hear, but I kept all of them to myself.

"If you are okay with it, it would also mean that I'd get to stay with you guys."

"Here?"

"Yes."

"Here in this house? You won't live at Olive's anymore?"

"No, I'd live here."

His eyes grew big. "You'll live with us? Forever?"

"Let's slow down there, little human. If he pisses me off, I'm not sure how I'd feel about seeing your father's face forever. Yours, though…" I bumped his chin with my knuckles. "Yours I wouldn't mind seeing forever."

Laughter filled the room as he ran off to tell his father I preferred him over Adam.

I had mentioned that he was the perfect little human before, hadn't I?

Adam laid another kiss on me, this one more forceful, more intense, somehow even more beautiful and pulled me back to the present.

"And this one?" I asked when he let me get in a breath.

"This one was because today is our wedding day."

The smile that was on my lips slipped away in an instant, and I took a step back from him.

"What?"

"It's our wedding day."

"Again…what? Did I somehow time travel and miss the proposal?"

He closed the distance between us and stopped me from moving backward—I hadn't even been aware I was moving backward.

"I've been proposing to you every day with every kiss, Lucy."

"You have?"

"It's not my fault you took your time giving me an answer. Now you don't get to ask for a proposal. It's too late for that."

"It is?"

"Yes, Lucy. I'm sorry."

"But I want a proposal, Adam. I really, really want it. Propose. Please."

He leaned down and brushed a gentle kiss on the edge of my lips. "I'm sorry, sweetheart."

"So no proposal? What does that mean exactly?"

"It means we're getting married."

"We are? When?"

"Today."

"What?" My voice was barely audible

Suddenly Olive came around the corner, and I froze in my place when I saw what she was holding.

A wedding dress. A *fucking* wedding dress, and I had to admit, a *very* fucking beautiful wedding dress.

My hands flew to my mouth, and I just stood there, taking it all in.

There were tears streaming down her face so, obviously, there were some streaming down my face too.

"I-I…" I stuttered.

Aiden moved, and I saw him reach for his father's hand as he smiled up at me. I still had no words.

Then Olive was by my side.

"I wish you all the happiness in the world, Lucy. I wish you all the smiles, all the laughter, all the love." She laughed and wiped away her tears. "You deserve so much, my beautiful friend. You deserve the best love story, you deserve the very best ending, and I'm honored that I'll be standing right next to you when you marry the love of your life."

I dropped my hands and a laugh escaped my mouth—but don't worry, I was still crying. "Who said he was the love of my life?" He totally was. "And I don't remember asking you to be my maid of honor either, my little green Olive."

She handed the delicate dress to Jason and flung herself in my arms. "You don't get to have a say. Try to remove me from your side, I dare you."

Just as she finished speaking, Jason stepped in and pried her out of my arms, holding her against his body as Olive relaxed against him. Neither one of us looked all that pretty with our red, crying faces.

"And I guess, since you never asked before you started calling me Daddy, I'm not asking your permission to walk you to this guy," Jason said before pressing a kiss on my cheek.

I laughed and looked up at his smiling face through my tears.

Aiden dropped his father's hand and ran to my side. He was still in his Super Man PJs.

"Don't cry, Lucy. Don't you want to marry us?"

"Buddy, you can't ask her that, remember?" Adam interrupted.

"But why? I don't understand."

"Yeah, I second that. I don't understand either. Why can't you ask me that?"

He walked to my side and cupped my face in one hand. I barely registered Aiden letting go of my hand and going to Jason's side. Adam always did that to me, always made it impossible to look away from him.

"Because I don't want you to think. Because I don't want you to have the option to say no to me. You're mine, Lucy. When there is only one answer to a question and you already know what it is, it's pointless to ask it. You *will* get married to me today. You will become my wife and you *will* always be mine."

His wife.

His fucking wife.

I gulped and nodded. "You're right. It's pointless to ask when you know the answer."

His other hand came up, and he held me still. "So, yes? You're going to do it?"

"I thought you said I didn't have the option to say no."

"You don't," he repeated in a low voice, his eyes moving over every inch of my face. "But I can never be sure of what you'll do."

"I understand. So…okay." I lifted my shaky hands and put them over his. "Let's get married. And why not today, right? It's as good a day as any, and if all my favorite people will be there, well, that means it will be the best day."

He smiled slowly, as if he had actually been afraid I'd say no, as if he didn't already know I couldn't.

Then as his smile got bigger, my eyes filled with more tears.

"That's enough, Lucy," he murmured, kissing my leaking eyes. "That's enough, my beautiful warrior."

My body shuddered, and Adam wrapped me up in his arms before I could slip away and meet the floor.

His whispers were the only things that were getting through to me.

"You'll never be like them, Lucy. You're not cursed, sweetheart. You never were. You were just waiting for me to find you." His voice was so tender, so loving. "Who am I kidding? You couldn't even wait for me to find you. You fell right into my backyard, got right up in my face." Still crying in his arms, I held on tighter.

He had found me.

He'd never acknowledge it, but yes, Adam had found me.

"I love you," I whispered into his now soaked shirt.

"And I love you, my Lucy." I felt his lips on the top of my head and closed my eyes.

He was perfect. He was everything I'd always been afraid to want for myself.

Lifting my head, I looked into his eyes and managed to give him a shaky smile. "You *are* the hero of my story, after all, Adam Connor. You are my unexpected prince who broke my curse. Who would've thought, huh? I think I'm glad it's you because I would've hated to start from scratch and teach someone else how to kiss properly."

He laughed, his eyes going soft. "I'm afraid you'll never get to kiss anyone else but me again. You okay with that?"

I nodded, my heart still feeling wonky in my chest. "I can live with that."

"Good."

"So, Lucy, will you marry us or not?" a voice chimed in.

I let go of Adam and leaned down to kiss Aiden's cheeks. "Thank you for asking, my little prince. My answer is a definite yes."

"Good. Now can we eat the pancakes? I'm really hungry, and I've been waiting very patiently."

I laughed and straightened. "Yes. Yes, we can eat the pancakes."

A now tear-free Olive sent me a quick wink and went to help Aiden and Jason with the pancakes.

Adam drew me back into his arms, and I welcomed his warmth and closeness.

"Thank you, Lucy."

"For what?"

"For spying on me. For being mine."

"That's a lot to be thankful for."

"And I plan on thanking you every chance I get."

"You should do that. Three times every time, please."

Adam smiled, and I melted.

He leaned down and whispered into my ear, "Thank you for trusting me with your beautiful heart."

So that same day, after pancakes, I said *I do* to Adam freaking Connor with stupid, happy tears in my eyes.

After our shockingly gentle first kiss, I pulled him down and whispered a little secret into his ear.

I'd never forget the look he gave me...the one that said I was his world.

His hand resting on my stomach, on our little baby, he gave me another perfect kiss, another one I could add to the list.

That little girl who had spent her days crying, who had tried her very best to figure out why her mother couldn't love her enough to hold on to her, who couldn't understand why her grandmother would never love her like she needed to be loved...that same little girl who along the way had understood and accepted that not everybody gets to have their own happily ever after in this world...that girl in me...that hopeful little girl in me just smiled that day.

She smiled, and smiled, and smiled, and smiled.

THE END

If you want to read more about how Jason and Olive ended up together, keep reading so you can glimpse into the first chapter. Trust me, if you've enjoyed, *To Hate Adam Connor*, you'll love *To Love Jason Thorn*. Olive is one of my favorite characters.

TO LOVE JASON THORN

Jason Thorn… My brother's childhood friend.
Oh, how stupidly in love with that boy I was. He was the first boy
that made me blush, my first official crush. Sounds beautiful so
far, right? That excitement that bubbles up inside you, those
famous butterflies you feel for the very first time—he was the
reason for them all. But, you only get to live in that fairytale
world until they crush your hopes and dreams and then stomp on
your heart for good measure. And boy did he crush my little heart
into pieces.
After the stomping part he became the boy I did my best to stay
away from—and let me tell you, it was pretty hard to do when he
slept in the room right across from mine.
When tragedy struck his family and they moved away, I was
ready to forget he ever existed.
Now he is a movie star, the one who makes women of all ages go
into a screaming frenzy, the one who makes everyone swoon with
that dimpled smile of his. Do you think that's dreamy? I certainly
don't think so. How about me coming face to face with him?
Nope still not dreamy. Not when I can't even manage to look him
in the eye.

Me? I'm Olive, a new writer. Actually, I'm THE writer of the book that inspired the movie he is about to star in on the big screen. As of late, I am also referred to as the oh-so-very-lucky girl who is about to become the wife of Jason Thorn.

Maybe you're thinking yet again that this is all so dreamy? Nope, nothing dreamy going on here. Not even close.

CHAPTER ONE
OLIVE

Up to the day I met Jason Thorn, my dreams were made of fluffy white clouds, pretty pink dresses, tasty apple pies, and of course, our neighbor Kara's big brother.

"I don't want to hear another word about this, Jason. You are always welcome to stay here, sweetheart."

I was about to go down to help my mom set the table when their voices carried up to me and I stopped.

"See, I told you it would be okay. Come on, let's go up to my room."

"Hold on, Dylan. Not so fast."

I heard mom's coffee cup softly clink on the kitchen counter a few seconds before I heard her speak again.

"Jason, are you sure you don't want us to call anyone? Maybe they should check on your mom and make sure everything is okay, or we can call your father and let him know that you are spending the night with us. I bet he would be worried if he called your house and couldn't reach either one of you."

My mom was a soft, compassionate woman—soft as in she carried a heart that was purely made of shiny liquid gold. I'd heard my grandpa tell her so countless times for putting up with my father, so as a child I knew it had to be true. There was also a side of her that could be seen as vicious at times, as she was fiercely protective of the ones she counted as her family.

Other than that, she was a sweetheart, as my father liked to call her. She had this secret way of making anyone smile, even when they were sad about something. I knew that because she always made me laugh when we were at the dentist, which was a big scary place for a six-year-old (almost seven!). If she was in the room, chances were she'd have you beaming up at her in no time.

It wasn't just me and my brother; she had the same effect on my friends too. Whenever it was her turn to pick us up from school, they all looked up at her with these big, silly smiles stretched across their faces. Actually, now that I think about it, they reminded me of Buzz, the puppy Kara had gotten a few weeks before. Oh, how much I loved watching Kara's brother Noah play with that puppy; I'd always thought we could rescue a few puppies for ourselves after he asked me to marry him.

Sigh...

Anyway, I hadn't been allowed to have the puppy in the house, and of course I would never ever sneak him in whenever my mom was out—*sshh, don't tell anyone*—but I did see the faces the little guy made when he wanted something from Kara.

All in all, back then, I believed it was tough to be a kid, but having a mom like mine made everything a bit easier. That's why I'd always wanted to be like her. I'd wanted to make people happy, make them forget about their worries for a while, be their sunshine, as she was ours.

There had been only one teeny-tiny issue...the blaring fact that I didn't have a golden heart because I was never good at being peaceful or graceful, where my mom, on the other hand, was the epitome of those traits.

It wasn't my fault though; it was always Dylan who made me

angry. If blame were to be assigned, it would fall squarely on Dylan's shoulders, not mine.

Dylan was my big brother, the one who kept ruining everything for me, probably since the day I was born. Unfortunately, I didn't remember those early years of my existence, but I was pretty sure that he'd been messing with me back then, too. According to my mom and dad, a few days after they brought me home from the hospital, he told them they should take me back to where they'd found me—next to the garbage cans.

Can you believe the audacity? My loving big brother.

It didn't even end with a cleverly veiled threat either. I remembered myself that he would steal my stroller and run around with me in the park. Why, he was probably trying to kill me with sheer excitement!

At an early age, I'd come to the conclusion that I would get to have my own golden heart when Dylan wouldn't be around to throw me off of my game. Whenever he was around, chances were he'd do something and I'd lose my cool, which would lead to us getting into a screaming match.

There was nothing graceful about screaming your little heart out at someone because they wouldn't play My Little Pony with you.

Jason's carefully chosen words brought me back to the present where I was plastered to the wall just to the left of the staircase, listening in on them.

"Thank you, Mrs. Taylor, but I don't think my father cares about where I'm spending the night. And…um…my mom will probably be okay in the morning. I'm sure she just fell asleep. It's my fault really; I should've checked the time and made sure I was home before six."

"We were playing catch on the street, Jason. Like, right in front of your house. I don't think you are the one to blame here.

And who goes to sleep at six, Mom? Even Olive stays up later than that."

"Dylan," my mom said in a low voice before sighing.

I grinned, feeling proud. I could stay up pretty late. Sometimes I could even go until nine.

There was complete silence for a few moments, and then the feet of the chair scraped the floor as someone got up from the table.

"Okay, Jason." I heard mom's strained voice breaking the thick silence. Who was this boy they kept calling Jason? Maybe he was part of the family that had moved in across the street a few houses down a few days ago?

How come Dylan hadn't introduced me to his new friend?

"You are always welcome in this house. I want you to remember that, okay?"

"Thank you Mrs. Taylor. I appreciate it."

"Why don't you go and get cleaned up while I get dinner ready? After dinner we'll call your dad and make sure he knows you are safe."

"That's not really necess—"

"Let's say it's for my own peace of mind."

"Come on, Jason." I heard my brother murmur. "I'll show you the new video game my dad bought me."

Oh, about that…I'd always thought it was quite rude of him to hoard all the toys. He never let me play with him.

I turned on my heels and was about to run back to my room to check out who the new boy was through the small opening of my door when my mom said, "Dylan, can you stay and help me set the table first? Then you can join Jason upstairs until I call you guys down for dinner."

"Sure, Mom," my brother answered readily. "The bathroom is the second door to the left, Jason. My room is next to it. I'll be right up."

"Is there anything I can help with, Mrs. Taylor? I wouldn't mind."

"Oh, you are too sweet, Jason. How about you be our guest for tonight, and any time you come by after today, you'll give me a hand, too, okay? And you call me Emily from now on."

"Okay, Mrs. Tay—umm…Emily. Thank you so much for letting me stay here tonight. I'll be in your room, then, Dylan." His footsteps started up the stairs.

I stood still and patiently waited for the owner of those footsteps to reach me. Since Dylan wasn't with him, I could say hi and welcome him to our neighborhood without getting into trouble.

Argh Dylan… Just because he was four years older didn't make him the boss of me.

Would he be blond? Maybe he would have dark eyes and dark hair and be all dreamy, exactly like Kara's big brother, Noah, who had turned eighteen just a few weeks before. My mom thought he was a little too old for me, but she had also once said a girl should always dream big. While I loved my mom dearly, clearly she wasn't right all the time.

Anyway, since this Jason seemed to be friends with Dylan, I highly doubted he would be something to dream about.

Suddenly my stomach got all fluttery for some reason. I frowned and smoothed down my dress. Dylan's friend or not, he would be a guest in our house and I thought I should be welcoming since he sounded very stressed out about staying with us.

Tommy, one of my best friends from school, believed that we would get married one day, but I'd never said yes to him. I'd never even gotten excited whenever we were on playdates.

First, I saw Jason's sneakers. I still remember: they were white and very clean for a boy his age. I thought maybe he wouldn't be that bad and make fun of me like Dylan's other friends.

Putting on my best smile, I slowly lifted my head up to meet his eyes. His steps faltered when he saw me hiding next to the wall. I got a good look at him and my smile slowly vanished as my mouth dropped open.

Jason? Jason what?

Butterflies? Were those tiny flutters in my stomach butterflies? The ones my mom had told me about? It sure felt like it. Thousands of them. Were these the same butterflies my mom had felt when she'd met my father?

What was his last name?

I wanted—no scratch that, I *needed* his last name to be my last name.

Not the day after, not ten years or twenty years later. I needed it to happen that day—right at that moment to be exact.

He seemed surprised to see me for a second, but recovered faster than I did. He gave me a stupidly cute smile with a dimple showing on his left cheek.

"You have a dimple," I breathed out, totally lost in that tiny little crevice. It was almost magical.

I closed my mouth and felt the heat rise up to my cheeks. I managed to return his smile with a wobbly one.

"Hey, little one. You must be Dylan's little sister. I'm Jason."

"Hi," I greeted sheepishly as I gave him a small wave.

His smile picked up a notch, and I felt my face flush again. Tucking a loose hair behind my ear, I smiled bigger.

Oh, boy.

He was so cute.

I cleared my throat and extended my hand, just like I saw my dad do when he was meeting someone new. "I'm Olive. My friends call me Liv or Oli because they think I have a weird name."

Quirking his brow, he looked at my hand then up to my eyes as he gave it a good shake. "Do they now?" he asked, and I nodded enthusiastically, hiding my hand behind my back again. "I think you have a good name, little Olive. It would be hard for someone to forget a name like Olive. You have very beautiful green eyes; I'd say the name suits you."

Beautiful?

Beautiful?!

I was never going to wash my hand again.

My smile got bigger, and I believe it was the first moment I fell in love with the mysterious boy who had an adorable dimple and was going to spend the night right across from my room.

"Are you our new neighbor?" I asked. He had to be our new neighbor. I had to see him again.

"Yes, we moved in last week."

I nodded. That was good news—more time for us to be together.

"Since you like my name, would you like to marry me?" I asked.

His face turned red and he opened and closed his mouth a few times.

Finally he laughed and said, "What?"

I shrugged. "My dad doesn't want me to get married for at least another thirty years, but I don't think we should wait that long. So, can we get married sooner?"

He scratched his head and even made that look cute. "I think we are too young to get married, little one."

Crushed, I looked down at my feet. "My dad says that, too. I've always thought I would marry Noah, our neighbor, but my dad is pretty set against that. Even my mom thinks he is too old for me. I think I can wait for you to get older, though." I nodded to myself. "Make sure you wait for me too. Okay. I'm gonna go down and help mom with dinner. Dylan always screws it up. You know," I started, clutching my hands behind my back as my eyes fell to his shoes. "I helped her bake the apple pie and the vanilla sauce earlier. I'll make sure you'll get the biggest slice. You'll love it, and I'll give it to you first."

I knew guys cared about food because my dad had always appreciated a good home-cooked meal. My little heart had fallen in love for the first time and I was hoping Jason would fall for me, too, after he tasted the pie.

He chuckled and touched his finger to my chin. Surprised at the contact, my head flew up, my eyes huge. When I saw his smiling face, I had to bite down on my lip so I wouldn't grin like a little girl, which would surely be a dead giveaway that I was in love with him.

"Thank you, little one. I'm sure it's delicious if you had a hand in it. I better let you go then. I'll look forward to seeing you at dinner."

Passing by me, he tugged a piece of my hair, his smile still going strong on his lips as he headed for the bathroom.

I fidgeted with my hands so I wouldn't wave him a goodbye and sigh like my friend Amanda did whenever she saw Dylan.

Inside, I was dancing on the clouds.

He had touched my hair.

He had touched my chin and looked into my eyes.

Jason.

Our one-dimpled new neighbor. Had. Touched. Me.

Ah...

I was pretty sure he'd fallen in love with me, too. I mean why else would he smile, look into my eyes, and touch me, if he hadn't?

Right?

Right?!

OTHER BOOKS BY ELLA MAISE

Lost Heartbeats
To Love Jason Thorn
The Hardest Fall
Marriage For One

THE HARDEST FALL

The first time you meet someone, you make eye contact. You smile, say hello. Should be simple, if you're anyone but me. The first time I met Dylan Reed, I found myself making eye contact with a different part of his body. You see, I'm very good at being shy, not to mention extremely well-versed in rambling nonsense and, unfortunately, rather highly skilled at making a fool of myself in front of a guy I'm attracted to.

At the time, I knew nothing about him and thought none of what I said would matter since I'd never speak to him again. Turns out, I was very wrong. He was the star wide receiver of the football team, one of the few players expected to make it into the NFL, and I ended up seeing him all over campus.

I might have also propositioned him, run away from him, attacked him with a cooking utensil…and…uh, maybe I shouldn't tell you all of it. It's pretty normal stuff, things you'd expect… from me. Eventually, the time came when I couldn't hide anymore—not that he'd have let me even if I tried.

Before now, he never knew I was secretly watching him. Now that we see each other every day, he knows when I have a hard time looking away. It doesn't help that I'm not the most subtle person in the world either.

He smiles at me and tells me he finds me fascinating because of my quirks. I can't even tell him that I think my heart beats differently whenever he's around.

He thinks we're going to be best friends. I think I have a big thing for him, and the more I get to know him, the more I don't care that I'm not allowed to be his friend, let alone fall for him.

The thing is, that's exactly what I'm doing—what we're doing, I think.

Falling.

Hard.

MARRIAGE FOR ONE

Jack and I, we did everything backward. The day he lured me into his office-which was also the first day we met-he proposed. You'd think a guy who looked like him-a bit cold maybe, but still striking and very unattainable-would only ask the love of his life to marry him, right? You'd think he must be madly in love.

Nope. It was me he asked. A complete stranger who had never even heard of him. A stranger who had been dumped by her fiancé only weeks before. You'd think I'd laugh in his face, call him insane-and a few other names-then walk away as quickly as possible. Well...I did all those things except the walking away part.

It took him only minutes to talk me into a business deal...erm, I mean marriage, and only days for us to officially tie the knot. Happiest day of my life. Magical. Pop the champagne... Not. It was the worst day. Jack Hawthorne was nothing like what I'd imagined for myself.

I blamed him for my lapse in judgment. I blamed his eyes, the ocean blue eyes that looked straight into mine unapologetically, and that frown on his face I had no idea I would become so fascinated with in time.

It wasn't long after he said I was the biggest mistake of his life that things started to change. No, he still didn't talk much, but anyone can string a few words together. His actions spoke the loudest to me. And day after day my heart started to get a mind of its own.

One second he was no one. The next he became everything.

One second he was unattainable. The next he seemed to be completely mine.

One second I thought we were in love. The next it was still nothing but a lie.

After all, I was Rose and he was Jack. We were doomed from the very beginning with those names. Did you expect anything else?

ABOUT THE AUTHOR

Writing has become my world and I can't imagine myself doing anything other than giving life to new characters and new stories. You know how some things simply makes your heart burst with happiness? A really good book, a puppy, hugging someone you've been missing like crazy? That's what writing does to me. And I'm hoping that reading my books will leave you with that same happy feeling.

Everything you'd ever want to know about me and my books is on my website. I'd love to see you there!

www.ellamaise.com

To get the inside scoop of my books, extra materials, and to be the first one to know when I have a new release, you can Sign up for my newsletter!
(Only sent a few times a year.)

Newsletter Sign Up

ACKNOWLEDGMENTS

My readers…There is so much that goes into writing a book; a story. So many people who help making it possible for me to reach so many of you. I'm not sure if Adam and Lucy will get the amount of attention Olive and Jason did, but I can genuinely tell you that I think they deserve it and a lot more. I had a blast writing these characters and fell even more in love with Lucy. Her heart has been broken before, but despite she is a very strong character and she deserved all the love. So…if you're reading this right now, if you've enjoyed Adam and Lucy's story; thank you… Thank you from the bottom of my heart. Your support means the world to me.

Thank you to all of the wonderful bloggers for giving me and my stories a chance. So many of you read and loved Jason and Olive's story and now (hopefully) Lucy and Adam. I have no idea whatsoever how I can show you how thankful and grateful I am. All the beautiful reviews, shares, comments, messages…all of it —thank you so very much.

Jasmine… You are *everything*. I think that pretty much sums it up. Thank you for putting up with me. Thank you for not yelling at me to go away when I bugged you relentlessly. Thank you for kicking my ass when I needed it. Thank you for putting the biggest smiles on my face. Thank you for getting my stories and helping me smooth everything out. Like I said you are everything and nothing I'll ever say will be enough. You're amazing and I'm lucky to call you my friend. Couldn't do it without you.

Caitlin... I must be your worst author ever. One day I'll manage to get my manuscript to you in time. Promise! Thank you so much for making time for me and turning my stories into a publishable book. You are an amazing editor.

Erin Bailey... Thank you for reading everything I write even when you barely have time for yourself and for always being there for me; whether it is to hold my hand when I'm freaking out or to cheer me on.

Natasha G., Suzette, Rita, Samantha, Natasha M., Laura Gladden H., Amy—if there are any I forgot, I'm sorry—thank you all for reading the ARC before the release. Can't tell how happy it made me to hear your comments as you were reading.